On Heaven's Hill

A NOVEL

KIM HEACOX

WEST
MARGIN
PRESS

Edited by Sarah Currin and Olivia Ngai

Cover photo of Chichagof Island, West Chichagof-Yakobi Wilderness, Southeast Alaska, by Kim Heacox

Photo editing by Tammy White/tammywhite.com.au • Steve Heap/Shutterstock.com

Library of Congress Cataloging-in-Publication Data

Names: Heacox, Kim, author.
Title: On heaven's hill : a novel / Kim Heacox.
Description: [Berkeley, CA] : West Margin Press, [2023] | Summary: "A novel told from three alternating perspectives-a former trapper trying to care for his son with muscular dystrophy; a young girl who wishes for her father to be rid of his PTSD from the war; and a wolf fighting for his and his pack's survival. Set in a small Alaskan town, the residents fight for the remote wilds they call home when plans for a building development threatens to upend the peace"-- Provided by publisher.
Identifiers: LCCN 2022040034 (print) | LCCN 2022040035 (ebook) |
   ISBN 9781513139111 (hardback) | ISBN 9781513141350 (ebook)
Subjects: LCGFT: Novels.
Classification: LCC PS3608.E226 O5 2023 (print) | LCC PS3608.E226 (ebook) |
   DDC 813/.6--dc23/eng/20220829
LC record available at https://lccn.loc.gov/2022040034
LC ebook record available at https://lccn.loc.gov/2022040035

Printed in the United States of America
27 26 25 24 23 1 2 3 4 5

Published by West Margin Press®

WEST MARGIN PRESS
WestMarginPress.com

Proudly distributed by Ingram Publisher Services

WEST MARGIN PRESS
Publishing Director: Jennifer Newens
Marketing Manager: Alice Wertheimer
Project Specialist: Micaela Clark
Editor: Olivia Ngai
Design & Production: Rachel Lopez Metzger

This was the god of beginning in the intricate seawhirl,
And my images roared and rose on heaven's hill.

DYLAN THOMAS

AUTHOR'S NOTE

This story, in part, is about wolves. And while I cannot occupy the mind of a wolf or embed myself in a pack, I can avail myself of many excellent sources that tell me much. We now understand wolves far better than we did fifty to a hundred years ago. With each new observation and study, we gain more certainty that wolves (elephants, orcas, octopuses, and other animals) occupy much of the same emotional and intellectual landscape that humans do. With this in mind, I have taken literary license to create wolves that possess the compassion and brotherhood they deserve.

PART I

CHAPTER ONE

Silver

Late again.

The wolf pup, far behind his pack, follows the river through a tangle of young cottonwood, the leaves golden medallions in the September rain. He works the ground with his big paws and keen nose. Wet ears. Searching eyes. Great heart. No stranger to hunger, he moves from one distraction to the next. A dusting of silver-black in the shoulders. A touch of russet in his lower flanks. All black in the legs and feet. "A real beauty," men will say of him. Men with a hunger of their own, their hearts made of light and stone.

He follows the scents of moose and geese, circles, and moves on. Hunting. Listening. Working the air with his nose. Were he among his littermates, born this past spring, he'd play all day. But he's alone now. As such, he must be mature for his age, mindful in a way that doesn't create panic but instead makes him smart. Far ahead somewhere, his family travels in single file, fast and distant with the distance growing. The rain has washed away all but the faintest traces of their passing. Whenever his pack travels like this, Alpha and Mother and the subadults all work together to keep Old One up front so as to not leave him behind. As tough and determined as Old One is, his age slows him down.

Silver hurries on.

Mother must have lost track of him. It's happened before. And she'd always come back for him and grab him by the nape of his neck—he was so little then—and carry him to where they needed to go.

He's bigger now, growing fast. And hungry. Often hungry.

He emerges from a willow thicket and climbs a gentle slope onto a long, flat nothingness that reaches from one horizon to the other, its surface lifeless, hard, and dark. And worse: foreboding somehow, with strange marks down the middle. He holds still for a moment, as if death might speak and tell him what happened here.

How far does the nothingness go? And to where?

He travels upon it a short distance, then drops downslope and rejoins the river—so exuberant and free-flowing by comparison—and heads downstream, unaware that by traveling over the flat nothingness, he's crossed the river where his family did not and is now on the opposite side from them.

He hears a strange sound, and stops. From behind a veil of willow he watches a shiny object cross the river over the flat nothingness, moving fast without wings or legs.

Silver continues on, following the river that's fed by many small tributaries, growing as it goes. Again, he gets distracted as he tests rounded stones underfoot—rolls them back and forth with a nimble paw—and picks up the scent of a bear, then something else. Otter, perhaps. The river bends in a set of rapids, uncoiling over ancient scripts and hidden texts from the Ice Age. This is where his family would chase salmon and pin them in the shallows— and feast. The pup feels an ache in his belly. Hunger.

He thinks all wolves eat salmon.

He thinks with his stomach.

ONWARD. The rain lightens. The sky brightens. A strong smell assaults the young wolf. He pauses as fear rises in his throat, a fear new to him yet somehow familiar from long ago. He's never smelled smoke. Never seen a man. Never tasted human kindness, cruelty, or greed, never mapped the soulful intelligence between their needs and his. That will change.

A raven flies low overhead, circles, and continues on.

The rain stops.

He climbs a cut bank, and sits, and begins to yip, his face turned to the somber clouds. Were he older, he'd howl and sing. Were he older, like his elders, he'd dream of mammoths, and of taking down a moose, and leading his pack through this wet, blue-green world of forests, glaciers, tides, and fish.

For now, though, he yips.

After a minute or so he stops, and listens. Then he yips again.

Soon it will come—the reply.

The chorus of his clan.

CHAPTER TWO

Salt

SALT D'ALENE STEPS back to admire his work.

The Sitka spruce wheelchair ramp climbs at ten degrees, makes a less than elegant 180-degree turn, and continues up to the deck, four feet off the ground, where Salt has yet to finish the handrail. He can hear Hannah already, hours from now, when she returns home with the boys. It's nice, love, she'll say. But won't the boys fall off it? Of course they will, Salt will tell her. They're rowdy and carefree. Have faith. They'll land on their feet. And if they don't, they'll land on their heads. They have hard heads.

The concern, of course, is Solomon in his wheelchair, with his brothers— especially Abraham, the eldest—racing him around, and Solomon laughing and screaming gleefully, asking for more, breathless without ever getting to his feet. Duchenne muscular dystrophy. One chance in thirty-five thousand that a boy his age will get it. And Solomon got it.

Why? Hannah asked one night in bed a couple years ago, not long after the genetic testing, the muscle biopsy, and Solomon's diagnosis. Would he even live to age twenty? Why our son? Our beautiful son. Why... why... why? She began to cry. He's exceptional, Salt told her as he fought back his own tears. That's why. He's one in a million, a gift from God. He's our son— our sun, the brightest star in the sky.

Yes, she said. Our sun. And she cried herself to sleep.

AGAIN, SALT TAKES stock of his carpentry. *Not bad*, he thinks. *Not so good either. Many of the joints could be tighter. But they'll hold. Structural integrity, that's the important thing.*

Later, while making a difficult compound cut with the chop saw and unsure of what he's doing, Salt takes a break. He's tempted to drive over to Willynillyville, the veteran encampment only a couple miles away, founded by the bush pilot Tyler Nash. There, he could ask for help from Nash's buddies, the McCall cousins, Chippy and Cap, former Oklahoma Thunderbirds who served in Afghanistan and are said to be the best carpenters in Strawberry Flats. People say Chippy uses old, gnarled shore pines to make beautiful bannisters and handrails; that he has a fully outfitted carpentry shop and enjoys giving tours. *How good it would be to get some strong advice; to build something beyond functional. To make art.*

Salt has never been to Willynillyville. Never had a good talk with any of the war veterans there. Never apprenticed himself to a true craftsman.

He could be there in ten minutes. Drop by. Give his regards. Ask a question or two. Maybe have a few laughs. Make new friends.

But he talks himself out of it.

"You're shy," his mother used to tell him in Idaho, back when he was a teenager. "And that's fine,' she'd add, "until it keeps you from realizing your potential."

The last time I was an artist, Salt tells himself, *I was a trapper.*

Rumors around town say Tyler Nash is down in Texas with his younger brother, a former singer/songwriter who had his own band and touring bus and recording contract until he joined the National Guard for some crazy reason—extra money, no doubt—and got shipped off to Afghanistan. Three weeks later, he got blown up.

AS HE REACHES to put his earmuffs on to make the compound cut, Salt hears a sound familiar to him from the cabin life he knew on Minto Flats, near Fairbanks. Interior Alaska, another world, where the winters aren't as cold as they used to be, and river ice cannot be trusted, and one wrong step is all it takes—for both wolf and man. Where wild animals know a hundred times more than we ever will. Be careful not to look them in the eye. They'll take your stare and turn it back on you.

Salt listens. Another howl—not distant, not near.

A third.

A fourth.

He smiles. *Now that's something I haven't heard in a while.*

CHAPTER THREE

Kes

"He's still in there."

Again and again, Papa's doctors say this down in sunny San Antonio, at the Brooke Army Medical Center, as if words themselves were bandages.

Eleven-year-old Kes Nash sits next to her stepmother, Rita, and feels the room begin to spin, her stomach turn. *Where in there?* she wonders. *Is he going to be okay?*

And now in another office, for another consultation, another doctor is talking about "blast concussive trauma" and Papa's "complicated impaired blood flow" and his "clinical picture" and "bilateral involvement." The doctor finally says, "Not to worry, Mrs. Nash. He's still in there. The shattered legs are stable right now, free of infection. We'll deal with them later. Our chief concern is the trauma to his frontal lobe and to his ear and eye, and any stenosis that may have caused anoxia."

"Anoxia?" Rita asks.

"Lack of oxygen to the brain," the doctor explains. "The SCA—the subclavian artery—doesn't directly provide blood to the brain. The left and right carotid vertebral arteries do that. But damage to the SCA can redirect blood from the vertebral arteries, resulting in vertebrobasilar insufficiency. That's why the shoulder wound concerns us. If you're going to have damage to the head, the frontal lobe is the place to have it because of all its redundant systems. In that regard, your husband is lucky."

Lucky? Kes looks out the big windows, hoping to see a butterfly, a bird, a tree.

The doctor adds that the field report from Afghanistan had noted that the first thing an Army medic told Papa as he lay dying on the dusty ground, blown to bits, was this: "Stay with me, soldier. Don't close your eyes. Because if you do, you might never reopen them."

Kes rocks with unease. Rita grabs her hand and says, "He's going to be all right, honey. Your papa... he's going to make it."

Don't lie to me, Kes wants to scream. At Rita. At everybody. At the whole stupid world. *Don't lie to me.*

She gets up and leaves, and joins Uncle Ty, Papa's older brother, out in the waiting lounge. A pilot with his own Cessna down from his homestead in Alaska, Uncle Ty wears a red bandana on his head and has a missing front tooth, like a pirate. She sits next to him, opposite her grandpa. Uncle Ty wraps an arm around her, and asks, "What's the latest?"

"They're worried about his brain."

Uncle Ty nods.

"Please don't tell me he's going to be okay."

Another nod.

"I hate lies," Kes adds.

Uncle Ty gives her a hard look. "People here don't lie, Kes."

She shrugs.

"He's still alive, isn't he?" Uncle Ty says softly, cajolingly. "He has no spinal cord injuries. He has no inner organ injuries... none that we know of, anyway."

But will he ever sing again? Laugh again? Play music again? Write another song? Take me hiking, river rafting, birding?

Grandpa sits opposite Kes and her uncle. He appears stone faced, much older than he was a few days ago. Kes hears herself ask, "Are you okay, Grandpa?" Her own voice sounds distant and weak, as if about to blow away, as if her body and soul were made of ashes.

"I'm fine."

Grandpa doesn't look fine. He looks like he might die of sadness, his face white as chalk. He fought in Vietnam and still thinks the US could have won over there if we'd dropped more bombs. He's the one who convinced Papa to join the Texas National Guard for extra money after little Kipper was born and Papa's music career stalled.

"We're a family of patriots," Grandpa had said one night many months ago in the kitchen, back in Lubbock. Kes had eavesdropped from around the corner, unable to sleep.

Later, Rita begged Papa not to join. The other band members too. Stringer, the bass player, Kes's favorite because of how he would read Dr. Seuss to her on the band bus, using funny voices that made her laugh. He always said Danny and Rita were just one hit song away from big money and fame, and nobody in Texas wrote better songs than Danny Nash. But Stringer had been saying things like that for years as he lived in an old funky trailer outside Lubbock and ate cold refried beans from a can.

Later, Uncle Ty, talking about Grandpa, had told Papa, "The old man is crazy, little brother. We all know that. Too much John Wayne and *Top Gun* and Agent Orange. Don't do it. Come live with me and the other guys in Alaska. Bring Rita and the kids."

"It's the National Guard," Papa replied to Uncle Ty, flashing his trademark Nash smile. "It's only one weekend a month. I'll end up defending Texas from Louisiana. Or piling sand bags on a levee. Or working crowd control at an Aggie-Tech game."

"You'll end up in Afghanistan," Uncle Ty said.

Sure enough.

Beginning in Germany, from what Kes had gathered, a team of Army doctors had worked to save Papa, to relieve the pressure on his brain. Keep him on oxygen. Save his eye. They'd rebuilt his face and ear by grafting in new bone, cartilage, and skin. They'd shaved his head, cut him open, and bandaged him up. More surgeries were yet to come, each one followed by CT scans and more tests. Days. Weeks.

And again, they said Papa was lucky. Others died, all in a single Humvee. He lost three brothers that day, men in the same unit. That's what the military does, Uncle Ty says: it forges men into a band of brothers.

SOMETIME LATER, asleep in a lounge chair, Kes startles awake when Uncle Ty takes a call on his phone. "Hey Chippy," she hears him say as he gets up and walks away, headed down the sterile Brooke corridor past legless men in wheelchairs, his collared shirt untucked, his blue jeans tattered and faded to gray. Flip-flops on his feet.

What time is it? Kes sees Rita thumbing through a magazine. Little Kipper sits on her lap, innocent as a baby bird. Kes rubs her eyes, gets up, and walks to a bathroom where she dabs her face with cool water. She stares into the unforgiving mirror and sees nothing new: burnished red hair knotted behind her neck, a lightly freckled face, sad, gray-green eyes. She wonders if she'll ever be pretty, and happy. From her small purse she pulls out a tattered photo of Papa when he was young, and of Mom—Kes's first mom, her birth mom—sitting in his lap, the two of them laughing. Taken the year before Kes was born, six years before her birth mom died. Long before Papa met Rita and they began writing songs and singing together, and drawing big crowds.

Kes bends down to drink and is startled to see bright drops of blood on the bathroom's white tile floor. She draws back and wills herself to stay calm. *Breathe.* She leans against the wall, closes her eyes, and lightly taps her forehead, temple, chin, and sternum with her middle finger—an exercise Rita taught her to help keep her heart from racing. She hears soft sobbing coming from one of the toilet stalls. Quickly, she leaves the bathroom and returns to the others.

She still hasn't seen Papa. "Is he still in surgery?" she hears herself ask Rita.

Rita strokes little Kipper's hair. Grandpa sleeps sitting up, his chin on his chest.

"Yes," Rita says, her voice thin. "Still in surgery."

Uncle Ty returns with his phone in hand. "I just heard from the guys up in Willynillyville," he says with a twinkle in his eye. "They heard wolves, a whole pack of 'em, howling from across the river. I'm telling you, Rita, wolves make music too. Alaska is the place to be."

"I can't think of that now," she says. "Danny's in surgery. You know that, right?"

"Absolutely," Uncle Ty says. "And I know my brother has a huge spirit, a huge will to live. He'll get better. He will. And Alaska is calling." When Rita raises her weary head and stares at him, Uncle Ty asks, "What's the worst that could happen?"

Rita thinks for a minute. "We could all freeze to death."

"Okay," Uncle Ty says with a grin. "What's the second worst thing that could happen?"

CHAPTER FOUR

Silver

SILVER FOLLOWS THE RIVER, its riffles and rapids a steady voice. Here and there he comes upon the tracks of an animal he doesn't know, impressions deep in the soft sand.

Two legs. Not four?

From the opposite shore, his pack watches him as he watches them—closely, and with great anticipation, all in deference to Mother, who is searching the river for the best place to cross. Silver observes how when she stops, they all stop. And wait. She stares intently, as if the treacherous water has something to say, something to tell her.

Days ago, far to the north, the pack crossed the river easily where it braided into many shallow channels and had less volume and force. Here, though, not far from the ocean, the river is big and fast and unrelenting.

Mother makes her decision and plunges in, and immediately the river takes her, sweeping her downstream. The pack follows and begins to yip and howl. Silver can see his siblings, all pups of the year—Sister, Strong, and Weak—spinning like leaves in the wind, jumping with excitement and agitation. Mother keeps her head high and works hard and gains the opposite shore to shake off and greet Silver with a long nuzzle and several licks to his face.

How to get back?

Mother grabs Silver by the nape of his neck, lifts him off the ground, and pulls him into the uncompromising current. Swimming with tremendous effort, Silver stays downstream of Mother, right next to her, as she takes the brunt of the water. He can hear her huffing and coughing. Water everywhere.

Danger.

Fear.

The instant Mother touches the rocky bottom, she grabs Silver and hauls him ashore where they shake vigorously. The pack surrounds them, joyous, all save for Old One, who lies down amid granite cobbles and the final flowers of summer—Siberian asters—and places his chin on his forepaws.

Fireweed seeds sail by in a gentle wind. Silver, Sister, and Strong chase after them and leap about, snapping their jaws and tumbling over each other.

The air smells faintly of salt and sulfur and a nearby low tide.

Two ravens fly by, watchful, while high beyond, small in the sky, a gale of gulls swirls and breaks, white on gray.

Soon the pack is moving again, single file, with Mother up front and Alpha in the back to catch stragglers. They follow the faded tracks of a cow moose and her year-and-a-half-old calf. Later, they fish in back eddies for coho salmon. Nothing.

That night, all thirteen wolves bed down in tall grass under the large boughs of a deadfall spruce and dream of food. Always food.

CHAPTER FIVE

Salt

DINNERTIME AT THE D'ALENE HOME is a rugby scrum, all elbows and sharp forks until Hannah calls for order. She had always wanted a daughter, and what did she get? Four rambunctious boys, themselves like wolves. After saying grace and reading from the Book of Job, Salt watches with mild amusement as the boys launch into their meal: halibut tacos with kelp salsa and a mountain of black olives and cheddar cheese.

Abraham, Jericho, and Joshua, ages fifteen to five, look like beanpoles. Give them a dozen sandwiches and they'd devour them in an instant. A star volleyball player, Abe is getting so tall he'll one day need to live in a grain silo. Salt tells Hannah that Abe and Jericho elongate just talking about food. The other night, after a slurpy pasta-eating contest, little Joshua asked his mom if he had spaghetti sauce in his eyebrows. They all laughed.

Only Solomon struggles, in his wheelchair, with saliva building up whenever he talks or eats. Less than a year after his Duchenne diagnosis, he was unable to walk. Now, a little more than a year after that, having just turned thirteen, his speech is failing and he has his own one-on-one special education teacher. "He requires more attention than our other three boys combined," Salt heard Hannah tell a friend the other day.

"You shouldn't say that," he rebuked her later.

"But it's true."

"He's our business, nobody else's."

"He's my business, husband. Remember what the doctors said? He got the bad gene from me. It will be me and always me who gives him his prednisone, deflazacort, and antioxidants." She teared up for the thousandth time. "Besides, you're never here."

Yes, and Salt regrets that. When he first started working at Derek's Garage, Derek told him it would be thirty to forty hours a week. Good pay. And it was. But then a couple guys quit, and Salt is now working fifty to sixty hours each week, though never on Sundays. And still, money is tight.

"Maybe I should start robbing banks," he told Hannah the other night as they climbed into bed, exhausted. She didn't laugh.

She's so thin these days, and always tired. Holding her is like holding a sack of bones. It breaks his heart. "Guess what I heard last week?" he says, brightening.

"What?"

"Wolves."

He feels Hannah go tense. "Where?"

"Here."

"Here, at the house?"

"Out west, beyond the river, on the day I finished the wheelchair ramp." One of the few days off from work Salt has enjoyed these past several months.

"That reminds me," Hannah says. "A mystery man called for you."

"A mystery man?"

"He didn't give me his name. He only asked if this was the number for Salt d'Alene, the wolf trapper."

"How could he know that?"

"I don't know, husband."

"What did you say?"

"I said yes, it was." Hannah wraps her bony arms around him. "I don't want you to trap again."

EVER SINCE HIS BOYHOOD IN IDAHO, Salt has found satisfaction from hunting and trapping and being in the mountains and the woods, learning the ways of wild things and the beauty of God's gifts. And, of course, from his faith. He believes that no school or university could ever inform him the way the Bible does—or the woods still do. He knows this to his core and cherishes it daily. He is unshakable. Uncomplicated. Blessed. And despite the challenges he faces raising his four sons, and the occasional wrongheaded tendencies of his beloved Hannah, and their chronic shortage of money, and Solomon's muscular dystrophy, all is manageable. Salt will make a good life for himself and his family in the eyes of a loving God—his savior Jesus

Christ—who will accept them all into His Eternal Kingdom with kindness, love, and understanding.

The Word of God is everything. His truth.

And wolves? Sometimes their beauty, viciousness, and vulnerability astound him, how they stare right through him and die with hard dignity. When caught in a trap they'll chew off their own foot to get free. Lions and tigers perform in a circus, but never wolves. He admires them for this. *Here they are... the wild dogs that many years ago refused our company and warm fire, that turned their backs on obedience and comfort and processed food, that want nothing to do with the soft sofa or the short leash. Who can blame them? Who cannot see ourselves in them? They are freedom, darkness, and light. They are cunning and playful, cooperative, giving, loving, predatory, faithful, social, and savage, and dedicated to family. Just like us. Admit it.* It chills Salt to see himself in every wolf he's ever trapped, the sun going down in its eyes.

Only after falling through January river ice in Minto and surviving because Abraham—filled with adrenaline and as strong as a bear—threw him a rope and fished him out and got a fire going and stripped him down and filled him with hot tea, and half-carried him back to the family cabin... only then did Salt tell himself he'd never trap again. What to do? Hannah came up with the idea to move to Strawberry Flats, near Juneau—where she was raised and the boys could be closer to their grandparents.

"Let's trade the tundra for the tides," she had said. She missed the ocean.

So, they moved.

And Salt stopped trapping and became a mechanic.

And the money? It disappears, mostly into Solomon's medical bills. The d'Alenes always seem one paycheck away from poverty. So be it. Salt would pay a billion dollars and rob a million banks to hear his son laugh one more day with his brothers. This, too, is his truth.

As she nods off to sleep, Hannah stirs and says, "The new wheelchair ramp is a marvel, husband. Thank you."

CHAPTER SIX

Kes

VETERANS DAY at the Brooke Army Medical Center in sunny San Antonio. Stringer and Sammye, the keyboardist from Papa and Rita's band, arrive from Austin with treats—mostly chocolate. For a magical moment Kes feels happy again, as if maybe one day she might get her life back. Papa's life too. Stringer hugs her fiercely and says, "You're getting tall, kiddo, like your dad. It's good to see you again."

Kes hugs him back. Many of her best memories are from the summers she got to ride with the band through Texas and Oklahoma, and into Kansas, Colorado, and New Mexico, touring by bus, stopping to eat roadside chilis or to hike along a beautiful river, or to skip stones and chase lizards and watch birds. And late at night, back on the bus, playing games before everybody took turns reading her to sleep from Dr. Seuss and, best of all, from T. H. White's *The Once and Future King*, about how Merlyn mentored the Wart—who would grow up to become King Arthur—by turning him into a fish, a hawk, and an ant. All to help the young king become a better leader of his noble knights.

Sammye hugs Kes as well and kisses her forehead.

"How's it going?" Kes hears Sammye ask Rita as they hold hands.

Back when Papa and Rita first fell in love, not even one year after Kes's birth mom died, they wrote a bunch of songs and produced their first album, got a good agent, and played a few large venues. A *Rolling Stone* critic said they were the best singing duo since Gram Parsons and Emmylou Harris "made the desert smell like rain." After that, when they formed a band and added Sammye on high harmony with her Georgia Peach accent, the same critic wrote, "Whoa Nellie, those voices could have saved the South at

Gettysburg." Papa and Rita named their band Whoa Nellie, and Papa joked, "We should pay that critic royalties."

He was serious. Rita once told Kes, "Your papa is the only man I know who would give his last dollar to a homeless person."

Their first CD sold more than ten thousand copies. Their second, more than thirty thousand. They started playing concerts, opening for big names. And still, money was tight. When Rita got pregnant with little Kipper, Grandpa told Papa the National Guard was a good source of extra income. And look what happened. Papa ended up in Afghanistan, what Uncle Ty calls "Again-istan, the place where empires go to die."

Kes thinks her Uncle Ty is the smartest and most quick-witted person she knows. He's always reading three or four big, thick books at a time, mostly nonfiction: history, biography, ecology. He studied geology at the Colorado School of Mines, joined the US Army as a "petroleum specialist" in Iraq, rose to the rank of major, and came home convinced that war is madness. That's why he argues with Grandpa about it. And other things. Mostly politics.

Rita has asked him not to argue with anybody in Papa's presence. No fights, no raised voices, no snarky remarks.

Uncle Ty agreed.

"HE HASN'T SPOKEN A WORD IN NINETY-NINE DAYS," Rita says to Sammye about Papa. "Since the day his Humvee rolled over that IED. Ninety-nine days. That really worries me. It worries all of us. The doctors keep saying to give him time, that he's still in there."

"What about his guitar?" Stringer asks. "Does he—?"

"No," Rita says. "He doesn't play anything. He just sits and stares, and sleeps a lot, and reads, and takes his pain meds one at a time. The TV is too loud and stupid and violent for him. Even with the sound off, the images disturb him. He's lost weight, almost twenty pounds. But at least he's off his IV and starting to eat more. He writes messages when he needs something, and writes responses to our questions. We've all learned American Sign Language... a little, anyway."

"And the pain?" Stringer asks.

"It comes and goes," Rita says. "Especially with each surgery. His legs are all messed up and hurt him a lot. The doctors have been trying to save them. For a while it looked like they could. But now... I don't know, they think his legs should come off below the knees and be replaced with prosthetics. They also think his silence is because of TBI, Traumatic Brain Injury."

Kes feels tears pool in her eyes.

Rita adds, "There's no guarantee that he'll regain his speech, his memory, or his full motor skills—ever. It's going to be a long rehabilitation."

Sammye hugs Rita again and says, "I love you, girlfriend. I'll do anything for you. You know that, right? Any of us will." She looks over at Stringer, who nods.

Pulling away, Rita says, "Do you remember Danny's older brother, Tyler?"

"The developer in Houston?"

"No, that's Charles, the middle brother. This is the other one, the eldest of the three."

"The bush pilot in Alaska?"

"Yes. He wants us to move up there with him."

"To Alaska?"

Rita nods as she dabs away her tears. "He thinks it would be good for Danny. Good for all of us, really. He's built a commune up there for veterans who have PTSD, a place he calls Willynillyville, with a big garden and lots of rain and a carpentry shop and a chicken coop and an apiary and two ponies, and wild birds and strawberries everywhere. That's what he says, anyway."

"And wolves," Kes hears herself say.

Sammye raises her eyebrows.

"And glaciers that go from the highest mountains all the way down to the ocean," Kes adds, feeling better as she speaks about a place Uncle Ty calls the Africa of America. "And whales and sea lions... really big ones that are named Steller sea lions, after the German doctor who sailed in search of America, a long time ago, from Russia."

Rita smiles. "That's my little scholar."

Kes shrugs. After Uncle Ty told her about the Russian discovery of Alaska, she looked it up on her phone. Anybody can research anything on their phone. It's no big deal. Vitus Bering, a Dane, commanded the expedition and never made it back home. Neither did the German, Dr. Steller. Both men died.

Rita says to Sammye and Stringer, "Later today, we're supposed to visit the Center for the Intrepid, to talk to the experts there."

"About what?" Stringer asks.

"Danny's new legs," Rita says as she picks up little Kipper, who sleeps in a blanket.

"THIS ROD IS MADE OF CARBON FIBER," Dr. Clark explains. He works for a pioneering orthopedic surgeon in what he calls "the rapidly expanding program of limb salvage."

Limb salvage? Kes feels her throat go dry. She looks around and sees artificial arms, hands, and legs hanging on the walls and lying on tables.

"The rod, when affixed, strengthens the leg," says Dr. Clark. "It extends between the upper calf brace and the ankle/foot holder, like this, see? It's an artificial Achilles tendon. It flexes when weight is put on it, then snaps back lightly to propel the leg forward." He hands it to Rita. "Of course, you and your husband might decide to remove his leg. Both legs, in fact. It's a viable option, as I know you've been told. It's often the best option for many of our patients. You'll need to make the decision with your orthopedic team, of course. Some veterans use what we call 'Cheetah Legs,' like this one. Others use more traditional prosthetics that give them strength and agility, and much less chronic pain and adjustment time."

Remove both legs? Kes feels her stomach turn. She regrets having had pizza for lunch. *Breathe,* she tells herself. *Breathe…*

Dr. Clark is just getting started, talking about state-of-the art artificial legs, feet, arms, and hands made of carbon fiber, titanium, and wireless remote adjustments, custom fitted to each "recipient." He directs his attention to Rita the way all men do. Even in her grief, she's pretty. Raised in Midland, the town Uncle Ty says smells like a gas station because of all the fracking, she got married at eighteen, and again at twenty-two, to Papa. The second marriage for both. They met at a music festival in Austin. He's six years older than her, but these days Papa looks ancient.

Kes struggles to hold her food down. But when Dr. Clark talks about "musculoskeletal care" and "adult reconstruction," as if Papa were a machine, or a man who will soon be a machine, it's too much. Kes runs out of the office.

She gets to the bathroom, opens a stall door, and throws up into the toilet.

Minutes later, Rita finds her there on her knees. She gets down on the floor with her and hands her a wet paper towel. Saying nothing, she gently rubs Kes's back between her shoulder blades, the way she does at home to help Kes forget about her school troubles and to help her fall asleep.

Sammye comes in with little Kip, who's crying. "Is everything okay?" she asks.

Rita gets up to leave and says to Kes on her way out, "We have to get back to Brooke, honey, for the big Veterans Day dinner with your papa.

We'll wait for you in the car. Be sure to clean yourself up a little, okay? And don't be long."

Kes gets a text from her friend Allison: *Where r u?*

Still in SA.

Celia's parents finally let her get her ears pierced for her bday, check out the earrings she picked. Celia is their mutual friend in Lubbock.

Still at the toilet, Kes shakes her head, thinking: *My dad got blown up in Afghanistan and might get both his legs cut off, and you want to talk about earrings?*

R u there? Allison asks.

Gtg. Will txt u later.

SITTING UPRIGHT in his fancy mobile hospital bed that's parked in the Rusksack Bar and Grill, his legs buried under blankets, Papa slowly eats his turkey, potatoes, and gravy with a faraway look in his one good eye. The other eye is bandaged from a recent surgery. Family and friends join him around a table. Rita strokes Papa's short-cropped hair that's just beginning to grow back and reminds him to drink water. Kes watches Stringer and Sammye throw worried looks at each other. This is the first time they've seen Danny since he returned to Texas. He hasn't even acknowledged them, as if they're complete strangers. Uncle Ty talks with two newcomer friends of his, both veterans headed for Willynillyville, one a big Black man named Tucker John, the other a nervous skinny white guy with greasy hair, named E. J., short, Uncle Ty says, for Ethan James Dunkirk III.

Grandpa tells Kes that the Center for the Intrepid cost fifty million dollars to build. All the money was raised from private donations through the Intrepid Fallen Heroes Fund. "More than half a million people contributed," Grandpa adds, "and I was one of them. We take good care of our wounded warriors here in Texas."

Uncle Ty works his hands in and out of fists as if trying to squeeze out his demons, especially his resentment toward Grandpa—"the old hawk," he calls him, but never to his face. Even now, he says nothing. Rita watches him.

Nobody else speaks as Grandpa goes on about a wounded warrior who got two new legs that were "the best."

Kes glances at Papa, who stares vacantly across the room, past damaged and medicated men who, like himself, eat with their families and friends. Big American flags hang on the walls. A banner proclaims: VETERANS

DAY IS EVERY DAY.

Another says: TEXAS STRONG.

And another: THANK YOU, WARRIORS.

"Now he can walk without much pain and play catch with his son," Grandpa continues about the warrior who got two new titanium legs. "And one day he'll be able to dance at his daughter's wedding. And remember Hector Martinez? His son was a sniper in Afghanistan. He could hit a six-inch target at three hundred yards."

"Until he got his arm blown off," Uncle Ty says. "Now he's learning to scramble eggs with a mechanical hand."

Rita glares at Uncle Ty.

Uncle Ty catches her silent rebuke and changes the subject. He talks about climate change and putting up a hundred solar panels in Willynillyville, and fishing for Alaska black cod, and planting potatoes, carrots, rhubarb, and marijuana. Not in that order. When Kes asks him if he misses Texas, Uncle Ty says, "I miss the girls of Lubbock. And Buddy Holly. Everybody misses Buddy Holly. Did you know that John Lennon and Paul McCartney studied his music when they were first learning to write their own songs?"

Kes manages a small smile. "Yes. Papa told me."

"But I don't miss Texas, the Christo-fascist, cow fart capital of America. Neither will you, Kes. I promise. It's only going to get hotter, drier, and nastier, with water wars and vigilantism everywhere. The Ogallala Aquifer is going down. It's a sad and greedy race to the bottom."

"I miss Papa," Kes says, glancing over at him. He's stopped eating and has his head down, chin on his chest. *Is he asleep?* When Kes first saw Papa, nearly two months ago now, she wanted to climb into bed with him. But the doctors said no. He was too fragile. Too weak. She held his hand all that night, sitting next to him, asleep in a chair. She softly sang to him. And later, when she played her ukulele, he moved his bandaged head in a slow circle as if trying to place something that was lost.

RITA GETS UP, releases the brake on Papa's bed, and begins to roll him back to his room. Tucker John helps her, followed by E. J.

"We all miss your dad," Stringer says to Kes. "But we're gonna get him back. It might take a while. But we will. We're gonna get him back."

"How?" Kes asks.

"Not with narcotics and painkillers," Uncle Ty answers. "They work in the short run but create huge problems in the long run. What we'll do is love him up big time. Love him to the moon and back. How does that sound?"

"That sounds good," Kes says.

"We need to help make him passionate again," Uncle Ty says.

"With music?" Kes asks.

"Yes. And with time outdoors in wild places, the world's best health care clinic. Don't forget, he still has that great big, beating, thumping heart of his. By the way, how's your dinner?"

"It's good, Uncle Ty. Happy Veterans Day."

Uncle Ty's face goes dark. "Do you know what happened on this day in 1918? Do any of you?" He scans the faces around the table: Kes, Grandpa, Sammye (who holds little Kip), and Stringer.

"World War I ended," Grandpa says. "It was a great day."

"Right and wrong," Uncle Ty says. "Two days earlier, on November ninth, the two sides agreed that the armistice would be signed sometime on the eleventh. Then at five o'clock in the morning of that day, they chose the exact ceasefire time."

"Eleven o'clock," Grandpa says.

"That's right," Uncle Ty says. "Word spread quickly to every battlefront. And what did the field commanders do? Did they hunker down and smoke their cigarettes and rejoice? Did they give thanks and wait it out to save lives? No. They ordered thousands of young men—boys, really, just kids—to charge into hailstorms of machinegun fire like lambs to the slaughter."

"Why?" Kes asks.

"To win ground and glory," Uncle Ty says. "More men died in those six hours than the total number of Americans who would die on the beaches of Normandy in 1944."

"I doubt that," Grandpa retorts.

"Do the research, Dad," Uncle Ty says. "Then at exactly eleven o'clock, like it was the end of just another workday, the church bells rang and the shooting stopped and everybody went home. Their job was finished. They'd done as much killing as they could."

"That's sad," Sammye says as she rocks little Kip.

Kes slowly brings her hand to her chest, and begins to tap her sternum. *Breathe.*

DAYS LATER, THE DECISION IS MADE. Both legs will come off.

Kes has dreaded this.

"It will be for the best," Dr. Clark says. "He'll be in much less pain."

Another doctor says, "Once we fit him with his new prosthetics, we can aggressively begin with core strength rehab and balance, and with other motor functions."

Motor? Is that what my Papa will be? A machine?

Kes naps fitfully that afternoon at Brooke and has weird dreams. In one, she's with her papa just before his Humvee rolls over the bomb in Afghanistan. Stop, stop, stop, she yells—to no avail. In another, she's an angel—then a vulture—flying over the carnage. When she wakes up, disheveled on the lounge sofa, Grandpa says Rita is in the doctor's office signing papers for her papa's double amputation.

Kes sits up and rubs her eyes. "Is Uncle Ty back yet?" she asks Grandpa.

He shakes his head no.

Uncle Ty flew his Cessna down to Mexico to run drugs, buy morphine, volunteer in an orphanage, swim with sharks… nobody really knows. People sure guess, though. Every time he flies down from Alaska, he goes on to Mexico. At night.

Rita returns with two green-and-black prosthetic metal legs in her hands. Looking tired but relieved, she holds them up for Kes and Grandpa to see. "Below-the-knee surgeries," she says. "Thursday morning. Both legs."

Breathe.

CHAPTER SEVEN

Silver

ALPHA MOVES WITH HIS EARS UP, TAIL HIGH. The others follow, but not in single file as they did many days ago when the pups were small and the pack traveled atop a summertime alpine ridge, southbound in the sparkling sun. Now they move in a braided pattern through dark woods. And hunt mostly by scent, reading the wet winter ground, following animal trails, and working with wet noses. Keen ears. They stop to rest and nuzzle each other. Earlier, in a meadow just west of the river near the base of a hill, they found a patch of overripe wild strawberries and ate every one. But not today. Today the ground is a patchwork of melting frost and plant decay. They haven't had a sizeable meal in days. No salmon. No moose. No deer. Deer are rare here. But on a distant island, they're abundant. The wolves have yet to learn this. One curious pup, his silver shoulders becoming more distinctive as he grows, often lives with hunger. Still, he has more energy and hunting prowess than his three siblings—one sister and two brothers—that now and then make poor decisions.

Alpha pees at an intersection of two animal trails. Silver notes how one trail holds a scent that's oddly pungent, almost sweet, perhaps dangerous in a way new to him and his kin. Onward, the wolves weave their way through a thinning stand of spruce, cottonwood, and pine. Soon they smell the ocean. Two miles later, they emerge onto a rocky, low-aspect coast where they've been before, and where a small island sits just offshore.

And where, above the falling tide, rest a dozen seals.

Meat.

Silver immediately begins to stalk them, his head down as he slips back into the cover of nearshore alder. Alpha joins him with a mild rebuke—teeth and amber eyes flashing. He'll lead this attack. He commands Silver to follow with two subadults. The foursome moves slowly toward their prey while Mother, the dominant female, waits with the others, silent, expectant. A steady onshore breeze puts the wolves downwind and gives them added advantage. Still, the approach is exposed once the four stalkers leave the alder fringe and begin to walk a narrow intertidal isthmus that expresses itself more with the falling tide. Silver takes note of the acrid smell of a thousand things living and dying—barnacles, limpets, algae, chitons—most too small to make an attractive meal.

The seals, however...

One hundred feet away, the seals sleep and snort, dreaming their seal dreams. Silver observes how at least one among them is always awake and looking about. But no single seal can see everywhere. They face in all directions. When Silver sees one look his way, he freezes. His kin do not—a mistake. The seal panics and lunges toward the safety of the water. The others stampede. Cumbersome on land, they make slow but determined progress. Alpha charges directly for them. The subadults follow. Silver runs an intercept route that aims for the waterline. Alpha and the others miss upslope while Silver plunges into the sea and bites hard into the last seal as it dives. Locked into the seal's rear flank, Silver is pulled down with tremendous force. Seawater floods into his mouth and down his throat, drowning him. He holds on, trying to tear flesh, but the force is too great and he lets go. He surfaces and slowly swims to shore, bedraggled, exhausted. Cold.

Alpha and the two subadults have already returned to the pack.

This is how it's been the past few weeks. Silver alone ate ptarmigan in the high country. He alone found a mountain goat kid dead at the base of a cliff and shared it with the others. He alone alerted the pack of an approaching brown bear sow and her cubs. Then one day while again at higher elevation, creeping up slowly and quietly on a marmot, he accidently dislodged a talus stone. As it began to roll, he reached out and stopped it with a paw, and stabilized it. Without a sound. He then moved on to score his prey. Only his mother knows that the others underestimate him; that he's already an artist, destined to be a better hunter than Alpha.

UNDER WINTER'S BROODING GRAY SKIES, the pack samples low-tide sea stars, then moves upriver to catch a few salmon on a late run. When two of Silver's siblings, Sister and Strong, make lunges for immature bald eagles perched on a beach log, they end up chasing the sky, hungrier than before. They track moose but make no kills. One massive bull stares down half of the pack as if they're bothersome mosquitoes. His antlers appear so big that he could easily throw a pup into the treetops. When one of the subadults— Silver's older cousin—makes an unwise lunge for the hindquarters, the moose kicks him so hard that the cousin limps back to a large spruce, lies down under a graceful green bow, and never gets up. The others nuzzle him tenderly and move on as the light leaves his eyes.

Days later, and back on the coast, Silver sees something out at sea, not far, floating on the surface. Motionless. The water is flat calm. He plunges in and swims after whatever it is. He grabs it by a fin and begins huffing his way back. Mother and his siblings watch. Silver struggles on, working hard, his voice filled with determination, echoing over the cold, still water. As he approaches, Mother, Sister, and Strong plunge in to help. It's a sea lion, dead by some mysterious means. Mother helps to stabilize the heavy animal on shore where the tide can ebb around it. Silver observes how its teeth and jaws are like those of a bear.

While the pups tear into the bounty, Mother raises her head and howls. Alpha and the others, back in the forest, half a mile away, respond. Soon the entire pack is yipping, howling, celebrating their success, all except Silver who cocks his head, smells a faint whiff of smoke, and listens for things beyond the obvious.

Things that could turn his world upside down.

CHAPTER EIGHT

Salt

HANNAH OPENS THE SHOP DOOR out behind the house, where Salt is building a bookshelf for Abraham's bedroom. He hopes his eldest son will read more books one day.

"Phone call for you," Hannah says. "It's that mystery man I told you about." His third call in three months. "I told him you were home. Maybe I shouldn't have."

"It's okay," Salt says.

"This time I asked him who I should tell my husband is calling."

"What did he say?"

"He told me to tell you he's an admirer."

They leave the shop and walk hand in hand up Solomon's wheelchair ramp, through the four-o'clock December darkness, casting long shadows under the overhead nightlight that illuminates Salt's latest attempt at fine carpentry—the handrail he finished only last week, with help from Abraham.

"Did he say anything else?" Salt asks Hannah.

"Only that he hoped he wasn't calling at a bad time."

"That's nice of him."

"I don't know if I trust him," Hannah says. "Don't agree to anything on the phone, okay? Just ask him what he wants, and tell him that you and I make all our decisions together."

Salt gives her a small nod.

Abraham, nearly six feet tall, his face riven with acne, stands against the kitchen counter. Solomon sits nearby in his wheelchair, rocking slightly, his head askew as he drools and grins. Joshua and Jericho burst in from the living room, pushing and shoving each other. "Who is it, Dad?" Abe asks.

"I don't know," Salt says. "Please take Solomon into the living room with Jericho and Joshua, and help him with his homework."

Solomon says loudly, "Oh boy… hoooooomewooooooork…" as Abe wheels him away. Joshua and Jericho burst out laughing and follow their brothers.

Tomorrow is the final day of school before Christmas break.

Finally, it's quiet. Salt picks up the phone. "This is Salt."

"Mr. d'Alene, I'm pleased to speak with you. You're a hard man to catch."

"I work a lot."

"Yes. You're a mechanic these days, but you used to be a trapper up in Interior Alaska, is that right?"

"That's right. I mostly trapped beaver."

"And wolves?"

"Sometimes."

"Do you miss it?"

"Parts of it, yes. Other parts, no."

"Why'd you stop?"

"Lots of reasons." *Solomon's diagnosis. The cold. The killing. The brutality and irony of it all, loving the country while also diminishing it… taking, taking, taking… always taking.* "How'd you find me?"

"Contacts in Fairbanks. You're highly regarded up there, and in Minto and Ester. People told me you'd moved to Strawberry Flats."

"I don't trap anymore." It surprises Salt to hear the resolve in his own voice. Hannah grabs his hand as he says this. Abraham appears at the kitchen door, his face creased with worry, almost grim. Lately he's become fiercely protective of his family, in particular of Solomon at school, and his mother anywhere about town. Salt adds, "The rivers up north don't freeze like they used to. People say it's climate change."

"Yes, everybody has a crazy opinion these days," the mystery man says. "Myself, I deal in providence and opportunity. That's why I've called you. Would you like to hear my proposition? It involves some nice financial security for you and your family."

"And your name?"

"My name isn't important right now. What's important is that we—"

"I think it is important," Salt hears himself say, more forcefully than he intended. "I'm sorry, but I need to know your name and who you work for before this conversation goes any further."

Silence.

Salt adds, "I can't do anything wrong, anything illegal... you see? I'm the sole provider for my family."

"Of course. Your reticence reminds me of Isaiah 50:2: 'Wherefore, when I came, was there no man? When I called, was there none to answer? Is my hand shortened at all, that it cannot redeem? Or have I no power to deliver?'"

"Behold," Salt adds, "at my rebuke I dry up the sea, I make the rivers a wilderness."

"That's right, Mr. d'Alene. Many things are about to improve. But only for those who boldly answer when called. Do you understand?"

"I think so, yes."

"The state house and senate are composed of many good men and women who are evangelicals, the best of Alaska. Their new governor-elect says Alaska will soon be 'open for business.' Are you aware of his Roads to Resources program?"

"A little."

"Those roads cannot be built if federal impediments stand in the way."

"Federal impediments?"

"Endangered or threatened species."

"Oh... you're talking about wolves."

"Yes. Right now, wolves in Alaska are not listed as endangered. But that could change. And if it did... if wolves were relisted as endangered or threatened, it would paralyze the governor's program and complicate things. I understand that wolves have moved into your area, west of town. Is that true? Have you heard them or seen them?"

"I've heard them a few times," Salt says, "out west of town, across the Menzies River. There's a hill over there they might climb up and howl from. I can't say for sure. I've never been over there. The river is not easy to cross. Other people in Strawberry Flats have heard them too. A group of veterans... guys from Texas and Oklahoma mostly, who live a couple miles from here, have heard them more than anybody else. They might have seen them too. I don't know."

"I can pay you a thousand dollars a day, up to ten days a month, to reconnoiter the area and report to me by phone when I call you back. How does that sound?"

"That's ten grand a month."

"Up to that amount, yes."

"Not for trapping? Just for looking around?"

"Yes. For detailed notes and maps that you'll keep to yourself. I'll pay you for your abilities, but also for your discretion. Is that clear?"

Salt stares at Hannah and Abe, thinking back to when he nearly drowned up in Minto and Abe fished him out of the icy river, and Hannah told her friends: "My husband tried to kill himself and our eldest son. We're done. No more trapping. No more cabin life at minus forty. Or even at minus ten."

"Mr. d'Alene, are you there?"

"Yes... I'm here. I understand what you're asking for."

"Good. It's wintertime, a good time for tracking. I'll phone you in March and we'll talk again then. You'll submit your notes by mail and be paid in hard cash."

"How can I trust you? I mean... not to be rude. This is a big commitment you're asking for. How do I know you'll pay me?"

"Wherefore putting away lying, speak every man truth with his neighbor—"

"—for we are members of one another."

"Ephesians 4:25. I look forward to meeting you one day, Mr. d'Alene. Merry Christmas to you and your family."

"Thank you. I still didn't get your name."

"In time, you will."

"WELL?" HANNAH ASKS when Salt hangs up. "What did he say?"

Salt feels a bubble of hope rise in his heart. "Remember that clinical trial at Johns Hopkins, the one we talked about for Solomon?"

"Yes."

"I think we might be able to afford it."

CHAPTER NINE

Kes

"Stop feeling sorry for yourself," Kes says as she lies in bed on the morning of her twelfth birthday, New Year's Day. Last night, she cried herself to sleep. Like a little girl.

Is that what I still am? A little girl?

She would have slept longer this morning, but a neighbor woke her up with his stupid leaf blower and lawnmower.

The January temperatures are twenty-some degrees warmer than they used to be.

"You're going to have to toughen up," Uncle Ty told Kes back in November. "It's simple, my young apprentice. You either muddle your way through your days, months, and years until you're half dead, or you stand tall and live, and give your papa something to return to and yourself something to be proud of."

Kes thinks of Merlyn and Arthur and the knights of Camelot who stood against the evils of the world; of Arthur when he was young, as the Wart who slept on battlements under a bearskin and imagined himself falling upward into the stars.

How old was Arthur then? Ten? Eleven?

"What have I done at eleven?" Kes quietly asks herself, still in bed. "I cried my eyes out when Papa first came home. But then I helped him to walk on his new legs and get his smile back—the beginning of a smile, at least." *That's what I've done.*

After the doctors amputated Papa's legs, they waited for the swelling to go down, then quickly fitted him with his fancy titanium prosthetics and had him up and walking by Thanksgiving. By mid-December, after a lot of physical therapy on fancy equipment, including a standing wave pool where

Papa learned to belly surf, he returned home to Lubbock. Everybody wanted to see him.

These days in Lubbock, they go for slow walks, usually around the block. Sometimes they drive to a local park to look at birds. Papa loves birds. Some of his best songs from before are about birds. Every week, Rita, Papa, Kes, and little Kip drive down to San Antonio for Papa's physical therapy, where the physical therapists at the Center for the Intrepid tell him he's excelling on his new legs and feet. Papa still has some pain, and probably always will, the PTs say. But nothing like before. For Christmas, the PTs gifted him a new pair of black-red-white Nike Air Jordans.

He smiles more than he used to, and the whole world brightens when he does.

"I'm proud of you," Uncle Ty told Kes on Christmas Day, just a week ago, when he phoned from Alaska to hear the latest progress about his little brother. "You're doing good work down there, Kes. Remember, none of us raised you to look for a knight. We raised you to pick up the sword and be one yourself."

Still, no voice for Papa. Not yet, anyway. Day number 150 since the bomb in Afghanistan, and he has yet to speak. Or sing. Or laugh.

BORN ON NEW YEAR'S DAY, Kes shares that distinction with Paul Revere, as Grandpa reminds her every year. He loves the American Revolutionary War and Paul Revere's ride to tell Americans the British are coming. He loves everything about American patriotism.

Instagram star Jessica Universe and YouTube cosmetics expert Alexandrea Garza have New Year's Day birthdays too. Kes knows this because her Lubbock friends told her. Celia, who got her ears pierced on her own birthday back in early November, recently texted: *Allison's mom says your mom says you might move to Alaska where your uncle can hear wolves from his front porch. Is that true?*

Yes.

Omg. R u scared?

No.

Allison says your uncle wears a bandana and has a missing front tooth and he flies his own plane.

Yes, a Cessna 207 Skywagon.

Omg. I just googled Cessna. Your uncle is badass.
Ikr.

Kes suspects it's big gossip that she might one day live with wolves and become one herself and eat raw meat and howl at the moon. And get killed by a bear.

Somebody raps lightly on her bedroom door.

"Come in, Grandpa."

He pokes his white-haired head inside. "The British are coming," he says. "How'd you know it's me?"

"It's always you on my birthday."

"Oh, is today your birthday?" He smiles mischievously as he steps into her room with a tray of cookies and tea. "Well then, happy birthday to my favorite twelve-year-old. Did you get any good sleep last night?"

"No."

None of them did because neighbors down the street got drunk and invited over a bunch of friends with motorcycles and big diesel trucks and guns, and blew off fireworks. And maybe shot off their guns. They do it every year on New Year's Eve and the Fourth of July. It's always been bad. But with Papa now sensitive to loud noises, last night was horrible. The cops finally came and quieted things down after midnight. Papa spent the night curled into a fetal position, wearing his bathrobe, headphones, and new legs, listening to Willie Nelson and the Traveling Wilburys to help mask the noise.

"Had your Uncle Tyler been here," Grandpa says as he sets Kes's birthday cookie-and-tea tray on her bed, "he would have gone down there and started a war with those fireworks nutballs."

"He hates war, Grandpa."

"A riot then."

Kes sits up and eats a cookie and sips her tea. It's almost too warm out—in January!—to drink hot tea. Crazy. "I've been reading about Alaska," she tells Grandpa. "Some of the islands up there have wolves, but no brown bears. And other islands have brown bears, but no wolves. How cool is that? It's called mutual exclusivity."

"Sounds fair to me," Grandpa says.

She knows that he loves it when she reads. He once told her: "Words are magic; they come in boxes called books." Her favorite subjects are wizards and lizards, galaxies and stars, rivers and rocks. And science. Always science.

Over and over she read *Jurassic Park* and *The Once and Future King*, and tales of riding the fossil byways through geologic time. Last year in school she memorized the rock strata in the Grand Canyon and learned how the Colorado River, much younger than the rocks, like a new kid in town, carved the canyon and exposed the rock layers into magical shapes that her teacher said Michelangelo couldn't begin to match.

"Alaska," Grandpa says. "You're thinking about it then?"

Kes shrugs.

"If your papa's getting better here in Lubbock, do you still want to go?"

"We're in the middle of a drought here, Grandpa. I heard on TV that five million trees have died in Texas. Uncle Ty says the aquifer is dying, that it's all messed up from fracking, and that Papa needs wild country and wild animals to really get better, a place where there's lots of rain and tall trees and clean air and good gardening."

"Your Uncle Ty says lots of things, Kes. Be sure to listen to others too, and not just to him. Moving to Alaska could be a serious hardship on Rita and little Kip. Think about that. You'd have to sell this house and go to a new school and make new friends. And it would probably be the end of Danny and Rita's band."

Kes eats another two cookies. She's already thought of this. She would miss Allison and Celia, and a few others. But not in how they gossip and giggle for hours, and irritate her in ways Kes never noticed until after her papa came home wounded. And not in how they talk about God and how everything is according to his plan, and for a reason.

If God is so great, how come Stringer's three-year-old nephew got brain cancer and died? What kind of God does that?

A couple months ago Allison and Celia and Kes's other friends formed a girls' club and gave themselves new names and talked about which boys were the cutest and funniest—all of which now seems trite to Kes.

Grandpa sits at the foot of her bad.

"Would you come with us?" she asks him. "If we moved to Alaska, would you come too?" She's been meaning to ask him for weeks. It wouldn't be right for them all to go north and leave Grandpa alone in Lubbock. He'd still have his Monday night bowling league and Friday night poker club. But Uncle Ty says the veterans at Willynillyville play poker too, all the time, and eat moose chili.

Grandpa runs his gnarled brown fingers through his white hair and says, "I'd give anything to see Danny be his old self again and make music. If

Alaska could do that for him and I could help in some way, then yes, I'd go. Besides, old farts like me need to shake things up now and then to stay alive."

To see Danny be his old self again and make music... Hearing this makes Kes smile. This is her dream too, her deepest hope.

Papa still hasn't hummed a note of music, or picked up his Martin D-28 guitar. But everybody is hopeful. Rita leaves the guitar standing in the corner of the living room. "As if it might jump into Danny's lap one day," Grandpa likes to say, "and beg him to be strummed." It's true, though Papa is more of a picker than a strummer, and a good one at that... like James Taylor, though nobody can really pick like James Taylor, also known as J. T. Papa used to say that J. T. invented a whole new style of syncopation.

After last night's fireworks, Kes is beginning to think she doesn't like Lubbock. But the band? She will miss the band. Summers on the road. How Papa and Rita would sit facing each other on the bus, their knees interlocked (Papa drinking his Corona with lime, Rita her margarita with salt) as they worked up a new song, their voices like poetry, but better. And Sammye adding her voice on top. Pure beauty.

GRANDPA SOMETIMES JOINS Rita, Papa, Kes, and little Kip on the trip to sunny San Antonio where the doctors and therapists continue to evaluate Papa. Kes wants to ask: Will he ever dance again? Laugh and sing? Write a haiku about Rita's smile? Tousle my hair? Play the guitar with his hummingbird hands? That's what Rita used to say: "Your papa plays with hummingbird hands."

Two days after her birthday, Kes gets a text from Allison: *I've been thinking.*

Uh oh.

Very funny. I'm serious.

About what?

Seconds later, Allison calls her and says, "Remember that scene in *Beauty and the Beast* when Belle escapes from the castle and rides her horse into the dark forest and gets surrounded by snarling wolves?"

"Yeah, I think so." Kes remembers that Allison loves movies, especially cowboy Westerns and animated Disney musicals.

"Don't get eaten, okay?" Allison says. "By wolves, I mean. In Alaska. If you go, I really do think they could kill you and eat you."

CHAPTER TEN

Silver

WINTER IS HARD, almost cruel in how the weather swings from snow to rain and back. The ground freezes solid in open meadows where Silver and his kin find dozens of dead voles that keep them alive, but nothing more. The big bull moose drops his antlers, yet remains a formidable foe, rebuffing the pack for three days as ravens watch from leafless cottonwoods. Even at night, the bull stays on his feet.

The next day, during one coordinated attack, two of Silver's older cousins take direct hoof hits to the shoulders and hips, and stagger off. As the moose runs away, Mother chases it, flanks it, and charges in at an angle. She runs up a fallen log, and with every ounce of her remaining energy launches herself onto the bull's back. The moose dodges and sends her flailing to the ground, then turns to finish her off. Silver charges in from behind. The moose swings a hind foot that clips his head. Everything goes dark. When he awakens, Silver sees half the pack around the moose, baring their teeth and snarling, their starvation apparent in their lean faces and fallen ears. They are many. They should prevail. They must prevail. But they are too long without substantial food, and this is no ordinary moose.

With a turn of his head, Alpha leads them back into the woods where the two injured subadults bed down with Old One, his age crippling him more each day, and with Weak, Silver's least capable sibling, also badly injured. Mother curls herself around him and licks his face. Weak would normally lick her back, but not this time. His eyes close, never to reopen, and Mother moans through the night.

TWO DAYS LATER, the pack is a short distance west of the river, and still hungry, when a sharp sound shatters earth and sky. The wolves freeze, wide-eyed.

Fear.

Twice again, the sound hits them.

Still alive? Yes. They look at each other keenly, ears up, breath rising in the cold winter air.

No snow.

No food.

No answers.

Alpha is about to lead on when another sharp crack rattles them, and they all take off, running through the open forest.

CHAPTER ELEVEN

Salt

SALT IS HALFWAY between the end of Menzies River Road, where he parked his old white Toyota hatchback, and the river itself—walking with caution as always, making as little sound as possible—when he hears gunshots. *Bam, bam.* Followed by two more. *Bam, bam.* Rifles, near as he can tell: 30.06 or .270. Moose hunting season is over. Deer season will end the last day of January, one week from now. But deer are rare here on the mainland. *What then? People sighting in? Adjusting their rifle scopes? Or just goofing off, shooting cans off logs?* Most everybody in town sights in their rifles at the gravel pits, near the airstrip. Not out here near the Menzies River, at the quiet end of town.

More shots. Different this time, closer. Small caliber. Handguns. Salt quickly leaves the trail and takes cover beneath a tall spruce with ample, low-sweeping boughs. No other vehicles were parked at the end of Menzies River Road twenty minutes ago, when he left his Toyota. *Who could this be?* Salt's best guess: the keep-to-themselves veterans who live nearby in Willynillyville, less than a mile away. They could easily walk here from there. Salt wishes now that he'd worn his Shoshone moccasins, the ones he'd gotten as a young man in Idaho and used all the time to sneak about when he learned to trap and hunt; how he would wear them when he watched deer in the meadows, and once saw a cougar that didn't see him, and many times enjoyed the Spokane girls who would skinny-dip in Priest Lake, a lifetime ago, before he brought Jesus into his life, and met Hannah, and moved to Fairbanks, and began to worry.

Worry, worry, worry... that's all Salt seems to do nowadays. Worry about Solomon and his muscular dystrophy. Worry about Hannah being too thin, and how Sol's death would leave her as a shadow of herself. Worry about his own health, coming from a long line of middle-aged men who have a bad habit of dying of heart attacks. How his own heart, just this last year—like clockwork, when he turned fifty—began to beat unevenly. And of course, worry about money. Always money. And about the river up ahead, how attractive it is to visit, flanked by summertime flowers and wild strawberries, but how difficult it is to cross, especially in winter, after the big earthquake that lifted the land twelve feet and steepened the gradient and accelerated the flow. And about Joshua being too unfocused and out of control, maybe having ADHD. And about Jericho and his eagerness to make others laugh without any regard for what's right and wrong. And about Abraham—in some ways, mostly about Abraham—with his dark moods and growing fascination with war and guns and religion and race; his outward contempt for Muslims and "stupid snowflakes" and "libtards." *Where'd that come from?* The other day Abe's social studies teacher at the Strawberry Flats Public School suggested that Salt and Hannah might want to restrict his time on his phone and on the internet, and talk to him about his "anger issues."

And now another worry. Gunshots from the direction of the river. Followed by a strange silence. No voices or distant laughter. No sign of other people. Yet.

All Salt intends to do today is look for wolf sign and earn one thousand dollars in secret. Read his Bible and eat his jerky and cheese. Sit still for a while and listen, and learn. He's always been a good listener. That's one thing he misses most about trapping: the silence. A silence so profound that he could imagine it stretching all the way from Alaska to Asia.

His mother named her only son Salt and her only daughter Light, from the Sermon on the Mount: "You are the salt of the earth... and the light of the world." And d'Alene? "I married your father," his mother once told him, "a wonderful man of French descent whose ancestors thought the Native people were tough traders who had Coeur d'Alene—hearts like the metal tool, an awl."

Once he knew this, Salt walked confidently through the world, untouched by the teasing he got by other boys who called him "Saltine" and "Cracker."

And wolves? "Beware of the false prophets," says Matthew 7:15, "which come to you in sheep's clothing, but inwardly they are ravening wolves." So, Salt learned to fear them; to despise them before he ever saw one, believing the world would be better off without a single wolf. And when he finally saw his first one, on the Minto Flats, caught in one of his traps, Salt could see the wolf was in pain, and afraid. He shot it without satisfaction.

AND NOW, FROM THE DIRECTION OF THE RIVER, he hears voices. Laughter. Lively banter.

Salt leaves the snowless trail and gets low behind a large and generous spruce bow that reaches nearly to the ground and makes a perfect veil. He goes stone still.

Sure enough, it's three Willynillyville vets moving down the trail, talking easy with their Remingtons over their shoulders, voices crisp and clear in the cold air. Salt recognizes the McCall cousins, with their neck tattoos and short-cropped hair. The other man has a striking red beard flecked with white. Cap and the red-bearded man wear ball caps and US Army green field jackets, with beige Carhartt pants and Xtra-Tuff rubber boots. Chippy is dressed in military-issue camo and black Army boots. Salt hears Chippy say to the other two, "It was a 1901 Colt .38 six-shooter, like the one Black Jack Pershing used when he went after Pancho Villa."

"Gold-plated, I'll bet," says the red-bearded man.

"Not at all. Pershing wasn't like that."

"He was a general, Chippy, like every other general."

"Meaning what?"

"Meaning he was an arrogant idiot who got his ass kicked in France one year later."

"The general who wins the battle is the one who makes the fewest mistakes."

"Whatever happened to Pancho Villa?" Cap asks.

"He opened up a Taco Bell in El Paso," Chippy answers.

They all laugh, then abruptly stop and appear to focus; to listen with heightened senses.

No more than forty feet away, Salt holds his breath.

"I'll tell you what," Chippy finally says. "Walk around the UT campus in El Paso on a warm afternoon and you'll break your neck looking at all the foxy ladies."

"Foxy Lady, like the Jimi Hendrix song."

"Eric Clapton says Hendrix was the best rock and roll guitarist ever."

"What about B. B. King?"

"He played the blues."

"I think a Hispanic gal from El Paso won the Miss USA pageant a year or two ago. Or maybe it was Miss World. Or Miss Universe."

"Why is Miss Universe always from Earth?"

"I don't know, cousin," Cap says. "Why do people think they're right even when they're wrong?"

"The truth is the truth, guys," Chippy says, "even if no one believes it. And a lie is a lie, even if everyone believes it."

"Thank you, oh great wise man of the Menzies River," the red-bearded man says.

Chippy takes a low bow and says, "You're welcome. I'll bet you didn't know I was a philosopher."

"Nope, just a gun nut."

"Wait until I get my van up here from Texas. It's an arsenal."

"Yep, a real gun nut."

"Hey, if guns were ostracized, only ostriches would have guns."

"We're all gonna die, Chippy. You know that, right?"

"Not me. I don't have time to die."

More laughter.

Salt hears a raven call from behind him, sharp and distinctive. As if on cue, the three vets turn directly toward him. *Do they see me?* Salt feels his heart beat like crazy. A long moment hangs in the air. The vets appear to stare right at him, or through him.

Don't move.

Another raven call, again from directly behind Salt, very near, but different from before. More of a signal than a call; more human than bird. The three vets turn and continue east on the trail toward the parking area, once again jiving each other, busy in conversation.

Still seated, Salt waits a long moment, then slowly turns to see one more Willynillyville vet staring straight at him—from behind. A Black man in military fatigues. The only Black man Salt has ever seen in Strawberry Flats. *Where'd he come from? How'd he outflank me?* Sixty feet away, he stands motionless until he finally tips his broad-brimmed Stetson, smiles as if mildly bemused, and disappears into the forest, headed east.

Salt feels defeated, nailed to the ground. And he hasn't even crossed the river yet, uncertain if he can, given how wild, forceful, and deep it can be. Not for another half an hour does he get up, slowly, stiffly, and begin to walk back to his Toyota. *I came out here to look for any sign of wolves. And what do I find? Men in a pack—wolves of another kind—who instead find me.*

"I'll pay you for your abilities," the mystery man told him when he called in March. "But also for your discretion. Is that clear?"

Salt shakes his head.

This is not going to be easy.

CHAPTER TWELVE

Kes

"Have you ever kissed a boy?" Kes's cousin Julie asks her as they walk along the Rio Grande, deep in Southwest Texas, with Allison and Celia lagging behind.

"No. Have you?"

"No. But this one boy at my school says he likes me."

This makes sense to Kes. Julie is crazy cute—a perfect boy magnet. She's also super religious, like her mom and dad in Houston.

"Look, a snake." Kes runs forward to catch it.

"No snakes." Julie stops in the intense heat; the sun is a furnace in the cloudless March sky. Earlier, she had freaked out when she first got dirt in her hair. But she later won Kes's admiration when she threw river mud like a maniac.

"This one's harmless," Kes says as she holds up the little snake.

"Kill it."

"No way."

"Throw it away then."

Kes gently releases it into the riverside reeds as Allison and Celia catch up.

Papa and Uncle Charles, Julie's dad, had started out hiking with the girls. But when Papa had trouble with his metal legs in the sticky river mud, he turned back toward camp. Kes was about to join him when Uncle Charles, in his bossy way, insisted that he would go back with Papa. "You stay with the other girls," he told Kes.

Celia thumbs her phone while Allison, lathered in sunscreen and wearing a sunhat, says, "In the movie *Lonesome Dove*, when the cowboys were crossing a river during their cattle drive, one of them fell off his horse and got bit by a snake and turned a weird color and stopped breathing and died. The other cowboys buried him and said a prayer and rode away and never came back. I stopped watching after that."

"That was a cottonmouth," Kes tells her. "This is a western ratsnake."

"The cowboys said it was a water moccasin."

"Water moccasins and cottonmouths are the same thing."

"I watched *Jurassic Park* too," Allison adds. "How all those dinosaurs got out of their cages and corrals and stuff, and started running around eating people."

"I love that movie," Kes says. "The book too."

"Not me," Allison says.

"Not me either," Julie adds.

"Those scientists on that island would have never been able to control the dinosaurs," Kes says, "no matter what they did. They should have known that. Reptiles can reproduce without having sex."

"Without sex?" Julie says.

"No way," Allison says in mock shock, as if trying to impress Julie.

Celia, wearing her new earrings, continues to fiddle with her phone.

"If things get really hard for reptiles," Kes tells them, "like really hot and dry, and if boy lizards can't find any girl lizards, then some girl lizards, if they're determined to have babies, can make copies of themselves... a whole bunch of little lizards exactly like the mom. It's called parthenogenesis. Michael Crichton should have known that."

"You mean the moms just get pregnant on their own?"

"Not really pregnant. It's called asexual reproduction."

"That's weird."

"Who's Michael Crichton?"

"He's the author of *Jurassic Park*," Kes says. "One day he was in a dentist's office when he read a magazine story about amber—you know, fossilized tree resin? How the amber sometimes oozes out of trees and traps insects. He suddenly realized that some mosquitoes that bit dinosaurs would land on a tree and get caught in the sticky resin, and be preserved for millions of years until scientists came along and discovered them after the resin had hardened into a glassy rock with a mosquito trapped inside. And inside the mosquito was dino DNA. Is that cool or what? He was so excited that he couldn't sleep for days. That's when he sat down and wrote the book."

"How do you know all this stuff?" Julie asks.

"My Uncle Ty tells me. And my Aunt Kathy. Her son has a girlfriend from Poland who went to school for a year in Lubbock. She told me too. She reads a lot."

"So, Kathy is… who again?" Julie asks.

"Rita's sister," Kes tells her.

"Oh, your stepmom's sister?"

"Yeah."

"Do you remember your birth mom?" Julie asks Kes.

Allison and Celia stop to listen.

"Only a little," Kes says. "She died when I was five."

"Yeah, I know," Julie says. "My dad told me."

Kes wants to change the subject. She says, "Let's look for more snakes."

"No," Julie protests.

Kes grins. "Just kidding."

Celia is already back on her phone, searching for a signal, as Kes takes a moment to drink it all in, the river cool on her bare feet, the cactus flowers in full bloom, the canyon wrens singing the river along, and white-throated swifts darting and dancing overhead, catching insects on the wing. Kes has always wanted to see this part of Texas, the Big Bend country, the place Uncle Ty calls "the jewel of the Chihuahuan Desert, the only piece of the original Texas as the Comanches knew it, free of cattle, oil, fracking, and ranches, and too many people and their urban sprawl." And now she's here, on spring break with her friends and her cousin Julie, and Julie's family, and many others. And, best of all, Grandpa and Papa. And while Papa still doesn't talk or sing or laugh or play his guitar or pull practical jokes like he used to, before Afghanistan, Uncle Ty believes Alaska will fix all that.

Will it? Will anything fix Papa? Ever?

THAT NIGHT, THEY GATHER IN A CAMPGROUND outside of Terlingua. As the setting sun warms the volcanic summits of the Chisos Mountains, a Cessna roars in from the northeast and dips a wing as it passes overhead.

Everybody waves except Papa, who cowers and pulls his hands to his ears. Rita holds him and says, "It's okay, Danny dear. It's your crazy brother, with good friends of ours. We'll soon have a real party, a real Texas barbecue. How's that sound?"

Papa raises his head and looks away at the mountains. Kes watches

Uncle Charles shake his own head in disgust. He's never liked Uncle Ty, his older brother.

Uncle Ty shows up an hour later in a rusty old truck. He must have parked his plane at a nearby airfield. With him are some tattooed men Kes has never seen before, though she's heard of them: Chippy and Cap McCall from Alaska—and before that, Oklahoma. "Nail-bitten veterans," Rita calls them, "a little messed up in the head." PTSD for sure. Post-Traumatic Stress Disorder. But nice men "once you get to know them," according to Uncle Ty. And joy of joys, Stringer and Sammye also climb out of the truck. Kes runs to them. Big hugs all around. Rita and Sammye hold each other for a long time. Uncle Ty tells Kes that he detoured through Austin to pick up Stringer and Sammye as a surprise.

They gently hug Papa and tell him he looks great. Papa nods.

Uncle Ty checks in with Papa as well, who sits in a lawn chair. He rubs Papa's shoulders from behind and kisses the back of his head where his hair is getting long. Uncle Ty then walks over to Uncle Charles, the Houston developer with six kids and as many Bibles, and shakes his hand with no show of affection. When Grandma was alive, all her sons and their families would get together once a year for a big reunion up on the Llano Estacado, west of Lubbock, where Kes fell in love with camping. But since Grandma's passing, the glue is gone. The family now sees each other maybe only once every three years, and it's a strain. Because Uncle Ty plans to "steal Danny and his family"—according to Uncle Charles—and take them to Alaska, and maybe take Grandpa too, a large gathering seemed in order. Best to make it a barbecue in Big Bend. Barbecuing is an art in Texas, and nobody does it better than Grandpa.

"Where to from here?" Uncle Charles asks Uncle Ty as everybody sits around a large campfire in the evening air, eating potato salad and barbecued beef ribs. Rumor has it that Uncle Ty and Chippy and Cap McCall, just arrived from Alaska, plan to fly the Cessna down to Mexico and maybe Central America, or all the way to Colombia, before they return to Texas in early July. Then, if all goes according to plan, Chippy and Cap will drive their van to Bellingham, in Washington State, and put it on a ferry to Alaska. If Papa is able and willing, he'll join Uncle Ty and Kes in the Cessna and fly north. Grandpa too. Rita and little Kip will come up a few weeks later, in August, by commercial jet to Juneau, and from there a small air taxi to Strawberry Flats, the little town where Uncle Ty has built a homestead, his so-called "Willynillyville."

Hard to believe. Kes gets dizzy at times just thinking about it, as if she were going to Africa or the rings of Saturn.

Uncle Ty ignores Charles's where-to-from-here question and says, "Hey Kes, have you checked out the night sky here? It's so clear that you can see the Andromeda Galaxy with your naked eye."

"Really?"

"Yep. It's near Cassiopeia. I'll show you later with a spotting scope." He opens a can of beer.

Chippy and Cap do the same.

Rita and Sammye softly sing a few of their favorite Whoa Nellie songs, the ones Papa and Rita wrote shortly after they first got together, back in the day, according to Stringer, when Papa was "at the top of his game." Papa's Martin D-28 sits quietly in a case nearby. Rita makes sure it goes everywhere with him. He ignores it and licks the last of the barbecue sauce off his fingers, appearing content. A few times in the last several months Kes and Rita have caught faint smiles on his face and have done their best to help it along. Whenever they tell him they love him, which is daily, he sometimes nods slightly, wraps his arms about his chest, and rocks. On his best days, he hums ever so softly, and plays on the floor with little Kip.

"Don't do anything stupid down in Mexico, brother," Uncle Charles says after Rita and Sammye finish a song.

Uncle Ty, the pirate, built like a coat hanger, thin and strong, grins back.

"I mean it," Uncle Charles says.

"Thank you for your concern," Uncle Ty replies.

"I just want what's right."

"Says the developer who builds homes in Houston floodplains."

"For people who are happy to live there."

"Can they swim?"

"And what building and zoning codes do you have up in Alaska?"

"No codes, no zoning, no covenants. We build however we want, willy-nilly."

"That's why you call your little hippie commune Willynillyville?"

"That's right, Charles. You should come up and join us."

"No thanks, Henry David Thoreau."

"Oh, so now you think—"

"Stop," Grandpa says. "We're not going to do this. We're not going to argue. Think of your mother, both of you. We're here for her, God rest her soul."

"Amen," Uncle Charles says.

"Amen," Julie repeats, sitting next to him.

"Amen," says her smaller brothers and sisters, who play on the dusty ground with little Kip, as sparks from the fire dance around them.

After an awkward moment, Uncle Ty asks, "Can you see the Milky Way, Kes?"

She looks up. "Yes."

"So, get this," Uncle Ty says. "If our entire solar system were the size of a single human blood cell, and you put it in, say… Colorado, the Milky Way Galaxy would be about the size of the entire contiguous US. All the lower forty-eight states combined."

"Really?"

"Yep. And if you then reduced the Milky Way down to the size of a sixty-watt light bulb and hung it in the blackness of outer space, the next nearest galaxy, filled with a trillion stars, would be another sixty-watt light bulb about ten miles away."

"Andromeda?"

"Yep. Can you see it?"

Again, she looks up. "You said it's near Cassiopeia?"

Uncle Ty gets to his feet, goes to the truck, and comes back with a spotting scope on a tripod. "C'mon, I'll show you."

Kes stands up to go with him. She turns and extends her hand and says, "Papa, you want to join us?" He takes her hand in his, softly.

They leave the crowded campfire and walk into the night. Stringer, Allison, and Celia tag along, followed by Julie, who runs to catch up, waving her flashlight into the night. "This is so cool," she says.

"Better than reading the Bible?" Uncle Ty asks her as he sets up the tripod.

"My dad says the Bible has all the answers," Julie says.

"Your dad is a Christian because of geography," Uncle Ty tells her. "Nothing more. Had he been born in Syria or Saudi Arabia or Iran, and raised to read the Koran, he'd be a devout Muslim. It's that simple, Julie. Please turn off your flashlight."

Julie turns it off. Everything goes dark except for the night sky that blazes overhead. So many stars. Kes stares with disbelief, feeling weightless, a part of it all.

"There she is," Uncle Ty says as he backs away to let the others look through the spotting scope. "Andromeda, what a gal."

"How far away is it?" Kes asks him.

"Two and a half million light years," Uncle Ty says. "That's how long ago the light hitting our eyes right now left that galaxy, back at the beginning of the Pleistocene here on Earth, the Ice Age, when saber-toothed cats preyed on North American camels, and massive glaciers began to carve Puget Sound and the Great Lakes, and a squirrel could cross all of Kentucky from tree to tree without ever touching the ground."

When Kes feels Papa squeeze her hand, she hugs him back with all her might.

CHAPTER THIRTEEN

Silver

LATE APRIL. Winter commands the mornings with frost and cold, but retreats quickly as the sun climbs high and each day stretches out longer than the one before.

Silver and his pack thrive after killing a subadult moose and finding a beached deer, a young buck that must have drowned while swimming Icy Strait. The pack is nine strong now, out of thirteen from a year ago, their numbers down but not critically low. Only Old One moves slower than before.

Tens of thousands of shorebirds string out along the tideline beaches and probe the sand and take flight en masse, as if each flock were a single organism and every bird a separate muscle or feather in that organism. Together they flex against the sky, darting hither and fro, flashing silver, white, and black before settling back down and chirping their delight to find more food, hungry as wolves. Soon, they will leave for the far north. A few days ago, hardly any graced these beaches. A few days from now, hardly any will again. But for now, they own the stage, moving as one, bound by laws stronger than gravity, navigating over great distances by continental shorelines and starry skies.

Geese and cranes arrive as well. They would make a full meal, but it's foolish to stalk Canada geese. Get anywhere close—as Silver and Sister have tried a couple times, sneaking up through last summer's rye grass, the tall, dry stalks noisy as rattles—and a single goose honks up the entire neighborhood and sends everybody flying, leaving the wolves earthbound, chasing their own tails.

Alpha leads the pack back into the forest, north along the river but not too near, keeping ample cover between them and anything that might see them from the other side. Beware. Something lives over there that makes smoke and noise and deep tracks that go everywhere and nowhere. Something two-legged, tall, and upright. Silver knows it. He can feel it. The signs this animal leaves speak to a hunger different from any other. Because of this, Silver, Sister, Mother, and the subadults show great caution, while Alpha and Strong, Silver's other remaining sibling, are wary but not consistently so. Strong can crush a moose femur with one bite, but cannot see a seal concealed and motionless on a gray rocky shore a short distance away. If he were to come upon a suspicious carcass, Strong would likely dig in before making a full inspection. And if he were on his own for a month or so, he'd starve. Old One too.

It's a beautiful, brutal existence, the only one Silver and his kin know, and they live it daily, far from the soft comfort of domestic dogs, but not without love. They flick their tails and twitch their ears and curl their lips, and bark, growl, howl, and whine, but mostly squeak—intimate sounds barely audible to others—to convey many complex emotions, as they do now, gathering up to end the day. Come nightfall, Alpha and Mother carefully choose a bed, and the family lies down in a circle, each wolf side by side with the others, stretched out in the warmer nights of spring. Unlike winter, when they curl more tightly into a ball and into each other, and wrap their tails over their noses, and let the snow cover them, leaving only a small breathing hole above each wolf. Mother is the last to lie down, after she walks the circle and checks on each member of her pack, and licks Alpha's face, and nuzzles Old One into his dreams.

THE FOLLOWING DAY, Alpha lets Silver take the lead as Mother and Sister sweep up behind Old One, who lags. Silver finds a route that turns back around to the south, still west of the river, and climbs through thick alder. The ground smells faintly of otter. Up he goes, his alert ears filled with the rhythmic breathing of his family close behind. Now the smell of alder assails him as pale green leaves unfurl themselves everywhere. Silver stops, hears a kinglet above, a sparrow below, and receives a confirming huff from Alpha. Onward he climbs. This is the first true elevation the pack has gained since coming over the mountains last year and following the river to the sea.

And now the route levels off, and the tree cover grows thin, and suddenly...

it's open. Clear. A summit. Silver and his kin stand atop a hill profiled by a gentle, though heavily wooded, route up from the north and a steep face—almost a cliff—to the south. The uppermost rocky promontory is covered in bird droppings and a strange material—a brittle wrapping of some kind—that Silver avoids but Strong samples and curls back his lips after one taste. To the south, east, and west, the pack can see for miles, and smell the ocean, and find the river sparkling in the sun, bound for the sea.

Silver sees it and thinks: salmon.

Mother appears to take it all in, as if mapping their world. To the west, beyond the forelands and a distant bay, tall white mountains stand bold against the sky, where they gather enough snow to birth great glaciers. To the east, smoke rises from wood-burning stoves and speaks to the presence of tall uprights, but will not alarm the wolves until they smell it and taste it. For now, the smoke goes south, driven by north winds out of the Yukon.

Lost in the moment, Silver is suddenly startled by a bald eagle that sails by, eye to eye with him and very near, the tips of its wing feathers flexing gently on the updraft. As quickly as it appears, it is gone.

Two of the subadults begin to yip and softly howl, covering one continuous note. Mother snaps her head to and fro, uncertain if this is the right time and place. Strong joins in and raises the volume on the same note. Things could go either way—end this now or do it right—until Old One walks out to the promontory, turns his gray muzzle to the sky, and finds a series of three long, descending notes that the entire pack can sing.

And they do.

IN THE TOWN OF STRAWBERRY FLATS, nearby to the east, people stop and listen, none more intensely than Salt d'Alene. And he wonders: *What am I going to tell those state of Alaska men in Juneau? And what are the doctors going to say about Solomon?*

CHAPTER FOURTEEN

Salt

THE MAN WHO CALLS HIMSELF KELMAR RADDOCK sits opposite Salt in the back room of a hole-in-the-wall restaurant in Juneau's Mendenhall Valley. Ruddy faced and older than Salt had expected, he wears horn-rimmed glasses and a blue blazer, and runs his finger over a topographic map that covers most of the table. "From everything you've told us," he says, "the wolves appear to travel here, here, and here, is that right?"

"Yes." Salt points. "And here."

"And this is where you've been crossing the river, due west of the road?"

"Yes." Salt fidgets under the harsh fluorescent light. He doesn't want this Mr. Raddock, if that's his real name, to press him on the difficulty of the river crossing, or if Salt has recruited any help, which Mr. Raddock—the mystery man now revealed—strictly forbade from the beginning. Only Hannah, Salt's wife, is to know that he's investigating wolves and will probably soon trap them.

"And you park your car here, every time, at the end of the road, and walk west?"

"Yes."

"Wouldn't that seem suspicious to others?"

"No. People drive out there all the time and park to go hiking and berry picking."

"Are there other places you could cross?"

"Yes, due west of my house, here. And much further upriver, where the road to Crystal Bay National Marine Reserve crosses a bridge. Going that far north would save me crossing by foot, but it would add twenty miles round trip of heavy bushwhacking to get to where the wolves usually are. Also, I'll still need to get all my leghold traps, chain, snares, and rolls of cable down from Fairbanks, then across the river."

Mr. Raddock says nothing as he studies the map.

"See this hill here, immediately west of the river?" Salt says. "It's the one I told you about on the phone. Our new pastor in Strawberry Flats calls it Heaven's Hill. I climbed it once. It gave me a good overview of much of the wolves' southern range."

Mr. Raddock makes notes on his phone and again says nothing. Two other men who earlier introduced themselves as Gary and Jack sit on the outside of the booth, pinning Salt and Mr. Raddock inside. They also busy themselves with their phones.

A waitress returns. "May I take your orders now?"

"A few more minutes, honey," Gary says, sending her away for a second time.

The four men nurse their lunchtime drinks: one whiskey on the rocks, two vodka tonics, and, for Salt, a Dr Pepper. Gary, the youngest among them, is a political hack, near as Salt can tell. Dressed in a suit and tie, he has an insincere smile and mud-brown eyes that give no definition to his pupils. Earlier, before they were shown to a booth, Salt overheard him say to Mr. Raddock in a soft but heated discussion, "C'mon, K. R., you and I both know how we handle that: the bigger the lie and the more often we repeat it, the more people will believe it. Just let me handle it." Gary then spoke to Salt about the governor's Roads to Resources program that will include "many exciting projects across Alaska to provide jobs and grow the economy." He also invited Salt to speak freely during this meeting, adding ominously, "After all, Mr. d'Alene, we're all in this together."

Jack, a heavy-set man who wears a tan-brown Carhartt coat, seems to be an engineer of sorts, probably with the Alaska Department of Transportation.

While Mr. Raddock appears consistently engaged with what Salt has to say, Gary and Jack do not. They drift in and out, and have quiet conversations of their own. Both call Mr. Raddock "K. R." in a way that tells Salt they've known each other for years. Salt has briefed them on everything he knows about the wolves: that for some reason the alpha male and female didn't mate or den this past winter and spring; that the pack feeds on salmon, moose, and an occasional sea lion or seal. "They travel as far south as Icy Strait," Salt says, "and maybe all the way north to Adams Inlet. And from the Menzies River west to Crystal Bay, in the marine reserve. That's about five hundred square miles."

"And you know this… how?" Mr. Raddock asks.

"Mostly from information posted online by the feds at the marine reserve. But also from my field time, mapping and inspecting the wolves' tracks and scat. I've crossed the river five times now." *And have almost fallen in and drowned myself every time.*

"We appreciate your work," Mr. Raddock says as he studies the map and makes more notes.

"Crystal Bay National Marine Reserve," Gary says. "That's our biggest problem—the federal government—until we straighten things out in Washington. The wolves will need to die on state land, near Strawberry Flats. You can do that, Mr. d'Alene?"

"Yes."

"Do you feel adequately paid?"

"Yes. My son, he's—"

"We know all about your son," Gary says. "That's why we're happy to help provide you with the finances you'll need to properly take care of him."

"Thank you."

Again, Gary and Jack sip their drinks and check their phones while Mr. Raddock studies the map. Nobody speaks. Salt fidgets, thinking about Hannah and the boys at Bartlett Hospital, getting the results of their tests. *And me here. I need to be with them.*

"My son, Solomon," Salt blurts out, his emotions rising, "he's my second boy… only thirteen, you know, and he has such a bright spirit and a wonderful sense of humor and a blessed way of seeing the world. He says funny things that make us all laugh. And to think that he might not live very long unless we… unless we find a cure for him. So, my wife and I… we're looking at an experimental program, a clinical trial, at Johns Hopkins in Baltimore."

"Do you believe in miracles?" Gary asks him after he takes another drink of his vodka tonic.

"Yes," Salt says, catching his breath, half embarrassed to be so forthcoming.

"So do I. So do we all." Gary looks around the table. "Jack, what are the onsite job projections for this Menzies River development?"

Jack scrolls through his phone. "Roughly ten to thirty high-paying positions the first year, half of them technical and skilled, the other half general labor, depending on how the field plays out. After that, six to ten full-time positions every year for the next five to ten years, maybe more, depending on development and production."

Production? Production of what? Salt feels his stomach churn. He loses track of the conversation. *Field plays out? What field?*

"...and yes," Jack says, "the road and bridge will go in at the same time, after the ground is dry. Otherwise, it'll turn into one big mud pit. But I have to admit, this is a guess. Nothing is normal anymore. Everything is topsy-turvy these days."

"Topsy-turvy," Gary says. "That's one hell of an engineering term, Jack."

"The ice road building season up at Prudhoe used to be two hundred days a year," Jack says. "Now it's not even seventy days. Permafrost is melting everywhere, and we've got a dozen lawsuits on our hands about the Arctic Refuge."

"It used to be the frozen north," Gary says. "Now, if you listen to the liberals, it's the goddamn 'delicate tundra.'"

The waitress returns and takes their orders, including another round of drinks. When she leaves, Gary says, "A man named Salt who drinks Dr Pepper. That's funny."

Salt stares into his mud-brown eyes, determined to make him look away first.

Gary checks his phone.

Mr. Raddock asks more questions about the wolves and takes more notes. Jack takes a phone call and leaves the booth, giving Salt a chance to slide out and stand up. A plate of spring rolls and colorful sauces arrive, but Salt has lost his appetite. The others dive in as he checks his phone and thinks again about Hannah and the boys.

"This development you're talking about," Salt finally says to Mr. Raddock. "Is it going to make a lot of noise at the west end of Strawberry Flats? With big machines driving bridge pilings and such?"

"Yes. We'll schedule hearings and take public testimony."

"I'm afraid you're in for a serious fight. You know that, right?"

"Yes. It's often—"

"I don't mean a typical kind of political fight with a few people getting upset and writing letters and calling the governor's office. I've seen that in Cantwell and Healy and Fairbanks. What I mean is... this could be a real fight."

Mr. Raddock and Gary stare at him as if lightly amused, because nothing can stop them, because nothing ever has.

Salt asks, "Do you know what I'm talking about?"

"You're talking about the overeducated, latte-drinking liberals of

Strawberry Flats," Gary says, "many of them employed at Crystal Bay National Marine Reserve. People who write clever Facebook posts and a letter to an editor now and then."

Salt shakes his head, still on his feet, ready to go.

"No lattes in Strawberry Flats?" Gary asks with a smirk.

Jack returns and waits for Salt to take his inside seat so he can slide in after him. Salt waves him in as the waitress arrives with their main dishes. Once she leaves, Mr. Raddock says, "Please, Mr. d'Alene, tell us what you're talking about."

Salt continues to stand and says, "At the west end of town, near the Menzies River, is a twenty-acre place called Willynillyville where a bunch of Iraq and Afghanistan war veterans live because it's quiet and peaceful. Most of them moved up here from Texas and Oklahoma to get away from construction and traffic and noise. Their leader is a man named Tyler Nash, a bush pilot who has his own Cessna and served in Iraq, and later worked on the North Slope, and now fishes for black cod. Some people say he runs drugs from Colombia and Mexico, but I don't believe it. I think he's in Mexico now, and due back to Strawberry Flats soon with some of his family. Anyway, he and his fellow veterans are a real band of brothers, like war veterans can be. Like … a pack."

"Willynillyville?" Gary asks. "Are you serious?"

"Yes. And so are they. They have guns, probably lots of guns. Maybe even some artillery. You talk about wolves… these guys are wolves. People in town say they survive on moose chili, potatoes, garden greens, and little money."

"Good," Gary says. "We'll offer them high-paying jobs with full benefits."

"Texas and Oklahoma?" Jack says. "They did the right thing coming north. Texas is hotter than blue blazes right now. My aunt lives there and says it's terrible. Cattle and trees are dying everywhere. It's their hottest June on record, and it's going to get worse."

"Says who?" Gary asks.

"Scientists," Jack replies.

"You mean the snowflake climate change scientists who say the sky is falling so they can scam more government research grants?" Gary asks. "Those scientists?"

Jack shrugs.

After a disquieting moment, Mr. Raddock looks at Salt, who's still standing, and says, "Are you going to join us?"

"No, thank you. I'm late to meet my wife." *She's too thin these days.* "She's at medical appointments with my sons. I have to go. I really do. I'm sorry." Salt puts a twenty-dollar bill on the table to cover his share of the lunch.

Mr. Raddock hands it back with a thick letter-sized envelope. "Keep your money, Mr. d'Alene, and please accept this, for all you're doing for us. Thank you for your good work. And please know that your efforts will soon contribute to many people having secure, high-paying jobs and brighter futures in a more robust Alaskan economy. Something you can be proud of."

"I hope you're right."

"You realize," Gary says to Salt, "that nothing can stop us. Delay us, maybe. Stop us, no. The governor and state house and state senate are all behind this. So is the White House. The president is a no-nonsense, law-and-order leader who will use the National Guard if he has to."

"Against American citizens?"

"If necessary, yes."

"Against decorated US war veterans?"

"Yes."

"Good luck with that," Salt says. "I'll trap your wolves, Mr. Raddock. I only ask that you take what I've told you as a fair warning. Not a threat. Just a warning."

"I do."

"I'm sure you also know," Salt adds, "that trapping wolves for money—for hire, I mean—could get me in trouble. It could be against state law."

"I'm state law," Gary says. "I speak for the governor. You have nothing to worry about, Mr. d'Alene. As for Tyler Nash, if what you say is true, we'll send out the Alaska state troopers to bust him for drug smuggling."

Salt glares at him.

Nobody reaches out to shake his hand, as they did when they first greeted him.

"Thank you for your time and for paying me as well as you have," Salt says to Mr. Raddock. The envelope no doubt contains more one-hundred-dollar bills, as he's been paid in the past via packages mailed from Juneau. "And thank you for inquiring about my son, Solomon. I appreciate it. God bless you and the earth you walk upon."

As he walks away, Salt hears Gary say, "Jesus, K. R., where'd you find that guy?"

SOLOMON AND ABRAHAM greet Salt as he comes through the double doors at Bartlett Regional Hospital, Solomon beaming in his wheelchair, Abraham unsmiling, standing guard behind his brother, circumspect as always, a copy of *Soldier of Fortune* folded into his back pocket. Solomon's smile melts Salt's heart. "Where's your mother?" Salt asks as he hugs both boys, then grabs Solomon's hand and presses it to his face—*my beautiful boy*. Solomon rocks excitedly in his wheelchair.

"She's still with the doctor," Abe says.

Just then Hannah, Jericho, and Joshua come around the corner. The two boys run to greet their father and begin to tell him that Mom is okay.

Hannah smiles. "I'm mildly anemic," she says, almost with a little laugh. "They think that's all that's wrong with me." She kisses Salt on his face and grabs his hand.

"Can we go home now?" little Joshua asks.

"Tomorrow," Salt tells him. They have a lot of shopping to do before jumping on the morning ferry for the four-hour run back to Strawberry Flats. Tonight, they'll stay with Grandma and Grandpa, Hannah's parents, who are mostly homebound these days with Grandpa's diabetes.

"Did you meet the mystery man?" Hannah asks as they walk out into the full sun. It's summer solstice, the longest day of the year. The boys horse around in the parking lot.

"Yes," Salt says. "I'll tell you all about it. What did the doctors say about Solomon and his coughing?"

"They said it's not unusual at this stage. They gave us a prescription for muscle relaxants. And they're going to write a letter of recommendation to Johns Hopkins."

Salt hands her the envelope. Hannah stares at it, then at her husband. "It's sixty hundred-dollar bills," he says.

Hannah hugs him. "I love you, husband. Thank you for taking such good care of us. All of us." She says nothing about his trapping, though Salt knows it worries her.

"I love you, dear wife."

"Are we going to be okay?" she asks him.

Just then Abe rolls Solomon back to within earshot, who says, "Okaaaay? Are you kidding, Mom? We're gonna be better than okaaaay. We're gonna shake it on dooooooown."

Little Joshua, with Jericho in pursuit, comes running back and flies into his father's welcome arms. Salt spins him around and nearly drops him, his weak hip and knee protesting from the weight.

Joshua squeals with delight. "Put me down, Dad. Put me down."

"Shake it on dooooooown," Solomon says, rocking again.

They all laugh as Salt takes the wheelchair from Abe—something Abe doesn't let go of easily—and pushes Solomon to their red van with the power fold-out ramp, the used one they got in Fairbanks for twenty-five thousand dollars, much of their family savings. Hannah holds Salt's sleeve. The sun dips behind a cloud then reappears, and the entire family turns to face it, speechless as they raise their faces, anointed by the light. Blessed.

CHAPTER FIFTEEN

Kes

THE FIREWORKS BEGIN SHORTLY BEFORE MIDNIGHT.

In the back room, Papa crawls onto the bed, curls into a fetal position, and pulls a pillow over his head. Kes gently affixes headphones over his ears and turns up the music as a dozen bottle rockets go off, pounding the San Antonio sky, putting Papa right back in Afghanistan. Kes is so mad she wants to scream.

This wasn't supposed to happen. First, Lubbock last New Year's Eve. And now, San Antonio on the Fourth of July. Nutballs down the street, making a racket. Uncle Ty had told Rita he was pretty sure this was a quiet neighborhood. Kes likes the San Antonio house—it belongs to one of Ty's Army buddies—but not the rude, noisy neighbors. Best of all, the house is only two miles from the Center for the Intrepid, where yesterday Papa had his final physical therapy session and checkout. Rita has little Kipper with her in Lubbock as she prepares the family house as a rental. So far so good, until a few hours ago when loud motorcycles and big diesel trucks began arriving down the street. That's when Uncle Ty suspected trouble and warned Kes there could be fireworks.

"Can't you make it stop?" Kes asks as she walks into the kitchen.

Uncle Ty sits at the table with Chippy, who thrums his fingers on the pink linoleum, and Cap, who lights two cigarettes at once. He passes one to his cousin who takes a long hard swallow from a Bud Light while Cap opens his own beer. Rita had said no smoking around Kes. And now smoke curls off their fingertips. The McCalls wear tank tops that show a blizzard of tattoos over their arms, shoulders and necks, some gothic, others beautiful, like the sunflower on Chippy's shoulder, and the night heron on

Cap's forearm. The air conditioner purrs in the corner while the outside thermometer reads 99°F. "Look at that," Chippy says, "It's dropped below one hundred. Time to bundle up."

The temperature had peaked at 112°F at five in the afternoon, when plastic garbage cans began melting onto driveways and sidewalks.

Uncle Ty gets up, walks down the hall to Papa's room, and comes back a minute later. He stands in the kitchen with a stern expression, his red bandana on his head.

"Did Rita ever walk this neighborhood—like she told me she would—and ask people not to set off fireworks on the Fourth?" he asks Kes.

"Yes."

"Did she tell the neighbors it would traumatize her husband?"

"Yes."

"That he's a decorated war veteran with PTSD?"

"Yes, Uncle Ty. She said all of that. She told me she did."

"And what did they say?"

"I think most people said, 'No problem.' But the people at that one house were mean and told her they'd do whatever they want because it's a free country."

"That's the same thing they'll say again, Big Dog," Chippy says.

"Okay," Uncle Ty says. "First, we'll go down there and reconnoiter."

"Then we'll blow their house to hell," Chippy says.

"And their motorcycles," Cap adds.

"Not if they're Harleys," Chippy says. "Harley-Davidsons are sacred."

Uncle Ty motions toward the door. "Let's go."

The cousins jump to their feet. Kes is startled to see Chippy pull out a handgun from behind his back, check it, and reconceal it under his tank top, into his jeans.

"Stay here," Uncle Ty says to Kes. "And keep a close eye on your father."

Before she can protest, the three men go out the door like commandos. She watches them huddle in the yard, then fan out into the darkness, two going one way, one the other. More fireworks: *Pffffffrrrrrrr… Ka-boom. Ka-boom. Ka-boom.* The sky lights up but does not illuminate Uncle Ty or the McCalls. They've disappeared.

She returns to the bedroom and holds Papa's hand, and rubs his lower back, and puts the Traveling Wilburys on his headphone music system.

When she hears the commandos return, she walks back through the kitchen and finds them in the garage, behind Chippy's large white van that he and Cap will drive to Bellingham and put on the ferry to Alaska. Nearly everything is packed. *Will it all go according to plan?* The doctors have said they see no reason why Papa cannot go to Alaska. Eagles, bears, and wolves. Whales that swim into your dreams. Trees that touch the clouds. Glaciers that calve columns of ice into the sea. Smoked salmon and moose chili. Sounds epic, the doctors also said. They wanted to go too.

The Cessna is at an airfield eight miles away and "eager to fly," Uncle Ty says. He often talks about his plane like it has emotions, ambitions, dreams. Maybe it does. Maybe nothing will ever again be the same.

R u still going? Allison texted Kes yesterday.

Kes texted back a "thumbs up" emoji.

This time Allison didn't write, *Don't die.* Instead, she wrote, *I'm jealous.*

Julie texted something similar from Houston: *I'm gonna pray 4 u. Maybe one day I can come visit u in Alaska.*

Cool, Kes texted back.

MORE FIREWORKS. *Pffffffffrrrrrrr... Ka-boom. Ka-boom. Ka-boom.*

"Goddammit." Uncle Ty slams the side of the van with his open hand, unaware Kes is watching.

Cap's head twitches as he takes another pull on his cigarette.

"I've got three RPGs in here," Chippy says with a maniacal grin as he zips open a long duffel bag in the back of the van. Kes watches carefully.

"You've got RPGs?" Uncle Ty says. "How'd you get three RPGs?"

"Contraband and connections, Big Dog. Everybody does it. You know the saying: 'Weapons adrift, must be a gift.' Rocket-propelled grenades fit into duffel bags—with launchers. These are Russian, designed by Bazalt, abandoned by the Taliban." Chippy grabs Cap's beer and takes a long drink. "I might have a bazooka or two in here too."

"And your Abrams?" Cap asks. "Where's your crazy-ass M1 Abrams Battle Tank?"

"Out back, next to my Nimitz-class carrier and my Big Ivan nuclear bomb."

Cap laughs.

None of the three have seen Kes.

"I ain't kidding, Big Dog," Chippy says. "With three RPGs, we could go down there and ask those guys how much they paid for their freedom."

"And steal their motorcycles," Cap adds. "It's okay to steal a Harley, right?"

Kes feels the copper taste of panic in her throat. She thought Uncle Ty was building a place in Alaska with men who were tired of fighting, tired of war. And here these guys are, arming themselves, ready to start World War III. Rita would be mighty angry if she were seeing this, hearing these bozos trash-talking in front of her daughter. Rita loves the word "bozos." Men are bozos, she says. Except your father, Danny Nash. He's an angel.

Uncle Ty now sees Kes in the doorway that opens from the kitchen into the garage. He walks past her and down the hall to find his brother still curled up on the bed. Kes follows. Uncle Ty sits beside Papa, who pulls off the headphones, taking special care of his rebuilt ear, the one near his droopy eye.

"The Traveling Wilburys," Uncle Ty says. "I can hear them through your headphones. George Harrison, Roy Orbison, Tom Petty, Jeff Lynne. Great band. Late '80s, if I recall. There was another member, right? Am I missing somebody?"

Papa offers only a haunted look, as if this night has set him back six months.

"Oh yeah," Uncle Ty says. "Bob Dylan. Who could forget him?"

Another bottle rocket goes off. Papa winces. Kes sits to the other side of him and gently rubs his back.

"Okay, little brother, here's the deal," Uncle Ty says. "We could stay here and let you sink into a half-life of safety, security, and Texas hospitality, surrounded by hornswoggled red-state evangelicals who ban books and sell baloney. The Army doctors and PTs have done a good job for you. They really have. I tip my hat to them. We all do. But we also think you're ready to go north and reinvent yourself along with the rest of us. Get wild. Get dirty. Eat moose chili. Grow kale leaves the size of dinosaur food. What do you say we leave this stupid house tonight instead of next week? I'll get you and Kes a quiet hotel room for the next day or two while Chippy and Cap and I finish things here. Then we'll go northwest, pick up Dad in Midland, and head to Alaska. How does that sound?"

Papa looks at Kes. How sad he appears, beaten and tired and maybe surrendered to the fact that it's never going to get better than this.

"Yes, Papa... to Alaska," Kes says as she squeezes his hand and digs deep for whatever resolve she might have, and feels it rise, thinking: *Alaska, where your brother says the lakes are jewels, and on a calm night you can row a boat through the stars and the northern lights. Where you can drink the rain, trust ferns, ponder bears, howl with wolves, and read the wind as it braids your hair. And more: whittle an alder walking staff, cook on a wood-burning stove, plant carrots and peas, go into the mountains and come back with moss in your pockets and birdsong in your ears. And most of all: make stories that fill your heart and the hearts of those you love, stories that shine like the full moon.*

Did Kes see a little blue flame of distant desire in Papa just then?

Pffffffffrrrrrr... Ka-boom. Ka-boom. Ka-boom.

Papa winces again, pulls the headphones back on, and sinks into the bed.

Uncle Ty is back on his feet. "Can we be out of here in one hour?" he asks Kes.

"One hour?"

"Yes, one hour." Uncle Ty goes down the hallway, moving briskly through the kitchen and into the garage where Chippy and Cap are busy with the RPGs. Kes follows.

"We'll need a stealth approach," she hears Chippy say. "They can't know where we came from. I'll cover your six."

"I'll cover your left flank," Cap says.

"No," Kes says weakly from behind, as fear coils in her belly.

"I'm going alone," Uncle Ty says. "No RPGs. No guns. Just talk... a friendly conversation. I don't want to end up in the slammer."

"The slammer?" Chippy shakes his head, his eyes on fire. "This is Texas, Big Dog. Those guys *will* have guns. And they're probably drunk. You could get shot. Here, take this Glock. No, wait... take this fifteen-round Beretta in case it turns into a firefight."

"NO," Kes says, loudly this time, but still the voice of a girl.

All three men turn to look at her. She's near tears. She knows she has no influence here. *Bozos. Men are bozos.* No influence or authority until two tender hands land on her shoulders from behind. Hummingbird hands. She turns to see her father in the kitchen doorway, steady on his titanium legs and feet, standing tall but with a sad appeal in his one good eye. He slowly shakes his head at the bozos preparing for battle.

No.

"YOU DON'T SEE THAT EVERY DAY," Uncle Ty says into his pilot headset microphone as he banks the Cessna to get a better view of Guadalupe Peak, bathed in midday light. "That's the highest point in Texas, a massive reef complex, mostly Capitan limestone filled with brachiopods dating back to the Permian Period. Isn't that right, Kes?"

"Yeah," Kes responds into her own mic, attached to her headset, as she stares from her backseat, her nose pressed to the plane's Plexiglas window. Last year she did school reports on Guadalupe Peak and the Grand Canyon. Her uncle knows this.

"You know," Uncle Ty says as Kes thinks: *Here comes a story; Uncle Ty loves to tell stories...* "One day, five veterans in wheelchairs showed up at a ranger station down there and told the district ranger they wanted to climb the mountain three thousand feet up a four-mile switchback trail. Not a good idea, the ranger said. The vets went anyway and ended up crawling through thorns and scorpions and snakes, and dragging their wheelchairs behind them much of the way. Three of the five made it to the summit. Can you believe it? The moral of the story: don't ever tell a disabled vet what he can't do."

Kes watches Uncle Ty glance over at Papa as he says this, hoping for a reaction.

Papa sits directly in front of Kes, in the copilot seat, "riding shotgun," Uncle Ty likes to say. Grandpa, fast asleep, sits behind Uncle Ty, to Kes's left. She rubs Papa's shoulders by bringing her touch to him gently, given that he startles easily. Uncle Ty banks the Cessna and enters the blue skies of New Mexico at 130 miles per hour.

Kes stares at highways, roads, and remote desert mines, and remembers the blue haze over Midland when they stopped to pick up Grandpa; the depressing gridwork of fracking pipelines and roads running for miles in every direction.

"Papa," she whispers now into his undamaged ear, "we're going to Alaska."

Uncle Ty says they'll fly west and then north to avoid what he calls "cornfield America with its thunderstorms, tornadoes, and millions of pitchfork populists who think anthropogenic climate change is a liberal hoax." They'll cross weathered mountains and vast deserts before heading up the green shaggy coast of British Columbia to Alaska. Leave God in the south. Find Heaven up north. Take breaks to get exercise and gas, and to recharge laptops and phones with small foldable solar panels. Study maps. Throw a frisbee. Eat cold pizza. Throw the pizza. Look for lizards and birds. Question the cosmos. Question the lizards. Eat cold frisbees. Laugh at stupid jokes.

Last night in San Antonio, Uncle Ty told Kes that during this epic trip north, he would land the plane often so she and her papa could go for walks. "Be sure to tell him stories," Uncle Ty said. "We are all made of stardust and stories. You never hear a parent say to a child: 'Let me read you some bedtime statistics.' It's not who we are. Statistics are just a tool, a valuable tool, but nothing more. Stories, on the other hand… they save us. Can you do that, my young apprentice? Can you tell your papa stories?"

"Yes."

"Oh, and Kes," Uncle Ty now adds through his mouthpiece and into her headset, and into the others' as well, "best not to tell your mom about the RPGs, okay?"

"RPGs? What RPGs?" Grandpa says, awakening from his slumped position.

"Nothing, Grandpa," Kes says.

Grandpa looks around at New Mexico, quietly takes it in, and falls back asleep, his chin on his chest.

WESTBOUND, they skim over mesas, escarpments, and old cinnabar-toned volcanoes. Everything becomes surreal, the passage of landscapes and random thoughts, ambitions and regrets, even the clock of time. *Do hours still exist?* Kes catches her freckled face reflected in the window, superimposed on the landscape below, and likes what she sees. *How strange.* She's never considered herself attractive, let alone pretty, though Rita campaigns to make her feel otherwise. "You are a masterpiece," she once announced in front of others. Kes nearly caught fire with embarrassment.

"See that?" Uncle Ty says into their headsets as he banks the Cessna gently. "That's Escudilla Mountain, Apache-Sitgreaves National Forest. We're now in Arizona."

"Cool," Kes replies.

Papa stares.

"Do you know the story about the wolf and the fierce green fire?" Uncle Ty asks.

"No."

"Right down near there, a little more than a hundred years ago, a young forest ranger was out with some friends on a rimrock when they saw wolves down by a creek. They unloaded their rifles into the pack, then walked down to see what they'd done. Most of the wolves were dead. But not the mother;

she was barely alive. This forester said he saw a fierce green fire in her dying eyes, a fire that made him question everything."

"Question everything?" Kes asks. "Like what?"

Uncle Ty laughs. "That's for you to find out."

SOMEWHERE OVER NORTHERN ARIZONA, as they approach the Grand Canyon, Kes asks Uncle Ty if his plane has a name.

"Nope. You'd better come up with one."

She thinks for a moment. "Claire."

"Claire? Why Claire?"

"For clairvoyant, the eye in the sky."

"All righty then, Claire it is. Hey, put your eyeballs in and wake up your grandpa. Here comes the Big Guy."

The Grand Canyon is just as Kes imagined it would be and more. All that layered rock laid down by an ancient ocean and much later sculpted and carved by a river. Uncle Ty tips the plane a little to each side for better views, and nobody says a thing. Best to let the canyon do the talking. At one point, Grandpa reaches over and grabs Kes's hand.

Everything is dreamlike after that: where they stop and camp and refuel and eat, from rimrocks to dusty little towns to fancy casinos on the edges of stark white salt flats. Uncle Ty knows people everywhere. He's flown this route many times. They greet him warmly and seem honored to meet his father, brother, and niece. Everybody offers them lodging and food. Papa walks easily—even briskly—on his new titanium legs. Kes tells him stories, and reads to him each night, and kisses his cheek many times a day, which makes him smile. Whenever she strums her ukulele, he taps his finger. Uncle Ty and Grandpa have no arguments, which is a relief. Rita must have told Uncle Ty to make this a positive experience for Kes. "And get her a nice hotel room now and then so she can shower and clean up," Kes heard Rita tell Uncle Ty. "She's an adolescent girl, after all."

Rita can be no-nonsense. Kes also once heard her say to Sammye, "If this Alaska experiment doesn't work, especially for Danny… if it doesn't help make him better, and soon, it'll be back to Texas in a heartbeat."

Over the high desert of Eastern Oregon, Uncle Ty buzzes a herd of cattle and yells, "Yeeeehaaaw… run for your lives, little doggies, before you become Big Macs with ketchup, pickles, and fries."

Kes laughs until she sees a boy on an ATV flip them off, take a rifle off his shoulder, and aim it at Claire. She holds her breath, half expecting to fall out of the sky.

In Post Falls, near Spokane, they pick up a thin, sad-eyed man named Mike, and several boxes of what Uncle Ty calls "contraband." Including morphine. Kes begins to think maybe her uncle really is a pirate. Or just crazy. Grandpa says he's both.

Mike tells Kes matter-of-factly, "I'm dying."

"Oh," she says, "I'm sorry."

"Don't be. I'm gonna do it right."

They refuel in Bellingham to avoid Canadian customs, and head up the coast. Everything is so green, as if green weren't just a color, but a texture. Kes stares with all her might, determined to miss none of it: the mountains and inlets, the fingers of land and sea that appear to grasp one another as if in greeting. Finally, in Alaska, Uncle Ty points out blue-ribbon glaciers and snowy peaks and granite pinnacles, and different kinds of fishing boats: seiners, trollers, gillnetters. They land in Juneau and stand about, inhaling the cool air. Already, Papa appears to stand more erect, be more alert. More alive.

When Kes hugs him, he hugs her back, fiercely.

Mike grimaces with pain and talks about the glaciers, how John Muir admired them many years ago, and dreamed of softly freezing in them, deep in a crevasse—what a glorious death that would be. Back in Claire, he takes a morphine drip and falls asleep.

Thirty minutes later, westbound, Claire passes over a beautiful snowy ridge, then drops down, down, down... to land in a little town on the edge of everything.

"Welcome to Strawberry Flats," Uncle Ty says. "You can set your watches back one hundred years."

PART II

CHAPTER SIXTEEN

Silver

HUNDREDS OF SALMON fight their way upriver, their dorsal fins flashing in the sun, attracting wolves, eagles, and bears. Having left their ocean home and just returned to the freshwater of their beginning where years ago they lived as fry, the adult salmon must now complete a final act before they die.

They must spawn.

And so they fight and swim with all their might, even though they are already dying. Even though the stresses on every cell in their bodies, going from saltwater back to fresh, take a daily toll. Some fish choose the riffles and pools of quiet, shallow channels where Silver and his kin await. Others dare the powerful central current.

No passage is without a challenge.

Every advantage comes with a disadvantage.

These fish are the one or two percent that have made it this far—that have survived disease and predation out at sea—and must now make it a little farther to lay their eggs and spread their milt in riverbed gravel and bring forth a new generation.

And so, they fight with all their might. Not each other. They fight against the odds they've been given by land and sea, hook and net, tooth and claw, no more, no less.

Silver watches with the eyes of a hunter, looking for patterns in the chaos, repeated behaviors, anything to improve the odds. He and Sister, now yearlings, work a shallow, nearshore area and do well, corralling many fish against gravel cutbanks. Nearby, Mother catches several and brings them to Old One, who sits on shore and eats only the choice parts and leaves the rest.

Alpha, Strong, and the subadults, now full grown, work somewhere upriver, all mindful that others could appear at any moment.

This river is not theirs alone.

Be alert.

Every time Silver eats, he can feel the fish's protein and fat flood into him, and strengthen him, and give him a power that no other food does. Not even moose. These salmon are the first cohos of the fall—delicious and life-giving beyond measure.

It's mid-August and already the cottonwoods are beginning to turn gold, the high-bush cranberries crimson. Already birds are heading south.

Last month, the wolves ate countless wild strawberries and two dead sea lions that washed up on shore, and some smaller, diseased salmon that made them sick.

Now finally, on the heels of summer, they get their prize: big, fat, feisty salmon.

HOURS PASS. Still no sign of Alpha and the subadults. The sun comes out and the wolves bed down, chins on their forepaws, the river murmuring nearby, singing them to sleep. When Silver snaps awake, he feels danger. He stands and turns to see a brown bear sow and her two cubs of the year. The sow rises onto her hind feet, impossibly tall. The cubs mimic her, looking about. Silver huffs to awaken Sister, Mother, and Old One.

Black bears are expected along this river and in this forest. Brown bears are not.

The sow and her cubs drop to all fours and walk to the river, downstream of the wolves but on the same side, not near but not far, the cubs tentative behind their mother, staying close, their eyes on the wolves. Silver watches the sow take in the river, how the salmon appear to come in waves. She plunges in but comes up empty, and again, and again. But now she moves to a back eddy, just as Silver and Sister did, and works the salmon up against the shore and catches one in her mouth. The cubs run to her as she walks to higher ground and places the gleaming fish on a bed of gravel. She pins it there with her long claws as all three bears dig in, the salmon still flopping, still fighting, still determined to live and reproduce as mightily as every other living creature.

Once they get a taste of the fish, the cubs keep their heads down and tear off long pieces of flesh and eat vigorously. The sow does not. She looks around, mindful of the wolves. Silver knows that if this sow were to ever come upon a moose kill that he and his kin earned for themselves, she'd do everything possible to displace them and take the meat for herself and her cubs. She'd fall asleep atop the carcass. And guard it for days. Or bury it. Only if wounded or weakened, or threatened with the well-being of her cubs, would she back off.

The wolves remain motionless, watching, unaware that other creatures are watching them and the bears.

When Old One huffs an alarm, Silver turns and this time sees something that truly alarms him: two beings across the river standing on their hind legs. Tall uprights.

Run.

CHAPTER SEVENTEEN

Salt

WORD SPREADS FAST IN STRAWBERRY FLATS. Two guys saw bears and wolves on the Menzies River. What two guys? Dunno. Where on the river? Dunno. How many bears and how many wolves? Dunno that either.

At Nystad's Mercantile—where people stand around and eat free popcorn and hot dogs (Saturdays only) grilled just right by Oddmund Nystad's pretty niece, Berit, and talk about everything from the weather to wolves, banjos to bears, politics to potato gardening—Salt listens without asking any questions and finally hears a better answer. Turns out it was two visitors from California, a father and son who are staying at a local place called Dave's Make Your Own Damn Breakfast. The father and son biked to the end of Menzies River Road, walked out the trail, hit the river and went downstream a quarter mile or so, and got lucky. The wolves ran off, but the bears—a mother and her twin cubs, cute little guys—fished there for an hour, caught several salmon, and finally walked away. The father and son got great photos, according to Rosie Goodnight, the school secretary and official town gossip, a title she bestows upon herself and works hard to retain.

"How come tourists get to see all the cool stuff and we don't?" Salt hears one man say to another.

"Because we're all working our butts off fishing and running lodges and taking tourists into the marine reserve to see cool stuff like whales and glaciers and eagles on icebergs, that's why. Summer is the money-making season."

Salt knows that visiting the Menzies River is one thing, crossing it is another. It might be shallow on its edges, made poetic here and there by back eddies, riffles, and pools. But at midcurrent, it's a beast.

He dreads crossing it every time, the cold, forceful water roiling off his chest waders, the rounded bottom rocks rolling under his feet as he totters his way across, exhausted when he gets there, heart jackhammering. He always unfastens the waist strap on his pack so that if he goes under, he can get free and not be drowned by his own gear. It happens all the time. People die. Young, old, tough and not so tough, experienced and inexperienced, Alaska gets them every year. And while his chest waders keep him dry, Salt knows that if he goes under wearing them and they fill with water in the strong central current, he's a goner.

Both his left knee and hip bother him and are getting worse. Not even Hannah knows this. He doesn't want her to worry any more than she already does.

Last week his friend Rolf, who has his own Fairbanks car dealership, drove to Haines and took the ferry to Juneau, where Salt met him and loaded four totes onto the ferry to Strawberry Flats. Totes filled with heavy leghold traps, cables, and snares that Rolf brought down in his truck. Before saying goodbye and getting on his southbound ferry to Bellingham, Rolf asked Salt, "So, you're trapping again?"

"I might. I'm thinking about it."

"What're you after?"

"Marten."

"Marten? Salt, you're a terrible liar. With leghold traps like these, you're after wolves. Get them all, man. Get every damn one of them."

KILLING WOLVES COMES EASY FOR SOME MEN. Salt remembers their faces, hands, and measured manners; their clean, scent-free, fur-lined anoraks, mittens, and boots; how their traps—sometimes rubbed with caribou fat, never oiled or soaked in solvent, and seldom touched by human skin—jangle softly in their hands. And how, after much attention to detail and care, their traps would lie perfectly hidden in a snowy trail. He remembers trappers buying snare cable in thousand-foot rolls and using a wolf's own instincts against it by hanging flagging in the trees, or setting a "stepping stick" to frighten the wolf off a trail—and into a trap. He remembers some of these men as callous-hearted old-timers; others as mere farm boys moved north from Nebraska and South Dakota, keen on wild country and being in the Last Frontier… the pride they took in outsmarting a smart animal that can smell one part per billion, and the deprivations the trappers suffered at minus forty. Tough. You had to be tough—Jack London's *The Call of the Wild* tough. The land showed no mercy. Yes, come winter the country would freeze up, and travel would get easy, and pelts would be thick. But winter up north was itself a trap, ready to prey on a single misstep, a flooded boot, an exposed hand. Make no mistakes. Anything out of the ordinary alerted the wolves. Never spit or smoke or pee on or near the trail. Never camp or rest near your traps. Boil them in water with spruce bows. And once out there, look and listen with the senses of your ancestors. It required artistry, precision, strength, and skill. And brutality. Maybe even hate, which can blind a man. Poison him.

Salt knows Rolf hates wolves but has never trapped one. Rolf won a seat in the Alaska state senate and introduced legislation to permit the aerial hunting of wolves two years after voters had approved a referendum against it. He attained considerable power, until he said terrible things about women, refused to apologize, and said God wanted him to be a senator. He lost the next election, blamed it on liberals, and wrote on Facebook that his opponent's green energy plan "made purfect since to an educated idiot."

Hannah never liked Rolf. She once asked Salt, "Why does religion make good people better and bad people worse?"

Rolf still has his Fairbanks car dealership, but now plans to live most of the year in Idaho. Sharpshooters contracted with the Alaska Department of Fish & Game in Interior Alaska do things Rolf's way to help manage every fur-bearing animal as a crop, and to make certain that caribou and moose are plentiful for human subsistence and sport hunters. How? By shooting wolves that prey on caribou and moose. And how to do this? Gun them down from bush planes and helicopters. "Not exactly sporting," Rolf once said with a laugh, "but damn efficient."

Salt remembers the story of one aerial marksman who killed an entire pack in less than two minutes as the wolves ran single file through deep snow. He got all but one. And what did that single remaining wolf do? It kept running with such determination that it launched itself off a cliff, its legs pinwheeling in midair until the marksman hit it in free fall—and watched the wolf go limp. The end of the line.

But things cut both ways.

Salt remembers one boastful wolf hater who loved what he called the "thrill of the kill"—shooting out entire packs from his bush plane, a Super Cub. The hater once had a photo taken of himself wearing his black cowboy hat with beaver felt earflaps, kneeling on river ice with a semicircle of dead wolves laid out around him like trout. He said the wolves had to die and we have to kill them, like duty. Simple as that. Then one day he crashed his Super Cub into another small plane, midair, as both were circling an elusive pack, and the planes fell to the earth. He died and never boasted again.

Soon after the crash, at a public hearing in Fairbanks, wolf trappers and bounty hunters ended up shouting obscenities at each other until a young woman stood up and berated them: "Listen to yourselves. You aren't decent men. You're bullies."

She's right, Salt thought at the time. *Wolves have better manners. And ethics.*

Less than a year later, he fell through the Minto ice and stopped trapping.

AND NOW HERE I AM, AT IT AGAIN.

How to get his heavy gear across the Menzies River without anyone knowing, all before winter sets in? Salt sees only one sure way: enlist his strong-as-an-ox eldest son, Abe—a distant boy these days, often sealed away in his bedroom.

"I don't know why he's like that," Salt says to Hannah one August evening while the boys play outside.

Hannah says, "I'm worried about him."

"You worry about all of them."

"That's my job, husband."

"Your job is to care, not to worry."

"One comes with the other, you know that."

Yes, Salt knows that. Hannah always wanted a daughter, and what did she get? Four rambunctious sons. Even Solomon is a tiger, pacing in his wheelchair, determined to be bigger than his actual self. Salt looks out the kitchen window to see all four barefoot, picking garden peas in the slanted light, the low evening sun swinging far to the northwest, its rays breaking through dark clouds heavy with imminent rain. Abe feeds a peapod to Solomon, who cannot feed himself.

Salt is about to tell Hannah of his intentions to enlist Abe, but thinks better of it. The last time Abe accompanied him, Salt nearly died. That's when it ended: the trapping and cabin living and bitter cold winters, but also the northern lights and great silence and making love by candlelight and knowing that your lives were extraordinary.

"You look better," Salt says to Hannah. "Have you been taking your iron pills?"

"No. Fish oil."

"Fish oil. You've been taking fish oil?"

Hannah slides in next to him for a hug.

"Well," Salt says, "it must be working."

Another thing he has not told Hannah, which feels wrong because they tell each other everything, is that on his first outing to look for wolves, he hid in the trees thinking he was furtive, part wolf himself, and what happened? Veterans from Willynillyville saw him and tipped their hats and walked on, leaving him feeling naked and embarrassed.

Out the window now, the boys throw small spruce cones at each other. It begins to rain. Salt goes out the door, hears something, and stops. As do the boys.

Little Joshua, his eyes huge, turns and says, "Dad, are those wolves?"

CHAPTER EIGHTEEN

Kes

ONE HOWL, NOT DISTANT, NOT NEAR.

From across the river?

A second.

A third.

Up in her cupola bedroom in Willynillyville, the walls made of untaped sheetrock, the floor of one-inch painted plywood, Kes stops playing her ukulele. Papa used to say he was never himself unless he had a guitar in his hands. George Harrison said the same thing. Papa also said nobody ever became a capable musician until they went through a period of obsession, when all they did was play an instrument for hours each day, months on end. Best done when you're young.

Another howl.

Kes cracks open the window and holds her breath. She hears the rain softly commenting on the shapes of the gables and eaves. And her heart. And the so-called Poker Pack downstairs laughing and playing cards and eating moose chili and drinking Uncle Ty's homebrewed spruce-tip beer, talking about how to stack firewood: tall, narrow stacks versus low, wide ones; short rounds versus long rounds; bark-side up or bark-side down? And movies. The Poker Pack always talks about movies: *Rio Bravo* versus *Red River*, *Ghostbusters* versus *Groundhog Day*... and so on. And *Gunsmoke*... who was the better deputy: Chester with his agile limp? Or Festus with his rumpled hat?

There again—faint, from a distance. Dogs?

No. Dogs mostly bark. Wolves mostly howl... in packs.

Kes doesn't want to make a fuss—interrupt poker night, which is sacred—because of mere dogs. Nobody in Strawberry Flats lives farther west than what Chippy often calls "our village, encampment, commune, cuckoo's nest, ashram, paradise, holdout, and fort all in one… our Willynillyville." Besides… Uncle Ty, Tucker John, Chippy and Cap, and many others have said they've heard wolves howling from across the Menzies River, though not for a while now.

Can't be dogs.

Again, more howling… faint but definite.

Coyotes? No. Coyotes yip.

Kes strums her ukulele lightly, figuring that if she practices daily and learns it well, Papa might pick up his Martin one day and jam with her and sing again. She should have started playing in earnest in Texas, but that all seems like a nightmare now, days on end of a horror show, the fireworks and surgeries and endless trips down to San Antonio. All her Lubbock friends so sad in their expressions, not certain what to say. Sorry about your dad. Hope he's okay. Please tell him we say thank you for his service. They'd bring over Hallmark cards filled with Bible passages and make small talk. "Queens of gossip," Rita called them. "They know everything about nothing."

And food. Lots of food. Potato salad, casseroles, and Jell-O. Church food.

Later, Rita took it all down to the San Pedro Homeless Shelter.

Then, just the other day in Willynillyville, maybe because Alaska is a good thing, the best thing, Kes noticed Papa clipping the fingernails on his left hand while letting his right-hand fingernails grow out. As if in preparation to play the guitar again.

She stops strumming.

More howling, closer this time. A chorus. So powerful she can feel it in her chest. A spiral of sorts, a mix of things she cannot fathom. *And harmonic?*

Impossible. Incredible.

Quickly she's on her feet, moving over the plywood floor and down the stairs, dodging the wooden joints that protest and squeak, softening her footfalls so as not to alarm Papa's shattered nerves, the remains of his musical soul.

WHEN THEY FIRST ARRIVED IN STRAWBERRY FLATS, over a month ago, Papa didn't join the poker games. But lately he has. Rita told Uncle Ty she didn't like Willynillyville with its mishmash of "half-built hovels" and "plywood palaces," the outside walls covered in Tyvek.

She arrived with little Kip one week after the others did in Claire, and two weeks before Chippy and Cap in their van (via ferry). She found little charm in the pallets, piles of lumber, sawhorses, rusty wheelbarrows, greasy chainsaws, sooty stovepipes, bags of cement, and piles of insulation everywhere. The whole place more of a construction site than a picturesque village.

"It's an unfinished symphony," Uncle Ty told her. "Like Beethoven, or Brahms."

Rita shook her head in contempt. That night, her first in Willynillyville, Kes heard Rita crying in her and Papa's unfinished bedroom through the closed door, and imagined Papa, himself still only a shadow of who he used to be, trying to comfort her, and Kes worried they might return to Texas even before school started.

Will I like school here, in Strawberry Flats?

Sometimes she feels a panic in her soul when she thinks about school, if she'll like her teachers, make friends, learn anything, or come home one day to see Papa worse than he was before and Rita packing to go back south.

But lately, Papa seems to be warming to it all: the chickadees and juncos at the bird feeder, the fish smoker and big garden and greenhouse, and him with his hands in the dark earth, pulling chickweed or an early carrot, washing it off and popping it into his mouth. Plus feeding the Manchurian ponies, Stardust and Golden (their names taken from the Joni Mitchell song "Woodstock"), and the chickens, and tending to the apiary, watching the bees come and go. And sitting contentedly on the porch with the floppy-eared bunny, Rabbit Downey, Jr., and visiting the woodpile when the other vets tell him there's a short-tailed weasel darting and winnowing its way through the stacks. Rita takes photos of her husband immersed in it all, smiling a little more each day, as if maybe to remind herself why they came here... and just might stay.

"Life is short," Tucker John told Rita and Kes one day. "You have to mix it up."

Kes likes to see Papa cock his musical head to hear the calls of ravens, jays, and geese, and the soft chattering of warblers as they move through, southbound. He and Kes love the brisk mornings and evenings, everything so lush and green. The air so brisk. Just yesterday, sandhill cranes flew overhead, very near, fluting their ancient calls, as if their own music could keep them aloft. And everybody stopped, transfixed, none more so than Papa. When he grabbed Kes's hand and squeezed it, she half expected her heart to jump out of her chest. So big was her happiness.

Add to that their walks to the river—Papa, Rita, Kes, and little Kip (on Papa's back), a family again—when they notice every little thing and take none of it for granted as they pick nagoonberries and find moose droppings, and talk easily while Papa signs with his hands. The other day he got down on his stomach in the moss to look closely at a mangy mushroom and a Siberian aster, and to photograph them with Kes's phone. When he threw a moose pellet at her, she threw one back and laughed and thought Papa might too, so radiant was his face, so big his smile. Later, as they stood on the banks of the Menzies River and tried to skip stones over the raging current, Kes told Papa and Rita, "I'm going to cross that river one day."

"I don't think so," Rita said. "It looks dangerous."

"Uncle Ty and Tucker John and E. J. have all crossed it. And some of the others too, I think."

"They're grown men, honey."

HALFWAY DOWN THE STAIRS, Kes sees Papa first—always has, always will. He looks up, cards in his hand, and gives her a faint smile. A more hopeful expression than she ever got from him this last terrible year in Texas.

The others look up as well: six veterans at the table, Rita in the kitchen, Grandpa with little Kip in the living room, playing with his Legos. Even Jasper, the old Irish setter stretched out on the floor, and Snickers, the cat with its lantern eyes. All stare.

Kes stops, facing a room filled with six Purple Hearts, five Army Commendation Medals, three Texas Combat Service Ribbons, one Bronze Star, and one Silver Star. Four wars altogether. More than twenty surgeries, and counting. "Damn near the entire March of Folly under one roof," Uncle Ty said at Papa's first poker night. Whatever that meant. Sometimes Uncle Ty says things that make no sense.

"What is it, Kes, honey?" Rita asks, stepping through the kitchen doorway.

"I think I heard wolves."

E. J. jumps to his feet, in part because he still has feet—his original feet, unlike Papa. "Wolves?" he asks.

"Yes," Kes says softly as she watches her father. And continues down the stairs.

"How close?" Uncle Ty asks.

"Close, I think." Kes feels the weight of her claim press against her. She approaches the table and sidles up next to Papa.

"Kick the fires and light the tires," E. J. says. "I've never seen a wolf."

"This side of the river?" Uncle Ty asks.

Kes faces her uncle. "I don't know. Maybe."

E. J. heads for the door with his cards in his hand.

"Hold it," Uncle Ty says. "We have to talk about this. We're in the middle of a poker hand here. Bets are on the table."

Papa puts an arm around Kes's waist and pulls her to him. She puts an arm around his shoulders and feels better. Safe. At home.

Everybody's talking:

"Somebody's gonna have to sleep with the chickens tonight."

"Not me."

"Not me either. I slept with them last night."

"How many times have we seen wolves on this side of the river?"

"Never."

"Tracks?"

"None."

"Well, there you go. Bets are on the table. Let's play."

"What about we just leave our cards face down and walk out and listen."

"How do we know this isn't a trick?"

"Because it's a twelve-year-old kid in PJs and pigtails."

"Somebody's gonna have to sleep with the ponies too."

"And the bees," Chippy says.

Cap laughs.

"First, we finish this hand," Uncle Ty announces, since he's the one responsible for this gathering.

Mike winces and rocks gently as he studies his cards.

Papa watches him.

More discussion:

"C'mon, guys. Did we move to Alaska to play cards or to hear wolves?"

"Play cards."

"I ain't movin'. I got three of a kind here. Maybe four. Maybe five."

"If it's really wolves, how come the ponies aren't making a fuss?"

"They're stupid."

"I'll tell you what's not stupid are bees. They understand the concept of zero."

"And fish can recognize themselves in a mirror."

"Good thing... given all the mirrors in the ocean."

"Okay, here's what we'll do," says a veteran named Captain Don. "We'll all put our cards face down and walk away at the same time. The dog will watch the table and report any wrongdoing."

"Or we'll just go out and listen, all of us, and take our cards with us."

"Jasper's blind."

"He sees fine."

"He walks into walls. He's a bazillion years old."

Sitting next to Grandpa on the floor, Kipper plays with his Legos.

"That's it." E. J. strides to the door, cards in hand, throws it open, and steps out onto the large deck built last year by Chippy and Cap. The others go still, listening...

Kes takes her father's hand. She knows every bone. "Papa, I heard them. It's not dogs. It's not coyotes. It's wolves. It has to be. And I think I heard them... they..."

"What, honey?" Rita asks.

"I think I heard them howling in harmony."

Papa raises his head and regards his girl with his one good eye, the soft metal of his dreams. He has so much light in him lately.

"Cammies and jammies," she tells him softly.

That's how they did it back in Lubbock, he in his military camouflage pants, the ones he wears now, and she in her pajamas, stepping outside to catch their breath. They sang like birds then, before Papa's seventy-two-hour deployment notice, when everything changed. They made up lyrics and serenaded the moon and jammed with Jupiter and fancied themselves rock stars in the Texas evening heat.

But now? Here? On this salmon-slippery, green-shaggy, ice-cut rainforest coast?

Wolves? Harmony?

Papa stands up. Together, he and Kes walk out onto the deck.

Everybody follows, cards in hand.

Kes sees Tucker John standing out by the garden, motionless. Late for poker, he must have heard the wolves en route to the main house.

"I hear them," Cap says. "Shh..."

Sure enough. Howling... from afar.

Chippy and Cap raise their heads and howl back, softly, and Papa raises his head too… his eyes closed, listening. On the edge of so much.

Then it stops. All goes quiet. And for a long moment nobody moves.

Tucker John makes a gesture with his hands to the west and looks back at Uncle Ty, who nods.

"Okay," Uncle Ty says, "bets are on the table. Back to the game. Nobody needs to sleep with the chickens tonight. Unless, of course, you'd like to, Chippy."

CHAPTER NINETEEN

Silver

NORTHBOUND. Mother and Alpha lead the pack single file. They travel not far from the river, but not within view of it. Their bellies full of salmon, they move swiftly through forest and meadow, leaving behind the faint but acrid smell of smoke. At twilight they cross a long, hard, lifeless surface that bridges the river: a death strip of some kind where nothing grows. Silver remembers it from when he and his kin came this way nearly a year ago, southbound, eager to explore new territory, and Silver, then a pup, fell behind the pack.

After a moment, the wolves melt into the forest and move on.

Old One struggles with the stopping and starting, his hips and legs protesting each time. Once up and moving again, he does well. The others take turns traveling with him. When Silver hears him rasping, he trots alongside shoulder to shoulder, offering his best support.

They sleep that night under a canopy of silent spruce. The next day they ascend a gentle ridge and stop. It's late summer. The former subadults, now fully grown, could leave the pack to find—or make—packs of their own. But Alpha and Mother had no pups this last spring. Because of this, the pack is strong, experienced, highly mobile, and without an active den. It also faces an uncertain future if Alpha and Mother, for whatever reason, no longer mate. This could doom them. Silver, Sister, and Strong are the yearlings now, and will one day be full grown and able to leave the pack. Mother licks their faces while Alpha walks up a long deadfall spruce that rises at one end, jammed between two other mighty trees. High above his pack, he lifts his nose into the breeze. The others can see that he senses something, how he moves his head back and forth, reading the air. Yes, something is out there. Now Old

One totters up the large, moss-covered log to join him, lifts his nose as well, and begins to show more excitement than he has in a long time.

Yes, something is out there.

DOWN THEY GO, THROUGH THE FOREST, headed for the ocean again, this time a large bay to the west beneath tall mountains defined by glaciers and bears.

They pass a clearing filled with voles. In the back of the pack, Silver pauses and takes note. Later, they cross a long, sinuous depression in the mossy, forest floor—a river otter slide, where the social, furry animals come ashore to cavort in the woods, sliding down the same track again and again. Silver pauses here as well, and takes note.

Onward, the air grows rich with the smell of the ocean, but also something more pungent, something Silver has never sensed before. Late again, he passes through a fringe of alder, moves quickly, and soon joins his family. There, not far away, a mountain of blubber and meat rises on shore, stranded by the tide: a beached humpback whale bloated and distended from its own dying and death, surrounded by ravens, magpies, eagles, and crows. Standing atop it, a male coastal brown bear is king of the mountain, feasting. The whale makes him look small. But he's not. Silver can see he's a huge battle-scarred boar not given to surrender or retreat—the kind of bear that can own a valley, swim a fjord, challenge a sow, and kill her cubs.

The wolves hold still for a long time, watching, licking their lips.

Finally, Old One steps forward and walks toward the whale. Alone.

Silver has seen something like this before, but where? In his dreams? Yes, dreams of him and his ancestors fighting to bring down mastodons and woolly mammoths from the Long Ago Time when wolves crossed glaciers and glaciers spanned continents and wolves threw themselves at their mountainous prey as if breaking themselves on rocks. And still they attacked, and sometimes got impaled, or hooked on a mastodon's huge tusks and tossed head over tail, high through the air, to where they landed on their backs and heard their own vertebrae snap. And so died a slow, painful death. And still... to build up strong jaws and teeth, young wolves jumped up and grabbed a tree branch and hung there, suspended, as if from a moose, for as long as they could. Longer. You never truly know who you are—what you're capable of—until you're hungry. Not belly hungry, but bone hungry… hungry to the marrow of your existence and all the way back to the beginning. It's the only way.

Watching Old One go now, Mother and Sister begin to whimper.

Alpha snarls them down. Quiet.

Old One doesn't hesitate. He walks straight toward that whale and the bear atop it, determined to eat or die.

CHAPTER TWENTY

Salt

ABRAHAM LISTENS WITHOUT MOVING, his head turned away from his father to look out the side window of the Toyota. He wears his Seahawks ball cap backward, and the sleeves of his T-shirt rolled tight up against his biceps.

When Salt finishes the small recruitment speech he's been preparing for days, he watches his son for any sign of conflict or doubt.

"So," Abe says, still looking away, "it could be against the law?"

"Not really," Salt assures him. "Remember, the man from the governor's office told me that—"

"Will the money really be enough to buy the treatment for Solomon?"

"It should be, if the stem cell surgery is approved. Remember, it's not a treatment. It's a clinical trial, the first ever. Johns Hopkins wants to do it. The chief surgeon who designed the trial wants to do it. It just needs approval from the FDA."

"The Food and Drug Administration?"

"Yes."

"It really could save Solomon? Save his life? Make him better?"

"Nobody can answer that, Abraham. But it's the best chance out there. It might be our only—"

"Why?" Abraham slams his fist into the dashboard. "Why does it have to be this way? Why can't we know anything for sure?"

Salt tells himself to stay calm as he drives the Toyota over the Menzies River Bridge and into Crystal Bay National Marine Reserve, ten miles northwest of Strawberry Flats. Abe has his head down now, as if in defeat. Hannah thinks he's never been the same since he pulled Salt soaking wet out of the frozen river up in Minto, screaming, "Don't die, Dad... don't die..." and began to half carry, half drag his father back to the cabin. Salt thinks Abe has never been the same since Solomon's diagnosis, when they all knew something was wrong... how Solomon began to stumble all the time, and then fall, and drool, and yet never lose his sunny disposition or funny ways. When Abe first watched his younger brother sit in that wheelchair, he cried for hours.

The other day Hannah caught him looking at tattoos on the internet and later said to Salt, "You have to talk to him. I don't want him to do that. I don't want him covered in tattoos. He's only sixteen."

Salt pulls the Toyota off the road and into a secluded spot in the forest. It's the Saturday before the first day of school. Traffic is light. Nobody should see them here. He lets a long minute drift by.

"So... there's a chance you could go to jail?" Abe asks, his head still down. "We could both go to jail? What happens if we both go to jail? What happens then?"

"Abraham, you're my son. I would never ask you to do anything that could jeopardize your future. Besides, you're a minor, under eighteen. The man from the governor's office told me state law is about to change. Nobody's going to know we did this, especially if you help me. The job is too big for me alone, and I can't trust anybody but you."

"I'll be your lieutenant?"

"Yes... okay, if that's what you want to call it."

Abraham nods lightly. He enjoys hearing this, being his father's trusty lieutenant. Lately he's been using more military terms in his daily speech, like captain, commando, operation, and lieutenant. Abe finally looks up at his father and says, "Dad, I'd do anything to help Solomon get better. I mean it."

"I know you do."

"So, let's do this."

They unload the four heavy plastic totes filled with traps, cables, and snares—one tote at a time, Abe on one end, Salt on the other—and stash them in the woods. Salt unfolds a large topographic map and spreads it out on the ground as Abe begins to stuff snares into his metal-framed pack. "Not too heavy," Salt tells him. They plan to go easy; carry the trapping gear through the woods a short distance at a time, stash it, then return home and come back to do more gear-hauling when they can. It will take days or weeks.

But it's better than risking drowning themselves hauling the heavy gear across the river due west of town. Yes, Abe could probably do it, given his strength and height. But one slip at midcurrent with all that weight on his back could be traumatizing, like Minto. Or worse, he could die. Abe had insisted that he give the river crossing a try with a fully loaded pack, but Salt said no. And that's final. They'll do it the longer way, the more time-consuming way. But also—and most important—the less dangerous way.

"Let's eat," Abe says, as he digs into a package of sausage, crackers, and cheese.

"Drink first," Salt tells him. Abe sometimes gets dehydration headaches because he doesn't drink enough. Last year he passed out during a school volleyball game.

Abe joins Salt, who is on his knees studying the map. Abe loads a cracker with a thick slice of sausage and cheese, and eats it. And another. And another. Finally, he drops the package next to Salt and takes a long drink of water. Had it been any of his other sons, Salt knows they would have prepared a cracker for their father first and handed it to him saying, "Here, Dad," the way their mother taught them from her favorite passages in Leviticus, Proverbs, Matthew, Luke, John, and best of all the words of the Lord Jesus himself, from Acts 20:35: "It is more blessed to give than to receive."

Salt feels his heart break when the package lands next to him. He takes a deep breath, points to a feature, and says, "See this hill here? I've been up it. The view is incredible."

Abe chews vigorously. "Is that the hill we can see from town?"

"Yes. The map says it's more than four hundred feet high. Pastor Anderson calls it Heaven's Hill."

"Pastor Anderson? He's been up there?"

"I don't think so. I don't think very many people have been up there. The south face is really steep, almost like a cliff. The east and west faces are treacherous too, heavily wooded. The north approach isn't steep, but it's loaded with devil's club and ankle-twisting alder. I found wolf hair when I finally got up there, and bird droppings, maybe bald eagle or peregrine falcon."

"Where are the wolves now?"

Salt chuckles. "I don't know, Abe. If I did, I'd be the wolf whisperer. My best guess is that they're somewhere along the river catching cohos."

Salt finally eats a little and drinks, and soon the two of them are working their way south with heavy packs, following the river.

"We'll need to do a really good job of hiding all this trapping gear," Salt says. But Abe is far ahead and disappearing fast, plowing through the forest. "Abe… slow down, okay?"

Salt's bad hip and knee begin to protest. His heart jackhammers. He stops, bends at his waist with his hands on his knees, and sucks air. When he stands erect again, he feels the shoulder straps dig into him with all the weight, and again he feels unwell.

Onward.

"Abe?" he calls. "Abe, slow down, okay…?" He feels funny. Not funny ha-ha, but funny peculiar. A bad sign. He walks on, stumbles over some roots, and keeps walking. *Where's Abe?* Salt thinks about what Hannah said the other day, about Abe maybe being sweet on Pastor Anderson's eldest daughter. *What's her name? Nice girl. Her younger brother plays guitar during the services… what's his name? Nice boy.* And then there's Pastor Anderson himself, a real storyteller who loves history and misquotes scripture but could never be accused of not being devout.

Salt stops and bends at his waist again to catch his breath and relieve the pain in his shoulders and chest. When he stands up erect, his head flops back and he sees the treetops spinning faster and faster—before everything goes black.

Abe?

CHAPTER TWENTY-ONE

Kes

THE LAST DAY OF AUGUST, first day of school. Rita offers to drive Kes both ways, but Kes wants to ride the red Schwinn Racer that Cap fixed for her. According to Uncle Ty, Cap can repair anything—except his own shattered life.

"School is only a few miles away," Kes tells Rita.

"I know. Did you find the bookbag I set out for you?"

"Yeah."

"And the carrots and hummus?"

"Yeah."

"And the jacket Julie gave you? The nice blue one?"

"Yeah."

"And the new Gro-Bra I bought for you? The soft one?"

"Yeah, Mom, thank you. Bye now." *Enough already. Geez.*

"Stand tall, honey. You look great."

"Thanks."

"Are the Anderson twins meeting you along the way?"

"Yeah, I think so."

"I like it when you call me Mom."

Kes shrugs. She can see that Rita struggles to be her real mom—*the mom I can barely remember.* She can see that Rita truly wants to make a happy home here in their new life under construction, one built with great heart by Uncle Ty and Chippy and Cap, and any of the others who can run a power drill, chop saw, table saw, chainsaw, and Skilsaw, and work on a metal roof without falling off and breaking their neck.

Uncle Ty likes to say there's something wholesome about having no mortgages and loan officers and all that; to build out of pocket instead, willy-nilly. Live with your mistakes. Oops, we miscalculated the rise-run on that staircase. Oh well, it'll do. Oops, we got that gable wrong. Oops, two weeks of rain just warped the floor before we got the roof on. Oops, we forgot to wire in the hall lights. Oh well, it'll do.

And the upside? Imagination. Experimentation. Creativity. Plus, no property taxes, no building codes, no covenants, and no law enforcement. No crime either, most of the time anyway. If anybody gets "cabin fever" and goes crazy in Strawberry Flats, the Alaska state troopers fly out from Juneau. Or the federal law enforcement rangers drive into town from Crystal Bay National Marine Reserve, only ten miles away. The troopers or rangers might make an arrest or write a citation. Or they might just talk the person down and alert a nearest relative.

"If we don't want troopers and rangers around here," Uncle Ty said once with a special nod to Chippy and Cap (who often talk about rebellion and revolution), "then we don't get crazy, okay?"

Chippy and Cap drove their white van from San Antonio to Bellingham loaded with—what? Three rocket-propelled grenades, ten thousand bags of Doritos, five hundred packages of Trader Joe's chocolate-covered cherries, and two dozen handguns? Nobody knows. They avoided Canadian customs by driving onto the Alaska State Ferry in Bellingham, sailing nonstop to Alaska, changing ferries in Juneau, and driving off a ferry in Strawberry Flats. Ten days total. They keep the van locked and parked behind their shed, near the apiary and the large solar array. Kes isn't sure if even Uncle Ty knows what's in it. All she knows is that Cap did a nice job on her bike and said, when he presented it to her, "The derailleur was all messed up. I oiled the chain and checked the spokes. Everything's better now. Have a good ride."

"Thanks, Cap."

Whenever Papa and Rita leave Willynillyville, even for an hour or so to run errands, Uncle Ty has Chippy and Cap trained to rush into their place to do carpentry. Tape up more sheetrock. Trim out the windows. Tile the kitchen counter one section at a time. Don't make a mess; get out fast. The rest of the time they work in the shop, making cool stuff like cabinets and rocking chairs without using a single nail or screw. Kes is beginning to warm to them, which is no easy task after the fireworks ordeal in San Antonio, them wanting to start a war with their stupid RPGs. Lately, they've been kind to her, though she still thinks they could go crazy at the slightest provocation.

THE POKER PACK LINES UP to send Kes off, high-fiving her as she peddles down the dirt drive. They're all there, near as she can tell: E. J., Mike, Captain Don, Chippy and Cap, Uncle Ty, and Tucker John. At the end of the line, she stops to hug Papa and smell his long hair pulled into a ponytail. The other day a chestnut-backed chickadee landed on his head while he was filling the bird feeder, and he smiled more radiantly than anybody could remember. The day before that he found bear scat near the river, and motioned others to follow him back through the woods so they could all see it. And the day before that he sat in the garden with Tucker John and Kes, and showed little Kip how to pull carrots, and for a moment looked as though he might laugh with the others when Kip ended up with a carrot shaped like a corkscrew.

Kes looks back to see Grandpa, Rita, and Kip, beyond the Poker Pack, waving her goodbye from the same deck where they all stood listening for wolves.

Howling in harmony? Impossible.

She rides easy down Menzies River Road, lost in thought, the cool morning air wet on her cheeks. A few vehicles pass her going both ways at ten or fifteen miles an hour. The drivers wave, and she waves back. That's how it is in Strawberry Flats, says Uncle Ty. People wave. If they don't wave, they're from out of town, forgive them. If they don't wave a second time, invite them to dinner. If they don't wave a third time, run them off the road. Uncle Ty loves the potholed, washboarded, alder-fringed, winding dirt roads here where people either drive slow and contemplate the cosmos, or they drive fast and ruin their shocks and suspensions. He also loves Mexico, where they have a saying: "Bad roads, good people. Good roads, too many people." Rita says Uncle Ty is devoted to a family in Mexico and once loved a woman there who broke his heart. But that he's also done some serious heartbreaking of his own over the years. He was married once, until something terrible happened that nobody talks about. When Kes tried to pry the secret out of Grandpa one night in Lubbock, he got sad and walked away.

THE ANDERSON TWINS meet Kes where Rusty Road joins Menzies River Road and the pavement begins. "Hey Kes," Tim says.

"Hey Tim. Hey Tia."

"I found huge moose tracks on Miller Road yesterday," Tim says as they ride. A somewhat heavy boy who gives all his energy to whatever he's saying, he's already out of breath. "I wonder if it's that legendary moose your uncle talked about."

"Big Al?" Kes replies. "I don't know. Maybe. I think he lives on the other side of the river... where the wolves are."

"The moose's name is Al?" Tia asks. "Why?"

"Because *Alces alces* is the scientific name of all moose," Kes explains. "They're all the same species. But I don't know if anybody has ever seen the one really big bull moose that my uncle talks about. He sometimes just makes stuff up."

"Why?" Tia asks. She rides more easily than her brother and looks just like him, though she's thinner and her hair is long.

"To trick people, to see how gullible they are. He's a lot of fun, actually."

"People say he's a good fisherman," Tim says, "and that he sometimes looks like a pirate."

"My mom, Rita, she says he's a reverse pirate because he gives instead of takes."

"That's cool," Tia says.

"All of Willynillyville is his idea."

The twins nod; they already know this.

Shortly after Rita arrived with little Kip, a little over a month ago now, Pastor Anderson visited Willynillyville with his plump wife, their eldest daughter, Tabitha, and the twins. They were new to town as well and wanted to welcome the Nash family to Strawberry Flats. They gifted Rita with a large dish of halibut caddy ganty and said matter-of-factly that the whole town was aflutter that Tyler Nash, fisherman, pilot, and founder of Willynillyville, had brought his family here, praise the Lord, including his younger brother, an almost famous Texas singer/songwriter who'd been injured in Afghanistan. Pastor Anderson thanked Papa for his service and invited the entire Poker Pack to his church every Sunday, adding that his services were nondenominational.

The veterans ate the halibut all in one sitting—"like wolves on a moose," E. J. said. The next day, a Sunday, nobody went to church.

During the visit, Kes noticed Tim eyeing Papa's neglected Martin, how it gathered dust in a corner. She'd heard about a boy—"just a kid," people said—"who rocked Pastor Anderson's church" every Sunday, that he was young, a protégé, the next Eric Clapton. And who does he turn out to be? Tim, the pastor's son.

"I liked all the big solar panels," Tia says as they ride, talking about Willynillyville. "And the greenhouse. And the ponies. Tim liked your dad's guitar."

"Those veterans are cool," Tim says. "They know how to make things."

"Yeah," Kes says.

"I went on the internet," Tim adds, huffing hard, "and listened to your dad's band. I love that song, 'Bird in a Cloud,' and the one with the long mandolin solo, 'Carry Me Home.'"

"I like those too," Kes says, feeling her heart swell as she thinks back to Papa and Rita composing their songs line by line on the bus while riding through the dusty plains. Papa with his guitar in his lap, Rita opposite him, testing the lyrics and melody lines, then kissing and falling asleep in each other's arms, or pulling the blinds in the back room for privacy, all before little Kip came along. And days later, or maybe even the next day, the band playing the new song in front of thousands, pouring their hearts into it, bathing in applause while Kes watched from backstage.

"Who sang the high harmony?" Tim asks.

"What?" Kes is a thousand miles away, back with the band, rolling through Kansas, laughing with Stringer and Sammye, stopping for ice cream that melts in the summer heat, the sun blazing overhead.

"Who sang the high harmony?" Tim asks again.

"Oh, Sammye Surreal. That's her stage name. She's the keyboardist. She and my mom are good friends. She's like an auntie to me."

"Cool," Tim says.

"Are you going to sign up for Battle of the Books?" Tia asks Kes. "Or for the spelling bee? Or the geography bee?"

"Science Friday."

"Science Friday?" Tia says. "That's for high schoolers, not open to us. My dad says that the new principal, Mrs. Cunningham, might end it."

"End Science Friday?" Kes asks.

Tia shrugs. "Yeah, I think so. I don't know. You'll find out today, maybe."

JUST THEN, three boys overtake them on their bicycles, riding hard as if racing. The older one, tall and powerfully built and riding upright with no hands on the handlebars, slows down to pace Kes and the twins. He looks them over with a hard expression, says hi to Tim, and asks, "Where's Tabby?"

"She went to school early to help set up the kitchen."

"My dad talked to your dad about his sermon on Sunday," the tall boy says.

Kes immediately likes nothing about him: his voice, posture, attitude—nothing.

"I know," Tim replies sheepishly. "Your dad said he doesn't like it when my dad speaks from scripture without using the exact words. He called it 'parrot phrasing.'"

"Paraphrasing," Tia corrects him.

"Yeah, paraphrasing," Tim says.

"He doesn't mean to be mean," the older, taller boy says, appearing to soften a little. "He just knows the Bible word for word and thinks your dad should too."

"Yeah," Tim says. "My dad felt bad about it. I think he apologized."

"Yeah, I heard that he did. You're from Kentucky, right?"

"Yeah."

"Have you been to The Ark museum? It's a huge replica of Noah's Ark."

"No," Tim says, "but I know about it."

"Have you been to the Creation Museum? It's in Kentucky too."

"No."

"You've never visited those museums?"

"They're not museums," Kes says with a glance at the tall boy, who is now flanked on his other side by the two smaller boys who must be his brothers.

The older boy glares at her. "What are they then?"

"Fantasylands."

"Says who?"

"Says science." *Forget the knight. Raise the sword yourself. Excalibur.*

The tall boy glares at her and appears ready to challenge her, when a red van zips by. "There goes Solomon," one of the smaller boys says. All three take off riding hard, with the tall, older boy down low on the handlebars, determined to beat his brothers and get to school first.

"Who's that?" Kes asks.

"That's Abraham d'Alene and his brothers Jericho and Joshua," Tim says. "Jerry's in our class."

"Tabby says Abraham is a star athlete, our school's best volleyball player," Tia says. "I think she likes him."

"She's stupid to like him," Tim says. "He's going to hate you for saying to him what you just did, Kes. You need to be more careful."

When Kes and the twins arrive a minute later, Kes sees all three d'Alene brothers standing at the red van, their bikes parked, as a fourth boy—in a wheelchair but the only one looking around, animated somehow, eager for the day—is lowered by a side ramp onto the school parking lot. "Shake it on doooown," she hears him say.

From afar, Kes feels drawn to him... to his open face and welcoming eyes. *He must be Solomon.*

Before the tall boy named Abraham can wheel his brother Solomon into the school, their father, wearing overalls, sunglasses, and a bandage on his face, directs his sons to kneel around the wheelchair and bow their heads in prayer, their hands clasped together.

Even then, Solomon raises his head, looks directly at Kes, and smiles.

TEN MINUTES LATER, Mrs. Cunningham, the school principal, a short woman with black hair, pasty-white skin, and blazing blue eyes, speaks to the entire student body in the multipurpose room. She mentions two students who qualified last year for regionals in the spelling bee and geography bee. "And let us not forget our star volleyball player, Abraham d'Alene, the top scorer in our region, who I'm told almost took our team to the state championship." Standing near Tim and Tia and her other new classmates, Kes watches Abraham step forward to receive applause as his brother rocks excitedly in his wheelchair. When Principal Cunningham calls for everybody to bow their heads in prayer and begins, "Our Father, who art in Heaven..." three adults walk out of the room, including one of Kes's seventh-grade teachers, Mrs. Carry.

AN OLDER WOMAN with long, gray hair pulled back into a turquoise clip, Mrs. Carry has arranged her classroom desks and chairs not in rows but in a circle that reminds Kes of Camelot. "This is how we'll study democracy and civics," she says. "Every day I'll expect you to arrive prepared and to express yourselves as best you can. Remember, a poorly written sentence reflects an ill-conceived idea. Be articulate, be smart, be kind. Is that asking too much?" She scans the students, making eye contact with each one.

No answer.

"I said: is that asking too much?"

"No," several kids say, Kes included.

"Good."

For weeks Kes worried that she might be tagged as the girl with the crippled father; the father with fake legs, the father who got blown up. But nobody says a thing or treats her out of the ordinary. Tim and Tia needle each other until Mrs. Carry separates them.

In the afternoon during geometry and biology, taught by Mr. Ringold, Kes works on theorems and truths with Tim, and suppresses a laugh—she's not the only one—when Jericho d'Alene makes funny faces. Mr. Ringold talks in a monotone and turns his back often to write on a whiteboard. When he does, Jerry rolls his eyes and sticks out his tongue as if dying from tedium.

How can one d'Alene brother be so funny, and the other so awful?

When school ends, Kes swings back into Mrs. Carry's classroom to get her coat.

"How was your first day?" asks Mrs. Carry, alone at her desk, typing briskly on her computer.

"Good," Kes says. She expects Mrs. Carry to say something about her papa.

"I like your name, by the way. Is it your full name? Or is it short for something?"

"It's short for Kestrel."

"Kestrel? Like the hawk?"

"Kind of. Hawks are accipiters, in the family *Accipitridae*. A kestrel is a falcon, in the family *Falconidae*."

Mrs. Carry slides back from her desk. "So then, you know your birds?"

"A little."

"Falcons are smaller than hawks, right?"

"Yeah, and faster. Their wings are bent more at the wrists. A merlin is a falcon, in the genus Falco, same as kestrels."

"If your parents had named you Merlin, you might have become a wizard."

"I know. I've read *The Once and Future King* three times."

"Three times? I'm impressed."

"There's a species of hawk in southern Texas, the Harris hawk, that hunts in packs, like wolves. They see lizards or snakes from the air and land and work as a group, you know, hopping around on their feet to flush their prey out from under a thorny bush. I saw them in Big Bend, near the Rio Grande, when my family went there on a camping trip in March. The night sky was amazing. We could see the Andromeda Galaxy. And my dad got better there. He used to be a singer and a songwriter and a good musician, and he had his own band, Whoa Nellie, with my mom. They wrote beautiful songs together. Anyway… Harris hawks are really cool. They mostly live in Mexico."

Mrs. Carry looks at Kes with new sincerity. "I want you to be comfortable in this class, Kes. I want you to feel free to talk to me about anything."

Kes studies the wrinkles around her eyes, the rebel strand of gray hair that's fallen across her brow. "Why can't we go outside to learn?"

"We can, and we will. We'll have at least one class field trip a month, some of them into the marine reserve. How's that sound?"

"Good."

As Kes pulls on her coat, Principal Cunningham bursts into the classroom and stares at the Camelot circle of desks. Ignoring Kes, she turns to Mrs. Carry and says, "I need to see you in my office."

Kes slips out the door and into the corridor as she hears Mrs. Carry say, "When?"

"As soon as possible."

"I have to finish this email," Mrs. Carry says. "I'll be there in five minutes."

Kes pushes herself up against the corridor wall, next to the lockers, as Principal Cunningham walks by only feet away, her face like concrete. She's several steps past Kes, en route to her office, when she stops and turns.

"Kestrel Nash?"

"Yes." Kes feels her heart begin to race.

"What are you doing here?"

"I'm getting my things… from my locker. To go home."

"You signed up for Science Friday, didn't you?"

"Yes."

Principal Cunningham walks back toward her, to within inches. "I know about your father, about his sacrifice. The sacrifice of your entire family. I'm sorry for your trauma. How's he doing here, in Strawberry Flats, your new home?"

"Good, I think."

Principal Cunningham smiles. "That's nice to hear. This is my new home too. I should tell you that Science Friday might not happen this year. It might be discontinued."

"Oh... okay. Why?"

Just then, Mrs. Carry steps from her classroom into the hallway.

Principal Cunningham ignores her. "We can have only so many extracurricular activities. I have to evaluate each one against the others. I'll make my decision soon."

"Okay," Kes says, feeling powerless and small. Pinned to the wall.

"I also saw you help Solomon d'Alene today, in the cafeteria."

"Oh... yes, he needed a straw for his drink, and I ate with him for a little. I like him."

"Of course, you do. He's a child of God. I also heard the disturbing news about what you said to his brother Abraham this morning, on your bike, coming to school. Remember, Kestrel, a girl your age cannot begin to know everything."

"Yes, she can," Mrs. Carry says.

Principal Cunningham glares at Mrs. Carry, as if ready to scold her, but then turns and walks away. When she's finally out of sight, her footfalls receding down the corridor, Mrs. Carry says, "Kes, you should leave now."

A MINUTE LATER, Kes rides home as fast as she can, peddling hard, fighting back tears. Home to Papa and little Kip. To the garden. Pulling carrots. Listening for wolves.

CHAPTER TWENTY-TWO

Silver

HIS BELLY FULL, Silver stands atop the dead whale—thirty-five tons of meat, blubber, and bone—and surveys his world. A sweep of sandy and cobbled beach curves to the north beneath tall, snowy peaks that climb into feathered clouds. A light rain falls, soft as mist. No wind. Ebbing tide. Water droplets hang in the needles of shoreline spruce. Rivulets of fresh water run downslope through the mossy forest and beach rye grasses and into the sea. Eagles, ravens, and crows come and go, partaking of the feast, getting their allotted morsels and more. Magpies too, though not as boldly.

All is quiet, save for the soft sounds of water.

The sky seems to hold its breath.

A tawny-colored coyote dashes out from the forest and steals a piece of whale blubber, but does so honestly, out in the open. Then runs away.

Every bird flies off when a wolverine arrives. The wolves back away a little as well, though not Silver, high atop the whale. The wolverine works the air with his nose, as a traveler might assess new ground. He then chooses a select piece of meat, rips it off ferociously at the tideline, and walks up the beach and into the forest.

FOR A LONG TIME, only Old One and the big male bear stayed on the dead whale day and night, with Old One at one end, the bear at the other, each refusing to yield.

But after many days, for reasons only they understood, both moved away.

When they did, others staked their claims.

Though just a yearling, Silver has achieved remarkable size. Deep chested, broad shouldered, and long legged, he moves with confidence and grace, no longer tripping on his oversized paws. He still plays with Sister and Strong, though not in the carefree manner of his early youth. Always watchful, he pays special attention to Alpha and Mother, and learns from them daily.

Other bears come and go, as do the tides.

Low tides leave the whale stranded on a mudflat and cobbled beach covered in barnacles, mussels, seaweed, and the occasional sea star. High tides surround the whale and make it a nearshore island, the water slick with whale oil, shimmering in the sun.

Two days ago, while feeding on the whale, Silver and his kin witnessed a strange birdlike object circle overhead and make an otherworldly sound, reminiscent of winged objects his family had seen before. But those earlier objects appeared much higher and weren't nearly so loud. They also didn't circle, but instead flew in straight lines.

Then yesterday, while again tearing into the whale yet being circumspect, Silver saw four animals emerge onto the shore far to the north. Mysterious in detail but not in profile, they were all black, with their ears up, shoulders back. Wolves. Drawn to the feast as any carnivore would be. Silver snarled his pack to attention and ran toward the intruders at full speed. Not to join them but to rebuff them; to protect his family and its bounty. The four black wolves hesitated, frozen in the moment as they watched Silver charge, then bolted into the forest and disappeared.

Such paw-twitching dreams Silver had that night. To see animals so familiar yet unknown, curious yet cautious. And hungry. Always hungry. Wolves from another pack, measuring up the country and the competition.

And now today, the quiet ends again when another otherworldly noise arrives, this time from two objects on the water.

Mother gathers the pack high on shore, near the forest fringe, and watches while Silver and Old One stand alone atop the dead whale.

The two objects approach slowly, touch shore on a flooding tide some distance down the beach, and stop. From them emerge five tall uprights who cluster together as the two objects from which they emerged back away, again making noise. Moving unlike predators or prey, apparently neither hungry nor afraid, the tall uprights approach the whale, pausing now and then. Silver senses no fear, feels no threat. He and Old One walk the length of the whale, head to tail, and step onto the wet shore. The tall uprights pause again, make chattering noises, and continue toward the whale.

The ravens and crows take flight.

As Silver and his family melt into the forest, he looks back one last time to study the tall uprights, now at the whale, all five turned his direction, where one raises a forepaw and holds it there. *A greeting?*

CHAPTER TWENTY-THREE

Salt

LIKE EVERBODY ELSE IN TOWN, Salt knows where to go to hear rumors. First: the Hi Tyde Bar and Grill, with its six-mornings-a-week Heart Attack Special of sausage, bacon, ham and eggs, hash browns, and biscuits and gravy, and its Friday and Saturday night pizza with extra cheese and crispy crust. Second: Nystad's Mercantile, where brothers Oddmund and Dag Nystad—Norwegians who live across Icy Strait in the town of Jinkaat, on Chichagof Island, and who recently opened a store in Strawberry Flats—offer "Any Second Item at 100% the Price of the First," as if it's a bargain. Need a water filter for eight bucks? Get two for sixteen dollars. Why buy one when you can have two for twice the price? And third: the Strawberry Flats K–12 Public School, where Rosie Goodnight, the school secretary, is such a bad gossip that her nickname is Miss Information.

And who should Salt and three of his sons run into as they enter the Hi Tyde Bar and Grill to pick up their takeout order of Friday night pizza? None other than Rosie and her husband, Paul, a heavy equipment operator, and the commercial fisherman Spike Wallace. And a flock of school kids that includes Tim and Tia, Pastor Anderson's twins, and the girl—Salt can't remember her name—whose father got badly injured in Afghanistan.

Kes. That's it. Kes Nash.

The same girl, according to Jericho, who on the first day of school looked Abraham straight in the face—a boy four years older than her and intimidatingly tall—and told him that The Ark and Creation Museum were fantasylands.

Like little birds now, the flock of schoolgirls flit about Jericho—they call him Jerry—and laugh at his jokes, which encourages him into greater antics, all of which makes Salt uncomfortable and leaves Abraham standing alone in his own shadow.

Salt hears the girls inquire about Solomon.

Jericho tells them he's at home with his mom, waiting for pizza.

The woman at the counter says to Salt, "Your pizzas are coming out of the oven and will be ready in just a few minutes. Would you like to pay with cash or credit card?"

"Cash." Salt hands her a one-hundred-dollar bill.

"I'm hungry, Dad," Joshua says as he pulls on Salt's pant leg.

Salt pats him on his head.

While more people exchange greetings and small talk as they come through the door and shake the October rain off their hats and coats, Salt sees Kes apart from the rest, staring at him as if studying the faint bruises on his face, his one eye still lightly discolored from when he passed out and fell hard onto the forest floor while hauling his heavy trapping gear. Once again, like up in Minto years ago, Abraham had to come to his rescue and helped Salt get back home.

This is not the first time Kes Nash has watched him.

When driving his Toyota back from the end of Menzies River Road a few days ago, Salt passed her going the other way on her bike. Both waved, as is customary in town. But in his rearview mirror he saw her stop and turn and watch him until he rounded a bend out of sight. And again, only yesterday, near where Willynillyville Drive branches off Menzies River Road, she did the same thing. *Why?* Many people go out there and park and hike to the river to pick mushrooms and berries, or to hunt moose or take photos, or in winter to cross-country ski. Half a dozen vehicles might be parked out there at any given time. Many people enjoy the area (state of Alaska land), though few cross the swift river. Salt always locks his Toyota and leaves no visible sign of his activities.

He's not nearly as nimble and strong as he used to be. He knows this. His heart is failing. And he's already been humbled by those Willynillyville vets who saw him when he hid in the woods off the Menzies River Trail and fooled nobody. *Did the vets tell this girl with the lightly freckled face and gray-green eyes about seeing me off the trail as I pretended to be furtive?* According to Rosie Goodnight, Kes's father—a former musician and recording artist—hasn't spoken a word in more than a year. Since Afghanistan. *Dear God.*

Rosie stands nearby, talking a mile a minute about the illegal moose that was shot by Carl Bankshe. "The distance between the antler tines needs to be fifty inches, you know, and this bull was forty-nine inches. The troopers fined Carl and took his hunting license for two years. And he had to forfeit the moose."

"And he still had to quarter it up and pack it out," Spike says.

"Friends helped him," Paul adds.

"And guess what happened to the moose?" Rosie says. "Well, let me tell you…"

Salt already knows. His employer, Derek Smith, told him earlier while Salt was working on an old Ford truck. The moose was taken to the school where every K–12 student helped to butcher it, aided by biologists from the marine reserve and the state. It took all day. A local photographer documented the whole thing and posted it on Facebook, saying: "Most schools confiscate knives… at our school we pass them out—even to the kindergartners." It went viral.

"And did you hear?" Rosie adds. "There's a dead humpback whale in Crystal Bay. It's being eaten up by wolves and bears."

"It's being scavenged, not eaten up," Spike says. "If it were being eaten up, you'd need ten T. rexes and fifty velociraptors."

Salt watches a smile crawl over Kes's face when she hears this. *She must like dinosaurs.*

"Dad," Joshua says loudly with another tug on Salt's pantleg. "When do we get our pizza?"

"We're boxing them up now," says the woman behind the counter.

"I heard the humpback whale numbers were way down this summer in Crystal Bay," Paul says.

"Forty percent down," Spike says. "Scientists think it's because the North Pacific has gotten too warm."

"Here you go," the woman says to Salt as she hands him four large boxes. Salt takes two while Abe takes the other two.

"Whoa, Salt," Spike says as Salt turns to go. "It looks like a party for you and the family tonight." Salt smiles and nods. He and Hannah have never ordered this many takeout pizzas before. Maybe he should be more discreet about throwing around one-hundred-dollar bills. As he goes out the door, followed by Joshua, Jericho, and finally Abraham, Salt hears Abe rebuke Kes through his gritted teeth. Salt doesn't get the words, but he can see shock register on the girl's face.

Ten minutes later, as the boys rush inside the house, Hannah greets Salt on the deck with a worried look, wet with rain.

"What is it?" he asks. "What's wrong?"

"The mystery man called. He wants to talk with you. He wants to meet with you in Juneau."

"Again?"

She nods. "He says it's important. He's already booked you a flight."

Salt feels his heart sink until from inside the house he hears Solomon whoop with his brothers as they open the pizza boxes.

"Shake it on dooooooooooooown."

Only then does Salt manage a weak smile and put his arm around Hannah and say, "It'll be okay."

SAME HOLE-IN-THE-WALL RESTAURANT in Juneau's Mendenhall Valley. Same table. Same map. And almost the same three guys: Mr. Raddock, Gary the political hack, and this time, instead of an engineer who builds bridges and roads, it's Jess Cleet, a wolf killer and lodge owner from Fairbanks, a good friend of Salt's friend, Rolf, the former state senator. Salt first met Jess many years ago and learned to avoid him.

And now the same Filipino waitress—*who deserves to wait on better men,* Salt muses—takes their drink orders and leaves.

After Mr. Raddock asks Salt about his family, and his progress so far with the wolves but not the faint bruises on his face, and Salt tells them he's staged all his trapping gear across the river, which is not entirely true, they talk about the wolves and bears on the beached whale in Crystal Bay, and when the wolves might once again occupy the Menzies River area. His face expressionless, almost inscrutable, Mr. Raddock then tells Salt there could be a change of plans. That's when Jess Cleet talks about denning, why the pack didn't have pups this last spring, perhaps because they were new to the area. If the pack were to den, or somehow be encouraged to den, given Salt's best knowledge of the west side of the river, where would that be?

"Where would they den?" Salt asks.

"Yes," Jess says. He has a full beard that's grayer than Salt remembered, a receding hairline, and a nasty scar that runs from one eye to his ear. Neither Mr. Raddock nor Gary look at their phones. Instead, they look intently at Salt.

"Here," Salt says, pointing at the map. "The whole area is glacial outwash except this hill, which is bedrock and about four hundred feet high. It's steep on the south side, almost a cliff, and gentle on the north side, heavily wooded, mostly alder. But on the east and west sides it has a nice slope, and lots of moss growing on finer sediments and glacial till, and some loose earth that could be easily dug out and shaped into a den. If I were a wolf in the Menzies River area, that's where I'd raise my family."

Mr. Raddock, Gary, and Jess all look at each other. Nobody takes any notes. Nobody checks his phone.

"Have you ever dug a wolf den?" Mr. Raddock asks Salt.

"No."

"Could you dig one?"

Before Salt can answer, Jess says, "Of course he can. I'll draw him a diagram."

"Why?" Salt asks. "Why should I dig a den?"

Jess smiles. "To make your job easier."

"How?" Salt asks, but the second he does, he knows, and he's appalled.

Jess Cleet pulls out a cardboard box, heavily taped, about ten by eight by six inches. "The instructions are all in here," he says. "Choose your time carefully and do exactly what the instructions say. You want to poison wolves, not yourself."

"There's also another payment in there," Mr. Raddock adds as he slides the box over to Salt.

When the waitress arrives with their drinks, Salt asks if she would please take away his Dr Pepper and bring him a whiskey on the rocks.

Gary chuckles. "It's okay, my friend. Just remember the greater good. There's something in Thessalonians about the greater good, right? About brothers not getting tired in their good work?"

Salt sets the box on the seat next to him and recites a passage he knows and loves: "But ye, brethren, be not weary in well doing."

"Thessalonians, right?" Gary asks.

"Second Thessalonians 3:13."

"I knew it," Gary says. "Hell, I should be a theologian."

CHAPTER TWENTY-FOUR

Kes

SOME PLACES IN WILLYNILLYVILLE are ripe for eavesdropping. The woodworking shop, for one, where the veterans build cool stuff and talk casually about all things past, present, and future. Add to that the front porch where Tucker John lives with Chippy and Cap. And don't forget the greenhouse. And best of all, the poker games, though Uncle Ty forbids any talk of politics or war if Papa is present.

From snippets of conversations in all these places, and from what she learned back in Texas (from phone calls, emails, and texts), Kes has pieced together what happened to Papa after he left home and ended up halfway around the world, expected to fight and kill. First came basic combat training at Fort Jackson, in South Carolina, what Tucker John calls a "hot and muggy flatland." Chippy and Cap went there too, and others with the Oklahoma National Guard, the "Thunderbirds." While Uncle Ty trained as an Army engineer in the Missouri Ozarks and went to Iraq, the others, like Papa, who served more than a decade after Uncle Ty, ended up in Afghanistan, and would later say South Carolina was fine for training except one thing: no mountains. "That's all Afghanistan is," Kes once heard Cap tell E. J. "Mountains and mountains and more mountains after that. Even if you hold the high ground, there's higher ground in every direction. It's a nightmare."

As far back as those dark days at Brooke Army Medical Center in San Antonio, when she first saw Papa (what remained of him), and later, after many surgeries, when he got his new legs and learned to walk again, and then back home, in Lubbock, something happened inside. Something made Kes resolve to get it right, because that might help him heal. She had to write it all down. A teacher encouraged her to write as a healing process. "Step into the darkness," he said, "and write to the light."

First came the acronyms; Kes saw them everywhere, and heard them, and was intrigued by them. The language of warriors. Even now, in Willynillyville, they pop up all the time, and she writes them down. Every one:

TBI: Traumatic Brain Injury

RPG: Rocket-Propelled Grenade

IED: Improvised Explosive Device

EOD: Explosive Ordinance Disposal

BDA: Battle Damage Assessment

MRE: Meals Ready To Eat

LAW: Lightweight Anti-Tank Weapon

SWS: Strategic Weapons System

DOA: Dead On Arrival

"What about KBO?" Captain Don asks as he and Tucker John walk by and pause to see what Kes is writing. Both men are carrying shovels, rakes, and digging spades en route to the garden that needs to be turned over and covered with kelp to help make it productive next spring.

"KBO?" Kes asks, looking up at them from where she sits on the deck. "I don't think there is a KBO."

"Keep Buggering On," Captain Don says. "It's British. It's what Churchill said to his people when Nazi Germany was bombing London. He even said it years before the war, when many members of Parliament wanted to appease Hitler and he did not."

"Appease Hitler?" Kes asks. "Why?"

"Because the British didn't want another war. The previous war had ended only twenty years before and had been devastating. They were sick of war."

Kes has to think about this. *Appease Hitler? How?* From everything she's heard and read, especially about Anne Frank, who went into hiding when she was only thirteen, a year older than Kes is now, Hitler was a very bad man. *Appease him? Why?*

"Churchill was wrong about Gallipoli and India," Captain Don adds, "but he pegged Hitler from the beginning, when not everybody else did. He saved Great Britain."

As the two men continue on to the garden, Tucker John turns a little and says over his shoulder, "That's a fine list, Kes, but you forgot the best one: SNAFU."

"SNAFU? That's funny. What's it mean?"

He grins—his white teeth and eyes dancing as he rocks on his heels—and chuckles. "You think I'm gonna tell you? You gotta work for it. And no fair lookin' it up."

Captain Don laughs as well, spins a rake in his hand, and says, "That's right. You have to make a SWAG."

Kes gets her mind working. *SNAFU? Signal Not Accessible For Use? Sudden Negative Altitude Failure Unknown? Smile Now And Fart Unapologetically? Come on, get serious. Signal Normal After... dang. And SWAG? What's that?*

Later, she walks through the Willynillyville twilight to where Tucker John lives with Chippy and Cap. A cloud of marijuana fills the place. "I give up," she says.

Chippy and Cap laugh to hear what she's been working on.

"Situation Normal: All Flubbed Up," Tucker John tells her with a big grin. "SNAFU."

"Really?" Kes says. "Flubbed?"

More laughter.

"Absolutely," Tucker John says. "Well... not quite. 'Flubbed' is a stand-in word for, uh... you know. Don't tell your mother we're talking to you this way."

"I won't. Thanks, Tucker John."

"You're welcome... Hey Kes, we all think your dad's looking better these days."

"Yeah, me too. Thank you for being so nice to him."

"You got it, kid. Sweet dreams to you."

Walking back home through the cool Willynillyville air, Kes remembers something and turns back. Tucker John is outside on the deck, his back to her, profiled by moonlight. She shouts from a distance, "Tucker John, I almost forgot. What's SWAG?"

"Scientific Wild-Ass Guess."

"Really?"

"Yes, really."

"That's so cool."

"I'll tell Don you said so. Now, off to bed for you."

Up late that night cruising the internet—everybody at Willynillyville gets their WiFi signal from the "slow dish" mounted on a nearby cottonwood tree—Kes finds more military acronyms. One in particular chills her. FUBAR: Fucked Up Beyond All Repair. *Was that Papa when he returned home: FUBAR? What must he have looked like in surgery in Germany? And in Afghanistan after the IED exploded under his Humvee?*

Later, curled up in her bed, she sings softly to herself and finally falls asleep.

EVERY SATURDAY IS HIKE DAY. Tim and Tia Anderson join Kes, Papa, Uncle Ty, and Tucker John on a quick walk to the river and back. Quick, Uncle Ty says, because he has lots to do before tonight's big poker game. And before he leaves tomorrow—or maybe on Monday, depending on sea conditions—to go black cod fishing in Chatham Strait with his good friend Zorro Brown, on Zorro's boat, the *Cinnamon Girl.*

Rather than walk down Willynillyville Drive and turn right onto Menzies River Road, Uncle Ty shows everybody a secret "angle trail" he's been blazing through the woods. It begins at the garden and angles southwest to the end of Menzies River Road, where it joins the main trail to the river. They stop to examine moose droppings.

"They look like Milk Duds," Tim says.

"Eat one," Tucker John says.

"They're smart pills," Uncle Ty says.

"Smart pills?" Tia asks. "Why smart pills?"

"Because once you eat one," Uncle Ty says, wearing his bandana and trademark missing-tooth grin, "you're smart enough to never eat another."

Everybody laughs.

As they walk on, Kes holds Papa's hand and tells him about her week at school, her classes; how much she likes her teacher, Mrs. Carry, but not the principal, Mrs. Cunningham, or Abraham d'Alene, who gives her the creeps.

It should be raining. October is the wettest month of the year in Southeast Alaska. But it's a beautiful day, crisp and clean, and Papa often stops to look at things: the bark of a western hemlock, an abandoned robin's nest, a red squirrel gathering spruce cones. Or he might just stand still, lift his head, and close his eyes to drink in the wildness, as if walking through the woods makes him taller than the trees. No sirens. No litter. No billboards or big-box stores or fast-food joints. No fracking or drought. When Kes asks her papa a simple yes-no question, he squeezes her hand once for yes, twice for no.

Tim and Tia walk with them while Uncle Ty and Tucker John, more fleet of foot, move on ahead, breaking trail, removing branches and such. Kes can hear them laughing.

Papa wears his Nike Air Jordans and moves well along the rudimentary trail. The doctors at Brooke had told Rita it would take months, "but in time your husband will come to appreciate his new legs, and he'll be as active as he chooses to be, depending on how hard he works and how much PT he does."

PT: Physical Therapy, the first entry in Kes's little book. Followed by the longer and more universal PTSD: Post-Traumatic Stress Disorder. The doctors at Brooke said PTSD applies not just to many veterans, but to their families as well, in fact anybody who's a victim of—or a witness to—a violent crime. *Maybe that's war—a crime.*

Uncle Ty never says PTSD. He calls it "shellshock." Like they did back in World War I.

As for Papa's droopy eye, Rita now says it makes him look handsome, like Marlon Brando. And with his hair so long and sometimes pulled back into a ponytail, it covers his rebuilt ear and makes him look like Kenny Loggins back when he was a lady-killer singing under the redwoods about peace and saving the earth and celebrating home.

At the river, the six hikers sit on the bank and eat their lunches. Uncle Ty talks about the times he's crossed the river, how tricky it can be, and how rewarding. "It's beautiful over there," he says.

"Can we cross it now?" Kes asks, forgetting, for the moment, about her father.

"Some other time," Uncle Ty says.

"See that hill?" Tim says, pointing northwest, across the river. "My dad says God put it there."

"It's a roche moutonnée, made of dolomite," Uncle Ty says. "It was carved by glaciers."

Tim thinks for a minute. "Maybe God directed the glaciers."

Nobody speaks.

Uncle Ty finally says, "When we hear the wolves howl, they're right over there on the other side, moving upriver and down, probably fishing for salmon. Not far downstream from here is where that father and son from California saw the whole pack."

"I thought wolves ate moose," Tia says.

"They do," Uncle Ty tells her. "But these wolves also eat salmon."

"And whales," Kes adds. Everybody knows about the dead whale in Crystal Bay.

Uncle Ty looks over at her and tosses her a big garden carrot. It's a perfect throw, arcing high through the air. As Kes reaches out to catch it, a hand comes from nowhere and intercepts it. Papa. Kes jumps on him. Soon, father and daughter are wrestling on the ground and grabbing for the carrot as everybody cheers them on. Kes finally wins, sits up triumphantly, and says to her papa, "You let me win, didn't you?"

He smiles.

She snaps the carrot not quite in half, and gives him the larger share.

"C'mon," Uncle Ty says, extending a hand to help his brother to his feet. "It's poker night tonight. I have to start cooking the moose chili."

"Did you hear that?" Tim says quietly to Tia. "Moose chili."

As they make their way back along the Menzies River Trail, Kes sees Tucker John point off-trail and hears him say to Uncle Ty, "That's where I saw the guy hiding in the woods, under that big spruce, right there."

Uncle Ty shrugs and keeps walking.

Kes wonders, *What guy?*

TIM AND TIA CALL HOME and get permission to stay in Willynillyville for moose chili. When Rita sees Tim eyeing Papa's Martin, she walks over, picks it up, and brings it to him, saying, "It's got new strings on it." The entire Poker Pack is there, gathered around the table and scattered about the adjoining living room, eating and talking before the cards come out. Papa sits in the corner with Snickers the cat in his lap. At his feet, little Kip is building another Lego masterpiece, what Uncle Ty calls "a multicolored, postmodern, reach-for-the-sky monstrosity," but what Tucker John says looks like "a mechanical, low-tide, butter clam–sea cucumber orgy."

The others laugh, none harder than Chippy and Cap.

Mike eats little, says nothing, and appears a million miles away. He hardly ever talks. Sometimes in the night he screams.

Tim sits pigeon-toed, turns the chair, cradles the Martin upside down, and begins to play left-handed, with the pick guard on top. He hits a few harmonics, thrums the blues, makes a few mistakes, apologizes to Papa, and moves on. He runs his right hand up the fretboard, easily managing things and getting better by the minute, playing with many nice touches. His chords, fingered so differently, are barely recognizable to Kes. It's like reading a book upside down in the mirror.

Everybody stares, fascinated. *This kid is good.*

"Look at that, Danny," Rita says. "He plays the way Doyle Bramhall does, left-handed, without restringing the guitar."

Papa taps his finger on his knee.

Tim builds into a smooth rhythm, his forefinger thrumming the base notes. "I like your song, 'Bird in a Cloud,'" he says to Papa as he keeps the rhythm going while hitting a lead run. "It's in G, right? G to C, and back again? But then it gets bluesy somehow."

"G to B flat to A minor," Rita says.

"Oh... wow," Tim says with a big grin. He picks up the progression and Rita begins to hum.

Kes watches only Papa, the light brightening in his one good eye, the faint smile, the finger tapping his knee just above where the prosthetic joins flesh and bone.

Tim transitions into a few more songs, or pieces of songs, and finishes with a shrug, as if hoping what he just did was okay.

For a moment, nobody says a word.

Kes watches Papa.

Mike shifts on the sofa and says, "Do you know 'Blackbird,' by the Beatles?"

"Not yet," Tim says. "Someday, I hope."

Just then the Lego masterpiece, having attained a height of three feet or more, topples to the floor and breaks apart, and little Kip bursts out crying.

AN HOUR AFTER TIM AND TIA HEAD HOME on their bicycles, and the poker game gets serious with penny and nickel bets, Taylor de la Croix arrives from Bartlett Cove, the headquarters and housing area in the marine reserve. She's Uncle Ty's latest girlfriend, what Rita calls his "soon-to-be next casualty of love."

Kes hopes not. She thinks Taylor is cool because she's a marine biologist who makes her uncle happy. She knows Uncle Ty has his regrets. Sometimes a sadness comes over him, and he gets quiet and distant. But then his quick wit returns. He once told Kes that to err is human, "but to 'arr' is pirate."

"Pull up a chair," Chippy says to Taylor, "and dare to get your butt kicked by the best poker players in Alaska."

"You know the whale that the wolves and bears have been feeding on?" Taylor says with excitement. "We set up three timelapse GoPros and got amazing footage."

"Cool," Uncle Ty says.

Taylor holds up a small jump drive on a cord around her neck. "I've got the footage right here. You're not going to believe what happened during the last full moon."

"The wolves howled in harmony?" Chippy asks.

"No," Taylor says. "Better than that."

CHAPTER TWENTY-FIVE

Silver

SILVER AWAKENS, startled by the moonlight and a deep-throated growling coming from the direction of the dead whale. On his feet in an instant, he travels fast through the shadowed forest, leaving his pack bedded down on the moss. He finds the big male coastal brown bear atop one end of the whale, near the head. Closer to the tail stands Old One, Mother's great-great uncle, snarling at the bear. Moonlight reflects off the indigo water and silhouettes the two determined predators. As Sister arrives and stands next to him, Silver steps into the cold high tide, the waters rising, and wades out to the whale's tail, and climbs aboard near Old One. He shakes himself dry and ascends the whale's spine, growling as he approaches the bear. The bear stands, bellows, drops to all fours, and charges. Silver retreats, ready to jump into the ocean. The bear stops midway, stands again atop the whale, near the dorsal fin, and bellows. Silver and Old One, now down near the partially submerged tail, their feet in cold water, make no sign of further retreat. The bear turns—mindful, perhaps, that a pair of wolves is a more formidable adversary than a solo wolf—and walks back to his domain at the opposite end of the whale.

An offshore wind picks up and the tide continues to rise. It floods the muddy flats and cobbled beach, and reaches far into the rye grass and nearly to the alder fringe and the red runners of last summer's wild strawberries. The dead whale, smaller than before, rocks gently, buoyed by its own design and reduced weight. It has provided a grand feast for Silver and his pack, and for other wolves as well, the pack of four all-blacks headed by an alpha male. The two packs, mindful that wolves can and will kill each other, have partaken of the bounty by turns, carefully skirting wide arcs around each other, now and then making bluff charges and darting away and stopping to look back.

And now, once more, the big male bear, his belly so huge it nearly drags, has claimed his throne.

Slowly the whale, unmoored, begins to float away.

Watching from the cobbled beach, Sister howls up her concern and Silver responds, their voices melancholy over the cold, indifferent sea.

BY MORNING, as sunrise anoints distant snowy mountains and sea otters cavort nearby, the dead whale—a massive raft carrying three passengers—is far offshore. At the head of the whale, the bear sleeps, chin on his paws, belly full. Near the tail, Old One chews on a piece of dark meat as if this will be his last meal, which it might, given his age.

Silver watches harbor porpoises roll to the surface and quickly disappear with delicate exhales and inhales. When two swans wing by, close overhead, Silver sits and watches until their white forms dissolve into the distance. He does his best to coax Old One into leaving. It's time to get off this whale or risk drifting so far out to sea that a swim to shore will be a death sentence. Old One refuses. He'll die here, riding the bounty. Fight the bear if he has to; kill or be killed. It's been like this for a long time, living and dying in the certainty of all that has come and gone and will come and go.

And the bear? He may leave later. Bears are stronger swimmers than wolves.

When his family howls from the distant shore, Silver responds. But not Old One. He stays silent, lying down, his breathing labored. Silver nuzzles him goodbye for many minutes and commits his smell to memory. Old One returns the gesture, though with less heart. Silver steps into the ocean and swims.

And swims.

And swims.

He can feel the tide working against him.

The cold weakening him.

His shoulders ache. His lungs burn. His paws go numb.

Swim.

When he finally reaches the mainland and staggers ashore, and shakes himself off, cold and exhausted, Silver is not alone. Mother, Sister, and the others cavort around him, and nuzzle him, and lick him, gleeful over his return. They all pause to look out at the whale, smaller now, rafting away into the distance. They howl in a mournful and musical way, and listen.

And howl again. And listen.

No response.

Time to go. They turn and head south, thinking of moose. In particular, one very large bull somewhere near the Menzies River.

CHAPTER TWENTY-SIX

Salt

CAN'T THESE BOYS MAKE THEIR OWN LUNCHES? *They have hands, do they not?*

Abraham, Jericho, and Joshua ransack the kitchen, looking for chips and salsa. Salt walks in and tells Abe to fetch bread from the pantry, and sliced meat, pickles, mustard, mayonnaise, onion, lettuce, and cheese from the fridge. There might be some garden spinach in there too. "Make sandwiches for yourself and your brothers. Your mother is busy taking care of Solomon." *And I'm buried in paperwork, trying to see if we can survive this year's medical expenses.* The trick: claim none of the handsome under-the-table earnings from what Salt calls "wolf work." Live below a specified annual family income to qualify for state of Alaska assistance through Lincoln Kid Care. And get Solomon back to Baltimore for the clinical trial at Johns Hopkins.

Hannah calls for help from the bathroom, where Solomon needs to use the toilet. Salt hurries to join her. When he returns, the kitchen is a disaster. Abe has made a mess of every counter, eating as he goes, while Jericho squirts mustard at Joshua because he stole the last pickle.

"Enough!" Salt yells.

The two smaller boys freeze. Abe keeps eating, having made a sandwich for only himself.

"Uh-oh," Solomon says, out of view but loud enough for everyone to hear. "Dad is mad again."

"Jerry started it," Joshua says.

"Like heck. You took the—"

"You pushed me."

"Enough!" Salt sweeps all the food, plates, and utensils off the counter and onto the floor. Hannah rushes in. The boys stand stone-still, stunned, as they stare at broken porcelain plates and glassware all around their feet. Food splattered everywhere.

Hannah pulls her thin, bony hand to her mouth, aghast.

Abe glares at his father.

"Clean it up," Salt says to the boys. "Then join me and your mother and Solomon in the living room for scripture."

THAT NIGHT, THE NIGHT BEFORE THANKSGIVING, Hannah makes burritos and begins to thaw a twenty-four-pound turkey, the largest they've ever had. When Joshua exclaims, "It's as big as a buffalo," Solomon does his funky chicken and says, "Buffalo-ho-ho-ho." And they all laugh. The six d'Alenes hold hands and pray and manage to tell a few stories and laugh more.

Jericho talks about Kes Nash's presentation at school for the first Science Friday. "She talked about the size of the universe, how big it is, and how it's getting bigger."

"How big is it?" little Joshua asks.

"Really big," Jericho says. "She said that if the solar system was the size of a blood cell, like, you know, really small, then the Milky Way Galaxy would be—"

"She's a liar," Abe says.

The table goes quiet.

"She thinks she knows what she's talking about," Abe adds, "but she doesn't."

Salt observes how Jericho hangs his head in defeat, knowing it's futile to ever disagree with his older brother.

Hannah serves up the burritos: tortillas, refried beans, cheese, olives, chilies, onions, and guacamole all piled in the middle of the table, with a special serving on the side for Solomon, who rocks with excitement. The other three boys dive in, each for himself, their hands and elbows flying. Though it's hardly fair. Salt notices how Jericho and Joshua make room for Abe, who dominates, then practically inhales his dinner, then sits back to quietly thumb through a photo book of the Battle of Stalingrad.

Volleyball season is over. It didn't end well for Abe, the star player. In the final game he missed several spikes and sent the ball into the net or out of bounds. He then got into a yelling match with a referee, and was benched for ten plays. When he returned, he did poorly, and Strawberry Flats lost the regional semifinal.

Yes, Salt knows his eldest son would do better in a larger high school in Juneau or Sitka, where athletes can play many sports. But those places are expensive. Both Salt and Hannah would need to work full time just to pay the bills. And who would take care of Solomon? Hannah's parents live in Juneau but are old, feeble, and ill. Derek offered Salt a mechanic's job in Strawberry Flats and said the slow-paced, friendly town would be good for Solomon. He further warned Salt that Juneau is a dangerously liberal town, "almost socialist," corrupted by too much government and Planned Parenthood and same-sex marriage and LGBTQ studies at the university, and constant nonsense talk about human-caused climate change and ocean acidification "when we all know only God can change the climate and the ocean."

Abe's discontent stems from more than a lack of competitive sports. People say he's sweet on the older Anderson girl, Tabby, who might not be sweet on him because of his worsening acne and quick temper. He's also brokenhearted over Solomon and his declining health. All the d'Alenes are. The other day Joshua asked Hannah, "Mom, is Solomon going to be okay?"

All Hannah could say was, "We hope so, honey. That's why we pray every day."

Salt regrets his earlier outburst in the kitchen, how the whole family, save Solomon, got out mops, sponges, and brooms, and helped to clean up his mess, with nobody speaking until Hannah said, "It's okay, husband. I didn't like those plates anyway."

After dinner, Salt finds time alone with Abe. "The Battle of Stalingrad," he says to him. "How'd you get interested in that?"

"Three of those veterans came into our history class today and talked to us about World War II."

"Three of the veterans from Willynillyville?"

"Yeah. One of them was an old man who brought his Silver Star and showed it to us."

"An old man? Was he Tyler and Danny Nash's father, Kes's grandfather?"

"I think so, yeah."

"He fought in Vietnam, didn't he?"

"Yeah. He was a Marine."

Salt has asked his boys many times to answer yes, not yeah, in the affirmative, but now is not the time to correct Abe.

"Hitler made a big mistake when he invaded Russia," Abe says, his head down as he thumbs his way through the Stalingrad book, looking at black-and-white photos of so much devastation and death. "He should have kept his armies in France to prevent the Normandy Invasion."

"The Battle of Normandy was a liberation, son. Not an invasion."

"But everybody calls it an invasion."

"That's because France was occupied by Nazi Germany. Nearly all of Western Europe was fascist then."

"I read on the internet that Hitler just wanted to make Germany better again, you know? He just wanted more food and jobs and hope for his people because the treaty that ended World War I... I can't remember its name."

"The Treaty of Versailles."

"Yeah, right. Anyway, it was cruel and unfair to the Germans, and Hitler just wanted to make it fair again, that's all. He just wanted to make the world a better place."

"Did he make the world a better place?"

"He would have, maybe, if people hadn't gotten so angry and ended up fighting and freaking out and everything."

"Abe, his Third Reich killed six million Jews and millions of other people."

Abe looks away, his jaw set, eyes distant.

"You disagree?" Salt says.

"People on the internet say that maybe some Jews died, but not six million. A lot of them just ran out of food because other people started the war."

"What people on the internet?"

"Just people, Dad. Everybody has a right to an opinion. One of those Willynillyville veterans said the Iraq War was a huge mistake that cost trillions of dollars. He called it 'a disaster in search of a strategy.' That's his opinion, right? Maybe he's right or maybe he's wrong, and maybe I'll join up and go to Iraq and find out for myself."

Salt catches his breath. Last week Abe turned seventeen, and nobody came to his party because he didn't have a party, because he has no friends, because he is who he is because he's an island of sorts, because—*Why? Because Hannah and I have ruined him? Because he's a dark and tormented soul who's angry at everything? Dear God.* Salt is tempted to remind his eldest son that if Hitler hadn't invaded Russia, he most certainly would have invaded England; that the d'Alenes had distant relatives, now dead, who resisted the Third Reich. And suffered. That the concrete shower walls in Auschwitz and

Bergen-Belsen are covered with scratches where thousands of Jews tried to claw their way out when the Nazis killed them by releasing poisonous gas, not hot water. Salt could shake Abe by the shoulders and rebuke him, but that would only isolate him more.

Abe heads upstairs to go to bed.

"Abe?" Salt calls to him.

He pauses without looking back.

"The military is not for everybody, son. It's not always the best thing, or the right thing. Please think carefully about joining."

Abe turns to face his father. "Think carefully?" he says. "Did you and Mom think carefully about living in a cabin in Minto all those winters? Did you think carefully about raising Solomon there and keeping him there even when you knew something was wrong when he started to stumble and fall all the time? Did you think carefully when you freaked out in the kitchen just now and knocked all the food and plates onto the floor? Did you think carefully about agreeing to trap wolves for dark money?"

Salt opens his mouth to respond, but nothing comes out.

Abe stares at him, then turns and continues up the stairs.

HANNAH PLANS TO DEVOTE HER ENTIRE DAY to the Thanksgiving meal. She's invited five guests: Derek Smith and his wife; Mrs. Cunningham and her husband; and Solomon's special education teacher. That makes eleven people total, by far the biggest Thanksgiving the d'Alenes have ever hosted. Hannah will recruit the boys when needed, to help with the preparations. Salt has already extended the table with two extra leaves. He's also convinced Hannah to serve the dinner at six o'clock, not three, so he can cross the river and work on the wolf den while everybody in Strawberry Flats eats their traditional dinner with family and friends, and watches football. It's a solid plan, Salt believes, though Hannah, who loves the additional money (all those one-hundred-dollar bills!), doesn't want him trapping again. She especially worries about him crossing what she calls "that dangerous river." Last summer three people got swept off their feet in midcurrent and nearly drowned. People die in Alaska's rivers every year.

When Salt comes into the kitchen to kiss Hannah goodbye, he admires her figure highlighted through her cotton dress in the morning light. "You're beautiful," he says.

She turns. "Are you hitting on me?"

"Yes. Where are the boys?"

"I ran them over to Pastor Anderson's. Solomon too. Tabby called earlier and invited them all for waffles."

"Tabby? I'll bet Abraham was happy about that."

"Abraham, happy? If he was, he didn't show it." Hannah turns back to the sink to work on the turkey, and asks, "What were you two talking about last night?"

"Everything. I'll tell you about it later." Salt knows it will break Hannah's heart to hear that Abraham wants to be a soldier. A friend back in Idaho once told Salt that good soldiers follow bad orders. They have to. The more he reflects on it—on all the kids he knew back then who joined up—the more he suspects that many were broken in some way before they enlisted; were wounded from their early childhood, maybe, or by some other family dysfunction. *Could that be Abraham? Hannah's and my Abraham?*

As Salt takes a breath, composes himself, and bends around her to kiss Hannah on her cheek, she says, "I Googled Kelmar Raddock and didn't find anything. I looked everywhere. He really is a mystery man."

"Lots of people aren't on Google. They're not anywhere on the internet."

"I Googled the governor's office too, his entire staff, all personnel, and found no Gary. And when I Googled Jess Cleet from Fairbanks, guess what I found?"

"What?"

"He was charged with domestic abuse three years ago."

Salt feels the blood drain from his face. "Really?"

"Yes, really. He's a wife beater."

"I didn't know that."

"I know you didn't, husband. That's why I'm telling you."

Salt pauses to look out the window at how the sun, low to the south, casts its winter light through the naked branches of cottonwoods. It'll be down by three o'clock, dark by four. Winter solstice is less than one month away. *I need to get going.*

Hannah asks, "What kind of man kills wolves and beats his wife?"

"A bad man."

"And now you're taking instructions from him?"

"Only this one time."

"We need the money, husband, but not at the cost of who we are. Please be careful."

"I will."

"And promise me you'll never become one of them."

"I promise."

NOVEMBER HAS BEEN UNSEASONABLY WARM, until now. Salt needs to dig the den before the ground hardens up. He began a week ago by choosing a good spot on the west-facing slope of Heaven's Hill, excavating a hole to the specifications Jess Cleet gave him: tunnel down five feet at a low angle, then up at the same angle. Get it started. The wolves will do the rest and build themselves a warm pupping chamber. Leave some bait—pieces of sausage, salami, whatever—to attract them to the area. Wait until the entire pack is in there, asleep, the alpha female pregnant, then release the M-44 cyanide bombs that came in the tightly taped box. Roll the bombs in, cover the entrance, and get away.

Later, return to mask it over—a death chamber now—with rocks, moss, and roots.

AT THE RIVER, Salt pulls on his chest waders, unstraps the backpack's hip belt, and uses a long walking stick to brace on his downstream side. It occurs to him that somebody should one day run a tightrope across this river. He thinks about a big bridge being here. Once the image comes into his mind, he can't get rid of it, like a bad song. *A bridge will change everything, and ruin much. Another wild place will die. And people will call it progress.*

An hour later, Salt digs at the base of the hill, pacing himself, lying on the ground, reaching deep into the hole with one arm and a small, foldable shovel.

When he hears a huff from behind, he stops. The air is different. Charged.

Slowly he turns while still flat on the ground. The light is low, getting dark.

Staring at him from nearby are five wolves, shoulder to shoulder, their ears up, heads low, trying to measure what they're looking at. They suddenly run away—all but one, a male yearling, not quite full grown, black on the face and flanks, russet in the legs, silver in the shoulders. A beauty. He stares at Salt with keen intelligence, his eyes fierce yet curious, almost transcendent. Then, like his kin, he disappears into the forest.

CHAPTER TWENTY-SEVEN

Kes

Is that howling? *Yes.*

Kes drops her armful of firewood and runs to the house to tell Papa and Rita. She bursts through the door, breathless. Nobody's home. She remembers now. Rita went to the airport to pick up her friend Jeannie—another veteran with PTSD.

Back outside, Kes listens as her heart pounds. *Again, unmistakable this time. Distant… from the west and south, across the river and toward the ocean. Harmonizing like before? Hard to tell.* She cocks her head and hears nothing more. Only the table saw.

Papa must be in the woodworking shop with Chippy and Cap.

She finds them cutting cedar trim with Captain Don, all four men wearing heavy ear protection, goggles, and face masks. They see her and stop working. Kes tells them what she just heard. Or thinks she heard. Already, she's having doubts.

Bless his heart, Papa removes his ear protection, takes Kes's hand, and steps outside. Chippy joins them with a wad of Skoal in his mouth—his way of trying to stop smoking. He spits dark tobacco juice on the ground and wipes his lips on his sleeve.

"You sure they weren't dogs?" Chippy asks. "Or coyotes?"

Kes doesn't reply. She keeps listening.

Her friend Tim rides his bike huffing and puffing up Willynillyville Drive.

"Hi Tim," Kes says. "Did you hear wolves a minute ago or so?"

"No. Did you?"

"Yeah, I'm pretty sure."

"Do you still want to study geometry together?"

Papa drops Kes's hand and walks from the shop doorstep out onto the drive as if to pick a song from thin air, something nobody else can do. Rita used to say that Papa's melodies were so warm you could swim in them; that he could tell a story just by digging into the guitar. He stands motionless, listening, his head turned, his one good ear tipped to the west, his lower arms raised ever so slightly, hands out, fingers spread, as if about to conduct a musical, waiting for the wolves to tune up. He wears his old Levis and Nike Air Jordans and stands near Tim, who straddles his bike and doesn't move.

Kes loves watching her father these days, how fluid and easygoing he's become, more at peace with himself than she could have imagined six months ago. Lubbock and San Antonio feel like distant geologic epochs. Everything is so different now, and school gets better each day, thanks in big part to Mrs. Carry. After meeting with several parents, Principal Cunningham finally approved Science Fridays. "As if science were a health hazard," Rita said afterward. "Ridiculous woman." Kes's first presentation, about the size of the universe, was based on what Uncle Ty had talked about when they camped down in Terlingua and studied the night sky and found the Andromeda Galaxy. Next, she plans to talk about the day the dinosaurs died. After that, the geology of the Grand Canyon.

Papa begins to walk around now. He smiles at Kes and moves his hands slightly as if to beseech the wolves. *Don't be shy. We know you're out there. Join us. We're all friends here. Let's hear it, you salmon-eating wolves. Music in the key of sea. You and me, set free.* He nods at Tim, who nods back as most people do when they see Danny Nash, unsure what to say. Jesus, what happened to you? Droopy eye, rebuilt ear, artificial legs. Kes knows kids in town privately call him Quiet Man and Metal Legs. Not out of meanness. They're just being kids. Whenever they see him, as Tim does now, their eyes betray an epic struggle between pity and thank-you-for-your-service admiration. Not that Papa's so-called "service" improved their lives one bit. Or anybody else's.

Uncle Ty always says it's sacrifice, not service. "And my brother didn't 'lose' his legs in Afghanistan, okay?" he said to Grandpa one night in Texas, not long after Papa's double amputation. "It's not like he can go back there and find his legs and go, 'Hey, look, my legs, still here in the dust with bomb fragments and dried blood,' and put them back on and be as good as new, right?" Uncle Ty was drunk. Rita began to cry. Uncle Ty apologized but later argued more with Grandpa, who brought up World War II, Korea, and Vietnam, and drank more, and this time Kes was the one who cried and ran out the door into the hot Texas night as fast and as far as she could. Running, running, running…

And look at Papa now. Not whole, but not broken either, with his long hair and Air Jordans and artful hands imploring Alaska's wolves to make music. He turns and smiles at Tim, who still straddles his bike, trying to look at anything but Papa's legs.

Just the other morning, Rita said, "Kes, honey, your papa laughed in his dreams last night. Not hard or loud or for long. But he laughed in a soft chuckle sort of way. It was the most beautiful thing I've heard in a long time. Maybe ever."

"He laughed?"

"Yes, he laughed. And he's sleeping better and needs fewer meds."

"Oh, Mom, he's in there. Like the doctors in San Antonio said. He's in there."

"Yes, he is."

"It's weird, isn't it? How it took a cold place to warm him up."

"We should hope for a long winter."

"With lots of snow. I've never seen snow."

KES LOVES GEOMETRY. This surprises her. She expected to enjoy her other subjects more: history, democracy, civics, and biology, and all she's absorbed from her uncle and grandfather, and from the books she's read about empires, religions, and wars.

"So, why geometry?" Rita asked her awhile back.

Kes had to think. Maybe it goes back to the plane ride north, in Claire, last July, flying over the American West, mesmerized by canyons, rivers, and roads, how Uncle Ty encouraged her to find "patterns in the chaos." Geometry in the geology. She remembers him talking about how everybody has their own truth these days, and how dangerous that is. "Any fool can be an expert in America today," he said after they stayed a night in a Nevada hotel/casino and watched too much cable TV. "And because any fool can now be an expert, there are no experts. Expertise is dead. And because of that, knowledge and logic and reason are meaningless. As are facts."

Kes said nothing. Same with Papa and Grandpa. Maybe because Uncle Ty flew the plane and had a certain authority when he did. Besides, Grandpa often fell asleep.

"We are adrift in a sea of fatuous opinions and bogus conspiracy theories," Uncle Ty added. "The more we depart from science and truth, the more our society persecutes those who actually speak it. Listen to right-wing media. Actually, don't. It's poison. All of it. I should have turned it off last night earlier than I did. I apologize for that."

"That's okay," Kes said.

"No, it's not. It fuels a world gone mad, driven by con men who are seldom right but never in doubt. Hucksters who are very good at what they do."

"What do they do, Uncle Ty?"

He thought for a moment. "They exploit people's prejudices and fears."

Kes would need to think about that. And write it down. She would need to think about many things. Already, Texas seemed like a page turned, a chapter far behind her.

The next day, back in Claire, Uncle Ty asked Kes how she was doing.

"Fine," she said.

"You've put yourself on an amazing journey, Kes. I don't mean just this plane ride, or this move to Alaska. I mean something deeper... a journey to find out who you are, who you can become, and what you can achieve. Maybe even to find out what's true and authentic. Let's call it your Journey into Open-Mindedness, a universe unto itself."

Papa nodded his head just then, in quiet approval, and reached a hand over his shoulder to find his daughter. She took it, interlocking her fingers with his.

Out the window, down below, entire mountain ranges rolled by.

MRS. CARRY, Kes's teacher, says that geometry doesn't care what you cherish or believe. It's the truth regardless, the birthplace of logic, built on theorems and proofs.

Kes loves it.

So does Tim.

"Check this out," Tim says, sitting next to her, pencil in hand, an hour after Papa went back into the shop, disappointed—but not defeated—to have heard no wolves. "I make a four-sided shape and make all four sides different in length from each other. Now I build an isosceles triangle off each of those four lines. See? Now I connect those four distant triangle points, and what do I get? A parallelogram. Every time."

"Every time, really?"

"Yep, no matter what the original shape."

"That's a truth," Kes says.

"Pretty cool, huh?"

"Really cool."

"I don't think you can call it a truth, though," Tim says. "It's just a theorem."

"No, it's a truth. You just said it happens every time."

"Oh, yeah, I guess I did."

"Geez, Tim. What's a truth then?"

Tim looks at her sheepishly. "You're not going to like it."

"What? Don't tell me… the Word of God?"

Tim shrugs. "Everybody knows you don't believe in God."

Kes feels her stomach turn over. *I never said I don't believe in God.*

Outside, two vehicles pull up. Kes recognizes the sound of both. One is Uncle Ty's light green truck named the Rolling Avocado. The other is the old Jeep everybody calls Sarge, the one that runs on three cylinders and has a mind of its own. If six gallons of ice cream show up in Willynillyville and nobody takes responsibility, Sarge must have done it. Late at night, Sarge drives himself to the store, buys the ice cream, brings it home, and puts it in the freezer. Same with pizza and chips and salsa and beer. Sarge did it. Not my fault, everybody says. Blame it on Sarge.

Rita comes through the door with Jeannie, a silver-haired woman who has on a leash a mild-mannered golden retriever named Skydog. Yesterday, Rita briefed Kes that Jeannie, the sister of Rita's best friend from high school, is a veteran who has a service dog to help her in many ways, but mostly to keep her anxieties at bay. Kes wonders where Jeannie is going to stay. Willynillyville is getting crowded: thirteen people in four buildings, some sleeping on mattresses on floors. Every residence has a big wood-burning stove, on-demand (solar-powered) hot water, a clean kitchen, and a good outhouse. Two homes have flush toilets and raised leach fields. And firewood is never in short supply. All in all, it's a cozy, quirky, funky village.

Jeannie's hands are delicate, but her grip is firm. She appears both grateful and overwhelmed. She compliments Tim on his geometric drawings. Rita says to Jeannie, "Follow me. I'll show you where you're staying. Then we'll get you something hot to eat."

"Mom," Kes says. "I heard wolves again, a couple hours ago, at a distance."

"Wolves?" Jeannie says, her sad eyes flickering. "I've never heard wolves."

That night, Kes remembers something a physical therapist said in San Antonio. If traumatized veterans are going to live full and happy lives again, it often comes down to one trait more than any other, one they either have or do not, deep inside: grit.

THE FIRST SNOWFALL comes on a Saturday in mid-December. The flakes start out small, testing the air, and soon get big and spiral down like cottonwood leaves. Kes goes out and catches them on her tongue. Papa and little Kip join her. Jeannie too, with Skydog. Others get involved. Mike watches the flakes gather on the moose fence around the garden. Chippy and Cap throw snowballs. Tucker John writes his name in the snow as if Alaska were a new book, a new beginning. Papa stands still with his hands out and palms up as if the snow were a gift from above.

Kes thinks again: *I never said I didn't believe in God.*

But do I?

"It's magical," Rita says as she takes photos from the deck.

Yes, it is.

Papa grabs Kip and swings him by the hands as the little guy giggles with joy.

So many things that used to be important aren't anymore.

What changed?

Papa.

Yes, Kes misses some Texas friends. Allison and Celia, mostly. And her cousin Julie.

It made Kes grateful for all the times Papa, Rita, Grandpa, Uncle Ty, Stringer, and Sammye read to her, and not just from children's books. She vividly remembers Uncle Ty reading passages from *Empire of the Summer Moon*, about the kidnapping of Cynthia Ann Parker, the daughter of a prominent pioneering Texas family, and telling Kes about it in his dramatic way a couple years before Papa shipped off to Afghanistan. "There she was," Uncle Ty said, "a nine-year-old girl, same age as you, stolen by the most powerful Tribe in American history: the Comanches. The year was 1838—"

"It was 1836," Papa corrected him.

Uncle Ty stopped. "You sure?"

"Yep. Same year as the Alamo. And I think she was ten, not nine."

"You want to tell this story, little brother?"

"No, no," Papa chuckled as he fingerpicked his Martin. "You're doing fine."

"And what happened?" Uncle Ty continued. "Years passed and the kidnapped girl became a Comanche. She forgot English and developed no love for money or Jesus or fine silk or indoor living. She married and communed with coyotes and wrestled cougars back in the time before Texas got ruined by barbed wire and roads." Uncle Ty paused. "Okay, she didn't wrestle with cougars. But she did ride horses, catch fish, bathe in creeks, and skin deer with great skill. She made love under the Milky Way and the huge summer moon, and sang with the stars, and had three children and raised them wild and free. One of her kids became the great chief, Quanah. And all that time, for more than twenty years, her original white family, the Parkers, never gave up searching for her."

"Twenty years?" Kes said in disbelief.

"Twenty-four years, to be exact," Uncle Ty said, "if my rock star little brother is right about 1836. Then, in 1860, Texas Rangers raided a village and killed every Comanche, except a woman and her infant daughter. They didn't know who the woman was at first. But it turned out to be Cynthia Ann Parker. For the rest of her life, while her white relatives washed her clean and dressed her in ribbons and silk, she moaned in sorrow, missing her Comanche family and way of life."

"She wasn't happy to be back with her original white family?" Kes asked.

"No."

"Why?"

"In the entire history of the United States of Amnesia, whenever a Native was assimilated into white society, he or she always suffered, and dreamed of being free again. And whenever a white Christian joined an Indigenous Tribe—Cherokee, Shoshone, Nez Perce, Comanche, whatever—and became one of them, he or she never chose to return to white Christianity."

"Why?"

"That's for you to figure out, my young apprentice. Someday it will make sense to you, but only if you touch the wild earth, your original home."

CHRISTMAS EVE DAY. Pastor Anderson drives over to Willynillyville with Tabby, Tim, and Tia. The kids make an elaborate track in the snow and spend an hour playing Fox and Geese. Rita and Jeannie have warm chocolate chip cookies ready when they come inside and stand sock-footed around the wood-burning stove. Pastor Anderson is on the floor with Papa, helping little Kip build another Lego monstrosity.

Tim breaks out his Taylor mini acoustic guitar and quietly plays a few bars of "Blackbird," saying, "I think I'll have it down in another week or so. It's an amazing song in G that goes to C major and C minor, and to F in the refrain."

Rita slips into her boots and hurries out the door, saying, "Mike needs to hear this." Weeks ago, Mike requested that Tim play the song. He's been terribly sick. Just yesterday, Uncle Ty flew him to Juneau and back for doctor appointments.

What happens next, Kes will never forget.

Papa gets to his feet, grabs his Martin, sits opposite Tim, and signals him to play it again.

"Blackbird?" Tim says.

Papa nods.

Kes stands nearby, breathless.

Tim launches into a smooth blues progression, strumming lightly in G major, as Papa begins to hit a few lead notes. Nothing fancy. Just little flourishes. They sit facing each other as mirror images, one right-handed, the other left, like early black-and-white photos Kes has seen of John Lennon and Paul McCartney, back when they studied the great Buddy Holly, son of Texas.

When Rita comes through the door with Mike, Uncle Ty, Taylor, the McCall cousins—the whole Poker Pack, in fact—and sees Papa with the Martin, she freezes.

Tears rise in her eyes; she bites her lip.

Kes feels oddly light-headed. Euphoric.

Tim slides into "Blackbird" and Papa follows, adding little garnishes. Tim stops playing, but Papa does not. He begins another song, one from Whoa Nellie's early years. Kes recognizes it, but can't remember its name. Rita walks over to him and puts a hand gently on his shoulder and begins to hum. He hums beneath her, faint but unmistakable, finding the low harmony. Now Rita sings, and wipes away tears, and smiles radiantly, but keeps on singing about a desert wind.

Kes remembers, yes, that's the song: "Desert Wind."

As the song gains power, Tim joins in, hitting some nice licks. Grandpa awakens on the sofa. Kes reminds herself to breathe, to never forget this moment. It could last forever and not be long enough.

When they finish, Rita bends down and kisses Papa, who smiles.

"Praise God," Pastor Anderson whispers just right.

"Welcome back, little brother," Uncle Ty says. He, too, wipes away a tear.

Papa hugs little Kip, and turns to embrace Kes. "We never gave up, Papa," she tells him softly. "We never did. We never will." She kneels beside him and buries her face into his chest and lets him hug her with all his might.

He hummed.

Later, he might sing. He might howl.

He might run with wolves and take me with him.

This is the best Christmas ever.

THE CELEBRATION LASTS for a couple hours, as Papa and Tim keep playing and Kes joins them with her ukulele. And Rita and Jeannie cook up a feast.

Uncle Ty's rules for living at Willynillyville get broken all the time. But one is sacred: quiet hours. Other rules apply to those things that must be done: poker night and philosophical ramblings at least once a week; recycling, composting, and gardening; everybody helping everybody else (when needed) with carpentry, firewood, plumbing, and electrical chores. Since many of the vets have taken local jobs in Strawberry Flats, ten percent of all earned income (including Veterans Affairs benefits) goes into the "Willynillyville Fund" to help with medical expenses and transportation costs. One more rule applies to Christmas Day: everybody must draw a name from a pool and make one handmade gift for that person. The names are kept a secret until the big day.

Uncle Ty now breaks his own rule and announces, "To celebrate my brother's arrival back to us all, we'll exchange gifts tonight, Christmas Eve."

With Rita's help, Kes has made a raven-black shirt with a red thunderbird insignia sewed onto it for Captain Don, who she hardly knows as he's in and out of Willynillyville all the time, caught in a custody battle over his four kids in Oklahoma. Uncle Ty says the war ruined his marriage. Like many others, Don joined the National Guard thinking he'd rebuild roads and public facilities hit by tornados or floods, and earn money for his kids' college fund. Instead, he got shipped overseas—first to Iraq, then Afghanistan—to fight radical Islamic terrorists who bomb schools. After he came home, what did the Pentagon do? It sent him back to Afghanistan again and again, until he was completely FUBAR.

"They call it a 'tour' of duty," Tucker John scoffs, "as if it's a summer vacation."

A nice man with a big scar up his right arm and a red beard that's turning white, Captain Don, when in Alaska, is 2,500 miles from his kids, with his ex-wife who is "already sampling the menu," according to E. J., who says she'll probably be remarried within a year.

"Thank you," Captain Don says distantly to Kes.

"You can try it on if you'd like," Rita tells him. She sits next to Papa, holding his hand.

"Later," he says with a reserved smile.

Everybody passes the shirt around and admires it.

Papa hands Don a cup of eggnog sprinkled with cinnamon.

Chippy then surprises Kes with a package neatly wrapped and tied with a ribbon.

"I hope you like it," he says.

She opens it slowly to find a laminated red-and-yellow cedar ukulele stand, a portable one that folds up for travel. She walks over and hugs Chippy and thanks him, smelling the Skoal on his breath. He shrugs and tells her it's nothing. But anybody can see he put many hours into it.

As the Andersons leave, the pastor invites everybody over to their house any time tomorrow, Christmas Day, and to church services in the afternoon.

"Thank you, pastor," Jeannie says. "I'll be there."

Papa looks tired.

"It's been a big day, a great day," Uncle Ty says, a little drunk.

Grandpa and little Kip are already in bed.

Papa, Rita, and Kes walk out onto the deck that Chippy and Cap built, and hold hands in the dark. A light snow falls through the deck lights and onto their heads and shoulders and all about, making everything perfect.

"No snowflake ever falls in the wrong place," Rita says. She and Kes hug Papa from opposite sides. "How is it," Rita asks, "that we can arrive here for the first time and feel like it's always been home?"

Papa raises his head and softly howls. Kes and Rita do the same. They stop and listen, and howl again. And listen. And hug.

Silence.

The wolves are out there somewhere, Kes knows. Out there living by their own constitution and wits and laws, or by no laws at all. No rules but their own.

Back in July, on the plane trip north, as Claire hummed along and everybody was quiet, Uncle Ty would sometimes fall asleep in the pilot's seat. After a minute or so, Papa would reach over and gently jostle him awake. Kes watched it all. Other times, Uncle Ty would talk animatedly about how hummingbirds can fly backward and trees have emotions and whales change oceans and wolves change rivers.

Really? When Kes questioned her uncle, he said, "Right over there, my young apprentice, due east of us on the other side of Idaho, is Yellowstone, the world's first national park. Back in the 1920s, rangers shot out all the wolves. And what happened? The elk got lazy and stood around like feedlot cattle, overbrowsing the riverside willow. But when wolves were reintroduced seventy years later, the elk became elk again, swift and agile. The riverside willows returned, and with them, beaver, muskrat, and all kinds of birds. Color and balance came back into the land. It was damn near a miracle."

Kes thought: *If wolves can change entire ecosystems, what else can they change?*

ONCE MORE, Papa softly howls and draws back a bit, smiling, as if his own newfound voice appeals to him. He and Rita go inside arm-in-arm while Kes lingers back and cries with joy. "Thank you," she says to the snowy night and to the wild vastness of Alaska. *But it's more than that, isn't it?* She knows who she's really thanking.

The wolves.

PART III

CHAPTER TWENTY-EIGHT

Silver

THE ISLAND IS RIPE WITH DEER.

Silver senses this. Sister too.

They stand at an old high tide line, near the mouth of the river, facing south toward an island that's not near but not far. Another world. Silver has sensed this abundance before, but never felt a compulsion to explore it. Until now. At their feet lies a dead buck, drowned, semi-frozen into the shore ice and a delicate kerf of snow. It renders tough meat mixed with hard fat that requires much chewing. The two wolves rip into it, taking breaks now and then to howl up their family.

Mother soon arrives with the subadults, frisking about. Hungry.

Always hungry.

But no Alpha. No Strong.

The wolves nuzzle and lick each other's face, and while the new arrivals curl their lips and flick their tails and dig into the deer, Silver once again walks down to the tide line to observe the island that's not near but not far. Bitter cold. No wind. No sound, save for the primal chewing and growling of his family crowded around the same meal. Wisps of fog move over the water and appear deceptively warm in the winter morning light. Silver looks back at the pack, then again out to the island. Mother and Sister join him. Together they work the air with their noses. Alone, Silver steps into the sea, ankle deep, to test the temperature. The water is warmer than the air, but still cold.

He can do this. He knows he can, from his recent swim to shore from the dead whale, when he left Old One out there to die, adrift, alone. But it's more than that. For months Silver has dreamed of a moment like this, of swimming fjords, crossing glaciers, climbing tall mountain passes to find something new. Something more.

He wades in belly deep... then up to his chest. Glancing to his right, he sees the small peninsula—an island at high tide—where he once charged after seals and came up empty and nearly drowned, hungrier than before.

Not again. Not this time.

He begins to swim without looking back.

Mother does a quick *yip-yip* from behind. Silver yips in return.

Later, the island appears closer, but still not near. Two small diving birds paddle out of his way. Another two. And two more. Then a bigger, long-necked bird takes flight, followed by a small raft of ducks. A sea otter mother and pup surface nearby, squeal an alarm, and dive. A single raven flies low overhead, circles once, caws three times, and flies on toward the island. This way.

Far to his left, Silver notices a small object moving along the water, headed the opposite direction, making a strange, high-pitched noise. The raven returns, circles once as before, caws three times, and flies toward the island. This way.

Huffing now, his voice echoing lightly over the water with each labored breath, Silver feels himself tiring. He paddles in a wide circle to see if he's being followed. And there she is: Sister. Not far behind, swimming hard. Silver continues on, buoyed to know that his favorite sibling is nearby. His lungs complain and begin to burn. His neck tires, his head drops. Seawater splashes into his mouth and down his throat. He coughs, flags, and begins to sink. He digs deep and pushes on. The island is near now, looming large.

He swims with everything he's got, all that remains, and when his paws touch bottom he slowly finds his balance and drags himself out of the cold ocean and staggers up the north-facing shore. Tired, he shakes himself dry and stands in the shadow of the forest, half-frozen, the sun too low to the south to crest the trees and warm him. The water on his fur begins to turn to ice, like a crystalline coat. He coughs, and shakes again, but the icy coat hangs onto him as a million small, glassy pendants.

Sister arrives, followed by the four subadults. But no Mother. No Alpha. No Strong. Silver knows Mother will not make the swim without Alpha, her mate for life, and without Strong, or at least without knowing their whereabouts and health.

Family is everything.

The subadults seem uncertain what to do without their parents. Every wolf is exhausted and cold, standing in the shadows, covered, like Silver, in pendants of ice.

Silver knows only this: they have to eat. And soon.

He leads them single file into the silent forest, peeing as he goes—the others do the same—to leave a scent trail for Mother, Alpha, and Strong. Soon thereafter, the six wolves arrive on the edge of a large muskeg that's dusted with snow and patterned with deer tracks. Here they fan out in pincer formation, and lie low, and wait.

CHAPTER TWENTY-NINE

Salt

SATURDAY IN STRAWBERRY FLATS. Salt finds himself again at Nystad's Mercantile, listening to what's being said around the hot dog stand and popcorn machine where blond-haired Berit Nystad serves up a steady stream of customers.

Today's special:

EARTHQUAKE LOG SPLITTER WITH A
HIGH-PERFORMANCE, EASY-TO-START HONDA 160
OVERHEAD CAM ENGINE. ONE PULL AND SHA-ZAM...
YOU'RE WARM FOR THE WINTER.
BUY TWO FOR TWICE THE PRICE!

As if any one person needs two log splitters.

Salt can't stop thinking about the wolf. Not just any wolf, but *the wolf*, the most arresting animal he's ever seen. Beautiful, yes. But more than that. Something beyond words. Call it grace. Silver, black, and russet red, with eyes that reflected the forest from ten thousand years ago and communicated in ways not even scholars could understand. It was six weeks ago when he saw the wolf, back in November, and still, during all that time, it has seemed so present, so immediate. Even after the wolf was gone, it remained.

Nobody should kill such an animal.

And all that time, Salt has thought about Solomon. And Johns Hopkins. Money.

Again, he thinks back to November. Thanksgiving Day. How, after lying on the ground for a long time on the other side of the river, next to the hole he'd dug, he sat up and wondered: *Why is this so hard?* He'd scattered a trail of salami pieces to the river's edge, where a tangle of old spruce lay fallen by a windstorm. As darkness overtook him, he set the only leghold trap he had. He then baited it, covered it with twigs and moss and pieces of bark, and chained it to an old log that was half-rotten.

By the time he'd recrossed the river, en route back home, late for the big holiday dinner, the night owned him. He tried to use his flashlight, but its light flitted across the fast current and created an image of confusion that made Salt dizzy, almost nauseous. He quickly turned the light off, took some deep breaths at midcurrent, felt the river pushing hard on his thighs, and moved on, holding steady to his walking stick. Praying. He managed to get across, fully aware that if he fell, he'd die.

Not until he reached the riverbank did he make a mistake. Neglecting to turn his flashlight back on, he climbed up the steep slope, slipped on ice, fell hard on his bad knee, and heard himself cry out. He lay there for a long time to let the pain subside.

It never did. Not fully.

All of this made him even more late.

He got to his Toyota and drove home with his knee swollen and getting worse. He limped into the workshop, got out of his coat and chest waders, dropped his pack, and pulled out a hidden flask of Jim Beam. He remembers taking a long drink and catching his breath and taking another, the whiskey coursing through his body like firewater. He then limped up the wheelchair ramp to the house.

Everybody turned to stare at him. Salt forced a smile and apologized for being late, as if he'd gotten tied up with errands. Nothing more.

Liar. I lied to my own family.

Hannah hugged him while Salt could see that Abraham, who quietly got up and fetched him some Ibuprofen, wasn't fooled.

He remembers eating like a starving man, and noticing that while the others talked animatedly and shared stories and finished their desserts, Principal Cunningham watched Salt with her intense blue eyes, determined to figure him out—where he'd been, what he'd been up to. As if he were a truant schoolboy.

"Isn't that right, husband?" Hannah said at one point.

"What?" Salt replied, miles away, back in the river, fighting to keep his balance.

"Mrs. Cunningham says that everybody loves Solomon," Hannah said, "that he's a real wonder. Solomon has always been popular at school, hasn't he?"

Before Salt could answer, Solomon rocked hard in his wheelchair and shouted, "Steeeeeeeevie Wooooooooonder, shake it on dooooowwwn."

And they all laughed.

But not Mrs. Cunningham.

So bad is his knee six weeks later that Salt has yet to recross the river to check the den or trap. His hip bothers him as well. And his heart continues to beat arrhythmically.

If only it could be tuned, he thinks, *like a carburetor.*

Berit Nystad hands Salt his hot dog and thanks him for his ten-dollar donation. While Nystad's Mercantile's hot dogs are free every Saturday, it's considered bad manners to not drop a dollar or two into the charity jar. This particular Saturday it's for a Strawberry Flats pioneer who can't afford insulin. Salt hears one man tell another that the price of insulin "has gone up three hundred percent in the past five years."

The other man says, "Did you know that the two scientists who discovered insulin gave it away for free, as a gift to society. It wasn't until some greedy capitalist came along and patented it that the price went through the roof."

"Don't be so hard on capitalists. Big Pharma CEOs made only fifty bazillion dollars last year."

"And paid no taxes."

"Hey Don," a third man shouts from down an aisle, "did Ty say he wanted water filters at ten microns or five microns?"

The man with the graying red beard shrugs. "I don't know. What's the difference?"

"Five microns."

"Get one of each. No, get two of each."

"Yeah, at double the price."

They laugh.

Salt realizes these guys are Willynillyville veterans and wishes he could laugh with friends like they do. *When's the last time I laughed hard? Really hard? Maybe once or twice with Hannah in Minto. But in truth, not since my youth in Idaho.*

Just then, two women come around the corner pushing a loaded cart and join the Willynillyville gang with high fives. One is a silver-haired lady Salt has never seen before, accompanied by a handsome golden retriever. The other is Rita Nash, a petite, dark-haired woman who's a fine singer, according to Rosie Goodnight, who read about her in a Texas music publication. She's also Kes's stepmom. The girl's birth mom died when she was young. How exactly she died remains a mystery that Rosie no doubt feels duty bound to discover.

The two women jive easily with the men, and disappear again down one of the aisles.

Salt finds himself strangely envious of their unity and friendship. He once heard Derek say that Tyler Nash is the kind of guy who'd build a baseball diamond in a cornfield. He's a rebel, a dreamer, a kind of hippie pirate, but also a trained geologist who served as a petroleum engineer and oil strategist with the US Army in Iraq until he resigned his officer's commission. Later, he went to work on the North Slope, and walked away from that too. He bought a Cessna and twenty acres in Strawberry Flats, and now fishes with Zorro Brown, and flies to Mexico and back once or twice each year, and builds solar panels, and does his best to help war veterans find peace and purpose in their lives.

A white van pulls up outside and two men get out, heavily tattooed and wearing ball caps backward on their shaved heads. Salt sees Chippy and Cap McCall come inside, grab their hot dogs from Berit, thank her and banter with her, put a twenty-dollar bill in the jar, and engage the other veterans. Derek once told Salt that Cap can fix anything, but he won't take work at Derek's Garage or anywhere else unless he absolutely has to. Maybe he has a big stash of money in that white van that he and his cousin drive around and always lock wherever they go, even now as they come into the mercantile. Which is strange, even suspicious, because nobody else in town locks their vehicles. *Except me,* Salt thinks dryly. Besides, if a car were stolen in Strawberry Flats, where would the thief take it? Bumper stickers say, *What's your hurry? You're already here.* And *I'd rather live here than have a career.*

The town has maybe fifty miles of roads—mostly driveways—that all dead-end. Whenever people fly to Juneau and to points south, they leave their vehicles unlocked at the airport, with the keys in the ignition. If somebody needs to borrow a car, they go to the airport and take one. If they don't return it before the owners come back, the owners take another rig. Pretty soon everybody is driving around town in somebody else's car or truck, until the next big potluck dinner or dance or music jam or sewing circle when everybody arrives in a borrowed rig and goes home in their own.

Not Chippy and Cap. They alone drive their van and always lock it, as if they're drug runners or arms dealers or bank robbers. Nobody really knows what they're up to. It drives Rosie crazy. She acknowledges that Chippy, an excellent carpenter, makes high-end rocking chairs and probably sells them for lots of money, mostly to buyers in Juneau and maybe down in Seattle. For a few months, Hannah worked part time at Fjord Flying (while the boys were in school) and saw Chippy ship out many chairs, all of them heavily protected in bubble wrap. He did a brisk business.

Salt would love to see the Willynillyville woodworking shop, reputed to be the best in town. And watch Chippy make his chairs. Salt could just show up one day. But he's shy, raised to be deferential, and would never ask. He heard Abraham once say that the Anderson kids spend time there, at Willynillyville. Tim and Tia, anyway.

"So, guess what I heard?" Cap tells the others as he dresses up his hot dog with mustard, ketchup, and relish. "Hank Barnes was out in his skiff and thinks he saw some wolves on the north shore of Archibald Island."

"That's nothing," another veteran says. "Rosie Goodnight says that Peter Metcalf found a dead wolf caught in a leghold trap that was chained to a dead tree that washed up on the beach not far east of the ferry dock."

Salt catches his breath.

"That doesn't make sense," Chippy says as he adjusts an unholstered handgun in his waist belt, at his stomach, under the tail of his coat.

"Jesus, Chippy," says a veteran the others call E. J. "Be careful with that thing or you'll shoot off your wangdoodle."

"Don't worry," Chippy says. "My wangdoodle is lightning fast."

Salt watches Berit flush with embarrassment.

"If wolves take up shop on Archibald Island," E. J. says, "they'll clean out all the deer in a couple months."

"There goes the good hunting," says another man, maybe a veteran. Hard to tell. More and more people crowd into the mercantile for hot dogs, popcorn, and gossip.

Salt stands back and watches it all and listens, keen to hear more about the wolves. He notices a bad palsy in E. J.'s right hand, and a nervous tic in another vet's eye. He knows that while some of the Willynillyville men live in the shadows and seldom leave their refuge on the west end of town, others, like the McCalls, get out all the time.

And then there's Danny Nash, who just last month began speaking again for the first time since Afghanistan. Principal Cunningham says it's a miracle.

Back in his youth, in Idaho, Salt knew lives devastated by the wars in Vietnam and Iraq. He watched marriages fail, families shatter. "If suicide doesn't get you," his friend Barry, himself a vet, once told him, "pain, depression, and addiction will. Some guys try it all: Paxil, Zoloft, Tofranil, Wellbutrin, Elavil, OxyContin, Metrazol, Parnate with lithium salts, Nardil with Xanax. And don't forget opioids and alcohol, and a little meth here and heroin there until, what the hell, man... the lights go out and you're just another dead junkie in the corner."

Salt's sister, Light, tried to save Barry with the Word of God, and cried for days when he rode his motorcycle into a tree and died. She had loved him since high school. Years later, after her own marriage failed, she confessed to Salt that if Barry had lived, she would have married him and been happy forever.

And now Abraham wants to join up and serve, and come home a hero. Another kid with haunted eyes and an Old Spice swagger, suckered into war, dying for oil while thinking he's fighting for freedom. Another kid who loves America, like most Americans, because he was born here and has never been anywhere else. Dear God.

AN HOUR LATER, Salt walks the beach east of the ferry dock. He reasons that if an uprooted tree—one with a dead wolf chained to it—were to get washed downriver to the ocean and caught in the current, it could end up here along the highest high tide line.

He finds nothing.

The sand is clean save for a few tire tracks that aren't unusual. People drive down here all the time in their big trucks and ATVs, smashing flowers and bird nests.

Salt remembers making quick work of setting the riverside trap in late November. *And then?* His best guess: *A strong wolf, caught in the trap that was chained to a half-rotten log, must have pulled hard enough to break the log. And when he did, the wolf, still in the trap and chained to the log, must have skidded down the steep embankment (with the log) and into the river. Wrapped up in the chain, he would have drowned while being swept downriver, kept afloat by the log that in time washed up on the beach.*

Walking back to his Toyota, limping slightly, Salt encounters the McCall cousins coming his way.

"Did you find it?" Chippy asks excitedly as they draw near.

"Find what?"

"The wolf. The one caught in a trap and chained to a log."

"Oh, no… I was just taking a walk. Getting some exercise for my bad knee."

Cap asks. "You work at Derek's Garage, right?"

"I do."

"He's asked me a couple times if I want to work there. I keep telling him no."

Chippy says, "That's because you're too busy running your multinational corporation and sailing your yacht and building your spaceship to Mars."

"Oh, yeah," Cap says with a grin. "I forgot about that."

"And driving that German Mercedes you bought from a Saudi prince."

"Oh, yeah, that too."

The McCalls laugh and walk on, as does Salt, going the opposite way. But a minute later, when the cousins are a good distance away, Chippy stops and yells back, "Hey, you're Salt d'Alene, right?"

Salt turns. "That's me."

"Solomon's dad?"

"Yes."

"He's a great kid. If there's anything we can ever do, let us know, okay?"

Salt nods and waves. "Okay. I will. Thank you."

PASTOR ANDERSON hits his stride midway through his sermon, which is more of a history lesson than anything else. He quotes not one line of scripture, but makes steady references to the teachings of Christ. He talks about the great American preacher Lyman Beecher, and his son, the even greater American preacher Henry Ward Beecher, who would often say there is no virtue without piety. Henry Ward delivered a famous eulogy at Appomattox after General Robert E. Lee signed the Confederate surrender.

"Why is it then," Pastor Anderson asks, his voice softening after hitting a crescendo, "that the great United States of America had no truth and reconciliation commission after our Civil War, as South Africa did after abolishing apartheid? And why is it that after the end of World War II, Germany banned the Nazi flag, the swastika, but after our Civil War, a war to end slavery, the Confederate flag still flies in many places? It is a flag of dominion and racial superiority and even violence, is it not? Many of our recent mass shootings have been committed by young men devoted to that flag. We have work to do, my friends. Let us be good to each other. Let us be tolerant, but not tolerant of intolerance. Let us be pious and kind, and find a way. And finally, let us be thankful that our own Danny Nash, back from Afghanistan, is speaking and singing again."

Pastor Anderson signals his son, Tim, to play his guitar, and soon a girl—Salt recognizes her but doesn't know her name—begins to sing "Amazing Grace."

As the entire congregation sings along, Solomon rocks excitedly in his wheelchair and moans along with the melody.

The d'Alenes always occupy the back of the chapel, where there's room for Solomon. And Abraham always holds his wheelchair. But not today. For the first time, Abe stands apart from his family, up front next to Tabby Anderson.

After the closing prayer, Salt makes his way forward to thank the pastor, as always, and to correct him on scripture—if need be. No need today. Many newcomers crowd the pulpit, including the silver-haired woman with the golden retriever, and the Black man, also a Willynillyville veteran, who saw Salt hiding in the woods off the Menzies River Trail. And Kes Nash, which surprises Salt. *Is her being here today the reason Pastor Anderson acknowledged her father?* Drawing near while keeping a distance, Salt hears Kes say to Tim and Tia, "We have to do something."

The twins appear alarmed.

"Do what?" Tia asks, her eyes large with apprehension.

"I don't know, exactly," Kes says. "But somebody's trapping wolves, probably on the other side of the Menzies River, and we have to do something."

Salt finds himself admiring her. In all his years trapping, battling the cold, the rivers, Defenders of Wildlife and the Sierra Club, he cannot remember ever encountering an adversary so feisty and young, and with so much fire in her eyes.

CHAPTER THIRTY

Kes

KES TIES THE ROPE over her chest waders, cinches it around her waist, and hands the other end to Tim.

"I don't like this," Tim says, his round face creased with worry.

"Just wrap it around that tree, feed it out as I go, and pull hard if I fall."

She studies the river, icy at its edges, and steps in. *Let's get this over with.* The cold current pulls at her and raises its voice to a soft roar. Pieces of ice float by. Kes looks back at Tim and Tia and the others and yells, "Feed it out just right, like we talked about… so if I fall in, you can pull me out."

"What do you mean, 'just right'?" Tim yells back.

"I don't know, Tim. Give me some slack, but not too much."

"I still don't like this."

"Stop. You're making me nervous."

"You're making *me* nervous."

"People cross this river all the time."

"Yeah, grown men. And not in January."

The current roils off her knees—and soon, her thighs—as she inches her way across. The cobbled bottom shifts under her feet. Less than one-third of the way, she begins to shake. She stumbles and catches herself. "The rope is dragging in the current and pulling me back," she yells over the roar of the water. "Take up the slack."

"We are," Tim yells back.

"More."

"We are, Kes. We are."

Glancing over her shoulder, she can see her friends holding the rope with all their might while the raging river conspires against them, against her.

IF KING ARTHUR COULD HAVE HIS KNIGHTS, Kes figures she can too.

"Little Bird," Papa used to call her back in Texas when she was small but agile, and loved to fly off a swing at its greatest height, all before the accident that killed her birth mom and Papa cried. They all cried. And time passed either too slowly or too fast. And the sound of her mom's voice faded, and every photo of her—no matter how warm or bright—made a poor substitute.

After the funeral, Kes overheard one woman say to another, "Has anybody told little Kes how her mom really died?"

"Higher," Kes would say as Papa pushed her on the swing. "Higher, Papa. Higher." But he didn't have his same energy as before. He stopped writing songs then, except for one—for Kes:

> *Little Bird, you learn to walk*
> *But flying is your gift*
> *Wear the sky on your back*
> *Little Bird... up you lift.*

Later, as his grief subsided and he pulled the band back together, he would sing "Little Bird" for her late at night, his Martin in his lap as the bus rolled down another lonesome highway. And Kes would fall asleep curled up next to him.

One of those nights she asked him, "It was a car accident that killed Mom, right?"

"Yes," Papa said. "Just an accident. Nobody's fault. Go to sleep now."

After Papa met Rita and they began singing together, he wrote songs for her, not for Kes. And carried himself in a whole new way, like a man in love. Rita joined the band and brought along her friend Sammye, and things took off. The band gained a whole new sound, and a new name, Whoa Nellie, and a larger following.

Kes was the flower girl in their wedding. Sammye was a bridesmaid. Uncle Ty flew down from Alaska. Uncle Charles and his family drove to Lubbock from Houston. After Papa vowed to Rita how much he loved her and would care for her, Rita told the small gathering that Danny Nash was her dream come true, and she would work hard to make a loving and meaningful life with him, and never stand in the way of his creativity. "But also," Rita said, looking at Kes, "I hope to be a good mother to his wonderful little girl right here with us, carrying our rings."

That was five years ago.

Kes might not really be a bird, or have a magical sword, but she's got friends—who she calls her "order of knights"—who now find themselves confronting an icy, raging river, feeding out a rope while Tia prays aloud, "Please, God, don't let this river kill Kes."

It's taken more than two weeks to assemble the order and mount this rescue, this expedition, this… whatever. "Maybe we're a Rogue One Delta Force Zero-Dark-Thirty Commando Navy SEAL team," said Kona Michael Marks, the youngest recruit, when they set out walking an hour ago from the parking area at the end of Menzies River Road.

Nobody laughed.

Tim and Tia joined first—or rather, were coerced by Kes. Next came Melissa Darling and Emily Patchett, two "soul sisters," as they called themselves, in Kes's class with Tim and Tia. Mrs. Carry, their teacher, once said they were "a bunch of twelve-year-olds in imminent danger of becoming teenagers." The world belonged to them, for better or for worse. Climate change. Proms. Driver's licenses. Rising seas. Green New Deals. Extinction Rebellion. Pandemics. Active shooter drills. Graduation. Fires, floods, storms, drought, and disinformation. The future was coming at them with full force. Kes could feel it. Melissa too. She had told Kes so.

"If we team up," Kes had told her friends at school, "we could really do something. We could make a difference."

She told them she had once heard somebody complain to the famous climate activist Bill McKibben, "I'm only one person… what can I do?"

McKibben replied, "Stop being one person."

TAYLOR DE LA CROIX, Uncle Ty's girlfriend who works with Melissa's father, a PhD ecologist at Crystal Bay National Marine Reserve, recently told Kes, "If your father's an ecologist, then you're going to grow up without any delusions." That's Melissa Darling, a darling in name only, who recently said to Mrs. Carry, "Our president lies all the time. He should be thrown in jail." The previous president, fully aware of the threat modern civilization posed to the world's oceans, created the US National Marine Reserve Service. This current president—"a real bozo," according to Melissa (and Rita)—thinks windmills cause cancer and fighter planes flew in the American Revolutionary War.

As for Emily Patchett, she can be so tough and cutting that some kids call her "Patchett the Hatchet." She once got into an argument with Abraham d'Alene and didn't back down as Abe towered over her and told her she was stupid.

Emily's mom is a law enforcement ranger at the marine reserve.

And finally, Kona, a fourth grader. When he heard the others talking about their order of knights in the school corridor, he asked to join, saying he was "ready to be a hero."

Emily said to the others, "How do we say no to that?"

ALL KES WANTS IS TO FIND THE WOLVES, release them from the traps, decipher clues about who trapped them, confiscate the traps, take photos, and save the world.

And how to release a wolf from a trap? Kes has no idea.

When she reaches the other side, she'll tie her end of the rope to a tree. The others will then do the same at their end. Thereafter, the rope will provide a guide, something to hold on to and steady themselves as they cross back and forth and rescue more wolves.

But already the rope, dragging in the river, is more hindrance than help.

It's another day of cold, spitting rain. Only modest amounts of snow and ice linger on the ground and along the river's edge, enough that Kes hopes she'll be able to track who's been out here. An hour ago, she and her fellow commandos found no cars in the parking area, about a mile away, where they left their bikes. Still, they have to be careful. She told Tim, "Others could be around."

"Others? Like who?"

"I don't know, Tim, maybe a solitary hiker or a lone trapper."

"Or Bigfoot."

"Or Elvis."

"Or the band Queen, you know... the whole band. 'We are the champions.'"

"Freddy Mercury is dead, Tim."

"Oh, yeah... so's Elvis. Dying is a drag. Don't die, Kes."

Kes told Rita she was going over to Tim and Tia's house for a few hours. How much trouble could she get into at Pastor Anderson's place? Rita had wanted her to stay home to study—it's an in-service Thursday at school—and maybe pull out her ukulele to jam with Papa. Lately they've been working up some good songs, with Papa beginning to compose again, his hummingbird hands taking flight once more up and down the fretboard of his Martin.

It's a strong temptation, to make music with Papa.

But first, this river.

"You don't need ferocious animals to get into trouble in Alaska," Kes remembers hearing Uncle Ty tell Chippy and Cap. "The rivers alone can kill you."

"Tim?" she yells over her shoulder.

"Yeah?" he yells back.

"The river bottom is shifting under me."

"You're just standing there."

"I know. I'm stuck… and I'm cold. I'm really cold."

"Okay, uh… turn around and come back if you can. Can you come back?"

"I don't know. I think my feet are numb." Kes begins to shuffle around to see her way back. The river thunders in her ears. The rope snags on something. Her pack? "Give me some slack," she yells.

"We are," Emily yells back.

"More."

"We are."

"The rope is snagged on something. I can't see—" And under Kes goes.

"KES!" Tim's voice is the last thing she hears before a thousand needles stab her entire body.

She comes up gasping, thrashing, fighting her way back, the cold river filling her chest waders and dragging her down, killing her, pulling every ounce of heat from her. She sees flashes of her friends digging in their heels, as if in a tug-of-war, the rope around the tree and in their hands. It rides high up under her armpits, tight as a cable, abrading her face. She's more horizontal than vertical, thrashing with her feet, taking in gulps of water.

Somehow, she gets to shore, coughing, heaving, spitting. She rolls onto her side, pulls her knees to her chest, and screams with pain. The cold is so intense, it knifes into her bones. She rolls onto all fours, coughing more. She hears a strange heaving cry, like that of a wounded animal, and realizes it's her. *It's me!*

Her friends help to pull off the rope… and her daypack… and chest waders.

She's never been this cold—so cold it burns.

"I… have… to… get… home…" she tells her frightened friends. Already her muscles are tightening up.

Shivering, she struggles to her feet and begins to walk, and falls. Her muscles are like wood. Again, she gets to her feet, stumbles forward, falls to a knee, rises again, and moves forward some more. Step by step she begins to loosen up and gain momentum, and now—more ferocious than she's ever been, and more scared—she starts to run. The faster she runs, the faster she can run, her limbs limbering up with each stride, adrenaline surging. Flying now, dripping wet. Running at a desperate speed, bound for her bicycle at the parking area, and from there—home.

Papa...

THE MINUTE TUCKER JOHN SEES HER RIDE UP and drop her bike, her skin porcelain white and her lips blue, he picks her up and carries her into the house. Rita gasps, then flies into action. She and Jeannie strip Kes down, wrap her in blankets, and set her next to the wood-burning stove. They fill three Nalgene bottles with hot water and place them in her armpits and groin, and serve her hot drinks.

Little Kip and Skydog stand in awe, watching it all.

Tucker John goes outside to get more firewood.

"Tell me what happened," Rita says as she dries Kes's hair. "I want the full story."

"Where's Papa?" Kes asks when her mouth no longer feels like frozen iron.

"He's in Juneau with your Uncle Ty and Mike and the McCalls," Rita tells her.

"Mike had another bad night last night," Jeannie adds as she sits next to Kes and strokes Skydog's soft fur. At one point, she reaches over and kisses Kes on her forehead.

Kes manages a weak smile, and takes her first deep breath. Were it not for Jeannie, a churchgoer who one recent Sunday invited Kes to join her, Kes would not have heard Pastor Anderson's amazing sermons. Or seen Tim tear into the electric guitar in a way the pastor said with a chuckle is "more Led Zeppelin's 'Stairway to Heaven' than Handel's *Messiah*." Now she can't imagine not attending the services.

"Not all preachers are like Pastor Anderson," Jeannie told her recently as they drove back to Willynillyville in Sarge the Jeep. "We're lucky."

"He should be a history teacher," Kes said.

"I don't think so," Jeannie said. "I think he should be exactly what he is.

He's one of those rare people who find their calling and know it, and are very good at it."

A KNOCK AT THE DOOR. Rita answers. It's the order of knights. Rita tells them to leave Kes's wet things on the deck. She invites them inside and serves them hot drinks as they sit around the warm stove.

Kona takes a sip of his hot chocolate and asks, "Are we prisoners here?"

"Only for the next hour or so," Rita says. "I'll let you go after I get a full explanation of what happened. How does that sound?"

"That sounds good." Kona looks at Jeannie. "Can I pet your dog?"

"Yes. Bring your hand to him slowly. Let him sniff it by way of introduction."

They take turns petting Skydog. The hot chocolate and wood-burning stove seem to work their magic on all but Tim and Tia, who glance at Kes as if to say: *We told you so. Crossing the Menzies is hard at any time. But in January, it's downright stupid.*

"Did you sing in a rock band?" Kona asks Rita.

"A band, yes. A rock band, no."

"Cool," Kona says.

"Totally cool," Melissa adds.

"What kind of horses are those?" Kona asks as he looks out the window at Stardust and Golden.

"Manchurian ponies," Rita says.

"The same kind of ponies Ernest Shackleton used on one of his expeditions to Antarctica," Jeannie adds. "Isn't that right, Kes?"

Kes nods.

"Cool," Kona says.

"Okay," Rita announces. "It's my turn to ask questions. Who are you, and what are you up to?"

After thirty minutes of tall tales of derring-do, near escapes, plans gone awry, and more hot chocolate, of Kes and her friends talking faster and faster and interrupting each other about why the wolf traps across the river have to be destroyed and the wolves saved because they helped save Kes's dad, sorta, kinda... to make him musical again with their cool howling and wildness and stuff, and after Kes, having finally warmed up, talked about King Arthur's Camelot and the evils of Might Makes Right and the Battle of Bedegraine in the ancient forest of Sherwood, adding how Merlyn would sometimes chew on his own beard and stare into a fire, deep in thought, Rita finally interrupts and asks, "So, hold on a minute... you, all of you, are an order of knights? Is that what I'm hearing? And you're prepared to invite adults to join your order?"

The kids look at each other and nod, then turn to Rita and nod.

"The Knights of Alaska," Melissa announces. "That's who we are."

"No," Kona interjects. "We're the Knights of the Menzies River."

LATER, AFTER DARKNESS HAS FALLEN, Kes awakens to howling and instantly knows it's not wolves.

It's a man. In pain. Mike?

She hears the door open downstairs... footsteps on the deck. Voices calling. Kes follows in her pajamas, down the stairs and out the door, across the cold ground to where Mike lives with E. J. and Captain Don. A crowd has gathered inside. Captain Don and Uncle Ty calm Mike with a droplet of morphine under his tongue. He looks wild-eyed, cornered, confused, but soon begins to relax. Uncle Ty rocks him in his lap and motions everybody to back away. Kes finds herself biting her lip. Rita holds her.

"It's okay," Uncle Ty whispers to Mike. "It's okay, buddy. We're all here and we love you."

Rita goes back to the house and returns with a large pot of soup and puts it on the stove. The others strike up a quiet game of poker while keeping one eye on Mike. They aren't going anywhere until he's better. Uncle Ty says this is how it is in a band of brothers. You take responsibility. You sacrifice.

He's such a complex man, Kes thinks of her uncle. *He hates war but admires the military brotherhood it creates.*

At the poker table, Chippy says E. J. is across town, "high-centered on the new preschool teacher, Cindy What's-her-name."

Kes watches Rita bristle. Her stepmom has never liked Chippy since the RPG incident down in San Antonio, which she heard about from Grandpa, who heard about it during the trip north in Claire. It so happens that Grandpa, like Kes, is a good eavesdropper.

ONLY A FEW DAYS AGO Kes heard Rita complain to Uncle Ty that she thinks Chippy is unstable. "And where are those stupid RPGs? Did he sell them? Throw them away? Give them to somebody? Or did he and Cap bring them all the way up here in his van?"

"I can't say, Rita," Uncle Ty said. "And I'm not going to ask him. We might need them one day."

"The RPGs? Are you serious?"

"Yes, I'm serious. Don't you see the shitstorm that's coming?"

"I do," Jeannie said as she joined them. "The whole planet is in trouble."

"Big trouble," Uncle Ty said.

"I pray every day," Jeannie added.

Uncle Ty shook his head.

"What?" Jeannie asked. "You think prayer is a waste of time?"

Uncle Ty thought for a moment. Kes could tell that he liked Jeannie. Everybody did. Kes could also see that he didn't want to offend her. She was a veteran with a cool dog. "Christianity is a bargain deal," Uncle Ty said. "It's transactional, more like business than altruism. You sign up with Jesus and live forever, right? How could anything so appealing be untrue? A few years back I ran into my old high school girlfriend in a Lubbock supermarket. It was New Year's Eve, like something out of a Dan Fogelberg song, but without the snow. She'd married an insurance adjuster and had five kids, and had never really traveled, never seen the ocean. Out in the parking lot, she commented on the full moon and how bright and beautiful it was. When I mentioned that it was all reflected sunlight, that the moon doesn't produce any light of its own, it's not a nuclear reactor like the sun, she scowled at me and said she believed in God, as if I'd offended her or lied. That's when she told me she was an evangelical and a patriot. We talked some more, and when I asked what she'd do if she found out her son was a *Homo sapiens*, she said she'd have him sent away to be cured, and if that didn't work, and if prayer didn't work, then she'd have to disown him."

"Disown him?" Jeannie said.

"Yep. She told me she'd kick him out of the house."

"That's sad."

"That's Christianity in America, Jeannie."

"Not all Christians are like her."

"But millions are," Uncle Ty said, "many of them filled with the moral certainty of the closed mind. Don't get me wrong. It's not Jesus who disappoints me. It's his fan club. He's a charismatic guy with delusional followers."

"*Homo sapiens,*" Rita said with a chuckle. "Are you serious?"

"Absolutely."

"Heaven forbid we should have any of those running around."

Uncle Ty laughed, and Rita laughed with him. It warmed Kes's heart. But when Rita noticed the disappointment on Jeannie's face, she grew serious. Jeannie reached for Skydog and ran both of her hands through his fur coat, then knelt beside him and wrapped her arms around his neck to take refuge there. Kes had heard Rita say "curse the heavens" more than once after Papa's return from Afghanistan. Maybe she had been religious once, and lost her faith. Kes didn't know.

"I'm sorry, Jeannie," Rita said. "I hope we didn't offend you."

"No offense taken. I've heard worse."

"Rita tells me you were a Mark Twain scholar at UT Austin," Uncle Ty said.

"Not a scholar," Jeannie said. "I just wrote my master's thesis on him."

"What about, specifically?"

"His relationship to the American Civil War, how it affected his writing."

"Are you familiar with what he said about religion? He said, 'Religion began when the first con man encountered the first fool,' or something close to that."

"I am familiar with that," Jeannie said. "Do you know why he wrote it? His beloved daughter Suzy had died at age twenty-four. It shattered him in his later years, and made him bitter about many things."

"I didn't know that."

Jeannie stood up then, walked to the door with Skydog, and said as she left, "You're a smart man, Tyler... a clever man... a good man with what you're doing for veterans here in Alaska. But a lack of faith can turn people bitter and mean. Be careful."

MIKE SLEEPS.

Tucker John and Kes make paper airplanes and fly them across the room while the others play cards. When Chippy and Cap light up joints, Uncle Ty tells them to put them out, then recants: "Oh, go ahead."

According to Tucker John, when Uncle Ty first got things going at Willynillyville, he forbade alcohol, but then remembered he liked to drink. He forbade swearing, but then remembered he liked to cuss. He forbade violent video games, until Chippy and Cap complained and threatened to leave, taking their building skills with them. He eased up on one rule after another. And how to deal with addictions to prescription meds? Or a love of marijuana? Should the vets smoke up in Kes's company? Rita thinks not and has told Uncle Ty so. She says Willynillyville is a veritable drugstore and weed shop.

"I'd die without my dope," Cap once told Kes. He has chronic back and neck pain from Afghanistan. "The Taliban are bloody artists when it comes to burying their makeshift bombs."

Two hours after Mike falls asleep, he awakens thrashing and screaming, "Stop the bleeding... check the perimeter..."

Kes startles awake, curled into a big chair with Rita. Others jump to their feet, panicked. Uncle Ty flies across the floor, grabs Mike forcefully, cradles him and rocks him like a child, and gives him more morphine. Ashen faced, Papa goes out the door. Rita squeezes Kes's hand and motions her to follow him.

It's cold out, but not as cold as it should be. Recent rains have washed away almost all the snow.

Back in their own home, Kes finds Papa stoking the wood-burning stove. He turns and picks up his Martin. Kes runs upstairs, grabs her ukulele, and skedaddles back down, breathless. He plays in that magical way, with the edge of his strumming hand lightly hitting the guitar bridge to create a gentle drumming sound. He capos up three frets and plays in A major so Kes can play open in C, an easy key for her. She strums through a 1–4–5 chord progression and Papa follows, playing lead riffs. He begins to sing, softly, making up a song called "Winter Rain," with an easy chorus. "Take the high harmony," he says to Kes, and she does, though she knows she can't sing as well as Rita or Sammye. Nobody can sing like Sammye. Except maybe Adele or Norah Jones or Tracy Chapman. Papa brings the song around again to the chorus, and once more they sing.

When they finish, Kes slides in for a hug. "Papa, is Mike going to be okay?"

"No," he answers softly. It's how Papa speaks and sings now, softly, slowly, in almost a whisper, as if easing back into the sound of his own voice. Taking his time. "He's loaded with stage-four cancer, sweetie. The only thing we can do now is to make him comfortable and help him die."

"Help him die? How do we do that?"

Papa looks across the room as his eyes go haunted and sad, and Kes feels that old fear come back… as if she could still lose him, as if Afghanistan is never far away. As if war, like love, defines who we are and there's no escaping it. Ever.

Papa looks back at Kes and says, "Your Uncle Ty knows how to help Mike die. That's why he brought him to Alaska."

Kes wants to ask about her birth mom. *Was it just an accident? Or was it more?*

Before she can, Papa smiles and says, "C'mon, let's play another song."

CHAPTER THIRTY-ONE

Silver

STRONG IS GONE.

Every night, Mother howls her sorrow, the notes long and mournful as they descend into unmistakable grief. Even after a bountiful meal, she remains forlorn, and leaves the muskeg and goes through the forest and down to the beach where she can cry over the ocean, alone.

Silver has only one surviving litter sibling now, Sister. They seldom leave each other.

The island deer are agile and fast, but no match for a pack of wolves. Were it just a single wolf hunting a single adult deer, the odds would shift in favor of the deer. But the pack hunts as a team in pincer formations and flourishes.

What happened to Strong?

When Mother and Alpha finally arrived on the island many days ago, Silver sensed a discord between them. Sister sensed it too. Something had happened on the mainland, something traumatic that stole Strong from this world.

Silver remembers with chilling clarity the tall upright lying on the ground next to the hill, not far from the river; how the two of them, man and wolf, fixed eyes on each other, and how Silver's kin ran away, for good reason, while Silver could not. Something held him there as it holds him there still, captured in his mind.

Sometimes when Mother goes down to the shore and howls up her grief, Alpha follows and circles her, keen on mating. Silver and Sister follow as well, and watch. With each day noticeably longer than the one before, the time is now.

Where to den?

Most alpha wolf pairs mate every year; some mate only in certain years when conditions are optimal. Some subadults stay with their original pack well into maturity. Others leave in search of distant horizons and a chance to find a mate, to achieve alpha status and to make a new pack of their own. Silver remembers one of the all-black wolves from the feast on the whale, the youngest of the four, a yearling female.

Silver will leave one day. He can feel it. He's made of salmon. And not all salmon follow their noses and return home to their natal stream. They wander. They explore. Within some populations exist a few fish that for reasons unknown and unknowable go their own way. They go elsewhere. It's a good thing they do. A natal stream might be destroyed by a landslide, or by an advancing glacier. If so, and if every salmon returned to find it gone and didn't know where else to go, the entire population might perish without reproducing. But if that run of salmon has a wanderer or two, the race will survive by finding a new natal stream, a new home.

Not all who wander are lost.

Alpha and Mother are wanderers from up north who crossed over mountains and pioneered new ground near a salmon river. Silver is a wanderer who swam to an island. And now, if Alpha and Mother are to mate, the pack will need a den.

After two days of heavy snowfall that forces a few final deer down to the beach, the wolves feast one last time on fat-rich meat and bone marrow to build up their strength for the swim back to the mainland.

Mother chooses the time: dusk on a windless evening, so the entire pack—eight wolves—can come ashore under the cover of twilight but still see where they need to go. Silver and Sister swim shoulder to shoulder, steady and straight. Off to their right, on the mainland, they see the glow of—what? Bright stars fallen to earth? This is what Silver thought when he and his kin first watched the lights appear every night from across the water, on the island. He now knows the lights to be signs of another existence where tall uprights come and go on land and sea, and make strange noises.

The wolves pull themselves ashore wet and exhausted, and quickly run up the beach, over the forelands and into an open forest of spruce, cottonwood, and pine, kicking up snow as they go, moving single file with Mother in the lead and Alpha in the back.

One of the subadults huffs and coughs all that night, with the pack bedded down under a large and generous spruce.

Moose sign is abundant. The bulls will be without antlers.

Silver and Sister, excited to be back, begin to howl up the night until Mother snarls them down. No howling. Not here. Not now.

Stay silent.

And find a place to den.

CHAPTER THIRTY-TWO

Salt

BAD HIP. BAD KNEE. WEAK HEART. Salt is a mess. Crossing the river and setting the traps would be impossible without Abe's help. Yes, Salt knows his eldest son is sullen at times, hostile even. He's also strong. And devoted to his brother Solomon as Paul was to Jesus.

Salt keeps checking his watch. They have to get this done and return in time to Zoom with the Johns Hopkins physician—the doctor with the strange name.

So much to do. First, walk to the river. Not from the end of Menzies River Road as most people do, but from a location farther north, bushwhacking through alder and devil's club, and trudging through deep snow due west of the d'Alene home. Second, cross the river arm in arm with Abe upstream. Third, retrieve the two backpacks loaded with trapping gear they carried through the woods two months ago when Salt fell and bruised his face. And now, fourth, set a string of cables, snares, and leghold traps in a snow track. This final task makes an artist of Salt as he sculpts the snow and covers everything with a delicate gloved hand, all while his son watches. "Okay," he tells Abe, "take the ends of the cables and lock them around those large spruce at both ends of the track. Be careful where you step. When you're done, I'll do a final bit of snow sculpting."

Before leaving, Salt checks the deadfall area where he set the leghold trap. The half-rotten log where he chained it has been snapped off. *Incredible.* The mossy forest floor under the remaining spruce tells a story of epic struggle where an animal, most likely a wolf, maybe two—one trapped, the other free and trying to help the first—dragged the log to the steep riverbank. *And then?* Near as Salt can tell, the log slid downslope and into the river where the wolf, chained to it, was swept away and drowned.

Salt tells Abe to wait at the river and eat more lunch. "I won't be long."

He travels west through deep snow, stops to marvel at the beauty and stillness and peace, and continues on around the south face of Heaven's Hill. As he nears the den he previously excavated, he pauses. No sign of wolves. No sound. He moves on but avoids approaching the den site too close. Snow means that wherever he goes, others can read his movements and history. Snow makes hunting—and being hunted—much easier. The land becomes an open book, one that can work for him but also against him.

The den site appears quiet. Unused.

From his pack, he pulls out the two modified M-44 cyanide bombs. *ULTRA-TOXIC. SODIUM CYANIDE. HANDLE WITH EXTREME CARE*. He touches the pull rings and waxy fuses, and wonders, when the time comes, if he'll really do it.

"Roll in the first bomb, wait one minute, then roll in the second," Jess Cleet told Salt weeks ago in Juneau. "You'll take out the entire pack and won't have to worry about disposing any bodies."

"No gunshots and no gravedigging," added Gary, the political hack. "Once it's done, you'll fill in the den entrance and collect a handsome bonus."

"And take your son to Baltimore to get the medical attention he deserves," added Mr. Raddock.

They all smiled, as if nothing could be better.

TIME TO RECROSS THE RIVER. Salt dreads it.

Tired and cold, he stumbles.

"I've got you, Dad." Abe takes Salt's arm in an iron grip. "Walk stride for stride with me. We need to keep our legs right together."

"Don't go too fast."

"I won't. You're doing great. Just stay focused."

Once across, they sit and rest and remove their chest waders. Abe ties both pair of heavy waders onto the top of his metal-framed backpack, and says, "Tabby told me that Tim and Tia came out here with Kes Nash when she tried to cross the river. She fell in, and they had to pull her to shore with a rope."

Salt straightens up. "When did that happen?"

"I don't know. Not that long ago, I think."

Kes Nash trying to cross this river in winter… why?

"Tabby says they've formed an order of knights, like King Arthur did. It's so stupid." Abe pauses. "Kes is unholy and doesn't know God. She gave that talk at Science Friday about the size of the universe, and another talk about how all the dinosaurs died. She said—"

"Did Tabby say what this order of knights is for?"

"What?"

"The order of knights. What's it for?"

"I don't know, Dad." Abe gets to his feet. "Kes is stupid, remember?" He hoists his pack and begins to walk back home via their secret route through the woods, on the trail he broke through deep snow getting out here. Home is about two miles away.

Salt follows, his head spinning with troublesome thoughts. He's heard that Kes attributes her father's improved condition to wolves along the Menzies River that howl in harmony. *Could this order of knights have something to do with that?*

"Why does it have to be so big?" Abe asks as they huff along, with Salt struggling to keep up. He can't afford to have anything go wrong right now: a sprained knee, a strained hip, his heart flipping into arrhythmia.

"Slow down, Abe. Please."

Abe slows and asks again, agitated this time, "Why does it have to be so big?"

"What, Abe? What are you talking about?"

"The universe. Why does it have to be so big? And dark? Kes said almost all the space between the galaxies and the stars is filled with dark energy or dark matter or something like that, and nobody knows what they are. But God knows, right?"

"I thought Mrs. Cunningham was going to end Science Friday."

Abe shrugs and keeps walking.

"Abe... please. Slower, okay?"

For some crazy reason Salt remembers a bumper sticker he saw on the white van that Chippy and Cap McCall drive: *In the beginning Pink Floyd created God.* The other day Salt ran into the McCalls yet again at Nystad's Mercantile, and ate a hot dog, and heard Chippy tell the crowd that Danny Nash is now singing and playing the guitar every day, and writing new songs, many of them about Alaska; that his voice is softer and raspier than before but somehow still a tenor, so he sounds like Don Henley of the Eagles, meaning "he could sing a shopping list and make it sound great."

Everybody laughed, and Chippy and Cap thanked pretty Berit for yet another hot dog extravaganza.

Salt has heard a lot of talk about the McCalls, that Chippy in particular is more than what meets the eye. Rosie Goodnight says he's a good guy, a little crazy for sure, a knight in search of a joust, a Don Quixote chasing windmills, but still a good guy who went through hell with the Oklahoma Thunderbirds in Afghanistan. One time, Chippy and his crack team tracked down a Taliban terrorist cell but hesitated to confirm a drone strike target because of a school next door. Confirm, said his commander from a thousand miles away, via satellite. Chippy gave a high CDE: Collateral Damage Estimate. We've got women and children in the kill zone, for crying out loud. Inconsequential, said his commander. Confirm now. So, Chippy confirmed. The drone pulverized everything. Women and children died. And Chippy, his heart broken, cried out loud.

Sometimes, late at night, when alone, he still does.

All this according to Rosie.

THE D'ALENE FAMILY gathers around a large computer monitor at nine o'clock at night in a private room in the Strawberry Flats Public Library to Zoom with the Johns Hopkins physician, a woman currently in London, England, where it's six in the morning. Solomon sits front and center in his wheelchair so she can see him and he can see her.

"It's nice to meet you, finally," she says to Solomon in an accent, even though she knows all about him. Juneau's Bartlett Hospital sent her a video of Solomon and a large file of his medical records. She has perfect teeth, olive skin, and long auburn hair. She wears dark, horn-rimmed glasses and a purple-green scarf, and is only thirty-eight (Salt researched her on the internet). She shines with beauty and intelligence.

"Nice to meeeet yoooou toooooo...." Solomon says, rocking in his chair. Hannah has combed his thick hair and dressed him nicely in a collared shirt and tie. The other boys listen intently, as if to a voice from another world.

Her name is Dr. Salama Hamadani. "As you inquired about in an earlier email, Mr. and Mrs. d'Alene," she says, "my given name, Salama, is Arabic for peace and safety. I come from Zanzibar and attended Faraday University of London, where I met my husband, who's Egyptian. We moved to Los Angeles, where I got my MD at UCLA, then to Baltimore, where I got my PhD at Johns Hopkins and did postdoc research in immunology, focusing on muscular dystrophy and other neuro-immunodeficiency diseases. That's where I developed this new clinical trial. Are you with me so far?"

"Yes," Hannah says. "We're with you."

"Where's Zanzibar?" Abe asks, somewhat brusquely.

"It's off the coast of East Africa, near Dar Es Salaam," Dr. Hamadani answers. "And I'm sorry to tell you that's part of the delay right now. I'm still awaiting approval by the FDA. But also, because my husband and I are Muslim, American immigration under this current administration won't let me return to Johns Hopkins."

"But they will eventually, won't they?" Hannah asks.

"Maybe. Meanwhile, Faraday has offered us teaching and research positions. That could actually solve the issue, because time is critical for Solomon."

Salt and Hannah look at each other. Salt turns back to the monitor and asks Dr. Hamadani, "What do you mean, 'solve the issue'?"

"I could operate on Solomon here at Faraday University Medical Center, one of the best facilities in Europe. Best in the world, actually. I've reviewed your son's files, Mr. and Mrs. d'Alene. His current condition aligns with the requirements needed to qualify for the clinical trial I'm leading. But before the stem cell surgery, Solomon will have to undergo weeks of chemotherapy and radiation. You'll lose that magnificent hair of yours, Solomon, and you won't feel well. But it will all grow back. The surgery itself should take only a few hours. If all goes well, you'll have a regenerated immune system."

Nobody says a thing.

"From a legal and ethical perspective," Dr. Hamadani adds, "it's important that I not coerce you into this. Will Solomon's condition improve? It might, and it might not. You'll have to sign many waivers. The surgery will be a clinical trial that's never been done before. You and about a dozen other patients will be the first, Solomon."

"Like Neil Armstrong on the moon," Jericho says.

Solomon rocks and says, "Armstrooong on the mooooooooooon."

"One last thing," Dr. Hamadani says. "As this is a clinical trial, you will not be billed for any of the medical procedures or tests. All you'll need to do is get yourselves to London and back."

Salt gasps and distantly hears Hannah ask, "Did you just say what we think you said?"

"Yes, Mr. and Mrs. d'Alene. There are no guarantees. But I'm going to do everything I can to help your son."

CHAPTER THIRTY-THREE

Kes

WARM IN BED, Kes thumbs her way through a tattered, dog-eared, paperback book Uncle Ty gave her: *A Sand County Almanac*, by Aldo Leopold, the famous conservationist who as a young man watched a fierce green fire die in the eyes of a mother wolf he had just shot. Kes wonders what kind of people would name their son Aldo. *But then, what kind of people name their daughter Kestrel?*

She texts with Julie in Houston, and with Allison and Celia in Lubbock, who text back that the Texas drought is so bad the Rio Grande has stopped flowing through El Paso. *It's all dried up. Really sad*, Celia adds.

Kes replies, *One of the Willynillyville veterans died today.*

O no r u ok?

He was really sick w/ cancer and in pain and wanted to die. He died on a glacier after my uncle took him there in his plane and left him. Crazy, huh? I really liked him.

R u serious?

Yeah.

Crazy for sure.

Kes expects Papa and Rita to show up any minute to discuss the Science Friday meeting with Principal Cunningham, scheduled two days from now, when she hears the phone ring downstairs. Nobody ever calls this late. Kes creeps out of bed and down the hall. She hears Rita say, "Yes, she's still awake. Of course, she's right here." Rita motions the phone to Kes, who's now halfway down the stairs in her pajamas. *Who could it be? Principal Cunningham? Tim?*

"Hello."

"Hi Kes, this is Berit Nystad. I don't know if you know who I am. I work at my uncle's mercantile."

"Yes, I know who you are."

"Oh… good. Well, I know who you are too. I know where you live and that you've heard wolves out at your end of town, and they mean a lot to you because they howled and your dad howled back and that was a big deal for your family because of what happened to him in Afghanistan, and that he's better now. He's a musician again."

"How do you know this?"

"Kona Marks."

"Kona?"

"Yes. He told me about your order of knights… your Knights of the Menzies River. He was excited and tried to recruit me. He's an adorable boy. I think he has a crush on me. I'm twice his age." She chuckles. "Anyway, if you want to keep your order a secret, you need to talk to him."

"Yes, okay… thank you. It's really not a secret. We just—"

"But Kes, you should know something else. I was going to tell your mom this, or maybe your Uncle Tyler. But maybe I should just tell you. I can't talk for long. I don't want these men to hear me or find me."

"What men? Tell me what?"

"A bunch of big equipment landed in town off a Juneau barge tonight, about an hour ago, on the high tide. That never happens. The barges almost always arrive during the daytime…"

Rita blows Kes a kiss as she heads upstairs to join Papa in bed. Kes blows one back and wonders why Berit is telling her about barges from Juneau.

"…but this barge was like a secret operation in a James Bond movie. I saw three big trucks pulling flatbeds loaded with an excavator, a bulldozer, and two huge steel I-beams that I think are used to build bridges. They parked in the gravel lot next to the mercantile, on state of Alaska land. Do you know where I'm talking about?"

"Yes."

"The mercantile was dark. I had already closed up and turned off the lights. I cracked open the back delivery door and heard men talking about extending Menzies River Road to the river and building a bridge, and building more road west from there, and I thought of all the noise, and of you and your family, and how you should know. All of you… you need to know. The men are still out there, tarping over the equipment."

"Thank you, Berit."

"Tucker John and Chippy and Cap are my best tippers, even though I know they don't have a lot of money. They're always funny and irreverent, but also kind. And they tell great stories."

"They're like uncles to me."

"Lucky you. Okay, Kes… I have to hang up now. Bye."

THE NEXT MORNING, riding her bike to school, Kes detours past Nystad's Mercantile. Sure enough, three flatbeds are covered with large tarps tied over what must be the excavator, bulldozer, and steel I-beams.

After school, Kes rides to the end of Menzies River Road and finds nothing suspicious. A foot trail/ski track runs through the snow, west to the river. But that's not unusual. People go out there all the time. Kes thinks about her near drowning and realizes she never wants to go through that again. There must be a better way to cross the river. But not by bridge. Or by road. If somebody builds a road to the Menzies River and a bridge over it, the noise will be awful, like back in Lubbock, where there's always construction. Or in Midland, the city that smells like a gas station because of all the fracking.

That night, Kes struggles with how to tell Papa and Rita and Uncle Ty and everybody else about what Berit said. *How to break the news?*

She doesn't have to.

Taylor shows up for dinner with a wildlife biologist named Mr. Robb who works for Conservation International in Washington, DC. He's staying at Dave's Make Your Own Damn Breakfast while he works with biologists at Crystal Bay National Marine Reserve. After some fun conversation around a large lasagna made by Rita and Jeannie, Taylor says, "We got an interesting email today at the marine reserve. It was an announcement saying the state of Alaska will soon be open for business through the governor's new Roads to Resources program, part of which is to develop coalbed methane in more than twenty areas around the state."

"And?" Uncle Ty says. He can tell she hasn't gotten to the worst of it.

"The West Menzies River area of Strawberry Flats is on the list," Taylor says. "The official announcement will go public on Friday. The governor expects full cooperation from the feds."

"Coalbed methane? Here?" Uncle Ty shakes his head. "Impossible. The geology is all wrong."

"I have news," Kes says. They all turn to look at her: Papa, Rita, Kipper (on Papa's lap), Uncle Ty, Taylor, Mr. Robb, Jeannie, and Grandpa. And just then, Tucker John comes in looking for a wine opener.

"A wine opener?" Uncle Ty asks him. Tucker John and the McCalls only drink beer.

"Yep," Tucker John says. "Chippy fixed Paul and Rosie Goodnight's kitchen door and wouldn't accept any pay, so they gave him a bottle of Chardonnay. We thought about watering the plants with it, or putting it in Sarge's radiator. But then Cap said we should drink it because that's what people do with wine, right?"

Laughter ripples around the table until Kes tells them everything Berit told her.

Nobody says a word. Even little Kip manages to be quiet as Papa moves him off his lap, gets up, and walks over to his Martin by the wood-burning stove.

Kes talks about her Knights of the Menzies River; she says adults are welcome to join. She recites the line from Bill McKibben and hears her own voice crack with fear.

Again, nobody speaks. Everybody appears lost in thought. Daunted. Afraid.

Papa softly fingerpicks his Martin.

"I know what can stop the whole thing," Mr. Robb finally says.

Everybody turns to look at him. He has dark eyes and wavy brown hair. "Wolves."

"Wolves?" Uncle Ty says. "The wolves across the river?"

"Yes. Odds are they're a separate subspecies of coastal wolves that eat salmon. We've found similar wolves along the British Columbia coast and on Prince of Wales Island. If we can get them listed as endangered, or even threatened, that will shut down any development on the west side of that river."

Uncle Ty shakes his head. "Not with this president and our current governor. Until the political landscape changes, the wolves are in jeopardy. It's that simple."

"Environmental groups have thrown lawsuits at this sort of thing," Mr. Robb responds.

"The state hasn't even held a public hearing," Tucker John says, "and they're already going to start building the road? How can they do that?"

"The state of Alaska loves to build roads," Uncle Ty says. "If building a road through the Grand Canyon or the Sistine Chapel created jobs and paid well, they'd do it."

Uncle Ty has a thing for the Grand Canyon. When he first heard that a developer wanted to build a tramway from the rim of the canyon down to the Colorado River, he said: "Anybody who thinks he can improve the Grand Canyon belongs in Las Vegas with a cigar in his mouth and a joker up his sleeve." And now, as Papa sets aside his Martin and goes up to bed without saying goodnight to anyone, and Rita follows with little Kip, Uncle Ty puts his head in his hands and softly says, "We can't let this happen. It will ruin everything."

Taylor gets to her feet, walks behind him, and begins to rub his shoulders. Kes thinks Uncle Ty looks older these days, at least in his face and hands. He's beginning to look like Grandpa. He'll declare war if he has to. The Menzies River will become a battlefield. Kes can feel it.

And the wolves? What will happen to them?

Later, when she tells Uncle Ty more about her Knights of the Menzies River, he looks at her with fierce resolve and says, "Excalibur, the sword in the stone, right?"

"Right."

"Poor King Arthur. He was noble and tragic at the same time, wasn't he?"

"Yes."

"Who are your knights so far? How many?"

Kes tells him, and lists others she's certain will join.

"Good. Train them up and make them tough. I'll do the same with my own recruits. We'll fight these fascists at every turn... you'll be my Patton. Now, off to bed with you."

"I love you, Uncle Ty."

"I love you too, dear girl."

THAT NIGHT, KES HAS TROUBLE FALLING ASLEEP. She looks again at the book by Aldo Leopold and thinks about the fierce green fire. She opens her window to let in the cool air. She thinks about Mike, how everybody seems to reflect on him, but nobody talks about him, not to her anyway. Except Rita, who said earlier as she gently stroked Kes's hair, "It was his choice, honey. Your uncle put retractable skis on Claire and put

Mike in the copilot seat, and gave him a grand tour, flying him over the glaciers. Mike was very sick and didn't want to die in pain, or waste away, or be a burden to anyone. You know how he loved the glaciers, right? From your plane ride north?"

"He loved how blue and beautiful they were."

"That's right. And how they shaped mountains and carved inlets and fjords."

Kes nodded. "He liked to quote John Muir about softly freezing in a glacier, what a noble death it would be."

"Your Uncle Ty gave Mike the opportunity to die on his own terms, and he did."

"Uncle Ty told me down in Brooke, in San Antonio, that we should live our entire lives in preparation to die with dignity, and without fear."

"Your uncle is a Buddhist, of sorts."

"Not Uncle Charles, though, is he? He's a devout Christian."

"You've got that right."

"Is Uncle Charles afraid to die?"

Rita had to think about this. "I don't know. He might be. Many people are."

"Are you?"

Rita smiled. "Sure, a little."

"I hope my first mom wasn't afraid to die."

"Your papa says she was a courageous woman, like you'll be one day, I bet. Why not try to get some sleep, okay?"

Minutes later, Celia texted Kes and told her that Allison's older sister's boyfriend got arrested for breaking into somebody's house.

KES THRASHES IN BED. When she finally falls asleep, she dreams crazy dreams about Texas and drought and terrible heat, and Papa wearing Cheetah Legs and running with dogs and cats and farm animals; Mike too, with a gray goat, running past crowds of panicked people who throw belongings into their cars and trucks and SUVs. A man yells to another man that all the churches and trees are on fire. There's no more water. Helicopters clatter overhead, carrying drop bags of fire retardant. A boy zips by on a motocross dirt bike. A truck speeds by, piled high with possessions. When it turns a corner too fast, a big flat-screen cartwheels off the back and shatters across the street. Another truck runs over it.

The dirt bike boy comes back, and stops.

Get on, he says.

Kes stands there, unable to move. She sees Allison sitting on a nearby porch, pigeon-toed, her knees together and her head down as she texts on her phone.

Kes calls to her: Allison, you have to leave.

The boy yells: The oil refinery is on fire and about to blow.

Kes asks him: Can you take my friend with you on your bike? She nods over at Allison, who's still texting, her thumbs dancing on her phone.

Yes, the boy says. What about you?

I'm okay. Please, take my friend.

A raven swoops down, calling... Caw, caw... Caw, caw... Caw, Kes... Kes—

"Kes...?" Rita says. "Kes, honey, wake up. It's time to get up. Time for school. It's way too cold in here. You need to shut this window when you sleep."

"What?"

"You were dreaming, sleepyhead. You've got a big day today, remember? The afterschool meeting with Principal Cunningham? Let's go. Chop, chop."

"What time is it?"

"Quarter after eight. I let you sleep as long as I could."

"What's that smell?"

"Tucker John's downstairs making you his sourdough pancakes with blueberries."

"Really?"

"You'd better hurry before Grandpa eats them all."

"Thanks, Mom."

Rita pauses on her way out... turns, and smiles.

"Are we going to be okay?" Kes asks. "All of us, I mean, here in Willynillyville?"

"I don't know, honey. I only know that I'll do whatever it takes to keep your papa well, and continue to make him better. If this place goes bonkers and turns into a war zone, and your papa suffers because of it, then, yes... we'll go back to Texas."

ABE D'ALENE STANDS LIKE A SEQUOIA in the doorway to Principal Cunningham's office and says to Kes, "I know about you and your stupid Knights of the Menzies River."

"You're blocking my way, Abe."

"Mrs. Cunningham knows too."

"Because you told her?"

"Everybody knows."

"You're still blocking my way."

Abe steps aside, and Kes walks in and takes a chair as previously instructed by Mrs. Goodnight, the school secretary. Kes taps her sternum to keep her heart calm.

Breathe.

Crazy Abraham. The other day Kes overheard Jerry say that Abe wants to join the Army and his mom is upset about it.

Papa and Rita arrive a minute later, followed by Kes's teacher, Mrs. Carry, who knows Papa and Rita, and engages them with lively banter. Papa looks at ease, but not Rita, who crosses her legs one way, then the other.

Finally, Principal Cunningham breezes in and shakes Rita's and Papa's hands after they stand to greet her. She thanks them for coming, then sits at her big desk and apologizes for being late. They talk about Kes's academic performance, which Mrs. Carry says is excellent, adding, "Kes is a strong student."

"We are in agreement thus far," Principal Cunningham says. "Now, let's talk about Science Friday, and Kes"—she looks right at Kes—"I want to explore your decision to talk about subjects that make other students uncomfortable."

"Uncomfortable?" Rita says, almost as a challenge.

"I've had complaints from their parents," Principal Cunningham says as she puts her elbows on her desk, with one elbow touching a free-standing Jesus-on-the-cross statue, and the other near a framed photo of two little dogs with pink ribbons in their hair. She tents her hands together under her chin and says to Rita, "Your girl talks about the size of the universe and the age of the Earth and the death of dinosaurs in a way that makes other students nervous and, yes… uncomfortable. I cannot allow that."

"If I may say something," Mrs. Carry interjects. "Education is not about making people comfortable. It's about challenging students. It's about pushing their boundaries and waking them up."

"I know what education is, Elizabeth," Principal Cunningham says. "I have a master's degree in education."

"I have a question," Papa says, quietly.

"Yes. What is it?"

"Just how old is Earth?"

Principal Cunningham blinks, as if to absorb what he just said.

"Give or take fifty million years," Papa adds with a smile.

Principal Cunningham sits up straight to increase her height. "You surprise me, Mr. Nash."

Papa chuckles softly. "I surprise myself sometimes."

"Thank you for your service, by the way... in Afghanistan."

"Kind of you to say," Rita replies. "But that war was a huge waste of lives and money, like our invasion of Iraq. For the cost of those wars, every student in the United States could get a free college education."

"And become a better critical thinker," adds Mrs. Carry.

Principal Cunningham leans back and says, "I think we're getting off subject here."

"I don't," Rita says. "I think we're right on subject."

"We appreciate your concern for our daughter," Papa finally says to Principal Cunningham as he stands and prepares to leave. Lately, he's started to play practical jokes again, the way he used to back in Lubbock. And the music, of course. The other day he talked about making a new album. "So," he adds, "about Science Friday. Kes loves it and works hard at it. And from what she's told us, many of her fellow students look forward to it."

"Are you going to end it?" Kes blurts out, surprising herself.

"That depends," Principal Cunningham says. "I'll need to think about it."

Mrs. Carry turns and says, "Kes, would you please go to the classroom and bring me your poster?"

Kes jumps up and dashes out. She made the poster herself and is excited to show it to Papa and Rita. In the hallway, she finds Solomon alone. School ended half an hour ago. *Solomon is never alone. Why now?*

"Hi Solomon."

"Keeeeeeesssss the beeeeesssst." He rocks in his wheelchair and grins.

Out a window, Kes sees Mrs. d'Alene, a thin, almost sickly looking woman, at her special red van—the one with the side ramp for Sol's wheelchair—talking with Jerry and Joshua. And Abe walking back toward the school, no doubt to get Solomon.

"I'd love to talk, Sol, but I have to go. It's great seeing you."

"Yoooooouuu toooooo..."

Kes returns, poster in hand, just in time to hear Papa respond to a question Principal Cunningham must have asked. "Oh... let me see. My favorite place of worship? I'd have to say the Santa Elena Canyon on the Rio Grande. Or Abbey Road Studios, in St. John's Wood, Northwest London." He turns to Rita. "What about you?"

"Easy. That patch of nagoonberries and wild strawberries out beyond the end of Menzies River Road, where we had lunch and watched the mama moose and her two calves." Rita is on her feet too, ready to leave with Papa.

Only then does Kes notice two more adults in Principal Cunningham's office, people she recognizes from Pastor Anderson's chapel. They must have arrived while Kes went to retrieve the poster.

"You know what fascinates me?" Papa says softly to no one in particular. "You take a group of kindergarteners and it's beautiful because they're filled with questions: Why is the grass green? How old is the sun? Why do trees lose their leaves? And so on. But in twelfth grade, those same students have none of that same curiosity." Papa turns to Principal Cunningham. "Why is that?"

She stares at him, her mouth slightly open.

One of the two new adults, a man in a nice, collared shirt and tie, says, "I think they're still curious. They're just self-conscious about asking questions."

"Yes, exactly," Principal Cunningham says.

Kes realizes then: the two adults must be school board members, brought in to support the principal. Kes hands the poster to Mrs. Carry, who unrolls it as everybody watches. Mrs. Carry says, "Each student in my class made a collage of a favorite person, favorite quote, and favorite place. This is Kes's."

It shows Aldo Leopold standing before a forest, and says: *Of what avail are forty freedoms without a blank spot on the map?*

Principal Cunningham studies it with a strange expression.

Breathe.

"Aldo Leopold is the ecologist who saw the fierce green fire," Kes says. "More than one hundred years ago... in the eyes of the dying mother wolf. It really touched him and changed his life. It changed a lot of things."

Mrs. Goodnight pokes her head in and says, "Your next appointment is here."

Principal Cunningham rises to her feet and addresses Papa and Rita:

"There's one more thing. Your daughter is organizing a group of students into an order of some kind, something I believe is a bad idea."

"Oh?" Papa says.

"Every student at this school needs to know their proper place... to one day play an important role in a productive society."

"Why assume that our daughter's order is counterproductive?" Papa asks.

Principal Cunningham stares at him.

"Four and a half billion years," Papa adds softly.

Principal Cunningham continues to stare.

"The age of Earth," Papa says, "give or take fifty million years."

Kes watches Principal Cunningham's face turn white.

"All of this according to my brother," Papa adds. "He's the geologist in the family... the one who thinks in epochs the way other people think in weeks, months, and years. Anyway." Papa reaches across the table and shakes Principal Cunningham's hand. "Thank you for your time. We'll await your important decision and take our daughter home now."

CHAPTER THIRTY-FOUR

Silver

MOTHER IS PREGNANT. The den is welcoming and warm, with the entire pack inside curled up together as one.

The wolves found it—the beginnings of it—many days ago on the west flank of the long tapering hill near the river, where much earlier Silver, Sister, and three subadults had seen a tall upright lying on the ground, staring back at them.

Initially suspicious of the den's crude opening, Silver later joined his kin to dig it out. They first tunneled in at a slight down angle, then up to where they excavated the sleeping and birthing chamber, designed to hold their collective body heat.

Every time Silver approaches the den, he stops, listens, and looks around to let the wind twitch his ears, the light sharpen his eyes, the shadows come into focus. He and Sister often bed down near the entrance to read every little verse of nature, and only then, when satisfied that all appears well, do they enter. This is the first den Silver and Sister have occupied since the den of their birth, far to the north, and they savor it, sleeping side by side.

Silver has learned much from Alpha and Mother, and the subadults. But also, and most important, he's aware that others defer to him ever since his pioneering swim to the island.

Alpha now shows some gray in his muzzle and moves with a slight limp.

One of the subadults huffs and coughs constantly since the cold swim back to the mainland.

Silver knows his family is never more comfortable than when they're bedded down together in their den. And never more vulnerable.

Every security comes with a hidden threat.

Every strength has its vulnerabilities.

Silver's littermate, Strong, was just that—strong. And often careless. Now he's gone.

One wrong decision. One mistake. One misstep. One kick to the head. One long swim through water too cold, waves too high. One tough fight with another wolf. One bad wound or broken tooth or infected eye. One fall into a crevasse or off a cliff. One swipe from a powerful bear. One icy, bitter night. One tall upright. One day like any other, until one thing goes wrong and it's over.

This is why Silver watches, listens, waits.

THE HUGE BULL MOOSE remains standing out there somewhere, eating willow, bedding down where even the ravens can't find him. He's undefeated, though not without scars. The pack has encountered him three times, and retreated each time.

Moose have it all. Massive antlers. Large bones. Powerful muscles. Surprising agility. High knees that propel powerful kicking legs even when they stand in deep, heavy drifts. High shoulders and flanks that are difficult to attack and disable. Long noses that smell everything. Big ears that hear everything.

Twice, the pack has brought down smaller moose.

Their trails run everywhere through the melting snow as the days lengthen and warm.

One moose trail, near the river, not far from the den, runs through snow between two stands of spruce. Silver and Sister found it many days ago, but hesitated to travel it. Something wasn't right.

Now, they return under the cover of another stand of spruce, and bed down side by side to watch and wait. Again. Something isn't right. More waiting. Soon they hear a high-pitched sound coming from above the treetops. In a neighboring stand of spruce, at one end of the suspicious trail, they see movement. Two tall uprights. Silver freezes. Something about them strikes fear into his heart, a distant something… intuitive and undeniable, a genetic memory of some kind, passed down from his ancestors. The ones who survived.

Sister gets to her feet, ready to run. Silver softly growls her down.

Stay. Don't move. Don't panic. Don't be seen.

One mistake is all it takes.

One mistake and it's over.

CHAPTER THIRTY-FIVE

Salt

SALT INTENDS TO COLLECT ALL THE TRAPS in a couple hours and be home by late afternoon. He's done trapping. Done waging war on wild animals that have done nothing to him. Done killing. Forever. But first, after another demanding river crossing that would have pulled him under were it not for Abe, it's time for lunch. Abe is on his third bagel with cream cheese and turkey jerky when they hear a strange sound. Not a plane. More like a large mechanical mosquito.

"What's that?" Abe asks.

The sound comes from the sky beyond the trees that provide them cover. Abe hustles to his feet and walks toward the strange sound, out from under the tall spruce.

"Stop," Salt says sharply.

"What?"

"It's a drone."

Abe assumes a crouched position and pulls his hands into fists, as if ready to fight. "Really?"

"Yes. Get back here." Salt remembers Mr. Raddock's demand for secrecy.

"What do we do, Dad?"

"We need to break camp, be invisible, and get out of here. Now."

Dear God, forgive me for ever getting myself and my family into this.

TWO DAYS AGO, Salt flew into Juneau to meet Mr. Raddock and Gary the political hack in the same back corner of the same restaurant to tell them he was done. He's no longer a trapper. "Don't let them change your mind,"

Hannah had told him. "I love you, husband. And I'm proud of you."

After Salt laid it all out, Mr. Raddock asked without emotion, "Why?"

"The stress," Salt replied. "Trapping has become too hard on me." *And I don't need the money.* "The river crossing is dangerous. I have a bad knee, a bad hip, and a bad heart. I'll have to cross it just one more time to get my traps."

"That river will have a bridge over it in three months," Gary said as he finished his vodka tonic and motioned the same waitress over to order another.

Salt told the two men he appreciated their trust and wished them well without saying a word about what they'd paid him, afraid that if he did, Mr. Raddock would ask for a refund.

Late one night, after a follow-up phone conversation with Dr. Hamadani, Salt and Hannah had penciled out a trip to London, what it would cost and when they could go. If either Salt or Hannah went with Solomon and took another son for assistance, and the other three d'Alenes stayed home, they could afford it and have Solomon home and mending—maybe even improved—in time for his birthday in August.

"How many wolves have you trapped?" Gary asked.

"One for sure. Maybe more."

"Are they denning?"

"I don't know."

"Did you dig a den like we talked about?"

"Yes, the beginnings of one."

"Then forget the trapping. Just get back over there and gas the whole pack."

Salt was afraid Gary would be difficult. "I can't cross the river anymore. I have a bad—"

"Yes, yes," Gary said. "You have a bad knee and hip and heart. But if you have to cross one more time to get your traps, then find out what the wolves are up to and gas the whole pack at once, at night. Job done. Collect your traps and a handsome bonus."

"I can't do that."

"But you said you would." Gary leaned into Salt from across the table. "You're a man of your word, are you not?"

"Yes. As often as I can be. Absolutely."

"And you're a devout Christian, correct?"

"Yes, but that should have no—"

"Genesis. Dominion over all living things. As a man of your word, Mr. d'Alene. Your task is clear."

"Genesis is from the Old Testament, written before the—"

"Exactly. So, finish the job. Gas the pack."

FATHER AND SON hold still in their little pocket of forest, sitting against a massive tree trunk under the cover of tall Sitka spruce while the drone moves overhead in a slow, circuitous manner, no doubt taking inventory of everything in view. At one point, as the drone can be heard going away, Salt begins to pack up.

"Who's operating it?" Abe asks in a low voice.

"I don't know. Let's hope nobody shows up and starts looking around and steps into one of those nine-inch leghold traps."

"Except Kes Nash," Abe says bitterly.

"You don't mean that."

Abe shrugs.

"Look at me, Abraham, and tell me you don't mean that."

"All right... I don't mean it."

"She's not a bad person."

"She's not a good person either."

"Because she thinks knowledge is more important than faith? You're going to have to make peace with that."

"Faith sees God, Father; intellect does not. I've been reading about this preacher in Alabama who says a free thinker is Satan's slave."

"Reading about him where? On the internet?"

Abe shrugs again.

"Is that where you read this... on the internet, where anybody can write anything and say it's gospel or the truth?"

"Thousands of people attend his church. He's like a rock star preacher who—"

"Shh... listen."

The drone returns, louder this time. Lower.

"I hate this, Dad. Let's get out of here."

The drone drops down over the snowy track that Salt and Abe built to deceive the wolves. The track that's filled with traps. Traps they intended to remove. But now?

Quickly, father and son pack up and move to the far side of the stand of spruce. While the drone is low on the other side, the two make a run for it, out into the open, headed for that damn river. The snow is not as deep as it was a week ago, but it's heavy and wet. Salt stumbles and falls onto all fours, and feels a shot of pain from his knee. He picks himself up, continues on, and falls again, this time face first, pulled down by his big pack. Abe is gone, moving like a deer, headed for the river where they've crossed the last two times, a couple miles north of where most people cross. For a moment, Salt cannot move. He lies in the granular snow, trying to breathe, his heart jackhammering. He feels inept, such a failure. *Hannah begged me not to trap again. And I did. Mr. Raddock told me to trap alone. And I did not. And now Abraham, my eldest, the boy who saved me on the Minto Flats, will soon be a man. An angry man, by all appearances. Dear God, why?*

The day after the family had Zoomed with Dr. Hamadani, Salt heard Abe joking upstairs with Jericho and Joshua about changing her first name from Salama to Salami. "You know?" Abe said. "Doctor Sausage? Doctor Lunchmeat?" They all laughed.

Salt hung his head.

And now Abe comes from nowhere, lifts Salt from the snow, takes his pack, and half carries him to the river. "The traps are still back there, Dad," he says, huffing.

"Leave them."

"Really?"

"Yes, just get me back across this river. Now. Please. Take me home."

CHAPTER THIRTY-SIX

Kes

MR. ROBB, THE SUPERCOOL WILDLIFE BIOLOGIST, operates the drone that's about eighty feet off the ground and more than a mile away. Kes and the others gather around him, next to the raging river, to see the images it sends onto the small-screen live feed. "Look at that," he says. "No wild animal made that track. Let's go down for a closer look."

He toggles the controls of what he calls the Quad—short for Quadcopter, because the battery-powered drone has four propellers and a built-in camera. As the suspicious animal track comes into detail, Kes stares. She's supposed to be glassing across the river with her new Nikons, the binoculars the Poker Pack gave her last Christmas. But she's mesmerized by the image from the Quad. As are the others: Papa, Captain Don, and Taylor, plus E. J. And the Knights of the Menzies River, some of them anyway: Melissa, Emily, and Kona. Tim and Tia had said they'd be here, but they never showed.

It unnerves Kes—embarrasses her, even—to see the river again, its willful current fortified by snowmelt, shifting between hypothermic blue and a silty gray.

Mr. Robb brings the drone down to forty feet and finds multiple tracks in all directions, some made by moose and wolves, no doubt, others that could be manmade. "I'm pretty certain this one track was created by people to attract wolves as a travel corridor through deep snow," Mr. Robb says. "And I'm pretty certain it contains hidden traps. Whoever did it probably used the trees for cover and crossed the river north of here to get back to Strawberry Flats."

"Or they're still out there setting more traps," Captain Don says.

Kes feels a thud in her chest. *We have to stop them.*

"Let's go," Captain Don says. "It's time to cross this river and do what has to be done. Operation Free Wolf, right, Kes?"

"Right."

AT FIRST, OPERATION FREE WOLF WAS TOP SECRET as Kes recruited her knights and found willing veterans in Willynillyville. Uncle Ty heard about it—he hears about everything—and wanted to be involved, but had to work with Zorro on the *Cinnamon Girl* and run errands with Tucker John, Chippy, and Cap. He told Kes, "If you go over there looking for traps, be careful. Take Don and put him in charge. Take your papa too."

That alerted Rita, who insisted that every parent of every kid involved had to know and give their permission.

"And there's this," Uncle Ty added. "Alaska state law says trapping is legal, while springing or removing another person's set trap is illegal."

"That's not fair," Kes remarked.

"Fair?" Uncle Ty said with his pirate grin.

"Life isn't fair," Kes recited, "and it's unfair that it isn't fair."

"That's right, my young apprentice. You've been reading Edward Abbey."

"And Aldo Leopold. And Rachel Carson."

"Good girl."

Later, when they were alone at home, Rita said to Kes, "Can your papa do this?"

"Cross the river? Yeah, I think so. Captain Don and E. J. have a plan to make it easy."

"Easy?"

"Well, I mean… not so dangerous."

Rita took Kes's hand in hers and said, "You know, honey, when I fell in love with your papa, how he sang to me and played the guitar, I fell in love with you too. His charming and feisty little girl. Did you know that? You really did it to me."

"Did what?"

"Stole my heart."

"I can't really remember my first mom… my birth mom. It makes me sad."

"You were only five. And now look at you. You're a teenager, all grown up, trying to save a pack of wolves, maybe even save the world someday."

"The Earth is on fire, Mom. That's what Greta Thunberg says. Mrs. Carry too. Species are going extinct way too fast. The oceans are rising and getting acidic and too warm. Kids my age are protesting everywhere. Remember that girl who came to Lubbock because she was part of a lawsuit against the US government for not addressing climate change? All of her friends back in Louisiana said she was unpatriotic, and they left her."

"Are you afraid the same thing could happen to you?"

"Not really. Not here."

"I heard somebody say that climate change is the new Holocaust."

"Uncle Ty says it's different. With the Holocaust, people had to commit evil acts. With climate change, all we need to do is nothing… just continue business as usual."

Rita looked away, deep in thought, her hair pulled back to reveal new caribou antler earrings gifted to her by Jeannie. Worry creased her brow. "It's not easy, Kes, to change business as usual. It's hard. It frightens people. It threatens them."

"Yeah, I know."

"Promise me you'll be careful and you'll listen to Captain Don."

"I promise. Are we going to leave here? Are we going to go back to Texas?"

Rita took a deep breath. "I don't know, honey. Your papa is much better these days. More relaxed and rested. Happier, really. He's a musician again. And now you've recruited him into your order of knights. Pretty amazing, right?"

"And he's writing new songs."

"Yes, he is."

Kes takes a deep breath and looks away.

"What is it, honey? Something else is on your mind."

"Julie says my birth mom died because she was drunk. Is that true?"

"When did Julie tell you this?"

"Back in Terlingua, when we all camped together. She didn't tell me. She just asked. She said that's what her dad said, and she wanted to know if it was true."

"Your Uncle Charles… I don't like that man."

"Is it true?"

"I shouldn't be the one to tell you."

"It's okay."

"No, it's not. You need to know the truth, but I can't be the one to tell you."

"Who then? Papa?"

"No. Your Uncle Ty. He—"

"And my grandparents... my birth mom's parents... why don't they ever call me or write to me?"

"Oh, honey, they will one day. It's hard, and complicated, and not my place to say. Ask your Uncle Ty. He's a good man... a very good man, actually. He'll tell you."

"Really? He will?"

"Yes, in time... I think he will. Just remember, everybody has their challenges and demons. That doesn't make them bad people."

Kes thought for a moment, and looked down to see her hand holding Rita's. They never held hands back in Texas. "You know," Kes finally said, "I don't really miss her anymore. My birth mom. Maybe I should, but I don't. Is that okay?"

Rita—no, Mom—hugged her and said, "Yes, it's okay. You're a big girl now, living a big life, tackling big issues, loving not just other people but the whole vibrant, imperiled world, from wolves to whales to chickadees and bees. I'm so proud of you." Tears stood in Mom's eyes. "You're the future. Don't let anybody take it away from you. Go cross that river and save your wolves."

KES AND HER FRIENDS WATCH, fascinated, as Captain Don and E. J. tie a length of rope to a come-along that's cabled to a massive cottonwood above the raging river. They wade the swift current, uncoiling the rope as they go. The water roils off their chest waders. One-third of the way across, and again at two-thirds, the two men tie a loop knot in the main rope. It's all confusing to Kes, but they seem to know what they're doing. Once across, they tie the rope to a huge spruce on the far shore. Mr. Robb, back at the cottonwood, cranks on the come-along to cinch the rope tight, like a cable that rises above the rushing water. E. J. is busy on the far side, walking upriver. When he returns with Captain Don, Kes sees the ingenuity of it all. The main rope now has two stabilizing ropes—what Captain Don calls "cavalettis"—tied into the loops, holding it firm from upriver positions. Operation Free Wolf can now cross as a unit, each person with their right hand on the main rope, and left hand on the shoulder of the person in front. E. J. tests it and leads them across, with Kes third, right behind Papa, who does great. She's amazed at the difference the rope makes, how the cavalettis keep it from sagging downriver under the strain of everybody holding on. The others follow, dressed in their chest waders, with Captain Don last, carrying Kona on his back.

They all high-five each other on the west side, and continue on.

Kes feels like she's in a new land—a world of wolves.

Papa beams. He looks like he could climb a mountain.

Using GPS waypoints established by the drone, Mr. Robb leads them to the long, narrow, suspicious snow track. Under a nearby huge spruce they drop their packs and hold still. Everybody is excited but apprehensive. Captain Don reconnoiters for ten minutes and returns. "Okay," he says. "Nobody gets hurt today, right?"

Silence.

"Right?" Captain Don asks again.

"Right," Kes says with a few others.

"I can't hear you," Captain Don says. "Nobody gets hurt today, right?"

"RIGHT!"

"Good. This spot here, in this thirty-foot radius, is our designated base camp and hangout area and kitchen. Beyond here, we walk only where I say we walk. Behind that tree over there with the big mossy branch is the bathroom. From here, you go straight there and straight back. No wandering or snooping around. Traps could be anywhere. We drink before we're thirsty, eat before we're hungry, and rest before we're tired. Nobody walks in the suspicious snow track ahead of Mr. Robb. We get this done right and get home feeling happy and accomplished. Are you with me?"

He requires that everybody look him in the eye and says, "Yes."

Kona salutes and says, "Yes, sir!"

The others laugh.

Mr. Robb finds a thin cable tied to a spruce and pulls it up. Sure enough, it parallels the long, narrow track under the snow. Tied to it are shorter cables connected to four snares and five leghold traps, also just below the surface, artfully placed, with their jaws open. Mr. Robb and E. J. dig them clear with small shovels. Everybody stares.

"What do we do now?" Emily asks.

"We spring them," Mr. Robb says. "With a stick."

"Do it," Captain Don tells him. As the others stand back, Emily and Melissa pull out their phones. "No photos," Captain Don says. "Put those back. I don't want to see any of this on Instagram, Twitter, Facebook, or whatever. No social media. And no gossip. This is a covert operation, not a school picnic. Understood?"

"Understood," they all answer.

Mr. Robb pokes the foot pad. *Whack*, the trap snaps shut.

"Look at that," Kes says. "It didn't break the stick."

"The jaws are set about three-eighths of an inch apart," Mr. Robb says, "so they'll trap a wolf above his ankle and hold him. If the jaws slammed all the way they'd cut off his foot and he'd escape."

"So, the wolf has to wait until the trappers return?" Emily asks.

"Yes."

"And then?"

"The trappers shoot it."

"Your turn," Captain Don says to Emily.

She shakes her head.

Kona steps up and says, "I'll do it." And he does. Cool as a cucumber.

Kes snaps the third trap. Emily and Melissa together snap the fourth and fifth, both holding the stick. Melissa still jumps each time a trap snaps shut, her eyes huge, hands shaking. When it's finished, she walks over and hugs Kes. Emily does the same. Soon the threesome form a tight embrace, fighting back tears.

MR. ROBB FINDS HIS DRONE right where he parked it by GPS, on the snow next to the stand of spruce. While the others eat their lunches, he sends it back up.

Papa hands Kes some carrots. She hands him some jerky. He offers her a drink from his water bottle. She takes it and leans into him, and makes a mental note to offer him some of her own water before they recross the river. The lunch scene is strangely quiet, with nobody telling stories or jokes, or sharing local gossip. Kes looks forward to Pastor Anderson's sermon tomorrow and hopes to see Tim and Tia and Berit; to quietly tell them about springing the traps.

At one point during lunch, Melissa says to nobody in particular, "I can't believe we did what we just did."

Nobody responds.

Even Kona is quiet, reflective.

They all hear the drone return, and soon Mr. Robb enters into their little forested lunch area and says, "I think I just found a den."

"A what?" E. J. asks.

"A wolf den… their home… for the whole pack."

Kes jumps to her feet, ready to go. Melissa, Emily, and Kona too. None of them have ever seen a wild wolf.

Mr. Robb looks at Captain Don and says, "I don't think we should approach it. Wolves will abandon a den if they feel threatened or compromised in any way."

"Where is it?" Papa asks in his soft voice.

"Not far from here. Around on the other side of that hill, the west side, at its base, under some alder and spruce. It's a good spot, with deep tracks coming and going out in the surrounding snowy areas. If I were a wolf, especially a pregnant female, I'd be happy to live there, with abundant moose and salmon nearby. It takes a fish to feed a forest."

"When will she give birth?" E. J. asks.

"Probably in April. Maybe May. Hard to say."

"Time to pack up and go," Captain Don announces. He says the traps will stay in the woods, piled up with the cables. They're private property, after all. Theft is a crime.

As they leave to head home, walking single file through the snow with Captain Don in the lead, Kes hangs back, takes one of the heavy leghold traps from the pile, and puts it in her pack.

She then hurries to catch up.

"IT TAKES A FISH TO FEED A FOREST?" E. J. asks Mr. Robb at the back of the line. "I don't get it. What's it supposed to mean?"

"It's textbook ecology on how everything is interconnected," Mr. Robb says. "It was first observed with bears in Alaska and British Columbia."

"And now wolves?"

"Yep. A salmon hatches in freshwater and swims out to sea and spends most of its life there, in the open ocean, in this case the North Pacific. It returns years later to the stream of its origin, to spawn and die. But before dying, some salmon are caught by bears or wolves and pulled out of a river and partially eaten and left to rot on the forest floor at the base of a tree, or in a stand of alder or willow."

"And when the salmon rots," Kes says as she catches up from behind, "it feeds the trees because the roots pick up the marine isotopes that were in the salmon."

"That's right," Mr. Robb says, carrying his drone. "And later, when a bird or a moose feeds on the willow, they pick up those same isotopes and nutrients. Everything is healthier and more robust."

"That blows my mind," E. J. says.

"If these wolves show a significant range of not just salmon-derived nutrients but of marine isotopes, as I suspect they will," Mr. Robb adds, "and if their numbers fall to critical levels, it will be easier to get them listed as threatened or endangered. And that could shut down any development near this river."

"But if we don't have the right politicians in office," Kes says, "it will never happen, right?"

"Well…" Mr. Robb says cryptically. "We'll see about that."

"Hey Kes," E. J. asks, "how do you know all this science stuff?"

"Science Friday, E. J. I'll invite you next time, if Mrs. Cunningham doesn't cancel it."

Pastor Anderson announces that his sermon is going to be "a little out of the ordinary again today."

Kes smiles, thinking, *Oh good, another story.*

Jeannie sits next to her, one hand on Skydog. It's the Sunday before the public testimony on drilling for coalbed methane out west of town, and Kes can feel the tension every bit as much as she felt the shoulder straps of her pack dig into her only yesterday, heavy with the stolen trap. *I'm a thief.*

The chapel is packed.

The sermon goes like this: On this day, March 15, in the year 44 BC, Julius Caesar was murdered on the Senate steps in Rome. This created a division of power that resolved itself with great bloodshed thirteen years later in the Battle of Actium between the strategic and diplomatic Marc Antony and the cunning and ruthless Gaius Octavius, Julius Caesar's great-nephew and adopted son and heir. All day the great battle roared. Marc Antony held the upper hand until the final hours when things turned, and Octavius prevailed. He became emperor, some said a god, named Augustus, and was succeeded by his stepson, Tiberius, who in turn appointed Pontius Pilate as the Roman governor of Judaea. If Pilate thought his job was going to be easy, he was mistaken when a dark-skinned, long-haired, radical Jew who lived with beggars and lepers and called himself Jesus, the son of God, began to speak to ever larger and more rapturous crowds on compassion, tolerance, grace, love, and the evils of prejudice and of moneylenders in the temple. What exactly happened next, nobody knows. The Gospels Matthew, Mark, Luke, and John, composed many years later, disagree on some points. Some say Pilate, easily threatened by beliefs outside his own, proclaimed this Jesus a menace, and so ordered him nailed to a wooden cross on a hill in or near present-day Jerusalem.

Kes feels Jeannie take her hand and squeeze it.

Kes watches Tim, who sits with his head down, guitar in his lap.

"Historians have speculated on how different things might have been had Octavius lost that day," Pastor Anderson says, "and Marc Antony won. Marc Antony and his lover, Cleopatra, were tolerant of a wide spectrum of races, religions, and beliefs..."

Did the pastor just say 'lover'?

"...Jesus may never have been crucified. But, of course, Octavius won and became Augustus, the most powerful and influential of all Roman rulers. And we have the world we have today. A good and kind world in many ways, though not as much as I'd like, and not as much as children everywhere deserve. I think we could always use more goodness and kindness even here in our little town. Wouldn't you agree?"

Kes hears a few people say, "Amen."

And from the back comes a boisterous "Hallelujah, Lord."

Kes grins. She knows that voice. It's Tucker John.

The entire congregation shouts, "Hallelujah, Lord."

Tim raises his head and smiles at Kes. It feels like ten thousand kilowatts flooding into her. Sunshine to a bee.

Scanning the congregation, she finds Tucker John in the back, standing near the d'Alene family, where Solomon sits in his wheelchair, overseen not by Abe but by his father, the man named Salt who never smiles. Once again, Abe has assumed a front pew place next to Tabby, Pastor Anderson's older daughter, near Derek Smith and his huge wife, and Principal Cunningham with her meek-as-a-lamb husband who, according to Melissa Darling, "is trained to agree with everything she says." And nearby, Oddmund Nystad sits with Berit, who winks conspiratorially at Kes.

Pastor Anderson offers a final prayer and Tim plays a closing song.

Afterward, Kes watches Mr. d'Alene make his way to the front like a man on a mission, determined to speak with Pastor Anderson and maybe correct him, even though the pastor hardly cited scripture. Maybe that's Mr. d'Alene's criticism: all history, no scripture.

Tim finds Kes and asks, "How'd it go yesterday?"

"Not now, Tim. Not here, remember?"

Tim gives her a puzzled look as Tia joins them.

Kes is about to remind them both that Operation Free Wolf is top secret, when from the crowd she hears a loud exclamation, "Cleeeeoooooopatra... woohoo. What a fooooooox." She knows without turning who it is.

Solomon.

The pastor laughs and everybody laughs. Not in a polite or accommodating way, as people might laugh at the off-kilter humor of a disabled boy who's not nearly as funny as he thinks he is. No, people laugh earnestly because Solomon *is so dang funny.* Cleopatra, a fox. Even poor, thin Mrs. d'Alene, after an instant of looking horrified, cracks up, as do Jerry and little Joshua, laughing mostly because everybody else is.

Kes notices that Principal Cunningham seems caught off guard, somewhat stone faced, as if uncertain what to do. Same with Mr. d'Alene. But not Abe. He looks angry in a way that frightens Kes.

CHAPTER THIRTY-SEVEN

Silver

SILVER DREAMS. The dead whale floats barely on the surface, suspended there as a raft of meat and skin and bone, smaller than before, rotting away. Old One stands his ground, still coughing, dying, refusing to leave. At the opposite end of the whale, the bear, equally obsessed, also refuses to leave. Silver paces next to Old One, ankle deep in the cold sea. A storm rises, pushing waves into them that break on the whale as waves would break over a shallow reef or shoal. Old One coughs up blood. Silver should have left many days ago. He's going to die out here. They all are. Gray sky. Gray sea. No land in sight.

More coughing. More blood.

Everything goes dark. Silver startles awake.

No wind. No waves.

He's warm. Safe.

He hears coughing, followed by a member of his pack rising from the comfort of the den, and leaving. Silver follows.

Outside, the day begins to express itself. Silver sees the subadult, the one that has been coughing ever since the cold swim back from the island. It stands alone, ready to leave. For the day? Longer? He looks at Silver, coughs again, shakes his head, and takes off northbound toward the distant mountains and the deep blue glaciers. Another world. Either to find a mate and to make his own pack and thus begin again. Or to die.

Probably die.

This is what wolves do. They disperse. They break away to form new packs, new families; they pioneer new ground. They die. And when they do, they often die alone, under the great sky and raven's eye.

Silver watches him go.

Juncos chatter from a nearby alder. Geese call from afar. Silver walks about to make certain nothing is out of order.

Reentering the den, he finds his family warm and dry in their sleeping chamber, just beginning to stir awake. In the darkness, he finds Sister and curls up beside her, and rests without falling back to sleep. He thinks about the all-black female, about his own possibilities. He thinks about the tall uprights, how different they are. Dangerous? He thinks about Mother. She needs to eat. A lot. He thinks about the huge bull moose, and how his pack, working together, could bring it down by forcing it up against a tangle of trees where one tree has fallen against the others, its trunk at an angle so Silver could run up it and launch himself from behind, like a flying squirrel, onto the moose's back.

Mother needs to eat.

Silver listens to his family now, as each wolf acknowledges the others in the dark den. Soon they will leave and enter the light, and know they are one fewer than before.

CHAPTER THIRTY-EIGHT

Salt

HOW MANY TIMES *in the Bible do men cross rivers? And subdue the land? And drive out their enemies and take possession? And make war?*

Always another war.

At lunchtime at Derek's Garage, Salt sits in his Toyota hatchback to enjoy a quiet thirty minutes, and to read from Joshua 1:11–14, and Numbers 32:21–32; of men "armed to battle."

Does it ever stop? All this fighting?

And the never-ending war of man against nature?

Jericho came home the other day, alarmed, saying that Mrs. Carry said that in the last fifty years more than half of all wild animals on earth have disappeared because of human beings and all the crazy things we do, building dams, cutting down forests, and spraying chemicals everywhere. Of all the mammals left on the planet, Jericho said, ninety-six percent are human beings and our livestock and pets. Only four percent are lions, tigers, wolves, bears, moose, deer, elephants, hippos, bats, and the like. Mostly bats.

Salt told Jericho that, no... he, Jericho's own father, doesn't want a world without wolves. *Back in my youth, maybe. All wild animals were fair game then. But it's not a game. And not fair. What changed?*

I did.

Salt remembers the first time he read Jack London's *The Call of the Wild*, back in high school, before social media, when people still read books, and his friends read it too and they all said they'd go to Alaska one day. But only Salt did, while the others bought big trucks and went to work at the lumber mill or a local restaurant or store, and married their sweethearts and had kids, and blamed their problems on anybody but themselves. The book's first line,

"Buck did not read the newspapers," made them laugh because Buck was a mild-mannered dog that would be stolen off a California farm and taken north by brutal men to work the icy Klondike goldfields and be exposed to vicious wolves.

How hard they laughed back then. Buck did not read the newspapers.

I never laugh like that anymore… like those Willynillyville veterans do. Why?

Tonight is the hearing and public testimony on the governor's proposed Roads to Resources coalbed methane project west of the Menzies River. Salt dreads it.

He often eats his midday sandwich with grease and oil on his fingers. But never does he open his beloved King James Bible with hands less than clean. So today he eats after a good soaping, and affords himself the smallest of smiles. *Maybe I should read my Bible every day at lunch. And find friends I can laugh with.*

When he and Hannah and the boys moved from Fairbanks down to Strawberry Flats two years ago, they heard about a wolf called Romeo that for many years befriended the people of Juneau. A magnificent animal— stately, black, and curious, even playful—Romeo would greet wintertime ice skaters and skiers out on frozen Mendenhall Lake, near Mendenhall Glacier, and romp a bit with their dogs, then disappear into the mountains only to reappear days later, as friendly as before. Romeo made statewide news before some loser shot and killed him. After that, Romeo made national news. *That's all it takes: one man with a trap or a gun. One man with a hole in his heart.*

I don't want to be that man.

I don't want Abraham to be that man.

Salt worries about Abe all the time, and wonders if love is enough. *Can love alone save a life? Turn a heart?*

DINNER THAT NIGHT IS SOMBER. Not even a story or a funny face from Jericho, or a clever retort from Solomon. Salt will leave soon for the hearing. Abraham has already said he intends to recross the river, check for wolves, bring back all the traps, and find out who operated that drone. He keeps thumbing through his book on the Battle of Stalingrad, making notes about how Hitler's man there, Field Marshal von Paulus, commander of the German Sixth Army, could have done better.

It breaks Salt's heart.

We gas Jews.
We gas wolves.
Dear God, who are we?

Later, as Salt is going out the door, the phone rings. Typically, he and Hannah let the boys answer, having taught them to say, "D'Alene residence, so-and-so speaking." But they're in the living room watching *Jeopardy*, so Salt picks it up. "Hello."

"Is this Salt d'Alene?"

"Yes, it is."

"Salt, this is Jess Cleet up in Fairbanks. Do you still have the two modified M-44s I gave you?"

Jess Cleet. Wolf killer. Asking about the cyanide bombs. Salt leans against the kitchen counter as he feels his head go light. "Yes, I have them."

"Good. Hold on to them. Tell nobody about them. I'll be down in your area soon to get them from you... to get the job done."

Before Salt can respond, Jess hangs up.

Hannah comes into the kitchen and asks, "Who was that?"

"Nobody."

She kisses his cheek and says, "We can do this, can't we, husband? For Solomon, I mean... for all of us? The clinical trial. It's the right thing to do, right?"

Salt and Hannah will have to sign waivers that say Dr. Hamadani and her medical team and the medical center—maybe all of London, Great Britain, and the manufacturers of every drug involved—cannot be held liable if anything goes wrong, no matter how horrible or unexpected. If Solomon shows no improvement, if new problems arise, or even if he dies, the d'Alenes will have no legal footing. No recourse, other than to grieve for the rest of their lives.

"Yes, wife," Salt tells her as he takes a deep breath, "it's the right thing to do."

"THIS HEARING WILL INVOLVE TESTIMONY ONLY," announces Gary, the same self-assured, nicely dressed, I-speak-for-the-governor political hack that Salt knows from the hole-in-the-wall restaurant in Juneau. Mr. Raddock is nowhere in sight. "We want to hear your ideas and concerns," Gary adds. "We accept both written and spoken testimony. The deadline is the last day of

March, two weeks from tomorrow. For tonight, we ask that each testifier limit your microphone time to two minutes. You'll be called forward to position yourselves on standby, to save time. Testifiers must live in Alaska and will begin by stating your name and place of residence. We ask that there be no outbursts or disorderly conduct of any kind. Two Alaska state troopers are here to keep things civil. The governor's Roads to Resources handouts you've received should answer most, if not all, of your questions about the specifics of this development and all its safety and environmental protocols, and the economic opportunities it will afford this town. This proceeding is being recorded and all testimony will be entered into the public record. We thank you for your cooperation and civic-mindedness. Any questions before we get started? No? Good. We have a growing list of testifiers, so let's get started."

Salt likes his vantage point, seated in the back row of the school's crowded multipurpose room, peering over a sea of heads. Every chair is taken, some by local kids with their parents. Another thirty or forty people stand along the sides and back wall, including a few dark-haired, solemn-faced Tlingits from the village of Jinkaat, across Icy Strait on Chichagof Island. Salt also sees several veterans from Willynillyville.

"I have a preliminary question," comes a male voice from behind, "one I'd like entered into the public record."

Seated up front, Gary says, "Yes, go ahead."

"Why are we here?"

"I just explained that."

"Isn't this just an empty formality? A dog and pony show? You've already barged in your heavy equipment and materials to build the road and bridge, right? Excavators, bulldozers, Ditch Witches, and pile drivers all parked next to Nystad's, in the empty lot, which isn't empty anymore. Or is all that equipment just big Tonka toys?"

"Nothing has been given a green light in this," Gary says. "I assure you."

"Really?" the unidentified voice presses on. "Then let me ask you this. In the history of the state of Alaska, has any testimony from a hearing such as this ever—and I mean even just once—changed the state's proposed actions on any major development?"

"That information isn't available to me at the moment," Gary says. "I suggest that we respect the audience and get started with the testimony."

The audience rumbles.

Salt hears another voice from behind: "Back off, Tyler."

And another voice: "Give 'em hell, Nash."

The first to testify is Derek Smith, who wears his John Deere cap crooked on his greasy-haired head, and says this new development will be good for American energy independence and for the local economy. "And the economy is everything, right? Where would we be without a strong economy? And don't forget that the state of Alaska has its department of environmental conservation to conserve the environment, right? So, we're in good hands. We should be grateful for this opportunity to grow our economy and to make it as strong as it can be." He saunters away.

A steady stream of testifiers says much the same. We need the jobs. If this operation can be done safely and properly and all that, let's do it. Let's get it done. Let's "jazz up our economy," says a commercial fisherman and Wall Street day trader who points out that methane is only bad for the environment if it leaks directly into the atmosphere, unburned. "This operation will extract methane from coal seams deep in the ground and capture it to be burned later to heat people's homes and such. Which means it's nowhere as bad as oil and coal, for global warming, that is… if there is such a thing."

Harry Bywater, the liquor store owner, points out that all the acreage west of the Menzies River is state of Alaska land, right up to the marine reserve, "…and the state can make big money by leasing that land to the oil and gas industry, and keep our taxes down. What we've got here, everybody, is a win-win situation if we've ever seen one. That's how I see it anyway, and I know I'm not alone."

The crowd jostles and grows with people pressing in on each other. More testifiers speak on the benefits of this methane project. Jobs, jobs, and more jobs. Real commerce. And the crowd continues to grow. Salt closes his eyes and wills himself to breathe deep and think about Dr. Hamadani. A chance to save Solomon. Right now, nothing else matters. *If Solomon were to die, I'd be crushed. The boys too, especially Abraham. But we'd survive. But my Hannah would never recover, and she's already weak. It could kill her—her spirit, at least.* The other night, during a private moment in bed, she told Salt quietly that Solomon was her favorite. Not just her favorite son, but her favorite person in the whole world. She felt terrible saying this, she said, because parents aren't supposed to idolize their children or have favorites. Yet it also felt wonderful to say… to speak the truth. "He's so magical and upbeat, in his own way, right? The irony. That God should touch him so. And yes, I remember the physical therapist in Fairbanks who said disabled people aren't supposed to be regarded as 'angels' or 'innocents' or 'beacons' and all that, because it can erase their humanity. So what are we supposed to do? Pretend that he's normal and is just like everyone else? That he'll walk again one day? Have children and climb mountains?"

As she trailed off to sleep, Salt opened his Bible to Galatians 6:9: "And let us not be weary of well doing, for in due season we shall reap, if we faint not."

LIKE A TIDE, the testimony turns halfway through the event.

"Good evening," says the same Willynillyville veteran who shouted hallelujah in church yesterday morning. "My name is Tucker John Jackson, and I came here by way of Stinkwater, Oklahoma, and Kiss-it-all-goodbye, Afghanistan, and before that, Africa, where they have a saying: 'The sheep will spend its entire life fearing the wolf only to be eaten by the shepherd.' Look around. Here I am, a Black man, speaking before a mostly white audience on how things ought to go. If this were the Jim Crow South one hundred or even just fifty years ago, I'd be dead by the next morning, hanging from a bridge or a tree. That's our history. Believe me, a lot of towns down south have been growing their economies for decades, even centuries, chasing one boom after another, and now have more of a past than a present, and no future, other than to blow away in the dust and heat that gets hotter every year. So, I have to ask: Are we here to suck every dollar out of the ground? To make the same mistakes too many other places have made? If so, too bad. Because it's a self-defeating prophecy brought to us by hucksters and shepherds who want to lead us to the promised land. Go see for yourself. Parts of Oklahoma and Texas are dying. That's why I came here: to build a life that's simple and pure. One I don't need to escape from. That's why I oppose this development. Drilling for methane is the wrong thing to do. Thank you for listening. I really appreciate it."

Frank Toons, a bush pilot who excels at video games and once told Hannah—who later told Salt—that higher education is a liberal trap that breeds socialism, counters Tucker John with a pro-drilling, pro-America, pro-patriotism testimony. Then Berit Nystad delivers an anti-drilling appeal, followed by a Tlingit man who states his name in Tlingit and says his people used to net and spear salmon in the Menzies River. "That river has another name," he says, "an older name, a Tlingit name. Building a bridge over that river is a bad idea. It's disrespectful. That's all I have to say."

Next comes Mrs. Carry and her husband, Bill, who surprise Salt with their appeals to leave things as they are. Mrs. Carry talks about the sixth extinction and recites some sobering numbers of species declines, like Jericho shared from school recently. The Carrys say they love the quiet, roadless places and going berry picking along that river. They've seen bear tracks out there and hope to see a bear itself one day, one undisturbed by traffic and noise. As Mrs. Carry and her husband rejoin the audience, Salt sees her smile at Kes Nash.

Gary calls for Zorro Brown to speak next, and for Kes to stand by.

Salt watches her grab her pack along the back wall where she stands with her mother and father and quietly move to the front; how she pushes a strand of hair off her lightly freckled face, and scans the room with her keen eyes. No wonder his younger sons like her. Jericho says Solomon adores her; that when Abraham is not around, Kes jives with Sol, and rolls him out to the playground, and gets him a straw for his drink, and makes him laugh and think. She's recruited a so-called "order of knights" to battle the governor.

Amazing. Maybe Solomon is one of her recruits, a secret agent of some kind. He would love that.

Kes's Knights of the Menzies River. That's what his boys call it.

Salt shifts in his chair, prays for Kes, and remembers Isaiah 11:6: "And a little child shall lead them."

CHAPTER THIRTY-NINE

Kes

BREATHE. KES SURVEYS THE ROOM as Uncle Ty's fishing partner, Zorro, a retired journalist with tousled blond-gray hair and wire-rimmed glasses, begins to speak. She concentrates: *I have to speak clearly and not too fast. Shoulders back. Head up. Eye contact... yes, make eye contact with people in the audience. And...* Suddenly, Zorro is finished.

"Thank you, Mr. Brown," the moderator says. "Next up: Kestrel Nash."

Breathe. Kes surveys the crowded room and finds her parents and Uncle Ty along the back wall, standing tall. Papa and Uncle Ty wear their pirate bandanas and give her thumbs-up. Emily and Melissa, seated with their parents, smile nervously, as if to say: *You can do this.* Emily records Kes with her phone. Tim, Tia, and Tabby stand along a side wall with Pastor Anderson, looking tense. No sign of Kona. Maybe his dad kept him home. According to Melissa, Mr. Marks has mixed feelings about Kona's participation in Operation Free Wolf, which is already less of a secret than it's supposed to be. No sign of Jeannie or E. J., or Grandpa. Earlier, Uncle Ty told all three they might not enjoy such a tight crowd. Chippy and Cap said they wouldn't attend because it's a rigged game. But just as Kes is about to speak, they come through the back door covered in neck tattoos, their ball caps on backward, wads of Skoal in their mouths.

Following them is Abe d'Alene, also with a ball cap on backwards.

The Alaska state troopers watch it all, stern faced, standing along opposite walls.

Breathe. Kes introduces herself, pulls the leghold trap from her daypack, holds it up, and says, "Somebody's been trapping wolves on the other side of the Menzies River." Her own voice sounds strange to her, strained, as if she's trying to be somebody she's not, something more than who she is. The trap is heavy. She lowers it onto the table next to the podium and feels the heat of everybody staring at her... into her. Nobody smiles. Everybody looks solemn, as if this were a funeral. *Maybe it is.* She glances over at the moderator, who looks back at her with lightly veiled contempt. *Breathe.* From the back wall, Papa makes a hand motion at her: two fingers in an inverted V, facing down and rocking back and forth like a swing—the same hand motion he used on Texas playgrounds years ago when he called her Little Bird because she would swing high and jump off, thinking she could fly. *You can do this, Little Bird.* Kes remembers vomiting in the Center for the Intrepid, down in San Antonio, bent over the toilet, feeling anything but intrepid. That was a year and a half ago. *I'm not that same kid anymore. Be strong. Breathe.* "These wolves are genetically rare because they eat salmon and marine mammals..." She talks about the wolves' howling, but refrains from saying they howl in harmony, or how she believes they reanimated her father and made him musical again. Instead, Kes closes by reading from a prepared statement. "Wolves have been trapped and killed across America for a long time, and still are every day. In many places they're extinct. Some people say they're God's dogs, maybe because they remind us of who we are and where we came from. Do they have to be killed here too, in Alaska? In this last wild place?" A wave of grief rolls through her. She steadies herself with both hands on the podium, pulls herself together and reads, "No, they do not. This is their home too. Because the wolves here eat salmon, they're probably genetically unique and could qualify as an endangered species. Whoever you are... whoever is trapping these wolves on the other side of the Menzies River, probably to get rid of the whole pack—an entire family— to make it easier for the state of Alaska to build this stupid bridge and development, I ask you to please... please stop."

After Kes grabs the trap and makes her way back to Papa and Mom, two men testify on her heels, both pro-coalbed methane. The first says wolves should be trapped because they kill a lot of moose and deer, and with the wolves gone, "that will mean a lot more moose and deer for families in this town who could really use the meat."

The second man says the economy is everything. "It's our lifeblood, and it needs to grow more than it has. I say bring it on... this project, I mean. Bring it on full steam ahead. And about those wolves. Nearby Crystal Bay National Marine Reserve is more than three million acres of designated wilderness.

Let the wolves roam and ramble there. If they're smart, that's where they'll choose to live. Not here."

The moderator nods and announces, "That concludes the testimony from everybody who signed up. Does anybody else have anything to say?"

Now four more men speak, none familiar to Kes. All four pro-methane. *Who are these guys?*

She feels her heart breaking. She catches glimpses from Melissa and Emily in the middle of the crowd. They look angry and ready to cry, but show no last-minute, come-to-the-rescue sign that they'll testify. Neither do their parents.

The hearing appears to be over when Principal Cunningham walks to the podium in her self-assured manner, gives her name and title, and says, "I just have just one thing to say. No... actually, two. First, have you ever noticed how all of our most vexing and damaging problems today began fifty years ago or so when prayer was removed from our public schools? That's why I'm thankful for this president and our governor, for their support of prayer in school. Second, about wolves. I see no reason why we need them. I have my two adorable terriers and love them to pieces. I know many of you here tonight love your dogs too, and are loved by them. Thank you."

"Very good," the moderator says as Principal Cunningham, looking triumphant, returns to her seat. "Anyone else?"

Silence.

"Okay then," the moderator says. "That concludes our—"

"Hold your horses," a voice calls from the back.

UNCLE TY WALKS FORWARD, weaving through the crowd, looking every bit the pirate. He steps up to the podium, scans the room, and says nothing. The crowd settles back down.

"The clock is ticking," the moderator warns him.

"I'll say it is," Uncle Ty says. "This world has only a few years to wake up and put an end to the predatory economy that's killing our livable planet. We have to vote the bums out, period. We have to leave nearly eighty percent of all known fossil fuel reserves in the ground and pretty much change everything. I'm Tyler Nash, by the way. I live here and am a professional geologist, and am positive there's no coalbed methane out west of the Menzies River. This thing is a bait-and-switch." He looks at the moderator. "True?"

"The clock is ticking," the moderator says without expression.

Uncle Ty turns back to the audience. "We all know why the dinosaurs went extinct, right?"

"They smoked too many cigarettes," Chippy yells from the back.

"Wrong," Uncle Ty answers.

"They put pineapple on their pizza?" Cap yells.

"Wrong again."

"Your uncle is crazy," Mom whispers to Kes.

"Yes, I know," Kes says.

"Sixty-six million years ago nearly every dinosaur was killed in a single day by an asteroid that struck Earth," Uncle Ty says. "Ten million years after that, the Paleocene-Eocene Thermal Maximum released a huge amount of methane into—"

"Get to the point," somebody yells from the crowd.

"Your time is up," somebody else yells.

Others join in:

"Drill, baby, drill."

"It's the economy, stupid."

"Let him speak," Pastor Anderson shouts amid more rumblings and stirrings.

"You know," Uncle Ty says as the crowd settles down, "the Bronx Zoo once had an exhibit called 'The Most Dangerous Animal in the World.' Guess what it was."

Silence.

Kes can feel her heartbeat in her throat.

"It was a mirror," Uncle Ty says.

No response. Not a sound.

Again, Uncle Ty scans the room, as if to inventory every face. "I saw a single-panel comic once," he goes on, relaxed now, speaking as if in casual conversation. "Yes, I admit that I'm a comic lover. This one showed a guy talking to some other half-starved survivors in a ruined landscape. You know what the guy said? He said, 'Yes, it's true. We destroyed the planet. But for a brief, shining moment we made our shareholders very happy.' Believe me, folks, this time around, we're the asteroid. There is no Tooth Fairy or Santa Claus or coalbed methane on the other side of the Menzies River. Our governor is a con man, like our president. He's deceiving us, or trying to. And these men up here"—Uncle Ty points at the moderator—"these men are his agents. Don't let them sucker you."

The audience stirs as Uncle Ty walks away.

Kes feels lightly euphoric when suddenly Papa grabs her pack and walks forward. She watches the exasperated moderator get to his feet to conclude the evening. But when he sees Papa coming his way, he sits back down, saying, "This will be our final testimony."

Papa steps to the podium, reaches into the pack, and pulls out the trap. He sets it on the table and, with some effort, pries open the jaws, and sets the trigger. He takes off his special Nike Air Jordan for all to see his metal foot and leg. Titanium. State of the art.

The room, previously agitated with everybody ready to leave, now goes silent.

Expectant.

Mom says under her breath, "Danny, what are you doing?"

Kes grabs her by the arm, thinking, *Do it, Papa. Do it.*

"My name is Daniel Emerson Nash," he says softly into the microphone. "I moved to Strawberry Flats eight months ago from Lubbock, Texas, by way of Kunduz Province, Afghanistan, and Brooke Army Medical Center in San Antonio. I came here with my family, for the peace and quiet. This here is a nine-inch leghold wolf trap."

He lifts his foot and steps into it. *WHACK!*

A woman screams.

Papa holds there for a long moment, looks around, then slides his foot off the table with the trap affixed above his metal ankle, its grip unrelenting. He walks through the stunned crowd and out the door, limping as he goes, dragging the trap behind him.

KES SLEEPS FITFULLY ALL NIGHT and falls into crazy dreams until she hears the phone ring. Something's wrong. She dashes downstairs in her pajamas as Mom, already in the kitchen, picks it up. Grandpa sits at the table drinking his morning coffee. Kes stands behind him and wraps her arms around his chest and kisses his rough cheek. He puts his hand to her arms and squeezes. Mom hangs up and says, "That was Jeannie. She says that Spike was just at Kelly's Coffee Shop when he saw two state troopers and heard them asking for directions to Willynillyville."

"The same two troopers from last night?" Grandpa asks. He's heard stories about the hearing and the epic testimony of his two sons.

Kes remembers the troopers in their flat hats, blue uniforms, and bulletproof vests—unsmiling, watchful. Big, imposing men with guns riding high on their hips.

Mom says, "Kes, honey, get dressed and go get everybody up and tell them to get over here. Chippy and Cap are in the shop. I'll call Jeannie back to see if she and Spike can get over here too. And tell Chippy and Cap they'll need to stay cool through this whole thing. No attitude and no guns."

"I don't know if I can tell them that, Mom."

"I will," Grandpa says, climbing to his feet.

"Your papa and Uncle Ty aren't up yet," Mom says. "I'll wake them. And I'll see if Taylor can delay going into work, maybe wear her marine reserve uniform."

Grandpa stops at the door and asks, "Should I put on my Silver Star?"

Mom thinks for moment. "No. That would look contrived. Just get everybody in here as fast as you can. I'll start making a big breakfast."

"Moose sausage?" Grandpa asks.

"We're out of moose sausage."

"We're out of ground moose, Mom," Kes says, "but not moose sausage. I'm pretty sure Chippy and Cap and Tucker John have some. I'll find out."

"Somebody needs to shoot Big Al," Grandpa says about the legendary moose.

"No, Grandpa. We've talked about this. The wolves need to get Big Al."

"Go now, both of you," Mom says.

"Blueberry pancakes too, Mom?"

"Absolutely."

"So... no school for me today?"

"This is school, honey. You're about to learn a lot about civics, law, and order."

"And the persuasive power of the human stomach," Grandpa adds.

"And civil disobedience?" Kes asks with a grin. Uncle Ty has told her all about Henry David Thoreau and his night in jail to protest slavery and a war.

"Out the door," Mom says. "Both of you, go. You have your assignments."

Grandpa says, "I feel like Paul Revere."

MOM OPENS THE DOOR and acts surprised. "Oh, good morning," she says. "My goodness. What can I do for you two gentlemen?"

"Good morning, ma'am. I'm Trooper Scott and this is Trooper Dryer. Is Mr. Tyler Nash at home?"

"Yes, he is. Please, come in and make yourselves comfortable."

They look at each other for a moment and step inside.

Mom shakes their hands and introduces herself as Tyler's sister-in-law. "We're just having breakfast and there's plenty."

Kes grins at Grandpa, who grins back.

Mom should win an Academy Award.

Kes watches the troopers take in the scene: a dozen people at the big table, eating like lions; a man sitting in the corner chair—the same man who last night stepped into the trap—now wearing two new titanium legs and playing the guitar and doing a fine job of it, his leg from last night leaning against a wall with the trap still affixed; a Black man on the sofa with a little boy and a book on his lap , the boy now mesmerized by the troopers; a floppy-eared rabbit and a big-eyed cat at the window; an old Irish setter in another corner that looks more dead than alive. A woman at the table wearing a blue National Marine Reserve Service uniform. And perfuming it all: the smell of moose sausage, sourdough pancakes, and spruce-tip syrup.

Taylor and Jeannie get up from the table and walk to the door and introduce themselves and shake the troopers' hands. The troopers reach down and pet Skydog. (Mom said earlier that law enforcement officials love service dogs.) Little Kip, now four, jumps off Tucker John's lap and runs up to Mom and puts his arms around her leg and stares. The troopers tower over him. Kip asks, "Are you superheroes?"

TEN MINUTES LATER, Troopers Scott and Dryer are bootless and hatless and sitting at the table with syrup on their fingers. Here's the deal, they say. Somebody in Juneau filed a missing person report and listed Tyler Nash as the last person to be seen with this missing person. Further investigation suggests that the last anybody saw of this person, one Michael Lipinski, was at the Strawberry Flats Airport, in Uncle Ty's Cessna 207.

Kes realizes, *Oh, no. They're talking about Mike.*

"He's dead," Uncle Ty says.

"And how did he die?" Trooper Scott asks.

"I flew him up to a glacier and left him there, as he requested."

"You landed on a glacier and left him there?"

"Yes."

"Where and when did this occur?"

"In the Fairweather Range." Uncle Ty answers each question without obvious guilt or regret. Kes watches Trooper Dryer write in a little black notebook, the pages sticking together from Uncle Ty's spruce-tip syrup.

"And he did this of his own volition?" Trooper Scott asks.

"Yes."

"Do you have a statement and witnesses?"

"Yes."

"Mr. Lipinski was not coerced, deceived, or encouraged in any way?"

"No."

"And he was coherent, self-aware, and of sound mind?"

"He was dying," Chippy snaps. "He had cancer everywhere."

"And was addicted to oxycodone, Percocet, and morphine," Cap adds.

"He'd been in chronic pain for more than ten years," Jeannie says softly, "from nerve damage from the war in Iraq. But the cancer might have actually been caused by toxic fumes from burn pits. Mike had trouble breathing."

Across the way, Papa stops playing his Martin.

"C'mon, you guys," E. J. says. "Mike wanted to die. He was ready for the next great journey. He said so a million times. And we helped him. We were his family and we helped him. He was miserable every damn minute of every damn day, remember? He dreamed of softly freezing, and that's where he is now, deep in a glacier, covered with snow. And we all loved him. What's wrong with that?" Big tears stand in E. J.'s eyes.

Chippy says to the troopers, "If you're looking for a guilty party, go investigate the politicians who voted that we invade Iraq. Because that's when Mike began to die, right?" He looks around the table.

Nobody speaks.

Mom hands E. J. a Kleenex. One to Jeannie too. And takes one for herself. She offers one to Chippy, who waves it off as he glares at the troopers.

"Mike signed a last will and testament," Uncle Ty says to the troopers. "I have three notarized copies, if you'd like one. He named a sister in Portland as executor."

"Yes, we'll take one," Trooper Scott says.

Again, nobody speaks.

Finally, little Kip says from across the room, where he sits with Papa, "Can I have another pancake?"

TROOPER SCOTT AND TROOPER DRYER put on their flat hats and lace up their black boots and thank Mom for a delicious breakfast after Uncle Ty signed a statement of confession and a death certificate in lieu of something called "habeas corpus" that Kes intends to research later. At the door, every Willynillyville veteran shakes the troopers' hands goodbye except two, Chippy and Cap, who stay at the table with sour expressions.

Mom, Papa, Uncle Ty, and Kes walk the troopers to their white pickup truck with the blue-and-gold insignia and thank them. Trooper Scott, who Kes sees as the more senior of the two, says to Uncle Ty, "Be careful out here."

"Meaning?" Uncle Ty asks.

Trooper Scott looks around at the scattering of buildings, the greenhouse and garden, the shop with all its tools, the firewood stacked neatly with the bark side up, the solar array and bird feeder busy with Papa's chestnut-backed chickadees; the chicken coop and pony corral; the apiary coming back to life, a dozen flower pots on each deck, ready for spring. "You have a lot to lose," he says. "If trouble comes your way, be careful not to cross a line. Because if you do, it's you who will suffer and pay. Not them. Don't let forces larger than you provoke you into defeating yourself."

"I know what you're saying," Uncle Ty says, "and I appreciate it."

"I'm a veteran myself," Trooper Scott says.

"Me too," says Trooper Dryer. "I was with the three-five at Al Kut."

"Three-five?" Kes asks.

"Third Battalion, fifth Marine regiment."

"My grandpa was in the Marine Corps in Vietnam," Kes tells him.

Trooper Dryer smiles. "Yes, we know. He was awarded the Silver Star."

"How do you know that?"

"We do our homework."

"Those two McCalls back in there," Trooper Scott says to Uncle Ty, motioning toward the house. "I've seen many like them. You'll need to control them."

Kes thinks, *How do we do that?*

"And one more thing," Trooper Scott says to Uncle Ty. "Two state of Alaska survey tripods and several dozen survey stakes have gone missing from the end of Menzies River Road. You should keep a close eye on your valuables around here."

Uncle Ty nods. "We will. Thank you."

"Might you have any information about them?"

"No."

That's a lie. Kes knows the Poker Pack took them, probably under instructions from Uncle Ty. They've all been reading *The Monkey Wrench Gang*, Edward Abbey's comic eco-novel about a band of saboteurs determined to destroy the Glen Canyon Dam on the Colorado River.

"And that leghold trap, the one from last night... who owns it?"

"I have no idea," Uncle Ty says.

Trooper Scott looks at Papa. "How'd you come into possession of it?"

Kes hears herself say without hesitation or fear, "I found it... in the woods, and brought it home." *What are you going to do? Arrest me?*

Trooper Scott stares at her for a long moment. She's afraid he's going to ask her if she sprang it. If she broke the law. Papa sidles up next to her. Trooper Scott motions Trooper Dryer to the back of the truck where they have a quiet discussion, away from the others.

Kes stands firm, next to Papa, her arm around his waist, his arm around her shoulder. She feels something powerful just then, a sense of determination and belonging, as if this were her ground, her home, her Camelot, her cause. Excalibur... as Merlyn would say to young Arthur. The sword in the stone. Or as Tucker John likes to say when he quotes Nelson Mandela, "It always seems impossible... until it's done."

Save the wolves and we just might save ourselves.

The troopers return and thank Mom for the fine food, and get into their truck. They're about to leave when Trooper Dryer says to Papa out the passenger-side window, "I'll never forget what you did last night."

Kes swells with pride. *Neither will I.*

Papa pulls her in closer to him.

"A storm is coming," Trooper Dryer adds. "And storms have a tendency to come on fast. Don't do anything you'll regret."

Papa nods.

As Kes watches them drive away, she thinks about doing nothing versus doing something, about playing safe versus taking risks, about staying in Texas versus moving to Alaska. Ground. Home. Cause.

Her knights are ready.

PART IV

CHAPTER FORTY

Silver

WATCH THE RAVENS. Work with them.

Silver learned this from Old One.

Ravens benefit wolves as spotters; wolves benefit ravens as killers. Ravens find moose and lead the wolves to them, then hold off and perch in trees while the wolves, as a pack, kill the prey. Unable to eat the entire bounty at once, the wolves rest. And when they do, the ravens move in for their fair share.

Silver knows that a pack can kill a large moose and lose less meat to ravens than to a single wolf or a pair of wolves.

This moose, the king of the Menzies River, stands tall and strong and indifferent to the weather and threats of predation.

Still, Silver has to eat.

So does Mother, back in the den, with new pups soon to be born.

Silver and Sister set a trap. They find a cottonwood, fallen this past winter by a storm. With spring coming, the cottonwood, even though it's on the ground, shattered in many places, still produces new leaves and buds. Many of the tree's upper branches that would typically be high in the crown and out of reach for a hungry moose now lie within reach, broken like sticks when the tree fell. The massive moose has already eaten as much as he can reach, a rare treat, perhaps more desirable than willow this time of year. Any chance to eat more should be a strong temptation.

Working alone while the rest of the pack hunts elsewhere, Silver and Sister use their powerful jaws to snap off cottonwood crown branches. They drag the bait and pile it nearby, under a fallen spruce that's propped up at a low angle by another spruce.

Will the moose go for it?

Under dim light, perhaps. If he's hungry enough, perhaps. And if Silver stays perfectly still, hidden in thick brush near the base of the fallen spruce, in attack position, and runs up it and leaps onto the moose at just the right moment, and holds on, and draws enough blood before he's thrown off... it could work.

Or Silver could get kicked to death.

He feels the danger. But danger is nothing.

Mother needs to eat. All the wolves do.

For hours, Silver and Sister wait, hidden. Night falls. Morning comes. Another full day. Another dusk. Another long night. Another morning. The ravens arrive, and soon thereafter, the moose. Silver remains as still as stone, not directly above the cottonwood branches piled on the ground, but some distance along the attack branch to make it a running ramp for a strong leap.

All is ready when a strange bird swoops in overhead, shredding the sky with large rotors, making the most terrible sound Silver has ever heard.

The moose panics, turns, and runs.

Silver holds his ground, and listens to his stomach growl. When Sister approaches a few moments later, he sees in her eyes something he's never seen before: deep fear.

CHAPTER FORTY-ONE

Salt

Solomon rocks in his wheelchair, excited to see the evening news about the encampment at Willynillyville. He's never been there, though many times he's asked his mom and dad if they would take him. Kes has said he's always welcome. It's magical, she likes to say, with cottonwoods, spruce, and pines, and the chickens sashaying around, and the chickadees that land on Kes's dad when he feeds them. And the occasional weasel working its way through the woodpile, and of course every spring and fall the sandhill cranes that fly right overhead.

Hannah picks up the remote to change the channel, but the boys protest. It's not often they get to see their own town on TV. And look what's going on out there. Wow.

"That's Jeannie," Jericho says. "The woman from our church, with her cool dog."

"It is peaceful and quiet here," Jeannie says to the reporter. "Well, it isn't now because of the state helicopter monitoring our growing resistance. A lot of good people have shown up here from near and far to protest this whole methane thing. I hope the governor is watching. The president too. People say he watches a lot of TV."

"Can you share some background on your military service?" the reporter asks her.

"No," Jeannie says. "This isn't about me. It's about preserving a quiet place and a way of life. It's about clean water, clean air, quiet living, and all that."

"Cleeeeeean aaaiiiiirrrrr..." Solomon says.

The camera zooms out to reveal two men standing next to Jeannie. Salt recognizes them as Tyler Nash and Zorro Brown. The reporter asks a question, but Salt misses it.

"There is no coalbed methane west of the Menzies River," Tyler says.

"How do you know?" the reporter asks.

"The geology is all wrong. Look it up. The area is all glacial outwash deposits atop accreted terranes. My guess is that the governor wants to build something else out there. A hotel, maybe. Or a fancy casino… for his buddy, the president."

"Or as political payback," Zorro adds, "for a big campaign contribution."

"You're a geologist?" the reporter asks Tyler.

"I used to be."

"You fought in the war in—"

"No… I never fought, never saw combat. I was an Army petroleum specialist in Iraq. After that, I worked for big oil on Alaska's North Slope until I saw it for what it is."

"And what's that?"

"A travesty. Burning fossil fuels will be the death of our livable planet if we don't wake up and end our addiction."

"Will we wake up," the reporter asks, "before it's too late… will we wake up and save ourselves from what you see as a global disaster in the making?"

"I'm not sure. I wish I could say yes. I really do. But to be painfully honest, we're a selfish species, one that thinks that because we're clever, we're wise. But we're not."

"Consider this," Zorro says. "Enough sunlight strikes Earth in one hour to power all of humanity's energy needs for a year. But what do we do? We burn ancient carbon and send millions of pounds of greenhouse gases into our atmosphere every second of every day. That's why the seven hottest years on record have been the last seven, due to a fossil fuel industry that prizes profit over planet, and buys politicians who haven't got the vision or courage to do what's right."

"Americans have to unlearn what's untrue," Jeannie adds, "and that's hard. The truth doesn't stand a chance against a sea of fools who are determined to believe a lie."

Salt is mesmerized and finds himself reflecting on what it means to live in a town with such intelligent, far-sighted people—the likes of which he never heard as a teenager in Idaho.

As the interview ends, he sees a sadness in Jeannie's eyes.

His sons plow through their chicken and potatoes as the reporter faces the camera and says, "This is Tanya Pantaletto reporting from Strawberry Flats, where a resistance movement composed largely of veterans, Tlingits, and local schoolchildren are determined to stop one of the governor's Roads to Resources projects, a proposed coalbed methane operation out west of here on the other side of the Menzies River. More to follow at ten tonight, including a report from our Anchorage affiliate on the US Army's Homeland Defense and Security Command at Joint Base Elmendorf-Richardson, and a possible convoy to be sent from there to Strawberry Flats for what the governor describes as a 'potentially volatile threat to Alaska's economic future and to US national energy security.' Also, at ten, a story about a pack of salmon-eating wolves west of this town that could be genetically unique and threatened by this proposed coalbed methane extraction."

Abraham huffs loudly and goes into the kitchen to get more dinner.

Solomon rocks in his wheelchair.

Abraham returns, his plate filled with seconds. He sits down and resumes eating.

"Did you leave any for your brothers?" Salt asks him.

"A little."

Jericho and Joshua dash away and come back with scraps, their faces hangdog.

"We're going to need a larger crockpot," Hannah tells her husband.

Solomon issues a faint high-pitched moan, his arms crossed over his chest, his body twisted.

"Abraham," Salt says, "please share your seconds with your brothers."

His head down, Abe keeps eating. Hannah and the boys sit stone still.

"Abraham?"

"Yeah?"

"Stop eating right now and share what remains on your plate with Jericho and Joshua. We'll make toasted cheese sandwiches if you're still hungry."

Abraham glares at his father.

"Go ahead," Salt says. "Say what's on your mind."

Hannah quickly gets to her feet and goes into the kitchen to start cleaning up.

"They stole our traps, Dad. Kes and her stupid friends... they stole our traps."

"Please share what's on your plate with your brothers."

Salt could recite from the Bible right now, but Hannah has asked her well-meaning husband to back off on his preaching to Abe. We don't want to make matters worse. We don't want him to build contempt for that which we love and hold dear, our family's devotion to scripture, the teachings of Jesus, the Christian purity of body, mind, and spirit. The other day Salt told Abraham that he mustn't partake of the flesh of Tabby Anderson until she is eighteen, and even then, probably not.

Abraham stormed off and didn't come home until late.

And now this.

Abraham sets his plate on the floor and kicks it across the living room toward his younger brothers. They don't move, other than to look at their father.

Salt feels his anger rise. He mustn't do what he did before, when he swept all the food onto the kitchen floor. He takes a moment to steady himself on Proverbs: "A fool uttereth all his mind: but a wise man keepeth it in till afterwards."

Jess Cleet, the wolf killer, will fly into Strawberry Flats tomorrow morning to do his dirty work. I'll meet him at the airport and give him the M-44 cyanide bombs.

I've called in a favor. I hope it works.

A favor from Chippy and Cap McCall, those likable cousins with Skoal in their mouths and guns in their pants... who often fly to Juneau for new tattoos, and might be just bold and crazy enough to send Jess packing without causing a fistfight or shootout. When Salt built up the nerve to call Chippy, only yesterday, he relaxed the minute he heard Chippy get excited and tell him that for his plan to work, Salt would need an incriminating phone message from Jess. "One we can play back for him," Chippy said. "To freak him out."

It sounded good to Salt—then. But now?

Chippy and Cap McCall. Dear God, what could go wrong? Everything.

LATE THAT NIGHT, after Salt surreptitiously called Jess, Hannah asks again, "Are we going to be okay, husband?"

"Yes, we're going to be okay. Every family has moments like this."

"Remember when the boys were small, in the Minto cabin, and Solomon was still healthy, and we'd all gather around the wood-burning stove to eat and read by candlelight and kerosene lamp, and Abraham would put Joshua to bed and softly sing him to sleep?"

"Yes."

"I didn't think I'd ever miss those times, but I do now, a lot."

"So do I."

JESS CLEET STEPS OFF THE TWIN-ENGINE Piper Navajo Chieftain and into the Fjord Flying air taxi area. He walks up to Salt and says, "Have you got them?"

"They're right here," a voice says from behind. Salt watches Jess turn to face Chippy, who stands next to Cap and Tucker John, who wears a Stetson and a big knife on his belt, and looks like he could gut and clean the Fairbanks man in less than a minute—like a fish. Salt is certain that Chippy and Cap have guns under their jackets.

Shortly before the plane arrived, Cap had said they were "ready to rumble." Salt's heart races.

Chippy hands Jess a small pack. "Your go-to-hell cyanide bombs are in here. Spiffy little killers, the sarin gas for wildlife, right? We've booked you on the return flight to Juneau that leaves in twenty minutes on the same plane you just arrived on."

Jess Cleet shakes his head. "You're mistaken, cowboy. I have work to do here."

"No, you don't. You're not welcome here." As Chippy says this, the others crowd around Jess.

"You think you can intimidate me?" Jess says. "You've got nothing on me."

Chippy takes Salt's phone and plays back a voicemail on speaker: "Salt, I'll be on the 12:05 Fjord Flying flight into Strawberry Flats. Meet me at the airport and give me the M-44s. I'll also need a rental car and a map that shows the exact location of the den."

"And oh, boy howdy... would you look at..." Chippy says as he shows Jess the phone. "The message has your number on it."

Jess looks around the crowded air taxi area, snapping his head to and fro.

"There's more," Chippy says as he opens text messages on Salt's phone. "Last night, our plucky friend Salt here... well, look at that... he texted you back. Remember? Here's your correspondence."

Salt: *I got your message. I'll see you at the airport.*

Jess: *Good. Thanks.*

Salt: *Do you plan to take out the whole pack?*

Jess: *Yes. At night... should be easy.*

Jess stares, and in his dark eyes Salt sees something of the man he himself used to be—a taker, a killer. Not for food, but for money.

Other veterans gather around, having flown in on the same flight to join the encampment and resistance. Some have long hair, some butch cuts; some dress in civilian clothes, some wear army fatigues and camo. Salt watches Cap and Tucker John greet them with handshakes and hugs, while Chippy remains toe to toe with Jess. "The M-44s are HAZMAT," Chippy tells him. "The air taxi desk already knows this. They'll fly your poison back to Juneau on a special cargo plane later today. You can pick it up then, back in the big city. It's been a real pleasure meeting you."

Jess glares at him. "I'll be back."

"No, you won't," Tucker John says from behind, his hand on the hilt of his knife.

Salt thinks, *Fish head soup.*

Just before Jess turns to leave, Salt sees his hardened face stricken with fear—the trapper trapped.

Other veterans gather around, "Hey Cap... Hey Chippy..."

"Hey guys," Chippy says to the newcomers while keeping an eye on Jess as he checks his cyanide bombs onto the cargo flight. "How are things in Texas?"

"Hot and dry as hell," says a new arrival who wears a black patch over one eye. "Thousands of Texans are moving into underground shelters."

"Why?" Cap asks.

"To survive the summers, man. It's too damn hot."

"What do they do in the shelters?" Chippy asks.

"I don't know... probably watch TV. Season twenty of *Duck Dynasty.*"

"Rednecks rule," Cap says.

"Yeah, until reality slaps them in the face. You guys should know that the president is building a secret police force and has his eye on what you're doing here."

"If it's so secret, how come you know about it?" Chippy asks.

They laugh, and Salt finds himself laughing too, or having a good chuckle at least. Watching Jess Cleet board the flight to Juneau, he feels as though he's able to breathe deeply again—for the first time in weeks. He feels happy... happier than he's been in a long time.

Chippy says to him, "Well, I think that went pretty well."

"Thank you," Salt says.

"My pleasure. The word is out about your big family trip to London. When do you go?"

"Soon. I'll stay here with our two youngest boys while Hannah goes with Solomon and Abraham, our eldest. Abe is strong; Hannah will need his help. They won't return home until August, if all goes well, hopefully in time for Solomon's birthday."

"You got enough money?"

"Yes, we think so. Thank you. And thanks again for this, for what you just did. It was hard for me to ask for help."

Chippy smiles. "Mother Earth and Brother Wolf, man... what more is there?"

"Why are you so generous to my family and me?"

Chippy stuffs a wad of Skoal into his mouth. "Oh, you can thank Kes for that. She says that if we don't do everything possible to help the world's few remaining wolves, and a kid like Solomon—who's probably part wolf himself, eh? given his spirit and light—then why are we here... right? I mean, honestly... why are we all here?"

PASTOR ANDERSON WAVES HIS ARMS to mimic the shorebirds down on Central Beach. "Have you seen them?" he asks his congregation. "They fly as if each flock were a single organism, the birds darting here and there, perfectly choreographed, flashing silver, white, and black as they suddenly shift directions and land all together, and then—whoosh!—they're up and flying and flashing again. It's a marvel, I must say."

Salt notes that the chapel is packed with many newcomers—veterans presumably, part of the growing resistance—who stand along the back wall, fidgeting and coughing, but otherwise quiet. Hannah squeezes Salt's hand with both of hers and turns to partly face him so she can rest her tired head on his shoulder.

"They'll be gone soon," Pastor Anderson adds, "headed north to raise their young on the tundra of arctic Alaska. Having said that, I'd like to tell a story. Not a parable from Jesus, or even a story from the Bible. But it is about birds, in a way...

"A little more than eight hundred years ago a child of God was born into wealth and privilege in a small town in central Italy. This boy grew into a boisterous young man who drank, chased women, and served as a soldier." Pastor Anderson smiles at the newcomer veterans in the back of the chapel. "In time, he was captured and thrown into prison, where he lived with rats for a year. When his nobleman father finally paid the ransom, the son did not come home. He went into hiding. He prayed. When his father hauled him into court for refusing to run the family business with all its rewards and responsibilities, the son stripped nearly naked and said money no longer interested him. The all-powerful church had grown too wealthy, he said. Too complacent and un-Christlike. Why, he asked, do the poor live in the malaria-infested shadows, while the bishops live high and mighty in their sunny splendor? This is wrong. Our young man grew into an ascetic, a saint. He gave away everything he owned, including his shoes, and devoted the rest of his life to helping the sick and the poor; to live in service to God and all His creatures. He delivered a sermon to birds. And best of all… are you ready for this?"

Salt sees Pastor Anderson pause to find Kes in the crowd, sitting next to the veteran with her tranquil dog. Again, the pastor smiles as if offering a blessing, and says, "He charmed a wolf that was menacing his town."

Salt catches his breath.

A wolf?

CHAPTER FORTY-TWO

Kes

KES CATCHES HER BREATH.

He charmed a wolf?

"Some said he was mad," Pastor Anderson says. "Others said he was brilliant. Everybody called him 'Il Poverello,' the Little Poor Man. As the years passed, he became a scrawny figure dressed in a filthy tunic, with sores on his skin and an infection in his eye. And still his popularity grew. He only asked his followers to do as he did: Give it all away. Let love be your riches. In his final years, this Il Poverello, this Saint Francis of Assisi, as we know him today, developed the stigmata, the wounds of Christ. He died at age forty-five with no army, no kingdom, no memoir, and no manifesto. He'd invented nothing. His followers were poor and powerless. Yet he changed the world, and continues to change it today."

Another pause. The congregation is all quiet save for one sound: Solomon rocking in his wheelchair and softly moaning. Not in pain, but pleasure.

"As many of you know," Pastor Anderson concludes, "the Pope chose to name himself after Francis of Assisi, the patron saint of Nature. He's the first Pope from South America. He studied chemistry, he understands the science of human-caused climate change, and he used to be a bouncer in a Buenos Aires nightclub. Don't mess with him."

Laughter ripples through the chapel.

"Pope Francis recently said that an altruistic atheist is more Christlike than a greedy Christian. He also said authoritarian capitalism, not democratic socialism, is what imperils our world. So, I ask: do we really need more roads? Nobody in this town will ever go hungry. Or die alone. We are here for each other. We are family. Let's remember that, cherish that, celebrate that, protect that. Oh yes, and one more thing about birds."

More light laughter.

"Any day now, sandhill cranes should come through our quiet little town, headed north. I've heard them before but have never seen them fly right overhead. I understand they sometimes rest and feed out west of the Menzies River, where the wolves live. Let's give them a warm welcome, shall we? Now, let's open our hymnals to number seventy."

EVERY DAY MORE PEOPLE ARRIVE IN STRAWBERRY FLATS. Mostly veterans, but also Native Americans and environmentalists. Kes notices several big diesel-burning trucks with *Drill, Baby, Drill* bumper stickers. And funky old VW hippie vans and new electric cars with their stickers *Go Insane with Methane.* Tents go up everywhere behind the shop at Willynillyville. Captain Don and E. J. build two new outhouses, with guidance from Chippy. Half a dozen Tlingits arrive from Jinkaat with camper trucks. Mom and Jeannie cook up mountains of spaghetti, burritos, and quesadillas.

And every day, construction men from Juneau and Ketchikan drive out Menzies River Road in their big trucks and hard hats to survey the site and stage their equipment and building materials: huge laminate timbers and rolls of cable, steel posts and I-beams and metal fixtures, all on pallets on long flatbed trucks, moved from the vacant lot to the end of Menzies River Road. And every day, en route home after school, Kes rides her bike out there to size it up, as instructed by Uncle Ty. And every day is less quiet and more crowded than the day before, and Mom gets more nervous. Papa and Grandpa too. And every day—but mostly at night—Chippy and Cap and others work in the shop making mysterious things. Battleships, maybe. Or F-15 fighter jets. Or atom bombs.

ZORRO BROWN, the former *Los Angeles Times* reporter who was twice nominated for a Pulitzer Prize, and who befriended Uncle Ty in Iraq, and who participated in Standing Rock and Arab Spring and Occupy Wall Street before he retired to Alaska and bought a fishing boat, arrives in Willynillyville late one afternoon to brief the growing resistance about civil disobedience: what works and doesn't work, how things can go well or unravel and escalate fast. "Remember," he says, "it's no picnic getting arrested or hit with tear gas.

Or getting tased… or shot."

The living room is jammed.

Kes sits on the floor with Berit, Emily, and Kona.

Tim, Tia, and Melissa should arrive soon.

Papa elects to go outside to feed his chickadees and work in the garden; it's almost planting time. He has his headphones in case a state or media helicopter flies overhead. Mom, Kipper, and Jeannie have gone into town to run errands, and to avoid the charged atmosphere. Earlier, Kes overheard Uncle Ty tell Tucker John and Captain Don that Chippy, Cap, and E. J. are likely more inclined to fight than to resist, and will need to be managed in some way.

"How?" Captain Don asked.

"I don't know," Uncle Ty said.

"My first piece of advice is this," Zorro says to the crowded room. "No weapons. No firearms. No knives. No rocks. Never get aggressive or violent. The minute you get violent, you're playing their game, and they'll crush you, especially if the governor and the president call in the military, which is a real possibility. Don't let your own zeal or fear make you crazy or stupid. There's too much of that in America already. You have to stay cool and calm. Stay focused and on message."

"What is our message?" Captain Don asks Uncle Ty.

Uncle Ty looks at Zorro. "What should our message be?"

Kes watches the others, including two Tlingit men from Jinkaat: One in his mid-twenties, muscular, with slightly offset eyes and a limp, his name Jimmy Wisting. The other older but not by much, hardened in some way, with cold arctic eyes until he smiles. Kona whispers to Kes that he has a cool name: Kid Hugh. They watch him open a pocketknife and cut a callus off his hand.

"Okay," Zorro says, "No message yet. We'll get to that soon. How many do you think you'll have in the resistance by the time the road building begins?"

Uncle Ty looks at the Tlingits. Jimmy says, "Twenty from Jinkaat. Maybe thirty."

Uncle Ty asks Kes, "How many kids do you think you'll get?"

"Fifty," Kona says impulsively.

"No way," Emily says.

"I can get half a dozen of my Jinkaat friends," Berit says. She graduated from Jinkaat High School two years ago. Kes detects sweet energy between her and Jimmy.

Uncle Ty looks at Kes, waiting for her answer.

"Forty," Kona says.

"Fifteen," Kes finally says. "Maybe twenty."

"Twenty-five," Kona says.

"As for veterans," Uncle Ty says, "I'll bet thirty to forty."

"And others from outside Strawberry Flats who might show up?" Zorro asks.

"Hard to say," Uncle Ty answers. "Maybe several dozen more. Maybe as many as one to two hundred. But then again, maybe only a handful."

Zorro says, "The house bill passed, so we have to assume the road building will begin soon. The state probably won't even wait for the EA…"

"What's an EA?" Emily asks her friends, quietly.

"An environmental assessment," Berit whispers.

"…and don't expect them to begin on a Monday," Zorro continues. "It could be any time. And once they begin, they'll work long days and stack the shifts to get it done fast."

Jimmy says, "They'll send two or three loggers down the flagged corridor to knock down the big trees, leaving high stumps. An excavator will follow and pull the stumps and logs. A Ditch Witch will dig a narrow ditch with guys laying power line and backfilling. After them, they'll roll out road fabric. A second excavator will ditch the north side to help drain the road and pile the organics off to the side with the stumps. After that, trucks will bring in full loads of gravel and dump it on the fabric. Bulldozers will smooth it out, and that'll be it—a new road to the river. Done in one week."

"The important thing will be to blockade them before they begin," Zorro says. "You'll need to be in place before they are. Can you do that?"

Everybody looks at Uncle Ty.

"Yes," he says. "We've already begun."

We have? Kes wonders. *How? When?* She feels her stomach lurch from excitement and fear. She taps her sternum.

"Another thing," Zorro says. "The men behind this coalbed methane initiative will lie. They already have. And when we call them out, they'll lie again and call us liars, and un-American, the enemy within. They'll call us socialists and radical leftists, just like other immoral men before them who disparaged suffragists, abolitionists, and union organizers. We'll need to stay calm and on message; be prepared to be roughed up and arrested. We're going up against an American legacy of conquest… a selfish, white nationalist, often brutal mindset that's marched across this continent for five hundred years, killing on an epic scale, eating up ecosystems, destroying cultures, forcing children to work long hours in dirty, unsafe factories. Our president has threatened to send troops to smash us. He's done it elsewhere, against similar blockades. Take it seriously. He and the governor will turn the entire right-wing media disinformation machine against us. Nine states have already made it a felony to do what we're about to do here."

Kes sees her uncle stroke his chin in thought, maybe even worry, something she's never seen before. "Will they send paratroopers?" he asks.

"I doubt it," Zorro says. "The area is too forested. And assets could land on the wrong side of the river. But supplies, yes. They could air-drop supplies and field markers. The president is an extremist, but he'll also defer to the governor."

"Helicopters?"

"No, the distance from Anchorage to Strawberry Flats is too far."

"C-130s or C-17s?"

"Yes, that's a strong possibility. The Strawberry Flats runway was built during World War II and is large enough to accommodate both C-130s and C-17s loaded with an infantry Airborne Brigade or the Alaska Army National Guard... and troop transport vehicles. One C-17 can also carry an M1 Abrams battle tank and two UH-60 helicopters."

Silence.

"When it happens," Zorro adds, "it will happen fast, and it will shatter our little town."

More silence.

"Don't let that discourage you," Zorro says, as if reading the room. "We don't resist because we think we can win. We resist because it's the right thing to do. We'll suffer setbacks and heartbreak, but over time the truth will prevail. It always does. Justice will win. Never forget that. A president or a governor can look desperate if not foolish by unleashing the military on American citizens. I've seen it before. But the court of public opinion is also fickle, and will turn on us if the kids we've involved get hurt. Remember that. People will not blame the road builders or the methane drillers or the military. If kids get hurt, they'll blame us."

Kes feels her stomach churn more. Emily grabs her hand.

Where's Tim?

As Zorro talks about the importance of producing resistance pamphlets,

Kes wills herself to calm down. She thinks back to her early years on the bus with the band, when Stringer would read *Green Eggs and Ham* to her. "Oh no," he'd say in his funny voice as she'd put the book in his lap, "not again." They'd laugh. And Sammye would harmonize above Papa and Rita, and even birds would stop to listen... so Kes imagined. Uncle Ty would fly down and talk about Alaska, how wolves up there inhabit your dreams and bring to life your four-legged shadow, the person you were always meant to be. He said the country was so wild and immense—more than twice the size of Texas— that if anybody could figure out a way to steal Italy, Alaska would be the place to hide it. Yes, modern civilization has many nice things: jazz and blues and rock 'n' roll, and laws to protect right from wrong and the weak from the strong. "But look around," he'd say to Papa. "I like Lubbock. You know that, little brother. We've had good times up on the Llano Estacado while Texas got hustled into one big Walmart, Big Mac nightmare. Right? I mean, vigorous economic growth forever on a planet that's only so big? Where do you want to be when it all comes crashing down?"

And so here we are, in Alaska. About to have a standoff.

Maybe a war.

After Uncle Ty told Kes that she would be his Patton, she researched General George Patton. He won big battles, and died in a car accident. *Crazy.*

THE SPRING DAYS BECOME VIVID yet dreamlike, filled with birdsong and warmth and everybody on edge and driving too fast. Mrs. Goodnight has so much to talk about, Uncle Ty thinks she might have a heart attack. Kes finds time in the garden with Papa, Grandpa, and little Kip, planting carrots and potatoes. It feels blissful until they hear the state helicopter, and Papa closes his eyes and slips on his headphones. She and Papa visit the beach at low tide to watch the shorebirds. Papa finds a hummingbird nest, shows it to Kes, and says, "Isn't that the most perfect thing you've ever seen?" He tells her that hummingbirds are found only in the New World... more than three hundred species, each with a heart that beats ten times a second. Early European explorers called them "Joyas Voladoras"—flying jewels. They had never seen such incredible creatures before.

Kes tells him about Science Friday, about rockets and microscopes and seaweed and art projects; how she always finds herself in a leadership role during Mrs. Carry's field trips, and how every presentation must now be approved by Principal Cunningham.

"I'm not surprised," Papa says.

Kes asks him, "What are Chippy and Cap making in the shop with all those ropes and nets and pulleys and stuff?"

Papa smiles. "You'll see."

THE FOLLOWING NIGHT, Kes can't sleep. From her bedroom window, she sees flashlight beams moving along the angle trail that runs from the shop past the garden and through the woods to the end of Menzies River Road. She sees the ponies hauling gear. She sneaks outside and into a gentle rain; takes a moment to fill her lungs with the cool, moist air. Overhead, she hears the winnowing of snipes in courtship flight. From one of the many camper trucks, she hears live music; from another, a smoker's cough; and from another, laughter. As she enters the dark shop, a headlamp beam hits her in the eyes.

"Oh... sorry, Kes," E. J. says. "What are you doing here?"

"I couldn't sleep." Kes's eyes adjust to see Jimmy Wisting and Kid Hugh, busy at work, also wearing headlamps. "Where are Chippy and Cap?"

"They're spiking trees along the proposed road route," E. J. says.

"Spiking trees? What for?"

"To ruin chainsaws and slow down the enemy."

The enemy? "But I thought we—"

"Back to bed, Kes."

Every night thereafter, men work in the shop until well past midnight. And every day, more resisters arrive until Willynillyville feels like a small city. And still, they keep coming. Uncle Ty gives one interview after another, mostly on the radio. He even talks to CNN and the BBC. And all the women seem to do is cook, cook, cook.

A WEEK LATER, Principal Cunningham calls Kes, Emily, Melissa, and Kona into her office and tells them they cannot spend school time raising and training "an order of knights... or whatever it is."

"The Knights of the Menzies River," Kona announces. "We're like the rebel fighters in *Rogue One*."

Principal Cunningham stares at him.

"The *Star Wars* movie," he adds, as if that makes everything clear—and acceptable.

"We're not going to fight," Kes tells her. "We're going to resist."

"We might fight," Kona says.

"How many of your classmates have you recruited or attempted to recruit?" Principal Cunningham asks.

The four students glance at one another.

"It's hard to say," Emily says.

"Everybody," Kona says. "I think every kid in this school knows about it because it's like wildfire, you know? I mean, it's pretty cool to get to serve with real veterans who have fought in real wars, and to cross rivers with them and to save wolves and maybe save the whole planet. That's cool, right?"

Melissa looks at Kes with her big eyes.

Principal Cunningham turns to face out the window. "Okay," she says, "we're going to end this silly thing right now. It's lunchtime. Everybody's in the multipurpose room. Mrs. Goodnight"—the kids look behind to see the school secretary appear in the doorway like a cop—"I want you to go ring the bell." Mrs. Goodnight disappears, the bell rings, and Principal Cunningham stands up and says, "The four of you, follow me."

Out the door they go, single file. As they walk down the hall, Kes asks Principal Cunningham, "You want them to drill for the coalbed methane, don't you?"

"It doesn't matter what I want."

"My uncle says you need to set an example for the entire school."

"I set an example every day by my decorum, Kes. I set an example by traits I learned when I was your age and attended a good Christian school filled with piety, kindness, and respect."

"What's piety?"

"Piety is being pious, being devoted to God."

"My uncle says the best place to find God is in a river... or in a glacier."

Principal Cunningham stops and turns on Kes, who is immediately behind her and nearly runs into her. They all stop. "Your uncle is not the man you think he is, Kes. You'll learn that one day, and it will be a hard lesson for you... to wake up and see things for what they really are. Now, follow me. All of you. And say nothing."

They enter the multipurpose room to find every student waiting, subdued, quiet, expectant. Before Principal Cunningham can begin, two teachers,

Mrs. Carry and Ms. Souther, intercept her and pull her back into the hall, out of sight. The kids love Ms. Souther because every fall she has her students write a constitution that directs their conduct throughout the year. It makes them feel like the Founding Fathers.

More kids begin to talk.

"Quiet, all of you," Mrs. Goodnight commands them.

Kona fidgets. At any moment Kes expects him to jump up on a table and give a speech like something out of *Rogue One*, which he's seen ten times or more. Sure enough, as if on cue, he says to Kes, "We have to do something. We're the rebels, right? We're the good guys. We need to fight."

"Be quiet," Melissa says.

"The Force is with me," Kona adds. "I can feel it."

"Quiet," Melissa repeats.

Kona scowls and says, "They all died, Melissa. All the rebels. But they got the plans for the Death Star to Princess Leia so she and Luke and Han Solo could save the galaxy."

"Kona... shut... up."

"QUIET," Mrs. Goodnight shouts.

Kes remembers Uncle Ty talking about insurgents from Libya to Somalia to Afghanistan to Iraq who saw themselves as Kona does now, as freedom fighters, like their favorite Hollywood heroes. *And who was their all-powerful adversary? The USA. Crazy.*

Principal Cunningham walks back into the room with Mrs. Carry and Ms. Souther, all wearing grave expressions. "All right, students," Principal Cunningham announces. "Lunch is over. Everybody, return to your classes and resume your studies."

As they disperse, the students appear confused, as if to ask: *What was that about?*

Kes catches Abe glaring at her.

Tim pulls her aside and says, "This isn't good, Kes."

Kes yanks her arm from his grip.

"You have to stop this," Tim says, his face flushed red. "Somebody's going to get hurt."

"C'mon, Tim," Emily says. "Show some courage."

"You're being stupid, Emily," Tim says. "You're all being stupid, pretending to be knights and rebels and stuff."

"Shut up, Tim," Kona tells him.

"You shut up, Kona. You don't know anything. You don't know if you're a rebel or a knight or a—"

"STOP," Kes says. She turns and says, "Tim, please... if you want, maybe you could pray for us." She expects him to say he will. But he doesn't. Instead, he shakes his head and walks away, and Kes feels her heart break.

THE NEXT DAY, Kes asks permission to roll Solomon outside into the sunshine. Abraham, always possessive of Solomon, is busy in the computer lab.

Solomon says, "I'm going to Looondoooon."

"I know, Solomon," Kes says. "That's so cool."

Kes parks Solomon's wheelchair atop the small rise near the school playground.

They laugh when they see Kona climb the monkey bars and shout to some kids below, "The Force is with me... and I am one with the Force."

Other kids dart out of school and across the street to the gymnasium. Kes hears thrushes and kinglets, and draws Solomon's attention to each song, how distinctive they are... until birds of another kind make a distant yet ominous sound, approaching from the northwest.

Military. Incoming.

Kes feels a thud in her chest. *This is it.*

Sitting next to her, Solomon blinks with incomprehension.

"Whoa, look at that," says Mr. Goodnight, stopping as he is walking across the school courtyard to bring lunch to his wife. Two massive planes lumber through the air with thunderous resolve. "Those are C-17 Globemaster IIIs," he adds. "Big suckers, made by Boeing... with PW2000 engines."

Kona jumps on his bike and rides up to Kes. "They're coming," he says. "The evil Galactic Empire. I'll ride out to the airport and watch them land."

"No, Kona. You don't need to watch them land. Go to Willynillyville and alert everyone, then take the angle trail to the blockade and get in position."

He rides off.

Kes watches teachers begin to shepherd kids from the playground into the school. Many break free and run to their bikes. Others jump into cars pulling up with nervous parents inside. It's mayhem, an invasion. For days, people have said something like this might happen, something like another Standing Rock. *Zorro was right.*

Emily and Melissa run up to Kes. "What do we do?" Melissa asks.

"We do what we've planned," Kes says. "Get to the blockade."

Solomon rocks excitedly. "Bloooockaaaaade…"

When Kes turns to speak with him and calm him, a vice grip grabs her by the wrist. The hand of Abraham. He towers over her. "You're a thief," he says.

Kes tries to break free. "You're hurting me, Abe."

"You're in big trouble around here," Abraham tells her through his gritted teeth.

"Noooo…" Solomon screams as he begins to rock hard.

With her free hand, Kes grabs Sol's wheelchair. "It's okay, Sol. I've got you."

"Don't touch him," Abe says. But he only grips Kes harder.

Her eyes begin to tear up from the pain.

The green Willynillyville pickup truck—the Rolling Avocado—pulls up with Captain Don driving. Tucker John gets out lightning fast. Abe drops his grip, unlocks the wheelchair brake, and quickly rolls his brother away.

"You okay?" Tucker John asks Kes.

"Yeah." *Breathe.*

"We have to go."

As they pull away with Kes in the truck bed, she stands up and pounds hard on the roof for Captain Don to stop. She yells across the schoolyard where dozens of kids watch the big planes come in. "Resist," she screams. "We need all of you. You know what to do. Follow Kona. Follow Emily and Melissa. Follow me to the blockade at the end of Menzies River Road. Resist. Now."

CHAPTER FORTY-THREE

Silver

NOT FAR TO THE WEST, beyond the Menzies River and the formidable but aging moose they feel capable of bringing down, Silver and Sister stop hunting and look up. Nothing has prepared them for this... for the thunderous mechanical birds that shatter the sky, coming closer, making an unnatural noise.

Nothing can explain this.

No hunt or story or dream.

From one of the noisy mechanical birds emerges a stream of small, billowing offspring, like the seeds of dandelions, black and threatening, drifting down... down...

Silver sees panic in Sister's eyes. He thinks of the all-black female, a member of the pack he displaced from the beached whale, but later saw again and again, always at a distance, and with each sighting felt more drawn to her. Will he ever see her again? Start his own pack? Have his own pups? Play with them? Hunt with them?

He thinks of Old One and his two brothers, Strong and Weak. Gone.

One of the mechanical birds continues straight while the other circles and releases more seeds.

The sky is falling.

What to do?

Her head low, shoulders up, tail down... Sister froths at her mouth. Frightened. Panicked. Silver wants to protect her. Protect them all. Family. Heart. Home.

What to do?

The noise is unbearable.

What to do?

Run.

CHAPTER FORTY-FOUR

Salt

DEREK STEPS BACK INTO HIS GARAGE and says, "Salt, get out here and look at this."

Salt wipes engine grease from his hands and follows Derek outside.

"Can you believe that?" Derek says. "Those are military planes. And are those paratroopers? I don't think so. I think it's a supply drop out west beyond the end of Menzies River Road. Tyler Nash is going to regret this... all of it."

Five minutes later, Salt speeds home in his Toyota while dialing Hannah on his phone. She answers. "I see them," she says. "The planes are huge. Rosie Goodnight just called and said that school has been canceled. We have to get the boys."

Salt arrives home, kisses Hannah quickly, then leaves for school in the red van. En route, he encounters a steady stream of vehicles and bicycles headed the other way, westbound, kids riding with determination.

"What's happening, Dad?" little Joshua asks when Salt arrives.

"Mr. Goodnight says it's probably an Army Airborne combat team," Abraham says excitedly as he rolls Solomon up to the van. "He says it's part of the Twenty-Fifth Infantry Division stationed in Anchorage at a combined Army and Air Force base."

"But why are they here?" Joshua asks.

"To smash the resistance and Kes's stupid order of knights," Abraham says, "so the governor can build his road and a bridge over the Menzies River to help make America energy independent and keep it great."

"Kes isn't stupid," Jericho says.

"Shut up, Jerry," Abe says.

"You shut up."

"Enough," Salt says.

"The governor needs the Army to beat Kes?" Joshua asks. "Is Kes a general?"

Solomon rocks in his wheelchair. "Keeeesss the beeeeest..."

THAT AFTERNOON, with his boys safely back home, Salt drives west down Menzies River Road toward the river. He finds it blocked by US Army Jeeps and soldiers in full combat gear, rifles at the ready, having arrived in the C-17s.

What to do?

Salt swings right onto Willynillyville Drive, private land, and soon encounters a huge encampment: trucks and camper vans parked along the road, tents and cooking grills and tarps erected in clever ways. Two bearded men he's never seen before stop him and ask for his name and his place of residence, and if he's here for the resistance.

Why am I here?

The other day, when Salt and Hannah went to the post office, Hannah jumped with fright and grabbed his arm when they walked by a parked car and two small dogs suddenly barked from inside, snarling and baring their sharp, little teeth. Both dogs wore pink ribbons and collars with bells. Mrs. Cunningham came out from the post office and said, "Winnie... Minnie... stop barking. Be good dogs."

Salt wanted to strangle them.

One of the bearded men asks him again, "Are you here for the resistance?"

"Oh... yes, I am," Salt says. "I used to be a trapper. Beaver, mostly, up in Interior Alaska. But I took wolves too. Lots of them. And I regret that."

The two men stare at him.

Salt adds, "Tyler is right. There's no coalbed methane around here."

More stares.

"Sorry, guys. Yes. I live in Strawberry Flats, and I'm here for the resistance. I can't stay through the night or get arrested. I have four sons and am the sole provider for my family... but still, I'm worried about my neighbors... Chippy and Cap and Tucker John and the kids, all of them. So... how can I help?"

"Are you a veteran?"

"No."

"Are you armed?"

"No."

One of the men hands Salt a resistance pamphlet and says, "Read this and park up on the right, just off the road, and check in with Zorro at the shop."

Salt drives up the road. Willynillyville is cluttered yet strangely quiet. He finds Zorro, who briefs him and tells him most everybody is at the blockade, at the end of Menzies River Road, where the new construction will begin. "To get there, follow this angle trail from here, at the shop. But before you go, check in with Rita and Jeannie about anything that needs to be taken by wheelbarrow or garden cart, especially food or water."

"You've seen this kind of thing before, haven't you?" Salt asks Zorro.

"Yes, many times."

"Are you frightened?"

"Yes, a little… always. Things can go wrong in a hurry. It's part of the chemistry. I heard about your confrontation at the airport."

"Things could have gone wrong there too," Salt says.

"But they didn't," Zorro says, "and here you are, right here, right now. Thanks for showing up."

In the main house, Salt finds Rita but not Jeannie. Instead, a woman named Sammye—who Rita introduces as a dear friend from her music days in Texas—is packing containers with food. Both women shake Salt's hand and load up his wheelbarrow with a small cooler and two totes.

"It's nice to see you here," Rita tells him. She looks exhausted.

"It's nice to be here," Salt replies.

Twenty minutes later, he arrives at the blockade. It takes a moment for his eyes to adjust to the spokes of sunlight that slice through the tall trees and render everything half in shadow, half in bright light. Looking up, he's amazed to see fifteen or twenty blockaders, most of them men, hanging in hammocks high in the trees—slated to be cut down—in the proposed road route, several with large banners.

CLEAN ENERGY NOW

THERE IS NO PLANET B

FRACKING NOT WELCOME HERE

GO INSANE WITH METHANE

Another one hundred to two hundred people—veterans, Tlingits, townspeople from Strawberry Flats and Jinkaat, and a few from Juneau, plus maybe two dozen kids, many with their parents and holding signs—mingle about, watching and waiting.

It's a standoff, all right. And like Willynillyville, it's strangely quiet.

Every veteran wears a red-white-and-blue bib that gives their tour-of-duty dates. *Iraq: 2004–05; 2007–08; Afghanistan: 2011–12; Vietnam: 1968–69, 1970–71.* Among the resisters are two very old men whose bibs read: *WWII, Pacific Theater, 1942–45* and *WWII, European Theater, 1943–45.* Salt observes Kes's white-haired grandpa with them, talking quietly.

To the west, behind the blockaders and under the command of a captain, Salt can see soldiers fanned out through the woods in combat fatigues, weapons ready, including tear gas and zip-tie handcuffs. To the east, in the parking area at the end of the road, a larger military unit is equally armed, under the command of a colonel. *They must have poured out of the C-17s that landed at the airport.* The colonel and the captain speak now and then by radio, and the colonel, near as Salt can tell, speaks by satellite phone with a command post in Anchorage, or maybe with the governor in Juneau, or the president in Washington, DC.

Nearby, Salt hears the Willynillyville veteran, E. J., say, "Kick the fires and light the tires, Tucker John. They don't know what to do. Not yet, anyway."

"That'll change," Tucker John says ominously.

"Where are Chippy and Cap?"

"I don't know, and that worries me."

E. J. turns to Salt. "You're Solomon's dad, right?"

"Yes."

Just then, Melissa Darling approaches with her father, the ecologist at the marine reserve, and says, "Hi Mr. d'Alene. Is Jerry here?"

"No... he's at home."

Melissa gives Salt a sour look and walks away.

Jericho and Joshua had asked to come along; Salt refused, thinking they could get hurt. He regrets that now because... *why? Kids can get hurt riding bikes and climbing trees; that's no reason to stop them. Animals are safe in cages, but only half alive.*

Not far away, he sees a TV crew interviewing Tyler, Danny, and Kes Nash, and again finds himself admiring the freckle-faced girl who created an order of knights... of sorts.

Behind them stand the soldiers.

Above them hang the blockaders.

In the parking area, the colonel, flanked by his men, talks with two state troopers while three Ketchikan loggers lean against a big Ford pickup, waiting to mow down the forest. Many protestors sit at the base of every large tree, some chained into position.

Salt takes it all in: people everywhere, some eating, others visiting, many fiddling with their phones. He watches three soldiers stand their rifles into a tripod, barrels up, and light up cigarettes. Things feel portentous but not imminent, and not at all dangerous. But as the resistance pamphlet warns: *Everything can change. Fast. Everything can go wrong. Be ready.*

Salt drops off his cooler and two totes, and heads back to Willynillyville for another load.

BACK HOME THAT NIGHT, Salt and his family gather in the living room to eat their chili dogs and to watch the Juneau Channel 4 News report on the "Standoff in Strawberry Flats." Nobody moves as Tyler Nash stares intently into the camera and says the standoff is "democracy and freedom at its best."

With amazing poise, Kes tells a story of a man who once shot a wolf and was forever changed when he saw a fierce green fire in its dying eyes. When asked how she manages to go to school, form an order of knights, and participate in this standoff, Kes says, "Not until our principal accepts science and allows our teachers to talk about climate change and the destruction of our biosphere, and how we can stop it, will my friends and I go back to school. Meanwhile, this is school now, here in the woods, standing strong. This is our classroom now."

The reporter turns to Danny Nash, who says, "I think my daughter just said it all."

Later, in the kitchen, Abraham says to Salt, "Kes is crazy, Dad. I heard Mrs. Cunningham talking about her, how she makes people feel uncomfortable."

"The way Jesus made the Romans feel uncomfortable?"

Abraham shrugs. "That's different. I think Kes and all those protestors should be arrested and thrown into jail."

"Jail? Really?"

"No more school? How stupid is that?"

A green truck rolls up to the house and parks. Salt and Abraham stare as several Willynillyville veterans climb out from the cab and the back. Next, an old Jeep pulls up with Jeannie and Kes, followed by Pastor Anderson's Subaru. Soon, a dozen people stand in the dusky light to admire the wheelchair ramp with its 180-degree turn.

Salt steps out with Abraham, followed by Hannah and Joshua, and finally Jericho who pushes Solomon.

"Did you build this ramp?" one of the veterans asks Salt.

"Yes."

"Has Chippy seen it?"

"No."

"He really should see this."

"We just saw you on TV, Kes," Jericho says. "You were awesome."

"Thanks, Jerry. You're always welcome to join our Knights of the Menzies River."

Abraham huffs loudly and goes back inside.

Hannah says, "Kes, Jeannie told me that your father's band is here from Texas."

"Yes. They drove all the way from Austin and showed up on the ferry two days ago, as moral support for my parents. Stringer the bass player, Sammye the keyboardist and singer, and Justin the drummer, who brought his brother and wife and kids. Sammye just finished recording her first solo CD. She has an amazing voice."

"Might we all get a concert?" Hannah asks.

Kes thinks for a moment. "I don't know about now. Maybe later. Everybody is pretty focused on the standoff."

"Why aren't all of you still out there, at the blockade?" Salt asks her. He realizes it's the first time he's ever spoken to Kes.

"We've all been given duty sheets with time schedules worked up by Zorro and my uncle," she tells him. "Night duty is light."

"Because loggers never knock down trees at night," adds a man in military fatigues that Salt doesn't recognize.

"Stringer volunteered for night watch tonight," Kes says, "up in a tree, in a hammock."

Solomon rocks in his wheelchair. "Stringer in a treeeeeeeeeeee."

"That's right, Sol," Kes says with a smile. "He's way up there."

"Why are you all here?" Salt asks.

Pastor Anderson steps forward and reaches up and hands Hannah an envelope. "This is for you. We've been raising money. We opened a bank account and just wrote our first check, something the Willynillyville veterans and our church put together for your time in London. It's expensive there. We thought we should give it to you now because, well… with the standoff, we could all get arrested soon."

"You did this for us?" Hannah asks. "For our family?"

"Yes," Pastor Anderson replies. "And there's more in there than just money."

With no more fanfare, they climb back into the green truck and the old Jeep, and Pastor Anderson's Subaru, and leave. As they drive away, Kes leans out the window of the truck and shouts, "Shake it on down."

"Shake it on dooooooowwwwn," Solomon yells back, rocking with excitement.

Back in the kitchen, Hannah opens the envelope. It contains three tickets to a Rolling Stones concert at Wembley Stadium, and a ten-thousand-dollar check written to "Salt or Hannah d'Alene" with "Saving Solomon" on the subject line.

Hannah begins to cry.

Salt wraps her in his arms as Jericho and Joshua join them. Salt grabs Solomon and wheels him into the middle.

Abraham walks away.

In a private moment that night with Salt, he says, "I'm going to pray, Dad. I'm going to pray really hard that you don't get arrested at that stupid blockade, because I know you're going back there tomorrow. And I'm going to pray for Solomon too, when Mom takes him and me to London and he gets operated on by that salami Muslim woman. Because we don't even know her, Dad. She's not even Christian, and we don't know her."

Salt feels his heart break. "And I'm going to pray too, son. For you."

Two FBI AGENTS motion Pastor Anderson down from the bed of the pickup truck that's parked at the end of Menzies River Road, near the middle of more than three hundred people: military, law enforcement, adult civilians, veterans, and kids.

"No more sermonizing," Salt hears one of the agents tell the pastor.

Day three of the standoff. When Salt told Derek yesterday that he wouldn't come into work because he had more important things to do, Derek stammered, "The standoff? You should think carefully about that, Salt."

"I have." *Mother Earth. Brother Wolf.*

With fewer than half the kids now showing up for classes, Principal Cunningham has canceled school indefinitely.

Salt has heard that the Knights of the Menzies River has grown threefold.

Last night, the Strawberry Flats blockade and standoff made national news, and the governor said his patience was wearing thin.

Now, as the pastor presents his hands to the FBI agents, as if in prayer, the agents pull his arms back and handcuff him from behind, slapping on the plastic restraints with such force that it makes Pastor Anderson wince.

"No," somebody screams.

"He's our pastor," somebody else yells.

"Go easy on him... please... go easy."

Salt finds himself rushing forward to help, hearing the pastor's voice in his head. *We are here for each other.* And he, too, is grabbed and handcuffed. As is Bill Carry, the husband of Jericho's teacher, Mrs. Carry.

Is this really happening?

The FBI agents frisk the three men, take their phones, wallets, and keys, and push them into a van.

The door closes hard behind them.

"Are you okay?" Bill Carry asks Pastor Anderson.

"I'm fine, thank you."

"These guys mean business," Bill says.

"At least it's not tear gas, Mace, and rubber bullets," Salt says.

"Not yet, anyway."

"Do either of you know what we're charged with?" Salt asks.

"No," Bill says. "Shouldn't they read us our rights?"

Pastor Anderson winces.

"Are you in pain, pastor?"

"Only a little. I'm fine."

"My eldest son," Salt says, "he worried that this would happen to me."

"Are your kids here?" Bill asks Pastor Anderson.

"Tabby was here on day one, but she hasn't returned. My other two, the twins, Tim and Tia... well, after they watched Kes fall in the river back in January, they stepped away from the whole Knights of the Menzies River thing. They thought Kes was going to die. Tim still thinks she could... or at least get badly hurt. He's worried about her."

"I'm not," Salt hears himself say.

"Oh?" Pastor Anderson says. "Why not?"

KIM HEACOX | 261

"I don't know… I'm just not."

"Neither am I," Bill says. "All those veterans are like uncles to her, one big extended family. What a childhood, right?"

"Speaking of family," Salt says, "I have to tell you, pastor, your sermons lately, they—"

"I know. They don't build off scripture very much."

"No. That's not what I want to say. They've been… I don't know. They've been really good for my family and me, really instructive. My three younger boys still talk about Saint Francis. They researched him on the internet. He's their new hero."

"Well, good. That makes me happy. Does Solomon still talk about Cleopatra?"

"Oh, no… not really. I apologize for that outburst of his. He—"

"He's a magnificent boy who's dearly loved in this town," Pastor Anderson says. "I hope you know that."

Salt feels his heart gladden as he says, "Oh, yes, I do. Thank you. Hannah cried when she opened your envelope."

"Tears of joy, I hope."

"Yes, absolutely. Thank you."

"It's the right thing to do, Salt. We have to help each other."

"Yes… I know. I've been meaning to say this for a long time. Those wolves out beyond the Menzies River, I'm the one who—"

Listen," Bill says. "Somebody's talking with a megaphone."

CHAPTER FORTY-FIVE

Kes

"It's time to go home, all of you," the colonel announces. "If you do not comply, you will be arrested. I've read your resistance pamphlet. It instructs you to bear no weapons of any kind; to not fight. It's good advice. Do not fight. Disperse now and go home and you will not be detained, arrested, or prosecuted. You will not have a criminal record."

Army infantrymen surround the entire resistance—every protestor they can see—and begin to close in and tighten the net.

Kes remembers Zorro Brown saying that it's no picnic getting arrested. Resistance is hard. The opposition wears you down.

After three days, she's exhausted. She struggles to focus, to stay smart, alert.

"If you do fight," the colonel adds, "I cannot promise the safety or well-being of any of you, children included. Do I make myself clear? My men are highly trained and unsentimental about your motives and cause."

Kes scans the large crowd and sees many familiar faces, but not Papa. He's supposed to be back at the house, wearing his headphones and listening to the Traveling Wilburys, avoiding all stress. Jeannie's supposed to stay back as well, but here she is in the middle of it all with Skydog, indignant at the arrest of Pastor Anderson. Her jaw is set. Anger burns in her eyes.

"Stand your ground, resisters," Uncle Ty says from the far edge of the crowd. "He has his own megaphone. "All you fine men of the Twenty-Fifth Infantry Division, these are your brothers and sisters in the woods with you today, decorated veterans from World War II, Korea, Vietnam, Afghanistan, Somalia, and Iraq. They are here to protect the same America you serve. They bear you no ill will."

Nearby, two bearded, long-haired veterans quickly peel covers off the backs of their jackets to reveal large yellow lettering: FBI. Undercover agents. Sneaky buggers. Kes recognizes them from the time they spent at the Willynillyville encampment, mixing with the others, throwing frisbees, playing guitars, talking shop, and eating spaghetti prepared by Mom, Jeannie, and Sammye. They even attended Pastor Anderson's sermon on Saint Francis and stood against the wall, looking nonchalant while no doubt missing nothing.

All business now, they lunge for Uncle Ty.

"I'VE BEEN THINKING," Uncle Ty said just last night as most of the Poker Pack and Papa's band sat around the dinner table with everybody talking and strategizing. "Maybe we should end this. The blockade, I mean. The resistance. Everything. Call it all off."

The table went deathly quiet, as if everybody was in shock. Kes was. She wished Chippy had been there to say, "No way, Big Dog." But Uncle Ty was serious.

Tucker John finally asked him, "Why?"

Uncle Ty looked around the table with something in his eyes Kes had never seen before: fear. "I don't see this ending without somebody getting hurt," he said, "or even killed. Do any of you see it ending otherwise?"

"No," Grandpa said quietly. "I think you're right, son. It's too dangerous. But I have to say that I'm proud of you for bringing all these good people together like this, for trying to protect what you love... what others love too. I've never seen a wild wolf, but I'm glad they're out there. I really am."

"Me too, Dad," Uncle Ty said with his missing-tooth smile.

Grandpa looked at Kes then, as if to apologize.

Too dangerous? Kes didn't know what to say. It was then that Uncle Ty surprised her a second time when he stood up, looked at Kes, and said, "We need to take a walk, my young apprentice."

"Me?"

"Yes, you. C'mon."

Kes looked at Papa and Mom then, who both nodded their approval, as if they knew what was about to happen. Out beyond the garden, illuminated by only the deck lights fifty feet away, Kes felt like a dam ready to burst. "What's wrong, Uncle Ty?"

"If anything bad were to happen to you," he said, "I'd die inside."

"No, you wouldn't."

"Yes, I would."

"Remember our trip north in Claire? When you told me to follow my convictions? You said I should find out what's really true, and confront it no matter how hard it might be. You said that only then would I find out who I am and what I can become."

"Yes, I remember."

"Well, isn't that what I'm doing now? Isn't that what we're all doing?" As much as she tried not to, Kes began to cry.

Uncle Ty didn't hug her. Instead, he lowered himself to one knee and looked slightly up at her in a way few adults ever do. "Rita tells me you've been asking about your mom, your first mom, your birth mom... and her parents, your grandparents."

Kes stared at him. "Yes."

"And I understand that Rita said you should ask me about it, is that right?"

Kes nodded slowly. "Yes. Why you?"

"Because your birth mom was the niece of a dear friend of mine who now lives in southern Mexico. When I first met her—the woman who would be your mom—I thought she was magical, and she should meet my younger brother. So, I played matchmaker and... it worked. And I have to say, Kes, watching them fall in love was one of the most beautiful things I've ever seen. That's why, to this day, I fly to southern Mexico. To help your mom's family who lives down there."

"They're Mexican?"

"No. They're farmers from Wisconsin, and they didn't really approve of your father—a penniless musician from Texas—marrying their daughter. Months after your mom died, the recession hit hard and they foreclosed on their farm, and your mom's mom got dementia. They moved to Mexico because it's inexpensive down there, and the health care is pretty good. Your papa can tell you more. He knows all about this. But here's the kicker, and it's not going to be easy to hear. The hard truth is that your mom loved to drink. And it caught up with her."

"So... Uncle Charles was right? My mom was a drunk?"

"No, your Uncle Charles was wrong. Your mom was a beautiful woman who partied hard now and then, when she could."

"I can hardly remember her."

"That's okay. You were young."

"But why—"

"When your papa was on the road with the band he had before Whoa Nellie, I had a party at my house in Lubbock. Your mom was there and drank too much. And I did nothing. I could have stopped her, but I didn't. Such a good time we had, all of us, and I let her leave alone that night, to drive herself home, and she never made it."

"She had her accident because she—"

"Because I was irresponsible, Kes. And I don't want to be irresponsible again. I have enough regrets already."

HOURS LATER AND UNABLE TO SLEEP, Kes got up to visit Uncle Ty. She rapped softly on his bedroom door once… twice… and finally peeked in. He was sleeping in bed with Taylor. They sat up, alarmed, and flipped on a light. "It's me, Uncle Ty," Kes said, standing in the door in her pajamas. "You talked about having regrets. Well, I don't want to have any either. I don't want to let everybody down. Including myself and the veterans and the Tlingits up in their hammocks in the trees right now. And my friends, and the wolves and all your friends too. We've all worked so hard. We have to do this. Please promise me you'll think about it."

"Kes, it's three in the morning."

"I know. I couldn't sleep. I'm sorry to wake you."

"No need to apologize."

"Please, Uncle Ty… promise me you'll think about it."

"I promise."

"Something else."

"Okay… what?"

"My grandparents in Mexico… Were they mad at you when my first mom died?"

"Yes."

"Are they still?"

"No."

"And that's why you fly to Mexico… to see them? To help them?"

"In large part, yes. There are other reasons."

"Do they ever ask about me?"

"Your grandpa does. Your grandma can't really remember anything."

"Was my papa mad at you?"

Uncle Ty thinks for a moment. "He was disappointed. He was sick from a broken heart. But he was never mad. Your papa is incapable of anger, Kes. He's incapable of revenge and even contempt. He's rare that way. He's the best of us."

Taylor said, "Are you okay, Kes? Are you okay being alone tonight?"

"I'm okay."

"Then we're good?" Uncle Ty asked her. "Do you think you can sleep now?"

"Yes."

"Excellent. Then back to bed with you."

"Uncle Ty, I just want you to know that if anything bad happens at the resistance, I'd never blame you. I mean it. Without you, I wouldn't be in Alaska. I wouldn't be who I am now."

THE FBI AGENTS SEIZE UNCLE TY, cuff him, and drag him toward a waiting van, but leave his megaphone on the ground.

Kes lunges forward. *This is it.* As she grabs the megaphone, the sun notches back a degree and everything seems to slow down yet speed up, as if nothing could go wrong yet everything is about to. "He tells us to go home," Kes announces, surprised by the authority of her own voice. "Look around. This is our home. This forest and this river... all of it. This is our home... the place we love. And all we want is to keep it the way we love it. Right? It's simple. The governor is wrong. The president is wrong. Everybody, stay where you are. Sit down. Chain yourself to a tree and padlock the chain if you can. Do it now."

The FBI agents hand Uncle Ty over to a state trooper and spin around, headed back for Kes. Mom had put Tucker John and Captain Don in charge of her safety, and they stand beside her now, weaponless. There's little else they can do.

Kes surveys her ground. *Where's Papa? And where are Chippy and Cap? They haven't been seen since two days ago, when the C-17s arrived.*

Other protestors, many of them kids, move in tight around Kes and Tucker John and Captain Don to help stop the FBI agents and soldiers, or at least to slow them down. Kes sees Melissa and Emily, both wearing expressions of fierce resolve.

Everything is getting louder and more crowded and confused. Kes sees the soldiers closing in, slowly corralling the resisters. The Ketchikan loggers pick up their chainsaws. *Are they going to cut down the trees with the hammocks still in them?* Kes begins to feel a heavy weight in her chest; her heart racing. Kona appears and says, "Kes, we have to do something."

Before Kes can respond, Mom appears, her face contorted with worry.

"I can't find your father," she says.

"He's back at Willynillyville," Kes tells her. "I don't think he's here."

"No, he's here. I can feel him, his presence... he's here."

"I think some of our veterans might have guns, Mom."

"We have to stop this, Kes. I know you don't want to. But we have to stop this right now."

"Attention, everybody," a voice booms over the crowd. It's the state man who moderated the hearing last month. He takes the megaphone from the colonel, who stands next to him. "This road corridor is a sixty-foot-wide section line. The state of Alaska has every authority to extend this road without an environmental assessment or an impact statement."

"That's a lie," somebody shouts from up in the trees. Kes finds him. It's a man she doesn't know. He has long, black hair and wears a T-shirt that says: *FIGHTING TERRORISM SINCE 1492.* He adds, "This is state land, but also a federally designated wetland."

The colonel takes the megaphone from the state man and says, "Here's what we're going to do. We're going to start up this Caterpillar boom forklift with a container pallet on the forks, and position it under those of you in hammocks so you can come down safely. If you do not comply, my men will be forced to pull you down or cut you down. The rest of you, leave now, all of you, or you will be arrested."

"On what charges?" somebody yells from the crowd.

The Caterpillar rumbles to life.

Kes feels helpless. She watches the soldiers confiscate the TV cameras and continue to close their human net, crowding the protestors into the middle.

Jimmy Wisting shouts from above. "We've got WiFi and cameras and video up here, colonel. We're filming and live streaming this. And we've got the governor's office on the satellite phone. He's worried about bad public relations."

More resisters sit down to make their arrests and removal difficult, as instructed in their pamphlets. Many take videos and photos with their phones. And selfies.

Kes sees Papa about forty feet away, in the crowd, wearing his headphones. Zorro stands next to him, as if to protect him.

"Everybody, go home," the colonel repeats, his voice booming through the megaphone, turned up to maximum to carry over the sound of the Caterpillar as it approaches the nearest tree with hammocks suspended overhead. "This is your last warning."

"This is home," somebody shouts. And others join in: "THIS IS HOME… THIS IS HOME… THIS IS HOME…"

"Colonel, the governor is asking for a stand-down," Jimmy says, using his own megaphone up in the trees. "He's on the line right now; he's asking that you and your men STAND DOWN. NOW!"

The Caterpillar advances, its forks about fifteen feet high and capable of going much higher; its huge knobby tires ripping up the forest floor.

"STOP THAT MACHINE," a voice screams. "STOP IT OR I'LL BLOW IT TO HELL. I SWEAR I WILL."

Chippy.

Mom points.

Kes sees him now. He stands at one end of the crowd with an RPG on his shoulder, aimed at the Caterpillar. *Men are bozos.* No soldiers can get a clear shot, so they charge him, weaving through the crowd.

The FBI agents advance.

The Caterpillar stops. The driver sees Chippy, panics, and jumps clear. Kes freezes, uncertain what to do. Then she sees Kona climbing up the Caterpillar as high as he can go, unaware of any danger. *Oh, no.* He stands on the forks, raises his fist and shouts, "The Force is with me."

Kes breaks away and rushes to him.

Mom cries, "Kes, no."

As Kes reaches the Caterpillar and begins to climb up after Kona, she sees Cap appear from behind a tree on the far side of the forest, opposite the position of Chippy. He, too, has an RPG on his shoulder. He fires. Kes hears the whistle of a rocket.

A scream. An explosion.

And everything goes dark.

KES DREAMS.

Am I dead? Is this Heaven?

She walks a rimrock above a stream in full sunlight and autumn colors. Up ahead, young men point down below, aim their rifles, and fire, taking many shots. *This is not Heaven.* Kes runs forward, trying to catch the men as they walk down to their kill.

Stop, she yells.

They ignore her.

At the stream, the men inventory a pack of dying wolves, moving from one to another, finishing them off. As they walk away, they turn and call back to one of their own—a thin, young man wearing chaps and a cowboy hat, still boyish about his face—who lingers near a streamside willow.

Hey Aldo, you coming?

Go ahead, he replies. I'll catch up.

Kes joins him. At his feet, a mother wolf lies dying.

Is this Texas? Kes asks.

No, he says without looking up. Arizona Territory.

He kneels and touches the dying wolf.

Kes walks away to give him time alone. As she does, everything turns gray. When she returns, Aldo is an old man with wire-rimmed glasses and little hair atop his head. He sits on a rock smoking a pipe, his legs crossed, pants hitched high, binoculars around his neck, boots laced to the top and neatly tied, like the photo of him on the back of his book.

You're Aldo Leopold?

I am.

Was this the wolf with the fierce green fire in her eyes?

It was.

She's dead?

Yes.

And all the color is gone now, from everything.

Yes. He stares at Kes, appears to study her.

My Uncle Ty gave me your book. I'm reading it. It's good.

Thank you. Who are you?

I'm Kestrel Nash. I live in Alaska.

Good for you. I always wanted to go to Alaska.

Did your mom and dad name you Aldo?

They named me Rand. Aldo is my middle name.

My Uncle Ty... he's the first person to ever tell me about you. He had a friend named Dash—only one letter different from Nash—who died in the war in Afghanistan.

We're at war in Afghanistan?

Yes. Uncle Ty said that for many people, a dash is all their lives amount to. In the end, they're just a dash on a headstone above their grave, a little line between the year they were born and the year they died. Nothing more.

Let it be a reminder to live your life to the fullest.

I'm trying to save a pack of wolves in Alaska.

Excellent.

It's not easy.

It never is. Kestrel is a strange name for a girl.

It's a species of falcon.

A North American falcon?

Yes. It used to be called a sparrow hawk.

Falco sparverius, he says, his face brightening. A bit smaller than a merlin, if I remember correctly, and much smaller than a prairie falcon, peregrine, or gyrfalcon.

My dad loves birds.

He's a good man then. I imagine we strangely named people ought to stick together, you and I, don't you think? He smiles.

People call me Kes.

He stands and shakes her hand. Then I'll call you Kes too, if that's okay with you. It has a nice ring to it... Kes... Kes...

"Kes... Kes, honey..."

"Mom?"

"Yes, I'm here."

"Where am I?"

"You're okay. You're in Bartlett Hospital, in Juneau."

"Where's Papa? What happened?"

"Papa is fine. So is your Uncle Ty. You have a concussion."

"I do?"

"What do you remember?"

"Uh..."

"Kona is okay too. He broke his arm and had a concussion, but he's okay. Everybody is okay. Well, maybe not Cap. He's in jail. We'll talk about that later."

"Cap's in jail?"

"Yes, honey. He fired the RPG that missed the Caterpillar but hit a cottonwood tree. Chippy was just a distraction, a decoy to draw attention away from Cap, who did all the damage. Chippy and your Uncle Ty got arrested too, but unlike Cap, they're out now, and shopping with your Papa. We've been taking turns here, watching over you."

"Can I have a drink of water?"

"Yes, of course." Mom calls a nurse. Soon Kes is sitting up and feeling better.

"I remember now," Kes says. "Jimmy Wisting said the governor was standing down."

Mom smiles. "And he did. He stood down. A quick poll says his approval rating has dropped by twenty percent since the standoff. So… he says he's canceling the project, for now anyway."

"And Kona is okay? He really is?"

"Yes, he's on pain meds and doing much better."

KES SLEEPS.

She awakens, and there's Mrs. Carry, right next to her. *Mrs. Carry?* And over sitting near the wall is Kona, the youngest of the Knights of the Menzies River. Like Sir Gareth of Camelot. He has a wraparound bandage on his head and a cast on his arm, and is looking at her tattered, dog-eared copy of *The Once and Future King*, the one she brought from Texas.

Night has fallen.

"Kona?"

"Hi Kes… you're awake."

"I guess I am. Your arm?"

He smiles. "It's okay. It's only broken in one place. This is a cool book."

Mrs. Carry asks Kes if she wants something to drink.

Just then, Mr. Robb and Zorro come into her room with contraband from the cafeteria: ice cream. "Your family is having dinner," Zorro says. "They asked us to watch over you. Most of your knights are with them. They all went to Bullwinkle's for pizza." Mr. Robb sets the ice cream on a table that's already filled with get-well cards.

"The Knights of the Menzies River are here?" Kes asks. "In Juneau?"

"In solidarity with you," Mr. Robb says. "Kona's parents too. The hospital said no pizza could be delivered, so we drew the short straws and stayed behind. Actually, we're honored. You showed great courage at that standoff, Kes."

"You both did," Zorro adds, with a nod to Kona.

"We wanted to tell you that," Mrs. Carry says. "The Knights of the Menzies River is all over the news and social media. The hospital has turned away reporters from the *Juneau Empire* and the Associated Press, and phone calls from the *Washington Post*."

"But the wolves are still vulnerable, right?" Kes asks. "Until they get protected by some kind of law, like the Endangered Species Act, right?"

"Wolf politics is complicated," Mr. Robb says. "Right now, the governor is backpedaling and—"

"He's the one who should be in jail," Kona says. "He's the one who's wrong."

A nurse comes in, stops, looks around, sees the ice cream, and says to Kona, "Young man, you should be in your room." Before Kona can protest, the same nurse checks the hall, closes the door, and says conspiratorially to Kes and Kona, "My nieces and nephews have been watching the news and have asked if I've met you, and if I could have my photo taken with the two of you. You're due to be released tomorrow, both of you. So, if it's not too much of a burden..." She hands her phone to Mr. Robb.

Kes and Kona grin at each other.

Kona turns back to the nurse and asks, "Do your nieces and nephews live in Alaska?"

"Yes."

"Okay, they can have their photo—"

"Thank you."

"...on one condition."

"Oh, what?"

"If they join the Knights of the Menzies River."

The nurse grins. "Done."

PART V

CHAPTER FORTY-SIX

Silver

SILVER PAUSES, STONE STILL, EARS UP.

Off his left shoulder, not far away on the calm waters of Crystal Bay, mergansers and goldeneyes take flight, whistling up the dawn. A great blue heron flexes against the pastel sky and lifts away, croaking. A short distance ahead, five river otters play on a mossy slope above the high tide line, sliding down and climbing back up, chattering and cavorting, unaware of any danger.

Silver waits for Sister. When she joins him, she offers a slight nod of submission that he accepts with quiet confidence, the very trait he'll need to become an alpha. They move forward slowly, cautiously. Sister goes high through the woods while Silver goes low along the shore, using large boulders for cover. At the same instant—with sharp instincts and a keen ability to read each other—they charge. The otters scatter. It's all over in minutes: three otters caught and killed.

Two escape.

In lieu of salmon and moose, this will do.

Silver and Sister drag the dead otters into the woods and eat one immediately. Overhead, high in a spruce, two ravens watch. Sister wants to eat a second otter, but Silver snarls her down. When Mother and the others arrive, they vigorously devour the two remaining otters, with ample portions going to the two surviving pups.

Strawberry Flats is far to the south.

Not for many days has Silver smelled the sweet and smoky odor of tall uprights, or heard the clattering sounds of their mechanical birds, or seen the huge moose that would feed his pack for many days. He still dreams of bringing it down, of finding a weakness and exploiting it: a bad shoulder, a weak knee. But the big bull will have developed huge antlers by now, with the rut coming.

He also dreams of the all-black female out there somewhere, and of Old One still on that whale, far out to sea, fighting that bear... if not long dead. He dreams of all things possible and true. Every mountain is a cemetery, every glacier a road, every crevasse a grave, every storm a threat where rocks break bones and peaks shred clouds. And still, he must go. In his deepest being, he feels it. He knows it. He wants it. He wants her.

It's time.

The leaves are turning gold, the berries crimson.

All five pups were born small, given the stresses on Mother when she was pregnant—the sky filled with mechanical birds and their shrieking sounds— and have since grown slowly, given her poor ability to produce milk. Three have died. The remaining two are playful but often listless and weak.

Sister has acknowledged with many small gestures that she will stay and help the others hunt, given her growing devotion to Alpha and Mother, especially to Alpha, with his lackluster spirit since Strong died. And this: no pups will probably survive their first year. The pack will need every capable hunter to make it through winter and hopefully breed next year.

Silver nuzzles them, every one, with special affection for Mother and Sister, who nuzzle him back at great length, as if committing his smell to memory forever. He then turns north toward the icy mountains and walks away at a steady clip, almost a trot. Many minutes later, out of sight and alone, he stops and howls, and listens. Soon it comes.

The chorus of his clan, lightly mournful.

Goodbye.

CHAPTER FORTY-SEVEN

Salt

ABRAHAM HAS STORIES. It occurs to Salt that his eldest son never had stories before he went to England. *Opinions and convictions, yes. Resentments and fears, yes. But stories? No.*

Back home now after fourteen weeks in London with his mother and Solomon, Abe effervesces as he talks. "Dad, you can't believe it. We bought fish and chips on the street corners, and in Trafalgar Square and Hyde Park, and at the Tower of London, which used to be a prison, and they just wrapped it up in newspaper and put a little vinegar and salt on it. It was really good. And we had to be careful crossing the streets—Americans, I mean—because we look the wrong way for traffic because everybody over there drives on the other side of the road. And when people say they're 'pissed,' it doesn't mean they're angry, it means they're drunk. They have different words for all kinds of things. Men call women 'birds.' And when women like you, they call you 'love.' Two of Solomon's nurses were from Ghana, in Africa, before they moved to England, and they called him 'love' all the time. After a while, they called me 'love' too."

"And the Rolling Stones?"

"Oh, man… incredible. Wembley Stadium is huge. It had a whole section up front for people in wheelchairs, so that's where we were. Mick Jagger just had heart surgery, but you wouldn't know it. He was amazing. Keith Richards too. He wears a bandana headband kind of like Solomon does to cover his scar."

Salt hears himself laugh, and say, "You know, Kes's father and uncle, Danny and Tyler Nash, they wear bandanas too. Like pirates."

"Yeah… I guess they do. Anyway, everybody sang along on almost every song. I think Solomon is going to talk about that concert for the rest of his life."

Another laugh spills out of Salt, so joyous is he to have his family back. The last time he felt this happy was the day Abraham was born.

"And Dr. Hamadani?" Salt asks.

Abe has to think about this. He looks out the kitchen window, bent slightly at the waist, his hands on the counter. He draws a deep breath and says, "I didn't like her at first. I guess she didn't like me either. I didn't trust her. Mom got mad at me early on and told me to be kinder. But yeah, she's cool. She's a really good doctor. Solomon loves her. I think he wants to marry her."

"He's too late for that."

"Yeah. She's really smart and articulate."

Did my boy just say 'articulate'? "Your mom wants me to talk you into going to Solomon's big birthday party."

"I know. Can't I just stay here and celebrate with all of you when you come home and we can be together, just the six of us? I'd like that."

"It's for Solomon, Abe. Do it for him, okay?"

Abraham looks out the window, deep in thought.

Salt adds, "There's going to be a lot of good food." Nutritious food. Not that Abe has ever been drawn to good nutrition. He's more of a volume guy. *And yes, my son, you'll need to be sociable. A little, at least.* "And Tabby Anderson will probably be there."

"And Kes," Abe says bitterly.

"Let it go, son."

"She stole our traps."

"And she put them down a long time ago while you're still carrying them like a burdened mule."

Abraham's eyes fill with tears as he continues to look away, out the window. Finally, he says, "'Come unto me... all ye who labor, and I will give you rest.' Matthew 11:28, right?"

Salt puts an arm on his shoulder. "Yes, but not just 'labor.' Jesus said 'labor and are heavy laden.' He's here for you, Abe. He loves you. We all do, very much."

HOW SULLEN ABE WAS when he left for England back in May; distant, as if on his own crusade, bunkered against any shred of reason that might upset his fundamentalism. Poisoned by rant radio and who knows what else, he talked about joining the military so he could get "over there" to straighten out "those stupid Arabs with their Mohammed this and their Allah that."

Hearing him say such things made Hannah cry. "After all we've taught him about love and tolerance and generosity," she said to Salt the night before they left, "now he seems to hate anybody who thinks or believes differently from what he does."

"He doesn't *hate* them," Salt said to her.

"What is it then?"

"He's just—"

"Don't delude yourself, husband."

"I don't think I am. To be honest, I think he's heartbroken over Solomon."

"So am I. So are all of us."

"I shouldn't have bought him that phone. It's turned him into a zombie."

"Maybe I should take Jericho instead and leave Abraham here with you."

Salt thought about it. He then remembered reading once about how travel can be lethal to prejudice, especially if you go when you're young, and not with the military or a ministry. If people wait until they're too old and comfortable and set in their ways, travel can work the other way and confirm their prejudices. But when they're young, it can be the best education in the world, and teach them things they didn't even know they didn't know. Salt said to Hannah. "No... take Abraham and expose him to four old hippies."

"Four old hippies?"

"Yes, the Rolling Stones."

Now, NEARLY FOUR MONTHS LATER, Abraham pulls back from the kitchen window, wipes his eyes with his sleeves, and says, "It's pretty cool when the whole town wants to give your brother a birthday party."

"Yes, it is. It's a homecoming too, of course. Everybody wants to see him."

"You know, Dad, when we were over there, in London, Mom told me that you almost sent Jericho instead of me."

"It's true. We did."

Abraham lowers his head for a moment, then looks directly at Salt, something he seldom does. "Thank you for sending me."

"You're welcome. Now, about Solomon's party?"

"When do we leave?"

An hour later the d'Alenes arrive at Willynillyville in their special red van. A big crowd greets them with *HAPPY BIRTHDAY SOLOMON* banners. Chippy stands front and center, and bows deeply and theatrically before the new ramp he just built for the main house. A while back, before Solomon's return to Strawberry Flats, he came over to study the ramp Salt had constructed so he could fashion one of similar design to make Solomon feel welcome in Willynillyville.

Abraham rolls him up it and onto the deck, where Solomon, wearing his bandana, announces, "Woohooooo... it's perfeeeeect." He's always wanted to visit Willynillyville, and now he's here. Triumphant.

"Shake it on down," Kona yells.

"Shake it on dooooooown..." Solomon yells back, and everybody cheers.

Look closely, as Salt has every day since Solomon's return. He's not nearly as bent as before, not as burdened by excess saliva. He sits taller, more erect in his neck and back. His arms are beginning to look like pistons. The other day he popped a wheelie and spun his wheelchair in a complete 360. Dr. Hamadani said his brain was already beginning to produce more dystrophin, a protein that protects his muscle fiber from breaking down when exposed to enzymes. Give it time. It's a clinical trial, after all. Near as she could tell, though, there's "measurable improvement." She plans to Zoom with Solomon once a month. And he'll need to go into Juneau for periodic tests. She also hopes to bring him back to London this time next year for a close evaluation.

Observing Solomon up on the deck and Abraham smiling with him, Salt fights back tears, thinking on Psalm 145:17: "The Lord is righteous in all his ways, and holy in all His works."

As are doctors and nurses halfway around the world.

CHAPTER FORTY-EIGHT

Kes

WHILE PAPA AND UNCLE TY take Solomon and his brothers on a tour of Willynillyville to show them the busy apiary and the ponies, and the garden peas bursting and eight feet tall, plus the rhubarb leaves "as big as Montana" (according to Papa), and the solar array working like a champ, Mom and Jeannie hug Mrs. d'Alene and invite her into the kitchen where they've been cooking for two days.

It warms Kes's heart to see things pretty much back to how they were before the standoff. She and others—most of the Poker Pack—help Chippy pick up his carpentry tools from off the new ramp and deck. He only just finished the railing minutes before the d'Alenes arrived.

"How's Cap doing?" Tucker John asks him.

"Not so good," Chippy says. "Prison sucks."

"It's nice to have you back, Chippy," Captain Don says. "But if you have any more crazy-ass weapons around here aside from a sharp knife and a handy toothpick, Tyler will kick your butt out of Willynillyville for the final time."

"I know," Chippy says with a sheepish glance at Kes. He coughs violently, finds his voice and says, "When guns are banned, only bands will have guns."

"Not funny," Captain Don replies.

"Like Peter, Paul and Mary with AK-47s. Or the Mamas and Papas with AR-15s."

"Still not funny, Chippy. Stick to carpentry."

"Just remember," Chippy adds, growing serious, "politicians love their citizens unarmed."

"Not true," Zorro replies as he walks by carrying two folding chairs. He puts down the chairs and levels with Chippy. "The most corrupt politicians—

and we have many—want their citizens uneducated, not unarmed. That way tens of millions of people will continue to vote against their own best interests by reelecting authoritarians who rant on about gun rights and illegal immigrants and same-sex marriage, all while giving tax breaks to billionaires and never raising the minimum wage, or addressing the climate crisis, or fixing income disparity, or working for universal health care, or ending poverty. What those politicians really care about, Chippy, is one thing: staying in power. Which they do by catering to fat cats who in turn finance their campaigns. That's why the South stays poor. That's why the Heartland will bake in an oven of its own making, having voted for pro-gun, climate crisis deniers for fifty years. Let them shoot the sun."

Chippy stares at Zorro, lost for words.

"Questions?" Zorro asks him.

Captain Don finally says, "Ignorance kills people."

"True," Zorro says. "Even worse, though, is the illusion of knowledge, which breeds arrogant ignorance, which America has in spades."

Chippy continues to stare. Kes takes note of the deep lines about his tired eyes, his pale skin and yellow teeth. More coughing. Chippy has moved from Marlboros to Camels to Red Man to Skoal and back to Marlboros, because that's what real cowboys smoke. She finds herself feeling sorry for him, something she would have never thought possible a couple years ago down in Texas.

"Those stupid cancer sticks are gonna kill you one day at a time," Tucker John tells Chippy. "Why not just light up a stick of dynamite and get it over with?"

"Maybe I'll do that," Chippy says, brightening. "Remember Hunter S. Thompson, the gonzo journalist that Big Dog always talks about? When he was dying of cancer and wanted to end it fast, he had his friends shoot him out of a cannon."

"Not true," Zorro says.

"Or maybe he was already dead when they shot him out of the cannon."

"Wrong again," Zorro says. "I have friends who knew Hunter Thompson."

"Or maybe they shot him out of the cannon to try to cure him," Chippy adds. "And now he's living in Mexico with James Dean and Marlon Brando."

That gets the other veterans talking:

"Nicolas Cage should have never made another movie after *Moonstruck*."

"What's Nicolas Cage got to do with Mexico?"

"Some actors should have never made their first movie."

"I'll say it again, guys: *Ghostbusters* is better than *Groundhog Day*."

"No way."

"And Festus was a better deputy than Chester."

"No way."

"*Gunsmoke*, slowpoke. Why didn't Matt Dillon ever get it on with Miss Kitty?"

Zorro walks away, shaking his head.

Kes lingers.

"You know, Chippy," Captain Don says, "I love my left-handed Remington .270 deer rifle as much as the other guy, and I don't want my government to ever take it from me. I also don't want citizens with military-grade assault rifles and kids afraid of being murdered at their school desks. Statistics don't lie. The most dangerous terrorists in America right now are right-wing white nationalists."

"Who mask their racism with patriotism," Tucker John adds.

Chippy takes a deep draw on his Marlboro.

"Two kids could have died, Chippy," Captain Don says. "A lot of people could have died. I was happy to see the FBI confiscate those damn RPGs."

Mom steps out on the deck and says, "Hey team, we need to set up another couple buffet tables and lay out those sheets of old plywood so Solomon can roll around easy in his wheelchair. And would somebody please help Kes's grandpa put up the last birthday banner? I don't want him up on any ladders."

The men take off.

Chippy heads for the shop, his arms filled with tools. All around, townspeople move about, carrying chairs and tables and trays of food.

"Oh, and Chippy?" Mom calls.

Chippy stops and turns. "Yeah?"

"The ramp and railing are beautiful, thank you."

"Any time, Rita." He turns and heads away with a little skip in his step.

When Kes checks in on Papa, she finds him at the bird feeder, putting sunflower seeds on his head. Solomon howls and rocks with delight to see the chickadees land there and grab the seeds and fly away. Papa then puts seeds on Solomon's head and says softly, "Be very still." The chickadees, accustomed to Papa but nobody else, hold off at first. "Don't move," Papa says. When the first chickadee finally does land on him, Solomon's eyes widen with wonder, and Kes sees a remarkable sight: Abraham smiling.

She decides then to give Abe something.

Not yet. But soon.

MR. AND MRS. D'ALENE have asked for no presents or speeches. Only friends, community, a good time for all, feasting on three venison roasts but no moose—Big Al is still out there somewhere—plus salmon, halibut, smoked black cod, Dungeness crab, garden potatoes and vegetables, more than a dozen pies, and unlimited ice cream and beer that Sarge must have run off and bought when nobody was looking.

People visit as if hungry to catch up and share their summertime stories and have a good laugh.

Later, Uncle Ty invites Abraham to the poker table, a rare privilege. Abe sits between Chippy and Captain Don, where Cap used to sit before the feds sent him to prison in El Paso. It's no small crime to fire a rocket-propelled grenade into a crowd.

Had anybody died, Cap would probably be in for life.

As Kes walks from the kitchen into the living room, she sees Papa and Tim jamming for the first time in months. It makes her heart sing. She also sees Pastor Anderson and his wife on the floor, playing Legos with Kipper—who's not so little anymore.

Back near the poker table, she pauses to catch snippets of the banter.

"Okay, then," Uncle Ty asks as they inspect their cards, "if not a drone, what's the most effective weapon in Afghanistan?"

"An IED," Chippy says.

"A girl with a book," Jeannie says.

Kes smiles and moves on.

Outside, she sees Emily and Melissa laughing with Solomon, Kona, and Jericho. And Zorro talking to Mrs. Carry. And Berit with Jimmy and Kid Hugh, Jimmy with his arm around her. Jimmy and Kid Hugh are just two of several people—Stringer included—who joined the resistance and have stayed, and now appear nicely rooted here.

As pastel evening light plays over the rooftops and trees and fireweed seeds drift about, catching the last light breaking, it occurs to Kes that you have to invent words for the way beauty expresses itself in Alaska. She remembers a similar evening from one year before, soon after she'd arrived in Strawberry Flats, when Uncle Ty told her that while the land is young and shaped mostly by glaciers, the processes are timeless—the rivers and tides, the seasons, the abundant life flowing and ebbing, the people rounded by water yet sharpened by ice, engaged in the country and committed to its flourishing. "All in all," he said, "it's a fine place to stand upon, and defend."

The other day Zorro surprised Kes by inviting her to join him and Papa and Uncle Ty for a week of fishing on the Cinnamon Girl before school begins. If indeed she'll go to Strawberry Flats Public School this year. It all depends on Mrs. Cunningham, the school board, and district superintendent. If they say no to Science Friday and science every day, the Knights of the Menzies River will probably boycott.

As for fishing, Uncle Ty says they'll longline in Chatham Strait. It'll be hard work. "But we'll also poke around the north shore of Chichagof to study coastal brownies, humpback whales, and sea otters. After that... who knows? We might head up into Crystal Bay for a couple days, anchor in rock-ribbed inlets, and hang out with harbor seals, kittiwakes, and tidewater glaciers. Sing with loons. Dance with storms. Put glacial ice in our drinks and slurp down the Pleistocene. How does that sound?"

That night, Kes was so excited. She jammed with Papa until one o'clock in the morning and talked about family in Mexico... her birth mom's family—*my family*—and heard so many life-affirming stories from Papa that afterward she could hardly sleep.

Slurping down the Pleistocene? Wow!

When she told Uncle Ty the next day, he chuckled. "It all used to be under one big glacier, my young apprentice. An icy sarcophagus. And now look how alive the land is, with wild strawberries growing out of solid granite, and moose swimming fjords, and wolves crossing icefields. It's a land and sea of rebirth, a renaissance place. And if you stay here long enough, and let it speak to you, and learn to listen... you'll be reborn too."

KES HELPS MOM and Mrs. d'Alene carry dishes inside to be washed. While the two mothers engage in steady conversation, Kes pauses again at the poker table, where everybody has something to say.

"Not true," Uncle Ty says. "Orwell was afraid of those who'd ban books. Huxley worried that there'd be no reason to ban books because people wouldn't read anymore, or question authority, or make any effort to understand others unlike themselves."

"We're already there."

"Ante up, everybody."

"What do you think the governor really intended to build out west of the river?"

"An Air Force base."

"A giant Taco Bell with fifty-five-gallon drums of salsa and guacamole."

"A Walmart. Every American town needs a Walmart filled with throwaway consumer goods to keep our landfills growing."

"A big oval racetrack, like the Indy 500."

"I've said it before and I'll say it again: a golf course, hotel, and casino."

"Not a coalbed methane operation?"

"Nope."

"So that means we can stop worrying now?"

"Never. Every defeat is final, every victory is provisional."

"C'mon, Big Dog. What's that supposed to mean?"

"It means the developer can lose many times and keep coming back until he wins, while the environmentalist only needs to lose once and a place is gone forever. Hey, how's it going over there, Abe? Or do you prefer Abraham?"

"Abe is fine."

"Don't trust any of these poker players, by the way. They all cheat."

"No, we don't."

"Yes, we do."

Kes studies Abe for any show of emotion. He looks around, catches her watching him, and returns his attention to his cards.

The front door flies open and Solomon comes through, pushed by Joshua and Kona. They stop. Everything stops. Poker. Guitars. Lively conversation. Everything. Kona sees Kipper's Legos and says, "Wow, what's that?"

After a minute, Kipper says authoritatively, "It's a space station."

Kes can see that, given its balance—what Mrs. Carry would call "symmetry." Turn it upside down or rotate it and it would look much the same.

"Cool," Kona says. He and Joshua spin Solomon around to head back out.

Pastor Anderson says, "Go easy, boys. You've got precious cargo there."

"Caargooo," Solomon says as they roll him out and down the ramp.

"I HAVE AN ANNOUNCEMENT," Jeannie says as they resume their poker game. "I'm starting graduate school next month. Criminal justice at the

University of Washington, in Seattle. I will miss you all."

"And we'll miss you," Uncle Ty says.

"Very much," Mom adds, standing there now, next to Mrs. d'Alene.

"Will Skydog go to graduate school too?" Chippy asks.

"Yeah, right," E. J. says. "What would he study?"

A grin crawls across Chippy's face. "How about dogma?"

Everybody laughs.

"And I'm going to run for political office one day," Jeannie says matter-of-factly. "Probably for a seat in the US House of Representatives. And after I'm elected, I'm going to work on getting a new amendment to the Constitution."

"An amendment for what?" Captain Don asks.

"Very simple," Jeannie says. "It will require that any politician who calls for US involvement in a foreign war must make their announcement from the middle of Arlington National Cemetery, surrounded by an ocean of white crosses."

"You've got my vote," Grandpa says.

Grandpa's awake? This whole time he's been sitting with his chin on his chest, cards barely in his hand. Maybe the boys with the wheelchair woke him. And he's always been pro-war, what Uncle Ty calls "hawkish." *What's the deal?*

"Can I ask a question?" Abe says.

"By all means," Uncle Ty replies.

"You all fought in Iraq and Afghanistan?"

"And Vietnam," Captain Don says, nodding over to Grandpa.

"But you fought to defeat Islam?"

"Not hardly," Captain Don says.

"Then why? To defeat ISIS? Al Qaeda? The Taliban?"

"We fought because we thought it was the right thing to do," Tucker John says.

"But why?" Abe asks.

This gets everybody talking:

"Because we believed the lies. We were young and naïve, and blinded by heroism and idealism and pride. Nothing more. It's been going on for thousands of years."

"What's been going on for thousands of years?" Abe asks.

"Wars started by pigheaded presidents, generals, and kings, and sustained by the suckers who obeyed them."

"Suckers who died young."

"Death is the journey. Life is putting on your shoes."

"Or taking them off."

"Hey, I made the best friends I'll ever have in the military."

"Me too."

"Too bad we were so convinced we were right."

"The less the ignorant man knows, the more stubbornly he knows it."

"Jeannie, I thought you wanted to go back to school for a teaching certificate."

"I did, but not anymore."

"There's not much income in teaching."

"You don't teach for the income, E. J. You teach for the outcome."

"Ante up, everybody."

"So, you..." Abe says tentatively, "all of you... you regret going to war?"

No response.

Everybody at the table stares at their cards. Finally, Chippy says, "We had some adventures. We grew up fast, that's for damn sure. We watched friends die. Women and children too. Over there in Afghanistan, Iraq, you name it... people love each other just like we do here. They laugh and sing and cry and bleed just like we do, and defend their homeland from invaders. Wouldn't you do the same?"

Kes watches Chippy's jaw quiver. She has never witnessed gravity like this at the poker table. Never heard the Willynillyville veterans talk about what it's like "over there." Jeannie wipes away a tear.

Mom says as she puts her arm around Mrs. d'Alene, "You can go over there with the best of intentions, Abe, but you're just meat to the grinder, a pawn in a game. And you'll break the heart and maybe the spirit of this fine woman standing next to me."

The table goes silent. Kes can see Abe processing this, how he looks at his mother, down at his cards, and over at Papa—his metal legs.

Papa and Tim have stopped jamming.

"I joined the Marines in '68," Grandpa says, slowly. "It was a terrible year."

"Martin and Bobby shot dead," Tucker John says. "Riots in Chicago."

"Riots everywhere," Captain Don adds.

"We all wondered if America would survive," Grandpa says. "We really did. And the Tet Offensive, and all the guys I knew over there, my brothers, good guys, so many so young, most of them teenagers... They all..." He chokes up.

"Grandpa." Kes goes to him and hugs him from behind.

"It's okay, Dad," Uncle Ty says from across the poker table.

Papa gets up and walks over to join Kes.

Grandpa digs deep to compose himself. Kes can feel him shaking. "It took me years to build up the nerve to go see that black granite wall," he says. "The one with all the names, in Washington. I had to make sure I wasn't on it. And make sure other names were. So many. And when I looked, I saw my reflection superimposed on every name. I'll never forget it."

After a long, silent moment, E. J. says, "Never get involved in a land war in Asia."

"That's a line from *The Princess Bride*," Chippy says. "Great movie. Not as great as *Ghostbusters*, though."

This makes Grandpa laugh, and soon everybody is having a chuckle. Kes continues to hug her grandpa, to savor the feeling of his rough, unshaved cheek against hers. "I love you, Grandpa."

"I love you, too, dear girl."

"You know," Uncle Ty says, "1968 wasn't all bad. Paul McCartney wrote three of his best songs that year: 'Blackbird,' 'I Will,' and 'Hey Jude.' And do you remember how the year ended, Dad? Apollo 8 whipped around the moon and gave us those amazing photos of Earthrise over the sterile lunar surface, framed in the blackness of space. I don't think we would have ever had our first Earth Day without those photos."

"'Blackbird' is Paul's tribute to the women of the Civil Rights Movement," Tucker John says. "The British call women 'birds.'"

"I didn't know that," Uncle Ty says.

"It's true," Abe says. "Men in England call women 'birds.'"

Everybody stares at him. Uncle Ty says, "So, you saw the Rolling Stones in Wembley Stadium... Pretty dang cool, I'll bet."

"Yes. Really cool." Abe smiles. "Thank you for that, for being so generous to Solomon and my family."

"You're welcome, young man," Uncle Ty says. "What song did they open with?"

"Gimme Shelter."

"See, E. J.," Tucker John says. "I told you. It's Keith Richards at his best."

From across the room, Tim says, "He plays it in open E tuning and mutes the intro with the side of his strumming hand... like this." Tim quickly retunes his guitar and launches into the opening riffs. Soon everybody is singing. Kes expects Papa to join Tim with his Martin, but he grabs Mom instead, and dances her across the living room floor, his metal legs and Air Jordans moving like poetry.

AT ELEVEN O'CLOCK, the d'Alene family loads up to leave. All the women kiss Solomon goodbye on his forehead and cheek. Others pat him goodbye on his shoulder. He drinks it up. While Papa and Mom hug Mr. and Mrs. d'Alene, Kes secretly motions Abe aside and hands him a piece of paper, neatly folded into quarters.

"What is it?" he asks.

"It's a map showing where your traps are hidden on the other side of the river."

He stares at her.

"And the trap from the hearing," she says, "the one my dad stepped into, is in a black bag in the back of your van. I put it there an hour ago."

"You know, Kes, you broke the law when you sprang and stole those traps."

"And your dad broke the law when he trapped for hire. Should we call it even?"

"Okay."

"Shake on it?"

"Okay."

Kes is surprised at the gentleness in Abe's hand. She says, "Don't ever trap out there again, okay?"

"Your uncle is really something."

"He's well educated and he reads a lot, Abe. He isn't anything you can't be."

Abe shrugs. "It's nice to see my mom smile again."

"I think your mom and my mom might be new friends."

As Kes turns to walk away, Abe says, "I'm still not so sure about you."

She turns back with a grin. "I'm not so sure about me either."

"Why does it have to be so big?"

"Why does what have to be so big?"

"The universe. Why does it have to be so big?"

"I don't know, Abe. It just is, that's all. It just is."

EPILOGUE

Three years later

Silver

SILVER LEADS THE WAY. All-Black—his mate for life—follows with two subadults, three yearlings, and four pups of the year. All in a line. Not for three winters and three summers has he revisited this area near the hill by the river. Not for three years has he found a moose like the one he remembers from here, a massive bull on borrowed time. He still dreams of it, and of Old One on the whale, and his swim to the island. And the first time he saw All-Black on his exuberant return, finding her; how she ran to him and circled him as he circled her, and how she licked his face and bonded her fate to his.

Small but mighty, Silver's pups remind him of his own youth, of Sister, Strong, and Weak. One pup in particular is often late, yet shows great promise. The other day, when the pup fell far behind, All-Black howled him home. And when he arrived, frisky and feisty and with a goose in his mouth, the pack howled together as one. A family.

Hunting has been good to the north, deep in the mountains, where All-Black was raised and winter ice has enabled Silver and the others to take seals and otters and moose during what would otherwise have been lean times.

But no salmon.

So Silver returns now to the river of his youth, where Mother pulled him as a pup across the strong current by the nape of his neck and never gave up. And where, now, five years later, Silver in turn will never give up.

He knows this forest, this ground.

No sign of Mother, or Sister... or any other wolves.

Silver works the air with his nose. When he stops, his pack stops. When he moves, they move... sometimes in single file, other times fanning out, hunting, searching... looking for food.

Always food.

Again, he stops. This time, he's alone in the forest.

He hears the river, smells smoke, finds tracks.

Voices.

Tall uprights.

Caution.

Salt

ABE LEADS THE WAY. The route proves not as steep as Salt remembers, but not as easy either. *One step at a time.* Salt will need a hip replacement one of these days. His heart beats fast, but also smooth and steady, obedient to the pacemaker the doctors put in his chest one year ago.

Abe, slow down… please.

Early June sunlight filters through a green canopy of spruce.

Birdsong fills the air.

The nine hikers bushwhack their way up the hill, through ankle-grabbing alder and the occasional devil's club; over thick, mossy logs that themselves support young hemlock and spruce. Salt stops to rest. He looks back down the route to check on Pastor Anderson and Danny Nash. They must be doing okay because he can hear them talking and laughing, drawing near.

Earlier, the wildlife biologist Kes calls Mr. Robb, up ahead now with Abe, passed word down the line, saying, "Wolves are nearby, remember? Be quiet. We don't want to frighten them away."

Abe is far out of view, all forward motion. *Probably on top by now.*

One by one, the lower hikers reach Salt and stop to offer him water and a snack. First Danny and the pastor, then Kes and Tim. All four gather around him to discuss the beautiful summer day. They know he has a pacemaker. It's a small town with no secrets—informed, like it or not, by Rosie Goodnight, Miss Information. While Salt can see that Tim and Pastor Anderson are winded and could use a rest, Kes and her dad appear fresh as daisies. They take off, breezing their way upslope through the tangled forest, with Danny's Air Jordans covered in mud.

E. J. and Captain Don bring up the end, deep in discussion about Tyler's friend, Zorro, the former journalist who, after the standoff more than three years ago, followed the money and discovered what the governor—now under formal investigation—wanted on this side of the river: a prison. The governor's brother, who had helped finance his campaign, was a major stockholder in a corporation that specializes in building private for-profit prisons in remote areas.

"A prison," Captain Don says. "How perfect is that? Maybe now both the governor and his brother will end up in one."

E. J. laughs and looks up to see Salt and the others. "Hey gang, is this the top?"

"Probably only about halfway," Pastor Anderson says.

ONWARD.

One step at a time. Be strong, dear heart.

Salt wishes Solomon could be here. Maybe next time. *Let us be hopeful but not delude ourselves.*

"The improvements we've seen thus far are encouraging," Dr. Hamadani said recently. "They might be all we get. Or they might be a preview of other improvements to come."

Salt tells himself daily to never forget how straight Solomon sits in his wheelchair now; how he does pushups off his armrests, and leg stretches. How he's free of excess saliva and speaks in full sentences, and works on his diction and punchlines, and takes great joy in making others laugh. How he calls himself a sit-down comedian.

Sol, our son, our sun, the brightest star in the sky.

Onward. Upward.

In time, the trees thin out, the sky opens up. Yes, Salt remembers now as everything comes into view. *This is my world, my home.*

No wonder Pastor Anderson calls it Heaven's Hill.

Below, the Menzies River courses its way south, free of bridges and roads, determined as always, bound for Icy Strait. Archibald Island commands the horizon, as does Chichagof Island, larger and farther south. To the west, beyond the sparkling waters of Crystal Bay, the snowy peaks of the Fairweather Range stand bold against the sky, while to the east Salt can see a few Strawberry Flats rooftops.

Mr. Robb is already breaking out his drone, spotting scope, and small parabolic dish, hoping to find wolves. Kes helps him. Salt hears Pastor Anderson say, "It's God's church up here, is it not? The Pristine Chapel. Wilderness in every direction. Have you ever seen anything more beautiful?"

"No," Salt says, catching his breath.

"Are you okay, Dad?" Abraham quietly asks him.

"I'm doing great, son. What's for lunch?"

Abraham hands him a cracker with cheese and jerky. "Eat that," he says. "I'll make you another… as many as you'd like. And be sure to drink."

Kes

THE NEW DRONE is ready to take flight when Mr. Robb surprises everybody by announcing, "You know, we don't need to do this. Fly the drone, I mean. We could just admire the view, eat our lunches, and enjoy the quiet. We might even see or hear the wolves through good old-fashioned observation and patience."

"I like the sound of that," Pastor Anderson says.

"Me too," Captain Don adds.

Papa nods his approval.

Mr. Robb says, "Be sure to watch for ravens."

Kes imagines the wolves down there somewhere. The Poker Pack heard them howl just last night, according to Papa, as the sky turned foxglove pink at ten-thirty. It was the first time people in Strawberry Flats had heard wolves since the standoff.

Papa hands Kes an apple. She gives him a cookie. He sits on the ground with his Air Jordans in the sun, metal legs glistening, ponytail down his back. *If only the doctors at Brooke could see him now.* He and Mom and Kipper are scheduled to tour five states with the band in July and August. Kes would love to join them, but as a new member of Extinction Rebellion, she cannot. She just returned home yesterday after a semester abroad in southern Mexico, near where her birth mom's father lives, and after getting to know him now has her own summer speaking tour. She'll travel by electric-powered vans with other young activists, with many scheduled stops, including one for several days in Yellowstone National Park to observe wolves. She tells Mr. Robb, "I've been reading about this one legendary wolf there, an alpha male called a 'super wolf.'"

"Wolf Twenty-One."

"Yes. You know about him?"

"Of course. Like you said, he's legendary."

"He never lost a battle," Kes adds, "but he never killed a defeated foe."

"Do you know why?" Mr. Robb asks her.

"Not really. I think scientists are still trying to puzzle it out."

"I know why," Papa says, his voice confident and strong. "If you let your opponent live, you appear merciful and wise. Others will follow you."

"A merciful wolf," Captain Don says. "I like the sound of that."

"I remember one time," E. J. says, "when Mike talked about wolves having souls. He said that if glaciers can be temples, wolves can have souls."

"And trees can have families," Papa adds. "Entire forests of them, all related and in steady communication with each other."

"Will the new president ask the Fish & Wildlife Service to relist gray wolves in Alaska as endangered?" Kes asks Mr. Robb.

"Yes, I think so. He's a good guy, an empathetic guy. It might take a few months… Last year we finally tested the wolves on Prince of Wales Island, not far south of here, and found that they eat a lot of salmon and are genetically unique. I'd like to test them here as well. I think wolves throughout much of the American West and the Upper Midwest could also get listed as endangered, or at least threatened. But what we really need, Kes, is to end this cycle of listing, delisting, more killing, and relisting. We need a Carnivore Conservation Act to protect all wolves, coyotes, mountain lions, and bears. But that's asking a lot of a country that's as cruel as ours."

Kes watches Abe absorb this, his face difficult to read. He sits next to his father as she sits next to hers and Tim next to his. Papa tosses Abe a carrot. Abe catches it one-handed, and tosses Papa a piece of jerky. Kes wishes Kona could be here. Last year, his family moved to Florida, where he says it's hot and muggy and flat, and ruined by too much concrete and traffic. He misses Alaska, and being a knight.

KES AND THE OTHERS hear lively banter and laughter coming up the trail. Soon, Tucker John, Uncle Ty, and Taylor emerge onto the summit. Everybody applauds, having heard the recent news that Uncle Ty proposed marriage to Taylor and she said yes. Uncle Ty takes a deep bow, then grabs Taylor, bends her low like in the movies, and kisses her. Taylor laughs and blushes.

"Look at us now," Pastor Anderson announces. "We're practically a congregation. I should deliver a sermon."

"Don't get ahead of yourself, pastor," Uncle Ty says. "Many of us up here are scientists, pagans, card sharks, and Buddhists."

"All the better," Pastor Anderson says.

"And Kes," Tim says, "did you hear that Berit and Jimmy are expecting a baby?"

"They are?"

Tim nods with a smile.

"Maybe they'll get two for twice the price," E. J. says. "Like at the mercantile."

People laugh.

"Have you seen or heard anything?" Taylor asks Mr. Robb.

"Not yet," he says as he scans the flats below with his spotting scope.

"I'm still hoping that one day you'll come to church," Pastor Anderson says to Uncle Ty. "We all miss Jeannie. You could take her place."

Uncle Ty smiles, but says nothing. Kes tries to imagine him in church. *That would be something.* He still flies Claire to Mexico once a year and plans to retrofit her with solar power, or stop flying if he can't. Just yesterday he brought Kes back to Alaska on another epic flight, starting each day by speaking Spanish:

"Que pasa, calabasa?" *What's up, pumpkin?*

"Nada nada, limonada." *Not much, lemonade.*

And they laughed.

"You do good work in this world," Pastor Anderson tells Uncle Ty.

"Amen," Papa says quietly to Kes.

She hears Mr. d'Alene say the same thing: "Amen."

Uncle Ty sits easily on the ground and digs out his lunch, hands a sandwich to Taylor and one to Tucker John, and finally says, "Thank you, pastor. I prefer questions that can't be answered to answers that can't be questioned."

"Ah, yes," Pastor Anderson says, "curiosity over conviction, the key to an open mind and a healthy perspective. I admire that."

"Hey Kes," Uncle Ty says, changing the subject. "Did you hear the recording your papa got of the wolves last night?"

"No... not yet."

"Did he tell you they howled in harmony?"

"Yes. That's the first thing he told me."

"Maybe you should recruit the wolves into your band, little brother."

"As backup singers," Tucker John says. "Gladys Knight had her Pips; you could have your Wolves."

"Or your Mosquitoes," Uncle Ty says. "Because, you know… Buddy Holly had his Crickets. Having insects in your band is cool, right? Texas cool."

Papa laughs.

Kes notes how full and animated his voice sounds. *He's happy.*

"Quiet, everybody," Mr. Robb says. He holds up his small parabolic dish that's attached to headphones and stands stone still, listening hard.

Nobody speaks.

A hermit thrush sings, and Kes sees Papa smile.

At the spotting scope, Taylor scans the forest below. Abe quickly gets to his feet and joins them atop the hill's southern clifflike face. Tim and E. J. as well.

Nothing.

"I'm sure I heard light yipping," Mr. Robb says. "They're down there. I know it… I can feel it."

LATER, AFTER LUNCH, the warm sun works its magic and massages Kes into a nap, with her head on Papa's thigh. In the middle of a dream, E. J. awakens her. "Kick the fires and light the tires," he exclaims. "I see them. I SEE THEM."

Kes and Abe jump to their feet and stand with E. J. and Mr. Robb. Her heart beats wildly. She has never seen a wild wolf. Papa, Tim, and Taylor join them. "They were right down there," E. J. says. "A whole line of them, under cover of the trees, moving toward the river. I only caught a glimpse. But it was wolves, for sure."

Tim grabs Kes's hand.

"Where exactly?" Mr. Robb asks. He fell asleep as well, and now enters waypoints into his GPS based on E. J.'s sighting.

"They appeared just briefly… right there," EJ says, pointing. "Hard to say how many. Four at least… maybe a whole pack."

Within minutes everybody is taking off down the hill's north side. "Don't chase them," Mr. Robb yells from behind as he packs up his gear. "Don't scare them off."

Kes thrashes through the forest, trying to keep up with Abe. Halfway down, she looks back, mindful of Papa. When she sees him coming with the others, helping Pastor Anderson and Mr. d'Alene over windfallen trees, she takes off again, moving fast. Tim is much taller than he used to be, thinner, more athletic, not far behind. On level ground, Kes pauses. Tim quickly joins her and takes her cue to stop and listen.

"Kes," he whispers after a minute.

"Yeah?" she whispers back.

"Where are they?"

"I don't know."

As she begins to take off toward the river, Tim grabs her hand again. "Kes, I have to tell you something." She tries to pull away. The wolves are near. She has to go. But Tim holds her tight. "Please, Kes… listen. Back when you fell into the river, remember? And you almost drowned? I couldn't be one of your knights anymore. I'm sorry. I've been sorry ever since. But I didn't want to watch you die."

"It's okay, Tim."

"I should have said something before now."

"It's okay… it really is." She pulls her hand free of him.

And off she goes.

A bit later, she stops. And listens. Mr. Robb and E. J. soon join her. Then Abe. But not Tim. *He must have waited for his dad.*

I wish Kona were here.

More listening.

Where are they?

Mr. Robb has dropped his gear, probably at the base of the hill. "Kes," he says quietly, "you and Abe work your way south. E. J. and I will go east. Move easy, and get photos if you can. All of you. Don't be hostile or aggressive."

Abe takes off, moving too fast. Kes hurries to keep up and soon intersects the route where the methane road was supposed to go. All the stakes and flagging are gone, courtesy of monkey-wrenching forest elves: Chippy, Tucker John, and Uncle Ty.

Watch for ravens.

Kes slows down, and is about to hurry on when her deepest knowing tells her to stop. *Breathe. Look.*

Color everywhere.

She turns.

And there he is. Her first. Tall, confident, wise. Stone still, staring at her. Studying her. Mostly black in the face with a touch of gray about the mouth. Russet in the legs, silver in the shoulders. Brother Wolf. Does she see a fierce green fire in his dying eyes?

No. This wolf is very much alive.

And so am I.

ACKNOWLEDGMENTS

Thank you to Sharon Alden, Paul Beattie, Dia Calhoun, Nat Drumheller, Carolyn Elder, Jen Gardner, Jared Posey, Jane Rosenman and Emily Wall who read the manuscript and made valuable edits. Hank and Linnea Lentfer also offered good advice. A sincere nod as well to the excellent team at West Margin Press: Jennifer Newens, Olivia Ngai, Alice Wertheimer, Rachel Metzger, Micaela Clark, and Sarah Currin. And always to my wife, Melanie.

Any mistakes or misrepresentations that remain are mine alone.

Q: What inspired you to write *On Heaven's Hill*?

A: Many things. The fact that we are capable of such deep love and never-ending war boggles me. You'd think by now, after tens of thousands of years of living together, we'd have figured out how to solve our disagreements more sensibly and peacefully. But we have not. How tragic is that? In response, I wanted to write a story about families, community, war veterans and the healing power of wild nature. *On Heaven's Hill* is what some readers might label "cli-fi," meaning "climate fiction," as it's something of a Standing Rock. My inspiration came from my friend and neighbor Linnea Lentfer, who, as a nineteen-year-old sophomore, helped spearhead a successful student movement to get her liberal arts college to divest from fossil fuels. And from the young Swedish climate activist, Greta Thunberg, who created a worldwide youth movement. Their vision and fortitude touched me deeply. As such, I patterned my preteen lead character, Kestrel Nash, after Linnea and Greta.

Q: How long did it take to write *On Heaven's Hill*, and what were the biggest challenges, rewards and joys?

A: It took me seven years. Actually, it took three years to complete the first draft. After that, I revised it many times. Some of those revisions were deep and intense, even heartbreaking. So while revising was difficult (taking something I'd already written and in some cases radically changing it), I'd say my biggest challenge was that I've never been a trapper, a preteen girl or a wolf. As such, it took a lot of research and resolve to put myself in their places—to write convincingly from their points-of-view. I did however get remarkable prepublication feedback from critical readers, including a physical therapist who works with war veterans suffering from PTSD (post-traumatic stress disorder). As for rewards: watching the story improve with every revision and edit and piece of productive feedback felt great. As for joys: seeing the published novel out in the world is gratifying.

Q: Does *On Heaven's Hill* explore some of the contemporary resource and political issues at play in Alaska today?

A: Yes. In the novel, the State of Alaska proposes to build a bridge over a river and into prime wildlife habitat to drill for coal bed methane. In real life, things like this happen all the time: plans to clearcut more old-growth forest, or to drill for oil in the Arctic National Wildlife Refuge (as if the climate crisis doesn't exist), and still other plans to build a mining road—pave the tundra—through our most pristine national parks and last remaining wild areas. It never ends. I read once about how Harriet Beecher Stowe, horrified by the 1850 Fugitive Slave Act, resolved to write a novel, *Uncle Tom's Cabin* (1852), unlike any written before; a story about the true evils and brutality of slavery. She said that to do otherwise—to write about happy slaves and their benevolent owners, which had been done many times—would be a moral failure. That's how I feel today about the climate crisis and global biodiversity crisis, the sixth mass extinction. I believe it is my responsibility, as a free writer, to address these crises, and others, including threats to democracy. If any one person inspired me to write this novel, it's Harriet Beecher Stowe.

Q: Do you use humor to help the reader swallow the serious aspects of the story?

A: Yes, humor is a wonderful literary device, and I enjoy writing it, though it can be hard to get just right (not corny, not flat, etc.). I remember reading *The Milagro Beanfield War* by John Nichols and laughing so hard I fell out of my chair. I thought: If I can even begin to write humor that well, I'll be on my way. My friend, neighbor and fellow author, Hank Lentfer, once told me that the bestselling novelist David James Duncan doesn't trust any work of fiction that doesn't contain humor. Why? Probably because embedded in the best humor are hard-to-accept universal truths. In *On Heaven's Hill*, I have a rogue's gallery of quirky, damaged characters, many of them war veterans, living in a place called Willynillyville, on the edge of a small town in wild Alaska. It's a perfect setup for Friday night poker, moose chili, and crazy banter. All the better when observed from the point-of-view of a preteen daughter of one of the vets, my protagonist, Kestrel Nash. As the poker games unfold and everybody gets talking, I'm able to create what I call "waterfall banter," where I can drop all dialogue tags (he said, she said) and let the comments cascade down the page. When that happens, it's like the entire Poker Pack becomes a single entity—a character in itself.

Q: Is anybody in *On Heaven's Hill* your alter ego? If so, who? And how?

A: Yes, Tyler Nash (Kes's Uncle Ty), the pilot and founder of Willynillyville. He convinces his brother's family to move to Alaska where he hopes the wildness—the sound of wolves howling from across a river—may be powerful and magical enough to heal them in the aftermath of the Iraq and Afghanistan wars. He wants Alaska to reanimate Danny (Kes's father) to become a musician again. It's not unthinkable. Decades ago, my own life was profoundly changed by Alaska. It's so big, wild, challenging and nurturing, it can really give a person a new start. Whatever plans I had for myself before coming to Alaska (as a young ranger with the US National Park Service) were forgotten after my first summer of sea kayaking off tidewater glaciers and eating wild strawberries and smoked coho salmon. Wild nature is our original home, where we find out who we are and what we're capable of. As for its healing powers: scientists say that listening to two hours of nature sounds every day reduces stress hormones and activates DNA segments known to heal and repair the human body. Uncle Ty knows this. He's studied science. I, too, studied science (not journalism or creative writing), and as such found it rewarding to create Tyler based on my own history and education. Also, about the time I began crafting *On Heaven's Hill*, I started writing opinions for *The Guardian* on the climate crisis, biodiversity loss and threats to US public lands. This raised my game as an activist writer just as I was creating Uncle Ty, who ends up challenging the State of Alaska and inspiring his niece to become a climate activist.

Q: *On Heaven's Hill* is set in the Icy Strait region of Southeast Alaska, a real place, as is your award-winning 2015 novel, *Jimmy Bluefeather*. Is *On Heaven's Hill* a sequel—or a sister book in some way—to *Jimmy Bluefeather*? If so, how?

A: *On Heaven's Hill* does reprise three characters from *Jimmy Bluefeather*. And it does take place a few years later. But mostly it's a stand-alone story. You don't need to read one before the other. I've thought about writing a third to complete an "Alaska Icy Strait Trilogy," but right now my work for *The Guardian* is my highest priority.

Q: You also write nonfiction, such as history, memoir and biography. Which do you prefer, nonfiction or fiction?

A: That's a tough question. I'm not sure I prefer one over the other. Both are exciting and rewarding. And both are hard work. Hemingway said, "Easy reading is hard writing." Here's the thing about fiction: nothing is more powerful than a good story. Think about *All Quiet on the Western Front*, *To Kill a Mockingbird*, *Anna Karenina*, *Moby Dick*, *The Yearling*, *The Grapes of Wrath*, *Uncle Tom's Cabin*, *Cold Mountain*, *The Pillars of the Earth*, and so on. Think about how novels—both famous and obscure—have shaped human consciousness and changed the world. Think about Shakespeare's sonnets and plays. Some people say the universe is made of stories, not atoms. I think they may be right. Long before books, our ancestors learned from direct experience (be careful, this plant has thorns) and from stories passed down by wise elders. Stories were everything. They informed and entertained, but also helped to expand our imaginations. They gave birth to shared myths, which enabled disparate peoples to band and work together and better survive. That's why nothing comforts us like a good story: one that transcends place and time. Also—and this is important—science tells us that reading fiction fosters empathy...the ability to walk in other's shoes. "Words are magic," Kes's grandpa tells her, "they come in boxes called books."

ON HEAVEN'S HILL
BOOK CLUB DISCUSSION QUESTIONS

1. *On Heaven's Hill* is written from three alternating points of view: that of Silver, Salt, and Kes. Did you find this compelling? Confusing? Can you think of other novels that use alternating perspectives?

2. The Author's Note before the story says this book is about wolves. Is Silver, the wolf, a convincing character?

3. Did you have a favorite character in the story? If so, who? And why?

4. Two prominent characters, Solomon d'Alene and Danny Nash, deal with disabilities. Did you sympathize with them and their families and their journeys?

5. At one point, Kes's grandfather says, "Words are magic, they come in boxes called books." Did you find *On Heaven's Hill* magical in any way? If so, why?

6. Uncle Ty calls Kes his "young apprentice." Does Kes admire her uncle? Learn from him? Think he's crazy? Reckless? Cool? All of the above? Does Tyler Nash see something promising and special in his niece?

7. Kes likes Willynillyville. Rita, her stepmother, does not...not immediately, anyway. Would you like to live in Willynillyville with a brotherhood of war veterans? If so, why? Or why not?

8. Kes loves the legend of King Arthur and his knights—which is both heroic and tragic—and sees herself as a knight, of sorts. Are elements of her story in Alaska also heroic and tragic?

9. What role does music play in *On Heaven's Hill*?

10. What character is most profoundly changed from the beginning to the end? How so?

11. If *On Heaven's Hill* were made into a movie, and you could have a role in that movie, what character would you like to play? Why?

12. Did you enjoy the humor in *On Heaven's Hill*? Is humor an important literary device?

13. In her review of *On Heaven's Hill* in the Anchorage Daily News, Nancy Lord, a former Alaska State Writer Laureate, says the novel might be best called "a book of ideas" and a "fable of resistance." Do you agree? Why? Or why not?

14. What one scene remains with you most vividly? Why?

READ ON FOR A PREVIEW OF

JIMMY BLUEFEATHER

the weight of air

USED TO BE it was hard to live and easy to die. Not anymore. Nowadays it was the other way around. Old Keb shook his head as he shuffled down the forest trail, thinking that he thought too much.

"Oyye . . ." he muttered, his voice a moan from afar.

He prodded the rain-soaked earth with his alder walking cane. For a moment his own weathered hand caught his attention—the way his bones fitted to the wood, the wilderness between his fingers, the space where Bessie's hand used to be.

Wet ferns brushed his pants in a familiar way. He turned his head to get his bearings, as only his one eye worked. The other was about as useful as a marble and not so pretty to look at. It had quit working long ago and sat there hitching a ride in his wrinkled face. The doctors had offered to patch it or plug it or toss it out the last time Old Keb was in Seattle, but he said no. Someday it might start working again and he didn't want to do all his seeing out of one side of his head. He was a man, for God's sake, not a halibut.

A wind corkscrewed through the tall hemlocks. Old Keb stopped to listen but had problems here too. He could stand next to a hot chain saw and think it was an eggbeater. All his ears did now was collect dirt and wax and grow crooked hairs of such girth and length as to make people think they were the only vigorous parts of his anatomy. He always fell asleep with his glasses on, halfway down his nose. He said he could see his dreams better that way, the dreams of bears when he remembered—when his bones remembered—waking up in the winter of his life.

Nobody knew how old he was. Not even Old Keb. He might have known once but couldn't remember. Somewhere around ninety-five was his guess, a guess he didn't share with any of his children, grandchildren, great-grand-children, great-great grandchildren, or the legions of cousins, nephews, nieces, friends, and doctors, who figured he was close to one hundred and were on a holy crusade to keep him alive.

All his old friends were dead, the ones he'd grown up with and made stories with. He'd outlived them all. He'd outlived himself.

He was born in a salmon cannery in Dundas Bay to a mother and father who managed to die before Keb had any memories of them. His mom was a beautiful woman (he'd been told), a Tlingit Indian with some Filipino and Portuguese thrown in, who got crushed by a tree that a good-for-nothing logger said would fall the other way. His dad was a Norwegian seine skipper who got drunk and walked off a pier and drowned. His Uncle Austin, his mother's brother, *du káak*, a <u>k</u>aa sháade háni clan leader, raised Keb and his brothers and sisters on the other side of Icy Strait from Crystal Bay, the memory place where long ago his people hunted and fished and picked berries and made the stories that held them together. All this before a great glacier got the crazy idea to come down from its mountain and swallow the entire bay like a whale swallows herring. Gone, every living thing buried in ice, the earth pounded silent beneath a cold carved moon. The hungry glacier evicted Old Keb's Tlingit ancestors and forced them to paddle their canoes south across big water where they built a new village—Jinkaat, Keb's home.

It's written in the rocks, Uncle Austin used to say. Nature doesn't lie. It might not tell you what you want to hear. It might be a brutal truth. But it is the truth.

Keb reached the outhouse and fumbled through the door and sat as he always sat, folded into himself. He thought he heard a *woolnáx wooshḵáḵ*, a winter wren, a walnut with wings, and so believing sketched in the missing notes with his imagination. Notes like water over stones. He thumbed through the catalogs and magazines on the bench next to him. Eddie Bauer, whoever he was. Cabela's. Good fishing stuff in there. L.L. Bean. Why so many catalogs? Why so many magazines? Why so many of so much? He found a big glossy report from the Coca-Cola Company. What the hell? Yes, he remembered now. He'd been to California a few years back to see Ruby's son, Robert, the sugar water man who worked sixty hours a week for Coca-Cola Company and was hoping to move to the big office in Albuquerque, Albany, Atlanta, Atlantis, something like that, some place far to the east. Robert was married to a white woman named Lorraine who had expensive hair, a poodle on Prozac, and a cat named Infinity. Boy could she talk. Talk all day, talk all night. Talk, talk, talk. She had a little phone attached to her ear and even talked in her sleep. The only thing she let interrupt her from talking to one person was the chance to talk to somebody else. She spent all her time at the mall shopping for time-saving devices and lived with Robert in a big house next to a million other big houses all different but all the same. Big houses on big streets with names like Shadowhawk Drive and Peace Pipe Lane. Big houses Keb remembered with sadness and fatigue, how the hot sun burned its way across thirsty country and stirred everybody up. Got them speeding in their shiny cars and eating so much fast food that—what? What happened? Keb didn't know. So many cars and people, all chasing the sun. A beautiful madness, California. Could they still slow dance after eating all that fast food? Slow dance the way he and Bessie used to?

"Eyelids," Lorraine told him. "People can tell you're getting old when your eyelids sag." She was scheduled to have hers lifted, along with everything else.

Robert the Sugar Water Man would spend all day Saturday in his driveway washing and cleaning his Mercedes. That's how it is in California, he said. Your car is half of your personality. He'd wax the cleaner and clean the wax and buff the wax and clean the buffer until Old Keb got tired just watching him.

Keb never did own a car. Just trucks. Fords, Dodges, GMs, every one a rolling box of rust that died and was stripped for parts at Mitch's Greasy Sleeves Garage. Come to think of it, he never did take comfort in a car or a truck like he did in a boat, out on the water, under the pull of the moon and tides. Skiffs, trollers, seiners, gillnetters, even the old gray punt he traveled in with Uncle Austin. All of his best memories were in boats, memories shaped like the boats themselves. Graceful, curving, and languid; exotic and erotic as a woman, the feeling of falling in love and falling beyond that.

Rowing with your heart.

And don't forget canoes. *Yakwt lénx'*, large canoes. And *yak-wyádi*, small canoes. And *yáxwch'i yaakw*, canoes with high, carved prows, and *seet*, a small, nimble canoe with a pointed prow. Canoes with flat bottoms, like *ch'iyaash*, from the up-north town of Yakutat, good for moving up a shallow river, and *xáatl kaltságaa*, the toughest canoes of all, with twin prows to push aside solid ice. Keb's best boats were the ones he learned to carve with Uncle Austin, and later, the ones he carved himself and gave away. The ones he built for friends, long ago.

Nobody traveled by canoe anymore. They didn't have the time.

Lorraine would keep Keb on the sofa talking all afternoon, talking until she gave him a headache. She told him that she wanted a pet bird, a parrot or a cockatoo or some damn thing in a cage. Pity the poor parrot that tried to mimic her. He'd be dead in a day. God loved the birds and invented man. Man loved the birds and invented cages. Best of all was little Christopher, Robert and Lorraine's delicate son, the boy with Down's syndrome and a defective heart, the sweetest human being Keb knew, the child whose smile could fill a valley. They would drive down to Malibu for ice cream. Keb tried rum raisin and found too little rum, too much raisin. He tried "death by chocolate" and an hour later was still alive. Next time he'd have a double scoop. Christopher ate "Killer Vaniller" and wore most of it on his chin. Lorraine stuck with "Sensible Strawberry." They sat on a bench, facing a sidewalk, and beyond that, a fine sand beach and the sea. Kids zipped by on skateboards and roller-blades. Lorraine held little Christopher and sang, "Puff the Magic Dragon." She said it was peaceful, the sea. "It's so tranquil and still, it makes you believe that everything will be okay."

"I don't dream here," Keb told her.

"What?"

"Here, in this California leaf-blower place, I don't dream here."

"Oh, Keb, maybe you do and you just don't remember. You have trouble remembering, remember?"

Back at her big house, Lorraine gave him the annual Coca-Cola report. On its cover, in large, bold print, large enough that Keb could read it without effort, it said, "A billion years ago intelligent life appeared on earth. A billion minutes ago Christianity emerged. A billion Coca-Colas ago was yesterday morning."

"Oyyee . . ."

Lorraine had insisted that Keb bring it back with him to Alaska; that he show it to Robert's mom, Ruby, Keb's older daughter. How proud she'd be.

Like all great literature, the annual report ended up in the outhouse.

Keb stood, or attempted to stand. His knees creaked. A sharp pain shot through his whole being. Next thing he knew he was leaning against the outhouse door, heavy on the rough wood, the sound of his own breathing ragged to him, his hips too cold, not right, made of plastic or fiberglass or Kevlar or some damn thing other than old Tlingit Norwegian bones. At least no pain cursed him when he pissed. Not this time. Sometimes things down there felt like they were on fire. Whichever one he was supposed to have two of—kidney or liver—the other one had been cut out and Old Keb couldn't remember why. Doctors had gotten in there, digging around for a swollen this or a funky that, and decided to take out the kidney because it got in the way or it didn't look right and that was that.

It began to rain. Keb stepped outside to inhale the wet earth, the May aromas of skunk cabbage, blueberry, alder, spruce. His nose still worked pretty well. In this regard he considered himself an old bear, a hunter with wild strawberries in his eyes, on good days at least. He had fewer good days all the time. Most days he was a pocket of a man, parceling out his vitamins and pills, staring into his own receding face. Awhile back he had caught himself in a mirror and thought, *When did I stop being me?*

A gust of wind caught his white hair and stirred the ferns. Back on the trail, he stopped to taste the cool salt mist blowing in from the sea, the fragrance of rocks. He tightened his arthritic hand around his walking cane and was about to go on when he froze. There at his feet, apparently dead, was *Yéil*. A raven.

A shiver ran through him, deep as a shiver can go. His heart jumped in his throat. For a minute he didn't move; he would say later that he didn't breathe then either. In all his years in Alaska, Old Keb could count on one hand the number of times he had found a dead raven. No other bird or animal was more storied to him and his Tlingit people.

He lowered himself to one knee, slowly, mindful in some ancient way of the rain falling harder, the storm filling its lungs. He bent forward to better see the sightless glare of the obsidian eye, the blue iridescence that shone and was gone. Minutes ago it had not been there, this bird that spilled nightfall off its wings, this bird that created the world and stole the sun. Keb looked into the sky and continued to look, unblinking, his face turned to the rain and the great somber trees. The wind stood and listened. Keb gasped. He could see now, see in a way new to him. Every branch and needle and raindrop falling with ten thousand other raindrops had extreme clarity. The sky cleaved open. The earth, wild on its axis, shot through space and pressed upon him the entire weight of its spinning. The stars, cold and conscious on the other side of the world, suspended themselves in the blackness where Raven got its shape and voice. Something had happened. Something bad. A small whining sound grew louder. A presence brushed his face, soft yet strong, the weight of air taking flight. The whining was big and getting bigger—shrill, serrated, sputtering. An engine? Yes, a motorcycle.

Old Keb didn't move.

The motorcycle skidded to a stop. A young man killed the engine and climbed off. He walked toward Old Keb, wearing a baseball cap backward over his long hair. His baggy jeans scuffed the ground. His loose-fitting jersey said, "L.A. Lakers, World Champions." He had the manner of a *jánwu*, this kid, a mountain goat grown mostly in the limbs, lanky, quick, unafraid of heights. He had cool, arctic eyes.

"There's been an accident," he said.

Old Keb nodded, "Yes, I know."

ABOUT THE AUTHOR

KIM HEACOX is best known for his memoir *The Only Kayak* and his novel *Jimmy Bluefeather*, both winners of the National Outdoor Book Award, and for his opinion pieces in *The Guardian*, where he writes in celebration and defense of the natural world, mostly on the climate crisis, biodiversity loss, and threats to US public lands. His book of essays and photographs, *In Denali*, won the IBPA Benjamin Franklin Award. A keen musician and photographer, and former ranger with the US National Park Service, he lives on eighteen acres in Gustavus, Alaska, next to Glacier Bay National Park, with his wife Melanie, two sea kayaks, a Martin guitar, and forty-some chestnut-baked chickadees. Learn more at www.kimheacox.com.